SISTERS ~of the~ SOUL

KRISTIN A. FULTON

ALSO BY KRISTIN A. FULTON . . .

Children's Literature:

Snake Food

The Haunting

Is THAT a Hat?

A Fable for All Ages:

Henry Bingle's Transformation

Dramatic Literature:

Chirstmas in July
(a humorous melodrama)

Short Stories:

Being There

All the Dog Wagons that Beckon

The Fish Pond

Sisters of the Soul

Published in the United States by
Broadway Pacific Press, Columbia, CA

Credits:
Cover by: 100 Covers

Author Photo:
Jennifer Ropoza, jenniferrapozaphotography.com

Interior Layout:
Melody Young, graphicdesignbymelody.com

Hardback: ISBN-979-8-9885977-2-8
Paperback: ISBN-979-8-9885977-1-1
Ebook: ISBN-979-8-9885977-0-4

Second Edition

First Printed 2018, Second Edition Published 2023

Sisters of the Soul

Kristin A. Fulton

Broadway Pacific Press, Columbia

"In thee my soul shall own
combined the sister and the friend."

–Catherine Killigrew

PART I

Sweetbrier

Addie Turner

Sweetbrier Plantation House

December 1837

You couldn't help feeling sorry for Mr. Hugo with his beat-dog look after Miss Lucille tried to stab him with the big silver carving knife—the very knife I'd used to slice up a smoked ham just a few minutes before. I put that turkey knife down on the table to sharpen it later, and Chemise and I started rolling out the biscuit dough. We was real quiet that morning. The only sound was a fly buzzin' around, plaguing us by landing on the backs of our necks and on our bare arms.

I was ready to go after the pesky creature when all hell broke loose upstairs. Miss Lucille was screaming like she had something after her, eating her alive, and Mr. Hugo was yelling at her to stop her crying, for God's sake, and would she please come to her senses and have relations with him like a normal wife would. "I'm mighty tired of you moping and crying in your room all day, Lucille. You've got to brace up, wife, and stop this nonsense!"

He must of tried to take her by the arm then, 'cause she screamed "Don't touch me," and we heard the Paris vase on the stair landing, that Hugo's mama brought from France some seventy years ago, smash into a million pieces, followed by the sounds of a scuffle with a lot of grunting and some more screaming. "Calm yourself, Lucille," yelled Mr. Hugo.

"Get away from me," she screamed, and before Chemise and I knew it, she'd run down the stairs on bare feet, right over the broken bits of the prized vase I'd dusted so many times I couldn't count. Chemise and I stood there with our mouths open as Miss Lucille whirled like a dust storm through the kitchen door, leaving bloody footprints with each step she took. She was as white as the flimsy nightgown she wore, her eyes red and puffy and her thick hair hanging in tangled mats around her. She looked kind of spooky, and I wondered if she was going more softheaded than usual from having the normal female troubles that women go through when they stop bleeding and so forth. Miss Lucille has never been what you'd call stable as a rock. She's more like quicksand, is Miss Lucille.

Mr. Hugo tried to drape a robe around Miss Lucille's shoulders and she screamed like he was killing her. Pouncing like a cat after a mouse, she grabbed up the big butcher knife off the table where I'd put it and tried to stab that poor man. I reached over and tweaked the knife out of her hand and it clattered to the floor. I wrapped my arms around Miss Lucille in a bear hug. "What's wrong, honey?" I asked. Miss Lucille looked up at me, her round eyes like a scared baby, and she sort of crumpled up so that I had to catch her from falling to the floor.

"I can't take this life anymore," said Miss Lucille, and she buried her face in my apron bib, sobbing to beat the band.

"You just tired out, Miss Lucille." I said, and I took hold of that skinny little thing and half carried her up the stairs to her bedroom, with Chemise on the other side holding one elbow and Mr. Hugo following behind us looking like he'd rather be anywhere but there on the landing with Miss Lucille nearly out of her mind, being led to her quarters by two nigger kitchen maids.

I felt sorry for Mr. Hugo; he looked so helpless and sad, but truth be told he is partly the reason for Miss Lucille's condition. Miss Lucille wasn't cut out to be alone, much less run a plantation house on her own, and Mr. Hugo was away far too much, starting in the early days of them gettin' hitched. The plantation covered a whole lot of acres and was split in a few places by a snaky stretch of swamp and a couple big streams. Mr. Hugo was a good farmer; his fields of cotton were the envy of other plantation owners, and his cane grew thick, bulging with sugar. He oversaw the whole place himself. Needless to say, he had plenty to keep him busy, so it wasn't really his fault that he was gone so much of the time, but he should have figured out how to make Miss Lucille happier.

I was eight years old when Miss Lucille come here from New Orleans some twenty years ago. She and Mr. Hugo had just got married, and he carted her and her things all them hundreds of miles from the city to Sweetbrier. Newlyweds should be happy, but not Miss Lucille. As soon as she got out of the carriage that bring her home a married lady I could tell she'd been crying but was trying not to show it.

My mama, bless her soul now in heaven, gave me the job of helping Miss Lucille unpack and get settled into her rooms. "We is short-handed today, so my Addie gonna help you put your things away. This girl is a mighty fine helper, plus she tall for her age," Mama said, pushing me forward and whispering in my ear to stand up straight. Miss Lucille nodded, and her and I followed after the men who was carrying three big trunks into the rooms that Mr. Hugo had painted fresh before he went to find a wife in New Orleans.

It was real clear that Miss Lucille had something upsetting her; she seemed nervous as a cat with a big tom following it. "What's your name?" she asked, trying to help unpack her trunks but mainly getting in the way.

"Addie."

"What?" She looked at me blankly, and I knew she'd forgotten her own question from a few seconds ago. That's how tight she was wound.

"My name, Missus Laurent. It's Addie."

She said what a pretty name it was, and she told me to call her Miss Lucille, then she sat down all of a sudden and started crying her eyes out. Mind you, this was her first day as Mistress of Sweetbrier, and poor Miss Lucille was a wreck. I didn't know what to do. I couldn't go around hugging a strange white lady, so I kept unpacking while she cried.

"I apologize," she said, finally. "I just can't help it." I felt sorry for her, and it must have showed in my face that she could confide in me. Pretty soon she's telling me all about her troubles with her father, who must have been a crazy old coot from what Miss Lucille said, while I was hanging up her fancy gowns, unpacking her shawls and handkerchiefs, and putting away her hat boxes and dainty shoes. I just listened and nodded, and said 'hmmm' now and then, and she laid her laundry down.

Honest to God and the Lord Jesus, I never met a white woman before or since who spilled out her guts like Miss Lucille did to me. I was just a know-nothing young black girl fillin' in for a lady's maid. But Miss Lucille was one to surprise you, keep you hoppin'. Even then, she was a little weird in the head. I wondered if she'd gotten it from her papa. Touched in the head or not, I liked that she respected me; at least she acted like she did. Miss Lucille was a whole new ball of wax compared to the rest of the folks I knew, black and white, and sometimes she told me some interesting tidbits, so I didn't mind listenin' to her at all.

She started crying again, and I handed her a fresh handkerchief. "Mother died when I was twenty, and afterwards father got as mean as a snake. Papa didn't believe in anything frivolous, like dancing or going to the horse races or having dinner guests. His idea of a good time was reading the Bible aloud and praying together for an hour every morning, noon, and night." Her hands were trembling, and so was her voice. "I became a prisoner in my own house, and it was so terribly lonely." She let out a big, shuddering sob and sort of gasped like she couldn't breathe good.

"Are you gonna be all right Miss Lucille, or should I get Mr. Hugo?"

"Oh, dear God, no!" The tears poured like rivers down both sides of her nose.

I waited until she calmed down some. "I gotta be getting back to my job helping Mama in the kitchen. Do you need anything else, Miss Lucille?"

She shook her head. "No, thank-you, Addie. You've been very helpful."

"Good night then, Miss Lucille." I stopped when I reached the door to tell her that everything would probably turn out fine and not to worry, but she was back to crying, so I just closed the door softly and joined Mama in the kitchen.

It wasn't the last time Miss Lucille poured out her soul to me. For the first few years she lived at Sweetbrier, I brought her breakfast most mornings. Miss Lucille had a habit of sleeping late in the morning, except the occasions when she made an effort to join Mr. Hugo for breakfast on one of his visits home. But more often than not, I carried up a tray. Some days she'd lay like a lump in bed and turn her head away. "Just put it on my dressing table," she'd say. On those days, I'd tiptoe out as soon as possible so as not to disturb her. On her good days she'd chatter away, and I could tell she enjoyed having the company. I'd stay for longer than I was supposed to, and Mama and Chemise would be crabby with me when I got back to the kitchen.

Miss Lucille told me about her mortal fear of bugs and dirt, and she confided that she was not much interested in beets or cane or the production of cotton. She missed New Orleans. It was plain as the nose on my face that she was a city girl, and life as a country wife was not her style. At Sweetbrier, poor Miss Lucille took on a life that was as foreign to her as if she'd joined a circus. She'd probably been happier if she had joined a circus, 'cause when she became Mr. Hugo's wife, she traded in her whole unhappy life with her mean papa for a new life that didn't suit her either. A circus would have given her more of the human companionship she needed.

We didn't get much company at Sweetbrier; being out of the way, it discouraged any old Joe from dropping by for a visit. The nearest town, Smithfield, was a generous hour's drive in the surrey down a rutted dirt lane. The only church in town, besides the Negro Evangelical Congregation, was the Catholics, and Miss Lucille wouldn't have nothin' to do with them. She told Mr. Hugo in no uncertain words that she didn't mind that he was born a Catholic, but if he expected her to convert, he'd still be waiting when he got put in the coffin. "The Catholic teachings are not true to the Bible. Father would turn over in his grave! I wouldn't attend if it was the last church in the world!" True to her word, she stayed away and did her praying in the side parlor, which she had made into a little chapel all her own.

Miss Lucille tried to help Mr. Hugo in his business affairs, but he chased her out of the office. "He told me that bookkeeping is a man's job," she sighed. "Addie, I don't know what to do! I feel useless here!" Since she was crying again, I handed her a fresh handkerchief. "Your mama and Chemise run the household perfectly, and they don't need me or want me to interfere," she said.

She was right, of course. Mama and Chemise had managed the kitchen and kept house for years, back when Mr. Hugo's parents were still alive. When Miss Lucille tried to help she tended to get in the way, 'cause she was about as suited to do housework as a white rabbit. I know that Mama didn't mean to be unkind, but she made it plain that Miss Lucille was just a visitor in the kitchen. After Mama had shooed her out a bunch of times, Miss Lucille got the message and stayed mostly clear.

Miss Lucille was left wondering what to fill her life with. I think she was bored to tears most days, which didn't help her mental troubles. She did her needlework, of course, and she read like she was starving for books. Every afternoon she sat in her armchair in the corner of her sitting room and studied the Bible. She'd invite me to listen while she read the passages aloud, and afterward we talked about what it meant. Half the time it was just a bunch of crazy words all jumbled together, but it was always a nice treat to listen and take a break from my chores, even if I got a scolding for being gone too long.

No matter what Miss Lucille did to keep herself busy, it wasn't enough to keep her happy. In between reading and knitting and so on, she took to pacing across her room, back and forth, muttering under her breath. I think she would have gone completely crazy even earlier if she hadn't finally gotten pregnant during the second year of her and Mr. Hugo's marriage. I never seen anyone happier to be a mother than Miss Lucille. It changed her into a person with a purpose.

Before the baby was born, I helped Miss Lucille sew a baby blanket and two patchwork quilts; "One for warm weather and the other when it turns damp," she said. Her eyes lit up, thinkin' about that baby. She crocheted little sunbonnets, and she and I sewed up a tiny white christening gown with a lace collar and hem. She was so excited and pepped up over the upcoming birth that sometimes I wondered if she was the same person who stayed under the covers a few days every week, crying to beat the band.

Miss Lucille went into labor on June 11, the same day I was born ten years before. Mama and Chemise delivered her wicked son, Hugo Bertrand Laurent, before midnight, which means we share the same birthday. That's a sore point, 'cause I have to think of that sorry, sick soul every time my birthday comes around, and I'd much rather forget about Mr. Bert until the end of time.

When Miss Lucille's birthing pains started coming close together, Mama and Chemise went upstairs to attend to her. I stayed in the kitchen, and they kept me busy running this or that up to Miss

Lucille's room. "Addie, bring some hot water," or, "We need more towels," they'd call down the stairs, and I'd rush whatever was ordered to Miss Lucille's door. "Stay out there, child," Chemise said, meeting me at the door, and I'd hand over whatever they'd wanted me to fetch.

It was late in the evening, ten o'clock or more, when Miss Lucille's screams took on a whole new tone. They was really piercing screams that echoed through the whole house and made me plug my ears. I thought maybe she was dyin', but about an hour later she gave birth to a baby boy. It was a sorry day in hell when that creature came into the world, for sure.

Mr. Hugo and Miss Lucille named the baby Hugo Bertrand Laurent the third after his daddy and his granddaddy. Against Miss Lucille's wishes, Mr. Hugo insisted on a Baptism ceremony. "You may not like Catholics, Lucille, but like his father and grandfather before him, my son will be baptized as a Catholic, and that is final." The following month the priest from Smithville rode out for the christening ceremony. That little boy looked mad as hell when he got a sprinkling of the holy water. His little fists were waving like he was in the boxing ring. After the ceremony was over, Miss Lucille handed me the red-faced baby who was shrieking at the top of his lungs. "It's time for his nap, Addie. Do you mind tucking him in?"

"No, Miss Lucille." I wrapped the child in a towel and carried him up the stairs to the nursery. On the climb up the stairs he grabbed my nose and twisted it with his little hand, hard enough so it smarted and made me wince. Even though he was just a baby, there was a mean look in his eyes, and I was careful to keep my nose out of grabbing range whenever I had the job of tending him.

So there wasn't confusion from having two Hugos in the house, Miss Lucille called the boy Bert, after his middle name. From the day he was born, Bert was the object of her deep and steady devotion. Never have I seen such catering to a child as Miss Lucille did to Bert.

She tried to satisfy his every passing fancy, and to relieve him of any pain or frustration. In plain words, she spoiled him rotten. Motherhood gave her life a whole new meaning. Too bad her love helped make the apple of her eye into a cruel monster.

Miss Lucille got out from her rooms and took Bert for walks around the grounds of the house, bundling him up even if the weather was warm. She fussed in the kitchen, insisting that special food be prepared for him. She began payin' more attention to the day-to-day doings around Sweetbrier. Mama and Chemise muttered and rolled their eyes when Miss Lucille decided to rearrange all the furniture; they had to move it around a bunch of times until she was happy, which she never was. When the furniture was more or less in the place she wanted, her next project was to make one of the first-floor rooms into a classroom with a real blackboard on the wall at one end.

I'll always be especially grateful to Miss Lucille for one thing; when she started schooling Bert, she let me sit in the classroom along with him, which is how I learned to read and to write more than just my name. Mama knew how much I liked learning, so she'd send me up to dust or mop or polish the wood paneling and the desks or bring a plate of cookies up to Bert and his mama. Miss Lucille was always real good to me, letting me hang around and listen to whatever lesson she was teaching Bert. Pretty soon, she just took it as a fact that I was her second student, and she threw herself into educating me.

"You're like a sponge Addie, the way you sop up information!" she exclaimed.

"I love to learn, Ma'am, and I appreciate that you're teaching me."

"At the rate you're going, you'll be reading Shakespeare on your own in a few months!" I was fifteen when she started Bert's and my lessons, and not quite two years later, I read through Mr. Shakespeare's Macbeth all by myself, just like Miss Lucille predicted.

She was a good teacher, Miss Lucille, and she was a saint to put up with her son in the classroom. Believe me, Bert was a handful. I think it was a relief to have me in the room when Bert threw his tantrums, kicking at his mama's shins and running from the room and slamming the door after him. Miss Lucille would shrug her shoulders and sigh, and finish teaching me the lesson anyway. I liked the days when Bert had one of his fits of temper and took off running. It meant that I had Miss Lucille's attention all to myself.

The lessons got harder as time passed. Miss Lucille taught arithmetic, grammar, history, and literature, which was my favorite. Miss Lucille was a dandy reader. She could make the words come alive off the paper. I loved listening to her and following along in the book with all them wonderful words.

We'd just finished reading *Great Expectations* and were starting *A Tale of Two Cities* when Mr. Bert ended my education. One day, he announced, loud and clear, that he didn't want me in the schoolroom any more. "Addie's an ignorant slave, Mama. Charles said it's not healthy for white people to be close up in the same room with niggers."

Miss Lucille's face flushed a shade pinker than usual. "Don't say that, Bert. You'll hurt Addie's feelings."

"Mama, you're breaking the law to teach niggers to read and write. Charles told me, and he said people can go to jail for it." Charles, an overseer's son, was a year or two older than Bert. They played together, the pair of them pulling the legs off insects or holding over the fire some little mouse they caught. When they got tired of torturing little animals, they went after the Negro children from the slave cabins in the woods out back. No doubt about it, Bert was the meaner of the two. His games ended in punishments that made bruises and drew blood. All the parents from the cabins warned their young'uns to keep clear of Mr. Bert, but he searched them out to practice his cruel tricks.

I was a few weeks shy of nineteen when Bert stopped my education. I hoped Miss Lucille would stick up for me, so I could keep on with my learning, but she disappointed me deeply. The next day, the closed door to the schoolroom let me know that I wasn't to come in anymore. I knocked softly on the door just in case, hoping she'd let me in, but when she answered the door she just took the tray of sliced ham and cheese I was carrying upstairs for her and Bert's midmorning tea. She didn't meet my eyes when she thanked me for the plate. I could see Bert smile like the cat got a canary before she closed the door. Bert walked all over Miss Lucille, which didn't teach him what he needed to learn: how to respect other human beings, slaves or otherwise.

I was awful sad over the loss of my education, but I put it all behind me 'cause of changes in my own life. A couple months after I got kicked out of the schoolroom, I married Garvus Washington, a neighbor in our settlement. We'd been sweethearts since I was twelve and Garvus was thirteen. I am forever grateful to have such a fine man in my life.

Between working in the big house and bein' newly married, I didn't have near as much time to yearn for things I couldn't have. I stopped thinking about Mr. Dickens and Mr. Shakespeare, and Garvus and I put our attention to making a family.

Lucille Bellingham-Laurent
Sweetbrier Plantation
1837

Hugo, my husband, disgusts me. I avoid him whenever possible, especially at night when wine sparks his husbandly desires. I know it isn't Christian behavior, but his touch is loathsome. I am a Godly woman, too much Father's daughter to stray from the teachings of the Holy Bible, but I cannot help the revulsion I feel when Hugo takes the privileges of a husband.

At Sweetbrier I am alone; I am a duckling trapped in tangled reeds, left behind by its flock. I wonder what life would have been like if my mother hadn't died, if father hadn't gone off his rocker, if I'd married Jim Wiggins when he asked. It was ludicrous, of course; Jimmy is far below the Bellingham's in status and three inches shorter than I. His height didn't matter as much as his crooked teeth and the unmistakable hunch growing on his back. I refused in my most haughty tones, and Sugar, our maid, showed him out. Jimmy glared at me fiercely over his shoulder, his face flushed with humiliation. "You'll be sorry someday, Lucille," he said.

It was a relief when the door closed behind him; yet, upon reflection, it marked the start of dark times to come. Mother died of influenza a few weeks later, and Father began a steady decline into madness. Always a pious soul and a staunch Baptist, Father grew even more besotted with Jesus and godliness and proper Christian conduct. His eyes glinted wildly when he was in one of his states, and his prayers and devotions were screamed at fever pitch. When he'd reach a certain height of zealotry, he'd tremble and speak in tongues. On those occasions he looked at me blankly as if he didn't know his own daughter. I began to feel frightened of him.

Father monitored my activities closely, forbidding attendance at any invitation or gathering outside our church. Eventually, even the sanctioned church meetings inspired suspicions of my supposed loose morals. He began to rage and accuse me of unseemly conduct, though I was ever innocent of misbehavior. I had to fight for his permission to attend any event remotely social in nature, and when I did manage to break free, upon my return he would accuse me of harlotry. No matter the measures I took to dissuade him from his delusional ideas, he was convinced that I was wayward, and the next stop in my shameless passage was the bawdy house.

One particular evening made clear Father's departure from any hint of reason and sanity. I'd gone to church to attend Bible study and stayed out past the usual time I was expected home. Sally Ann Tilson, my dearest friend who lived a few blocks away, accompanied me. After the study, we walked at a leisurely pace, our elbows linked together, engaging in the sin of chatter.

"I have a secret, Lucille. Can you keep it?"

"I will keep any secret of yours to the grave."

"Have you heard of the Mormons and their wonderful new religion?" I nodded; I'd heard of the sect through Father. He viewed them as madmen and charlatans, but I refrained from mentioning that to Sally Ann.

"Well, you are looking at a newly converted member of The Church of Latter Day Saints! I am going by wagon to the new City of Zion. The convoy leaves in ten days, with thirty fellow converts. I'm terribly excited!"

My heart sank. Sally Ann was my only true friend, and I loved her more than she or anyone knew. The idea of her leaving made me feel ill. "What about your parents?" The Tilsons were almost as devout Baptists as Father; I was sure they would forbid Sally Ann from going if they knew.

"It's a secret, remember. I am taking items from the house one by one, to the Mormon meeting hall. When the time comes, I will sneak out of the house, and everything I need will be waiting for me."

We stopped and sat on a low bench in the shadows of the giant elms lining the driveway to her house. Mary's eyes glowed when she talked of golden tablets, Zion and the Angel Moroni. I listened quietly until darkness fell. "I'd better go. Father expected me home an hour ago. I will miss you, Sally Ann," I said, tears in my eyes.

"And I will miss you, Lucille."

We cried with our arms around each other, and I shocked us both by kissing her, a long kiss on the lips that caused unspeakable desires to rise in my body. Sally Ann pulled away from me, and the puzzlement in her eyes told me her feelings were quite different than mine. "I've been promised a husband when I arrive in Zion," she said softly.

"I'm happy for you, Sally Ann." I rose abruptly and walked away without looking back.

I hurried home, consumed with guilt about my unnatural yearnings for Sally Ann. Scripture is clearly against carnal love for the same sex; such sinners are eternally damned. I knew that I must eradicate this memory and suppress any dishonorable passions lurking in my nature.

The house was not lit with the usual lanterns when I arrived home. A feeling of unease crept up my spine as I climbed the front steps. I hesitated before turning the heavy knob; Father was waiting on the other side of the door. His eyes had the peculiar glint that signaled he wasn't thinking clearly. "Is anything wrong, Father?" I asked.

"Why are you so late, girl?" he snarled.

"Bible study lasted longer than usual." I attempted to slip past and escape up the stairs.

"You are a liar." Spittle flew from his mouth and landed on my face. I lifted my hand to wipe away the drops. Father yanked me so that I stood directly in front of him and slapped me hard across the cheek.

"You've been consorting with men. I can smell it on you. You're a whore, just like your mother."

"Mother was no such thing!" I cried.

"She was a wanton! God's voice has told me so, and he tells me you are just like her! Now, admit your dalliances, you sly hussy!" He struck me across the other cheek.

The pain made tears well up in my eyes. "I swear I haven't had anything to do with a man, Father."

He tightened his grip on my arm, dragged me up the stairs and pushed me into my bedroom. "You shall stay in this room until it's proved that you're not carrying a bastard." He locked the door and gave Sugar instructions to bring meals to my room. Thus confined, I had ample time to reflect on the wickedness inside me, as well as the injustice of Father's accusations. It was three long weeks before the evidence presented itself, and Sugar showed Father the rag with blood on it. He unlocked my door, but ever after, he eyed me with distrust and something akin to malice.

I strove to make my already demure behavior even more Christian, more proper, but after my confinement, Father rarely gave permission for me to leave the house alone. Church services on weekends and Holy Days were the only allowable social activities. Sally Ann had made the pilgrimage to Zion by then, which left me bereft and lonely. Jim Wiggins's proposal looked better from the perspective of my narrow existence, but Jim had signed up as a Merchant Marine and shipped out. I was distressed to hear he died on a ship bound for the Far East. His warning that I'd be sorry had come true.

There was no bargaining with Father. He ruled our household with quiet tyranny; I lived in fear of displeasing him. Any infraction on my part, real or imagined, resulted in grueling penances. The time he suspected me of lying, my punishment was kneeling before the altar in our home chapel until I fainted. When I woke, I couldn't feel my legs until blood coursed through them and caused such throbbing and cramping that I cried out in agony.

"God will punish a liar every time! Let that be known to you, Lucille!" Father screamed.

The safest course of action was to cooperate fully with him and do nothing to raise his ire. I became an expert at compliance as the years passed in a quiet, inflexible routine; Father led prayers three times a day, and every afternoon I played devotional music on the pianoforte while Father read the Bible. Other activities were restricted by Father's ideas of seemliness: study of scripture was allowed, novels and casual reading, forbidden. Games and puzzles were the work of the devil; needle arts were permitted. Boredom resulted in endless pairs of crocheted infant socks and baby gowns to donate to charity. Our frugal meals were eaten in silence, and even Sugar grew grim and withdrawn.

I awakened to my 25th birthday with the desperation of a woman whose only escape is death or marriage. How I would accomplish either option was the plaguing question. Although the Bible says it is a sin to take one's own life, it seemed like death was the easier thing, and I began to lie awake at night thinking about how I might induce eternal rest.

Father was in good health. He walked every day, bathed regularly, attended to his teeth faithfully, refrained from the evils of smoking tobacco and drinking spirits, and banned sugar from our kitchen. All signs indicated he was hearty enough to live past the age when most are in their graves, which made his death all the more surprising. The unexpected happened at the dining table on an otherwise ordinary day in our household. Sugar's roasted chicken, a favorite of Father's, was his last supper. My own part in Father's demise will haunt me forever, for I am guilty of standing by and watching while he choked to death on a chicken bone.

All the usual measures one might take to help a choking victim ran through my head, yet I didn't pound his back, I didn't reach into his mouth to dislodge the bone choking him, I didn't loosen his collar. From my seat across the table, I watched Father's face turn red as a cherry. He clawed at his throat, all the while glaring at me with bulging eyes. Finally, frothy pink foam came out of his mouth, and he fell face first onto his dinner plate.

I felt no grief, only relief that I didn't have to kill myself after all. I'd grown to hate father, which is a cardinal sin and one that will be buried with me when I die. Hating Father is merely my first sin: in my soul I know the truth. I am a murderess and an aberrant.

Father revenged me from the grave. Mr. Pruitt, our family solicitor, arrived the day after Father died to present the specifics outlined in his Last Will and Testament. With the exception of the pianoforte, my bedroom set, and a meager annual allowance, everything was bequeathed to the church. "Your father's will dictates that the house and all furnishings will be sold on the open market with proceeds going to Saint John's. Do you understand the conditions, Miss Bellingham?"

I nodded, though the injustice of the disposition of our family belongings wounded my already battered soul.

"With such a modest sum bequeathed to you, Miss Bellingham, you may want to seek a position as a governess or domestic. Or perhaps you could seek service in one of the holy orders. I can make inquiries if you wish?"

"I'm a grown woman, Mr. Pruitt, and capable of making decisions on my own behalf, thank-you."

"Of course. Forgive me. I am merely concerned for your future."

"Until the sale ensues, I assume I can remain in occupancy here?"

"Of course, Miss Bellingham, however I must warn you; instructions in your Father's will state incontestably that the sale of the home and contents be initiated promptly after his death. As his solicitor, I must comply with his wishes. A notice will publish in the newspaper next week, and an auction will take place in a month's time."

I showed him to the door. I was free from father at last. Now, I was the prisoner of poverty.

I praise the Lord God for His intervention in the course my future took. Hugo Laurent was in New Orleans looking for a wife when he came to the estate sale at our house on Chartres Street. Mr. Pruitt requested my presence at the sale. "You can answer any questions buyers might have about the furnishings," he said. Mr. Hugo inquired about Father's secretary; a handsome piece of furniture made from solid oak; Father had spent many hours at the massive desk scratching out his religious philosophies with a narrow-tipped pen. "Father had the secretary made by a cabinet shop in Tennessee. I was a little girl when it was delivered. It took two carriages to carry the pieces."

"I intend to buy it for my office. I need something larger than the piece that's there now, and this would fit nicely."

I showed him how to release a hidden compartment in back of one of the slots for stationery and the trick to unlocking the lower drawers. We struck up a pleasant conversation, and he was by my side an hour later when Mr. Pruitt closed the sale for the day. I was surprised and pleased by Hugo's attentions. No man since Jimmy Wiggins had taken any notice of me. Father's profound piety demanded that I dress in severe, high-necked gowns with no adornment, and wear a cap covering my best feature, my hair. Since Father's death I'd enjoyed the freedom of dressing my hair in an attractive and modern style, and a rouge pot I found in Mother's dresser improved the usual pallor of my skin. Pride induced me to dress for the auction in my dead mother's best gown, a fitted navy suit with accents of silk ribbon around the neck and hem. It suited me, and I was pleased when I caught sight of my reflection in the hall mirror.

"Would you take a walk with me, Miss Bellingham?" Hugo held my hand as we stood on the porch. "I've found a decent tea shop not far from the canal. We could stop there afterwards if you'd do me the honor."

I nodded, hardly daring to speak.

"Are you free tomorrow afternoon?"

"I believe I am," I murmured softly.

"I'll come by at two."

At the side of my bed that night I knelt and prayed to God, my true guide. I begged for his forgiveness in the matter of my sinful feelings for Sally Ann Tilson, and though I didn't love Hugo Laurent, I begged God for marriage to him. Marriage was my only chance of escaping a life spent in the service of others, and I resolved to become Hugo's wife, whatever it took. I promised God I would grow to love Hugo.

Perhaps the failure to fulfill that promise is why demons plague me with morbid thoughts: I lie awake hours every night dwelling on the darkness in my soul, the impurity and wickedness of my thoughts. The guilt I feel drives me to despair. I have a better understanding of Father's madness now that I recognize signs of it in myself. I am, after all, my father's daughter.

Hugo's favorite topic of conversation was his family's plantation. "Sweetbrier, the main house, is a little over eleven miles from Smithfield. The plantation holdings cover some three thousand acres. My father believed in expansion; the tracts he bought are on both sides of the river."

"Three thousand acres! My! That sounds like an awful lot of land. How do you take care of it all?"

"The slaves help, of course. Couldn't do it without them, in fact. I have a handful over a hundred darkies living in three different settlements. They keep breeding, so I expect that number to go up some. I'm overseeing in the field quite a lot, particularly during planting and harvesting seasons." He fell quiet for a minute. "I need someone to manage Sweetbrier when I'm gone. I'll admit to you frankly, Lucille, I'm looking for a wife." I gazed down at my hands. They were trembling slightly, and I pressed them together so he wouldn't notice. "I know it seems quick, Lucille, and you might refuse, but would you marry me? I am in sore need of a wife and family."

I didn't want to appear too eager. "May I think it over and tell you tomorrow?"

"Of course. Should I stop by in the afternoon, around 3:00?" I managed a nod. Hugo Laurent proposed in the afternoon the next day, and I accepted. A week later, we were married in the sanctuary at Saint John's.

"Your father was such a generous benefactor, there will be no charge, Miss Bellingham." Pastor Gustavson inclined his head graciously, and I restrained myself from answering with an acid reply about Father's bequest to the church leaving me little more than a beggar. I merely nodded and smiled. He performed the ceremony speedily. Mr. Pruitt and his wife were among the small group of witnesses, which I thought was very nice of them both.

That night, in my girlhood bed, I was initiated to the animal nature of my husband. I lay still as he climbed on top of me and parted my legs. I tried not to cry when his blade pierced the most private passage. I hoped it would end soon, but it took forever as he heaved up and down, battering and ramming his target until a stinging fluid spilled down the insides of my legs. When he was finished, I felt every inch the names father called me: a slut, a whore, a common trollop.

The move to Sweetbrier didn't lessen my aversion to Hugo. I endured the shameful activities of the marriage bed as long as I could, waking in the morning with my woman's parts on fire. The smell of his sweat lingered on my skin and made me gag into the washbasin. With my marriage vows in mind and my aching need to have a child, I forced myself to accept his attentions. After Bert was born, I began to lock my bedroom door. Only when he pounded and implored angrily did I let Hugo in. Fortunately, as time passed, the unpleasant nightly skirmishes occurred rarely.

Hugo must have been enormously disappointed; I was entirely unsuited to run the plantation, and I couldn't bear his touch. I did my best to pretend, I did my best to fit into life at Sweetbrier, but I was desperately unhappy, as trapped in the big house as in our house on Chartres Street. I never realized how much I would miss New Orleans until I moved to this God-forsaken spot on the edge of a swamp.

The only success I've had in life is being a loving, devoted mother. Bert is my savior, my darling. Hugo spoiled our bond when he sent him away to school. It made me hate Hugo even more. How could he tear away the reason for my continued existence? Now I live for Bert's visits home from school. My son is the only reason I keep putting one foot in front of the other.

Addie Turner

Sweetbrier Plantation

1837

Bert was ten when Mr. Hugo put his foot down and insisted on sending his son to a boarding school for young gentlemen. I was polishing the silver tea service in the pantry, and I heard a bunch of shouting from Mr. Hugo, and Miss Lucille moaning and screaming like someone was sticking her with needles. "The boy can't grow up to be a man if he's being mollycoddled by his mother," Mr. Hugo yelled, and no pleading on Miss Lucille's part would change his mind.

When Bert's boarding school started up in the fall Mr. Hugo had a carriage hitched up, and he drove Bert to school all the way up to Baton Rouge. Mr. Hugo forbade Miss Lucille to go. "You'll upset the boy, the way you're carrying on," he said. As soon as the carriage left the driveway, Miss Lucille turned into a regular fountain of tears. As for the help, we were happy that Bert was gone.

Miss Lucille turned back to her old ways, before Bert was born, burrowing in her bed for most of the day like a boll weevil in a bud of cotton. I started taking a breakfast tray up to her, and more often than not, she'd pour out her sorrows and do a whole lot of weepin'. Then she'd have me light enough lanterns so she could read scripture.

No doubt Miss Lucille was lonely and downhearted, and there wasn't nobody around to relieve her from being bored. She only came to life when Mr. Bert visited on school holidays. Those times, she was a terror, bossing everyone around, making sure Bert's bedroom was freshened and the house sparkling clean. Mama and Chemise would be busier than usual with the extra chores and orders to make all of Bert's favorite foods.

Every time Bert went back to school, Miss Lucille dove into misery just like clockwork. Eventually that woman got so gloomy you could almost catch the feeling from being around her. Mr. Hugo tried to cheer her up, but Miss Lucille already had trouble loving him, and it only got worse with him sending Bert to school. Relations between them got frostier, and Mr. Hugo avoided her if he could.

Us who helped in the house suspected that Mr. Hugo was denied normal marriage rights, and like most red-blooded men, he had needs. He spent more time away than ever, overseeing the planting and harvesting, coming home late if he came home at all, and who knew who he visited on his way home. There were rumors about him bedding a Cajun half-breed down at the lower settlement, and if he did, who could blame him. I missed Mr. Hugo when he was gone. He was dependable, which made a welcome change from the crazy moods of Miss Lucille.

Not a single soul besides his mama missed Bert. Even Mr. Hugo didn't seem to like his own son much. Whenever that boy was home he played his same mean tricks on the slave children. His favorite punishment was to twist a little finger until it broke or hold a twig he'd lit on fire to someone's hair. Our folks told the children to stay away from him; just try to disappear as quick as possible when he came around. "But don't let him know you're avoidin' him, 'cause then he be sure to come after you."

Bert didn't mess with me, maybe 'cause I was older than him, or maybe 'cause I'd been part of the big house since I could walk, but tales of his meanness were told in most every cabin on the plantation. Luckily, he wasn't home near as much as he was gone away at school.

When Bert graduated from his boarding school, Mr. Hugo paid for him to go to college to study up on business. "You'll run this plantation someday, Son, and you'll need to learn about the new ways of agriculture," said Mr. Hugo.

"Bert's been away at school far too long! He belongs here at Sweetbrier." Miss Lucille begged and argued, but Mr. Hugo was like a bulldog with a bone when he decided something. Bert was goin' off to college, and what Miss Lucille wanted didn't matter. For the weeks he was home, Miss Lucille went all out fussing over her boy. The way she spoiled him was sick, and I determined never to do that with my own children.

The day he left for college made another big puddle in Miss Lucille's weeping hanky. "Good-bye, Mama," Bert yelled from atop the coach piled high with his trunks.

"Good-bye, darling." Miss Lucille's voice quivered. As soon as that coach turned the corner, she ran up the stairs, collapsed into her fainting chair and refused to leave her room for a month. I was the one who finally coaxed her to come out and get some fresh air. "You need to stretch your legs, Miss Lucille. Smellin' the pretty flowers is bound to make you feel better." On our walk around the yard she leaned on me like she was an old lady, but she was younger than Mama who worked her tail to the bone.

Bert's trips homes were farther and farther apart, and Miss Lucille started having conversations with people who weren't really there. She'd talk to someone named Sally Ann, and sometimes she'd plead with her daddy to forgive her for who knows what. She'd read the Bible aloud for hours at a time in a shaky voice, and sometimes she wouldn't comb her hair for days. I'd have to untangle the mats and try to calm her down.

She got so bad I thought she was goin' crazy for once and for all, but Miss Lucille still managed to rise up and be normal when

Bert dropped in like a swarm of locusts. "I know some day you'll finish college and come home to run the plantation." She hung onto her precious son, plastering him with kisses before he climbed into the carriage to go back to school. All of us working in the big house rolled our eyes. None of us could imagine lovin' Mr. Bert like she did.

"Don't Miss Lucille have any idea how mean he is?" Chemise asked.

Mama shrugged. "Love has a way of makin' roses from a pot of ash, I guess."

Miss Lucille practically busted a seam when her precious darling came home halfway through his second year of college and announced he was leaving school. I was serving pot roast and potatoes to the three of them, and Bert looked through me like I wasn't even there. To him, us Negroes weren't people who mattered.

"I'm not going back, Father. It's a waste of time and money, since I plan to work a plantation. There's profit potential beyond your wildest dreams in some of the upcoming cash crops. I'm ready to put to use what I've learned."

Mr. Hugo nodded enthusiastically, and Miss Lucille's face beamed out in the biggest smile I'd seen on it for years. "Wonderful, Bert! I'm so happy you're coming home, darling."

"Well, the thing is, Mama, I'm not coming home. I've asked a girl to marry me, and she said yes."

Miss Lucille turned white as mashed potatoes and clutched at her collar. "Who?" she said, gasping for breath. I patted her on the back 'cause I thought she was choking, but she was just being Miss Lucille.

"Her name is Sara Pierce. Her father owns Pierce Place over in Natchitoches, and he is giving us a deed of ownership of a thousand acres on the plantation," said Bert. "Someday, I'll run the whole place."

"But what about Sweetbrier?" squeaked Miss Lucille.

"Father can take care of Sweetbrier. Until he can't, I'll make my start on the Pierce place, where Sarah can be with her own people."

When Miss Lucille realized her precious boy wasn't never comin' home, she reminded me of a trout that's been fished out of its home pond and is about to have its throat slit. She said that she needed to lie down because of a pounding headache. I was sent up with damp towels to drape over her forehead. Miss Lucille was crying bitterly. "When you have your baby, you'll understand." She nodded to indicate my belly, which was growing larger by the day with our unborn child. Garvus and I had been trying to have a nice little family since we been hitched. Finally, our hopes for a child had come true.

"A son means the world to his mother, but he ends up breaking her heart." Miss Lucille let out a whimper and dabbed at her eyes, trying to sop up those tears that wouldn't stop falling. It was an especially bad spell for Miss Lucille. She ordered all the curtains be kept closed in her rooms, and the murky light matched the gloomy attitude she had. For weeks that woman moped around, moaning and complaining about the aches and pains she conjured up. She could snap out of her crazy moods though, if the occasion called for it.

Miss Lucille got up and acted just fine when Bert brought his bride-to-be, Miss Sarah, home to Sweetbrier to meet his parents. As soon as Miss Lucille read the note about their comin' to visit, she got out of bed, put on some regular clothes instead of one of her dressing gowns, and had me fix her hair into a tidy bun. She set out planning the menus for their visit, and she ordered Mama and Chemise to air and dust the nicest upstairs bedroom for Miss Sarah. It was always a wonderment to us around her, how she could pull herself together and act like a whole different person.

Come to find that even though Sarah Pierce was stealing away Bert, Miss Lucille and she got on like they was relations. Miss Sarah's mama was dead for a couple of years now from a wasting disease, and

Miss Lucille got all motherly and close to Miss Sarah. It just goes to show that a lot of Miss Lucille's troubles came from pure loneliness.

Miss Sarah loved Miss Lucille, and she loved Sweetbrier. The old place was awful pretty to behold, especially in the springtime, when all the blossoms let off their scent and the air smells so sweet, like the finest perfume. "I'd like to be married at Sweetbrier," she said to Bert, and a couple months later, on an Indian summer day in October, the wedding was held in the back garden under the grape and jasmine arbor that Miss Lucille begged Mr. Hugo to build in the early years of their marriage.

In the weeks before the wedding, Mama and Chemise worked late every day, cleaning the house until the windows were crystal clear and every last dust particle was swept away, preparing breakfast, lunch, and a fancy wedding dinner for seventy-five guests. The three of us washed a ton of linens and bedding and made up the rooms with extra cots; some thirty relatives from the Pierce side planned to stay the entire weekend. Since I was swelled up like a watermelon with our baby, Mama insisted on doing the heavy work alone. I'll never forgive myself for letting her work so hard.

On the wedding day we ran our tails off. Mama was sweating over the stove as usual and bossing around the dozen girls who were called in to help in the big house. I was awful hot from being pregnant and close to bursting, so Mama gave me the easy job of puttin' the place settings on the table. "Martha, you go along and help Addie set up the tables," she said to one of the girls. The dining table was extended as far as it could go, and extra tables were set up in the room 'cause of feeding so many people. I taught Martha where to put the salad forks and the water glasses and such. The table looked real pretty when we finished.

Miss Lucille flitted around like a butterfly to make sure the knives and forks were where they were supposed to be and the flowers on the tables looking just so. When she was satisfied, Mr. Hugo rang the big dinner bell that called everyone in from the garden. Mama, Chemise and the girls served the guests plates of green salad and bowls of tomato bisque and set baskets of buttermilk biscuits on the table. For the next course they carted out long plates piled three deep in big ol' crawdads, with bowls of butter for dipping and more bread to sop the juices up.

The crawdad course went on for a while, everyone messin' with cracking the shells and so on. When the plates were cleared, the help brought out trays of steaming washcloths for folks to tidy up with. Then came heavy platters piled high with turkey and roast beef, tureens of gravy, huge bowls of potato salad and green beans. Nobody left that table hungry; especially after eating a slice of Mama's spice cake and drinking a glass or two of Mr. Hugo's sweet port wine.

When the guests were finally snoring in their rooms, Mama, Chemise, and I finished cleaning up all the china and silverware. "Let's leave these pots and pans to soak and sit down a spell," said Mama, "My back needs a rest." Chemise brought slices of spice cake for the three of us, and we sat at the kitchen table. Mama took one bite and said she was too tired to eat the rest, which was surprising since Mama loves her sweets. I looked at her carefully; she did look awfully tired. I was glad the wedding was over; Mama needed a rest from working so hard.

The next morning the wedding party cheered and lit Chinese firecrackers to celebrate Mr. Bert and Miss Sarah riding off in their coach to the Pierce Plantation. Mama and Chemise served up a nice big breakfast, and after eating like they was a bunch of starving dogs, the guests packed up and called for their carriages. The stable boys were busy as flies on dead meat, buzzing around to get the horses harnessed up and the luggage strapped aboard.

It took two full days for the wedding excitement to fade completely. All of us around the place was waiting for the storm clouds to come rolling in, and when they did, Miss Lucille was worse than ever before. Now, she was sayin' she wanted to die, and since she barely touched the trays of food Mama sent up to her room, it seemed like she was heading for the grave.

"Come on, now, Miss Lucille. Ain't you gonna eat a little something?" I'd say, trying to get a spoon of this or that into her mouth.

"I am ready to go, Addie! If only God would take me from this mortal sorrow!" she cried. Dr. Brisco came out and said there was nothin' in the world wrong with her, but that didn't put a damper on her thinking she was sick and near dying. Usually, I could coax Miss Lucille out of the blues, but I was busy with my own life, and slowed down by my condition. Plus, Mama wasn't feeling good, which worried me to no end.

Mama never complained, so I knew it was bad when she said she ached in every bone of her body. "My head feels like it's about to explode, it's throbbing so bad." It was nothin' like Miss Lucille, whose head hurt her whenever she chose it to hurt. You could see in Mama's eyes the pain, and it was real. Mr. Hugo was decent about when someone felt sick, always letting a person rest 'til they felt better, but Mama went to work in the big house as usual instead of staying in bed like she should have. I've felt guilty ever since, wondering if she went to work that day to cover for me, 'cause I got lazier the bigger I got.

"You don't look so good," Chemise patted Mama's hand. "You kind of gray in the face. You feeling all right?"

"Probably just the usual aches and pains of gettin' old," Mama said. "Now, instead of talking, why don't you help me fold up the linen?" Sometime after noon, Chemise and Mama and me were making sausages when Mama all of a sudden said she needed to sit down. "I'm plumb tired and my head's about to bust into pieces. I got to put my head down and close my eyes."

An hour later, when Chemise tried to wake Mama up from where she was slumped on the table with her head buried in her arms, she was burning hot with fever and limp to the touch. Garvus and three of the stable boys rolled her onto a flat pallet and carried her home to the cabin.

I tended Mama through the night, tryin' to bring down the fever, but no amount of sponging with cool water helped. By early morning she was trembling and twitching through her whole body, and when I tried feeding her a spoonful of mush it dribbled down her chin. Garvus went to fetch Doc Spivens, the old, drunken excuse of a doctor who attends to the darkies and the farm animals, but he couldn't do a thing except say that he was mighty sorry, and the Lord had a way of taking someone when she was ready, and Mama must have been waiting in line to get a chance to live in paradise. "Good luck and God bless you," he said. "I got another call to make for a sick cow."

I started in again sponging her with the cool water. "Mama," I whispered, "please don't be sick! I need you to help with this baby that's gonna be here any day." Mama opened her eyes and looked at me so sad before she shut them.

It was the last time Mama opened her eyes. A few hours later she was dead.

I never believed much in heaven and hell and God; I always thought it sounded like a bunch of hokum pokum, but I hoped what the Doctor said about paradise was true. Mama, of all people, deserved to be in paradise.

I mourned so hard that I swear my Sophie popped out early to take Mama's place and stop me from crying. Our baby girl saved me from drowning in sorrow. No matter how sad I was about losing Mama, just holding Sophie in my arms made me smile. I only wish Mama could've got to know her first grandchild.

Not long after Sophie was born, I went back to work in the big house to take Mama's place beside Chemise. It made sense, 'cause I knew Mama's chores backwards and forwards. Mr. Hugo asked me to take her place right after Mama's funeral, which he turned out for, standing in the background with his hat in his hands. Miss Lucille felt too faint to come, but she did tell me later that she was mighty sorry for my loss. "Your Mama was the finest cook I ever met." She patted my arm and handed me a cotton handkerchief to dry my tears.

Every day, I carried Sophie with me to the big house, tucking her crib into a corner by the pantry door where she was warm and out of the way. I fed her between chores. That baby girl seemed to know her place in the big house; she was quiet and didn't draw attention to the fact she was there. I counted my lucky stars, for she could scream like crazy if she woke up in the middle of the night back at the cabin.

I still took Miss Lucille her breakfast when I could, but more often than not, Chemise's bird-witted cousin who helped in the house was sent up with a tray. The kitchen and housekeeping kept me busy, and on top of that, I had my precious child to tend to. Sometimes, I wondered how my sweet mama did all those chores and cooking at the big house, and then done the same thing at home in the little bit of spare time she had. Mama was truly good and kind, and it gives me inspiration whenever I think about her. But this story isn't about Mama as much as it's about the falling apart of Sweetbrier, a falling apart that was long and slow but moving always towards the end of a way of life for us who lived there. It would take another twenty years, and at the end, the plantation would lie in ruins and my family'd be torn apart forever.

Miss Lucille carried on with her crazy moods, every day worse than the one before, until that morning in December when Mr. Hugo tried to talk sense into her and she went after him with the butcher knife. Sophie was in her crib in the corner, and Lord bless, she slept through all that screaming and caterwauling. That's when I grabbed the knife out of her hand and half carried Miss Lucille up the stairs to her bedroom. "You ought to send someone to town to fetch the doctor," I said.

Mr. Hugo nodded with that sad, beat up look. "Tell Garvus to go. I'll be in the office if you need me." I didn't doubt that he poured himself a shot or two of the whiskey he kept in his desk drawer to get some relief from his troubles with Miss Lucille.

Doctor Brisco arrived on horseback later that day. I was in the room when he examined Miss Lucille. Ever since Chemise and I laid her on her bed, she'd been curled up like a prawn, moaning and talking gibberish. The doctor leaned over the bed with his hearing tube dangling from his neck. "What's hurting you Lucille?"

"I can't go on. I want to leave this mortal world. There is nothing to live for anymore!" She started shaking with sobs.

"You're just hysterical, Lucille," said Doctor Brisco. "I have something that will help you." He poured a whiskey glass full of dark tonic from a tall bottle he'd pulled from his satchel. "Now drink the whole thing down." He held it to her lips and she gulped.

Miss Lucille hiccoughed. "Why, that tastes awful."

"You'll get used to it in time. It's an opiated tonic, to help calm your nerves. Now try and get some rest." Doctor Brisco drew up the coverlet and tucked it around Miss Lucille. "Where is Hugo?" he asked.

Miss Lucille shrugged and turned her head away. "I don't know, and I don't much care," were her last words before she started snoring like a drunk sailor.

"Mr. Hugo is in his office downstairs," I said.

"Well, take me there, girl."

I didn't much like Doctor Brisco or his tone of voice, but that was what you had to expect from white men. I nodded and led him to the office. "Mr. Hugo, the doctor wants to talk to you," I said real soft, through the inch or so that the door was cracked open.

"Come on in." Mr. Hugo was sitting at his shiny oak desk with his head in his hands, a half empty bottle of whiskey and a shot glass next to him. His eyes were red and tired looking, but he stood up and shook the doctor's hand, smiling like nothin' was out of the ordinary. Mr. Hugo poured Doctor Brisco a tumbler of whiskey, and my mouth fell open when he even poured an inch or so in a little glass and handed it to me. "You earned this, Addie." I thanked him and took a sip of the stuff. It made my eyes water, and I set the glass back down on his desk. "Did you know, Brisco, that Addie here saved me from being stabbed to death by my own wife?"

"You don't say!" Doctor Brisco swallowed the whiskey in one gulp.

Mr. Hugo poured him another glass. "I'm at my wit's end of how to make Lucille happy and well," he said.

"Lucille is suffering from a nervous condition, Hugo. I've left her a tonic that will soothe her for the time being. Besides that, I think it wise to hire a lady's companion. Lucille needs some company from a woman of her own kind and color." The doctor finished his whiskey and handed the empty glass to me. "I've seen this condition before in women of Lucille's age and temperament. We'll see how the tonic works on her nerves. Other than that, Hugo, you should put some effort into finding a suitable woman to be a friend to your wife." The doctor shook Mr. Hugo's hand on his way out the door. "Don't despair, Hugo. Lucille will snap out of this in time."

"Do you think so?

"I am quite sure. These cases of female hysteria are often merely a phase." He shook Mr. Hugo's hand again and closed the door softly behind him.

Mr. Hugo let out a big sigh. "Well Addie, I guess I better work on finding someone who can help Lucille." I nodded and gathered the dirty whiskey glasses to take to the kitchen.

It was only a few weeks later that Fern Dumond came to the plantation to be Miss Lucille's companion. Mr. Hugo brought her to Sweetbrier from Mercy House Orphanage in Baton Rouge. She was a pretty girl, her soft face filled up with big, soulful blue eyes that looked like they'd seen the sorrows of the ages. They were old eyes in a young face and it kind of confused you when you looked at her because otherwise she was like a child. Later, Fern told me she was twenty years old, but she looked more like she was sixteen. I got to say that I liked Fern from the beginning. Chemise did too, 'cause Fern had a sweet nature and you couldn't help liking that girl. Chemise and I carried her trunk to the room next to Miss Lucille, and I was surprised at how light it was, like there wasn't nothing but dreams and hopes inside, and maybe a few clothes.

"You got anything else coming?" I asked her.

"No. This is it," she said with a friendly smile. "Thank you both for carrying it up the stairs."

"You're welcome, ma'am," said Chemise.

"Oh, please call me Fern," and she gave us each a hug, which was mighty surprising coming from a white girl. Fern was like that though. She didn't care what color a person was. It was one of the ways about Fern that got me to truly love her like a sister by the time she joined Mama in paradise.

Fern Dumond

Sweetbrier

January 1838

I am free from Mercy House at last!! It is undoubtedly unchristian—even blasphemous—to feel so exhilarated at escaping the orphanage and the nuns, but I don't care! Let blasphemes shout from my lips! I'm free, I'm free, I'm free! And nothing will make me go back; I swear to it on a stack of Bibles a mile high!

Sweetbrier is paradise compared to Mercy House. The orphanage was such a grim place: heavy, glum, endlessly gray. Perhaps it isn't true of all orphanages, but the very atmosphere at Mercy House dampened the spirit. I suspect the whole place was haunted by sadness and despair.

When I was nine years old I was taken to Mercy House and forgotten by any mortal soul outside the orphanage grounds. All my relations were dead, and I hadn't a penny to call my own. I wept as my head was shorn for the precautionary control of lice, and I was given a cast-iron-gray jumper to change into. The sister conducting the demeaning ritual to which new girls were subjected wasn't sympathetic. "We don't take to tears around here, young lady. You'll have to strengthen up if you're going to last at Mercy House."

The Sisters of Mercy adhered to a quiet order; meals eaten in silence, work performed without conversation, life lived without affection. Though I tried to make light where there were only shadows, the place quieted my soul and began to smother any spark of fun or laughter. The only joy was singing in the church choir. It was a tiny bright offering among an otherwise colorless existence. Over the years I yearned for adoption, but no one offered. People tended to adopt younger children on the rare occasions anyone came looking for a child.

Before Mr. Laurent inquired about a companion for his wife, I worried I might have to join the nuns. A female orphan with no money and no living relations has little chance for life in the world outside the church. Many of the girls in my predicament follow the nuns into service, becoming gray-robed ghosts with dull eyes, unless they are lucky enough to secure employment as a governess or lady's maid. Some take to the streets to earn a living in the oldest profession available to females. That's often a death sentence. The nuns have us pray for the failed souls who strayed after leaving Mercy House.

When I turned twenty, Sister Judith called me to her office and made clear the grim realities: "You are past the age of a dependent orphan, Fern, and to remain here you are expected to join the order and perform the same services you received as a ward of Mercy House. You could eventually teach the children once you've completed your vows."

"I am afraid I'm not suited to a cloistered life," I murmured.

"You must accept your fated lot if it is all you are offered, Fern. Otherwise, how will you live?"

A week passed, with Sister Judith waiting for my answer. Everywhere I turned I felt her watching me with her round bird eyes. "It's time for you to make a decision, Fern. I'll wait until the weekend, then we must have clarity about your plans." I felt trapped by Mercy House and my poverty. I considered striking out on my own, yet the reality of an uncertain future frightened me. At the last minute, on the Friday before I was to hand down my decision, a blessed opportunity saved me from plunging into the precipice of the holy order.

Mr. Hugo Laurent's offer was nothing short of a miracle.

Sister Judith summoned me to the office to meet him in person. "Your duties would involve being a companion to my wife, Lucille, who has a fragile nature," said Mr. Hugo. "The job pays twelve dollars a month, plus room and board and every other Sunday off. You would have your own rooms down the hall from my wife." He met my eyes and smiled for the first time. "Does this interest you at all?"

"Yes, it does, Mr. Laurent. I'd like very much to take the position."

"And what qualifies you for the job, Miss Dumond?"

"I am well educated in history and literature, and skilled in the needle arts. I am friendly and helpful by nature and am willing to do whatever tasks are necessary for the job. My aim is to please, Sir."

Mr. Laurent nodded his head and looked at me thoughtfully. "You seem lively and cheerful, which is what Lucille needs. I think she would like you very much. The job is yours, Miss Dumond, if the terms suit you."

"Thank you, Mr. Laurent. I accept the terms and will do everything in my power to not disappoint you."

"How soon can you be ready to join us at Sweetbrier?"

"I could be ready within the hour."

Mr. Laurent looked surprised. "Even better. I thought you might need a few days. Very well then, why don't I ride to town to do some business, and swing back around by midafternoon to pick you up? Give you time to pack and all."

I nodded. "That would be perfect, Mr. Laurent." He shook my hand. "I will plan to arrive here around two, Miss Dumond." He bowed to us as he departed.

Sister Judith pressed her lips together tightly, and her piercing eyes searched my face. "Well, it looks like you've gotten what you wished for, Fern. Go on and pack then. Be careful to leave behind any property of Mercy House. You may take your brush and comb, but not the hand mirror. Your clothes are yours to take, but the aprons and the bedding on your cot stay." She stood up from her desk and inclined her head dismissively. My hand was on the door ready to exit when she called after me. "Here, Fern, is a Bible for you to carry wherever you go and wherever you end up in life." I took the compact leather-bound volume from her. "If the position doesn't work out, you can always return to Mercy House and become one of us. You know that, of course."

I nodded politely, but inside I shouted that I'd never return to this miserable place. A god-sent miracle in the form of Hugo Laurent saved me from what had seemed an inevitable fate. I would dispose of the Bible at the earliest possible moment.

Mr. Hugo and I are kindred spirits! It took the better part of two days to travel from Mercy House to Sweetbrier. We talked a mile a minute the whole way, and I made him laugh with my tales of the orphanage and funny imitations of the nuns. It was past eight and getting dark when we stopped at an inn near Midway Ferry. "We'll stay overnight here and take the ferry in the early morning," he said. "I'm sure you're tired, Miss Dumond, and wish to get some rest. Shall I ask the innkeeper to send a light meal to your room? Or would you care to join me in the dining room?"

"I'm not tired in the least, Mr. Laurent. I'll be delighted to join you."

The inn fare was plain; a plate of bread and cheese and a second plate of sliced meats and pickled vegetables. "Sorry, but you'll have to make do with cold cuts. We served our last hot dinner an hour ago." The innkeeper's wife, a large, red-faced woman wearing a soiled white apron, put the plates on the table. "Will the Mr. and Missus enjoy a glass of beer?"

"Please," said Mr. Laurent, not bothering to correct her mistaken impression that we were man and wife.

Our meal confirmed the ease between us. We had no lack of conversation, and the few quiet spots were comfortable, as if we'd known each other for years. Mr. Laurent was a kind and understanding man, and genuinely interested in me as a father might be. When Mr. Laurent suggested that I join him in the barroom for a glass of sweet port, I agreed.

I was not used to spirits and drinking them gave me a boldness that was not usual. When the fiddler struck up a tune in the barroom, I asked him if he knew *Sweet Afton*, and I stood and sang it all by myself! I didn't even mind the handful of folks listening in the dimly lit room and was surprised and pleased when they clapped and asked me to sing another.

Mr. Laurent walked me to my bedroom door. "You have a lovely singing voice, Miss Dumond."

"Thank you, Sir. I had a lot of practice singing at church."

"The ferryboat boards at eight in the morning. Good night. I hope you sleep well."

I shut the door softly and prepared to climb into the metal-framed bed. It took a long time for my heart to stop beating in my chest like a hummingbird in motion. It was excitement causing the fluttering sensation, I decided at last. A half an hour later I was asleep, dreaming of white knights and enchanted wonderlands.

Mr. Hugo asked me to call him by his first name on the ferry ride down the river. "Mr. Laurent makes it sound like I'm ninety years old. You'll be living with us in the house, and Mr. Hugo is not so stiff and formal sounding." I nodded and replied that he should use my first name in addressing me as well.

Thereafter, he addressed me as Miss Fern until the night a few months later when we lay together on a blanket spread over a pile of hay in the barn. That night, he called me darling. He kissed every inch of my body starting with my toes and working his way up my legs to the wet place that thrills and quivers whenever he touches me.

"You're as soft and velvety as a rosebud," he whispered, slowly penetrating my throbbing part with gentle thrusts. Hugo moaned, and his hot love spilled into me. Afterward, he resumed kissing my top half, pressing his lips to my eyes, nibbling and tickling my ears with his tongue, gently sucking my breasts, pressing his nose into my armpit.

I might have felt embarrassed, but his earnest enjoyment reassured me. "Your smell sets me on fire, Fern," he said. My excitement grew, and once more he entered me, thrusting until I burst into an electricity of sensations I'd never before experienced. We lay in each other's arms afterwards, weak and trembling.

It is wicked, I know, to experience such bliss and ecstasy, and a mortal sin to engage with another woman's husband. Whatever the cost to my salvation, Hugo's love and attentions made my fall from grace a ride of sheer pleasure. When Miss Lucille put an end to our intimacy, I wanted to die from the sorrow. Carrying our love child was the only thing that stopped me from jumping into the great Mississippi.

Addie Turner Washington

Sweetbrier

1838

Fern loved living at Sweetbrier and being out of the orphanage. "I can't tell you how awful it was, Addie. Everything was gray: the nuns, the walls, the blankets, even the food had a grayish color." Fern shuddered. She was standing at the counter, helping Chemise roll out piecrust. That was another good thing about her; she'd pitch right in and help and be mighty cheerful about it.

"How'd you get stuck in that orphanage, anyway?" asked Chemise.

"Both Mama and Papa died of yellow fever when I was six years old. After that, I lived with my grandmother until she went soft in the head and burned down the house."

"Burned the house down? What in hell for?" Chemise flipped the piecrust over and started rolling it until it was paper-thin; the way Miss Lucille liked it.

"It was an accident. Grandmother was getting confused. She'd get up in the middle of the night and get dressed, thinking it was time to feed the chickens. Then she forgot which cupboard the flour was in, and where the outhouse was."

"That's like old Mavis," said Chemise. "She takes a walk and she don't know how to get back home. Her daughter said she gonna have to tie her up, so she don't get lost." The three of us shook our heads about poor old Mavis getting so mixed up.

"That sounds a lot like what happened to Grandmother," said Fern. "The day the house burned down, she'd started a fire in the kitchen cabinet instead of the wood stove. I came home from school and our house was burnt to a smoking pile of rubble. Grandmother was standing in the front yard, and when the neighbors brought me over to her, she didn't know my name. After that, they put Grandmother in a home, and I was sent to Mercy House. I never did see her again."

We were quiet for a minute, rolling out the dough in time with our thoughts. "How old were you?" I asked.

"I was almost ten when I was put in the orphanage, and I'm twenty now, so I spent a little over ten years there." She shook her head like she couldn't believe it. "They weren't such good years. I hope the next ten are better," she said. All of a sudden, she started singing, and she grabbed my waist and waltzed me around the table. I about laughed myself silly. Fern could spice up a room like that, make people laugh and sing and feel happy. She craved affection, probably 'cause there weren't much of it at the orphanage, and she gave out kisses and hugs freely.

Miss Lucille perked up from Fern being her companion and friend. "You're the daughter I always longed for," she said. Privately, I thought Miss Lucille was sweet on Fern, the way she leaned on her when they walked together, the way she pressed against her when they worked on the tapestry, the way she kiss and hug and fuss over Fern. I thought it was curious, but you could always expect the unexpected with Miss Lucille, particularly when she took too much of the tonic Doctor Brisco prescribed. Fern lapped up affection like a dog with a bowl of milk, and she loved Miss Lucille like she was her own dead Mama. I don't think she really noticed a thing about Miss Lucille being a little too affectionate.

At seven every morning, Fern took Miss Lucille's tray upstairs. She'd help her dress, brush her hair and pin it up in the soft coil that Miss Lucille wore on top of her head. For the rest of the morning, Fern read to her, or the two of them did needlework on a tapestry Miss Lucile started the year she and Mr. Hugo got married. Towards noon, Fern took Miss Lucille for a walk in the gardens, which was good for that woman, being cooped up like a roosting pigeon in her fancy rooms. Chemise and I would see them from the kitchen window, stopping to look at one or other flower or bush, with Miss Lucille taking ginger steps, leaning on Fern's arm like she was an old woman, and Fern chattering away like a magpie.

Fern served Miss Lucille lunch at noon, and following Doctor Brisco's directions, she poured her a dose of the tonic. I'd noticed by now that the tonic made Miss Lucille kinda floaty, like she in a dream world instead of the real place of flesh and blood. The tonic also made her sleepy, and she usually took a long nap in the afternoon.

When Miss Lucille woke up and rang her bell, Fern took a tea tray to her room. The two of them would chatter while Miss Lucille took sparrow-sized bites from the tea sandwiches. The rest of the afternoon was spent playing card games or checkers, crocheting or knitting, and studying the Bible. Occasionally, Fern played the pianoforte and sang hymns and spirituals, which sounded real pretty from what we could hear in the kitchen. Miss Lucille took a second dose of Doctor Brisco's medicine with an early dinner served in her bedroom, and most nights she was asleep by dark, leaving Fern free again. It didn't seem like much of a life for Fern, but she was plain happy being away from that orphanage.

"It was little better than a work camp," Fern told us, describing the long days filled with chores, the schoolroom, and a lot of praying and church services. "Nobody smiled at Mercy House. Can you imagine? A world of frowning nuns and quiet little girls." Fern took me and Chemise by the hands. "I swear to both of you, I'll never let a child of mine end up in such a place," she said, her eyes filling with tears.

"Well, you don't have to worry about it right now," I said. "You ain't even married yet."

She got a dreamy look on her face. "When I do get married, I want to have six children, three boys and three girls."

"Well honey, you don't have much choice whether a baby come out a boy or a girl, but good luck." I said. She hugged me and ran off to Miss Lucille's room to do her afternoon duties. I gave a big sigh; 'cause somehow I had a feeling things were gonna get all mixed up.

I ain't gonna tell nothin' but the truth 'bout Fern's being on the edge of love, ready to jump off the maiden's cliff. Her body was ripe, and the moon's moods played through her so that anyone nearby could get caught up in her heat. I know that's what happened with Mr. Hugo. Here comes a pretty young thing who wants babies and a family of her own to make up for losing her parents and her grandma.

The sad part was that Fern didn't have any husband prospects at Sweetbrier, which opened her up to what happened between her and Mr. Hugo. Fern couldn't help her wants, which were born of sorrow and the hope of filling up an emptiness inside. Mr. Hugo should of been a bigger man and put a stop to what was happening between them, but I reckon he was longing for love with a woman of his own color, being banned from Miss Lucille's bed for so many years.

Come evenings, Fern took to dining with Mr. Hugo, which after a while made Chemise and I roll our eyes at each other. Mr. Hugo wasn't a bad man, and he was handsome and still in his prime. Fern acted like she did because she'd been closed up with the nuns all those years, and then she came to Sweetbrier, a young, beautiful woman. It was bound that something should happen between those two hungry people, and it did.

At first, it was just talk. They talked like they was starving for conversation; like they'd known each other for years. I'd come from the kitchen with the next dish to serve and neither one of them would notice, 'cause they were so busy talking away and drowning in each other's eyes. I know that neither one wanted to hurt Miss Lucille, but the current between them was a whirlpool pulling them down hard and fast. "Somethin' like a two-headed snake gonna come outta this," I said to Chemise.

"Well there ain't nothin' we can do 'bout it, and it ain't none of our business anyway," said Chemise.

"You'd think Mr. Hugo'd stop himself instead of stirring up the feelings of a poor little orphan girl!"

"Fern ain't entirely innocent herself. I think you takin' too much of an interest in that girl, Addie. It's just gonna wind up breakin' your heart," said Chemise, and in the end, she was right.

We sailed right through spring with the talk between Mr. Hugo and Fern growing more familiar every day until it changed from just talk into forbidden sin. It was a hot night towards the end of May. Garvus and me were in our little cabin trying to get some rest, but it was much too warm to sleep. Garvus climbed out of bed after a few hours of tossing and turning. "I got to get some fresh air, see if I can cool down."

"Good luck, honey." I stretched out, glad he was gone for a while 'cause he is like having a burnin' coal next to you in bed. It must have been over ninety degrees, the kind of wet heat that makes you drip and feel like jumping out of your skin 'cause it's too hot to wear it. With Garvus gone, I was hoping that I'd be able to drop off and get a little shuteye. I did fall asleep pretty quick and was havin' a nice dream when Garvus came back to bed an hour or two later and shook me awake.

"What in the wide world is so doggone important you got to wake me up in the middle of the night? Can't it wait 'til the morning?"

"You ain't going to believe what I just seen." He was whispering so he wouldn't wake Sophie up, 'cause if she was startled out of sleep too soon she was one to cry and scream like she was being killed. I worried about waking up our neighbors in the nearby cabins, so I put my finger to my lips to shush him. "I'll come out to the porch. You can tell me there."

It was wet outside from one of the fast-moving storms that tear through our part of the world most summer nights, and it was a whole lot cooler out on the porch. I sat next to Garvus on the front steps and took his big, blistery hand in mine. "What'd you see, honey, that you want to tell me about?" I asked.

"Well, you ain't gonna like it, but since you want to know so bad, I guess it's gotta be told." He went silent then, looking at me with them deep brown eyes that made me fall in love with Garvus in the first place. I squeezed his hand and waited for him to go on.

"When I got up from bed and went outside, I decided to take a walk over to the pond, to jump in and get cooled down. I stripped bare and dog-paddled around for a while, and man, it felt mighty good, getting wet all over. You should've come with me, Addie."

"We couldn't just leave Sophie on her own, honey. What if she'd woke up and we were gone? She'd have screamed the whole place down!"

"That child sure does have a pair of lungs on her. Maybe she'll be a singer like my mama was," said Garvus.

"Maybe so." I wanted him to hurry and finish telling his story so's we could get some sleep. It wasn't more than a couple of hours 'til I was due at the big house and Garvus at the new cornfield. "So, what did you see in the pond, honey?"

Garvus shook his head. "It wasn't nothin' in the pond that I seen. When I got out of the water, I put my clothes back on and was comin' back to lie beside my sweet wife when all of a sudden, that crazy thunder and lightning hit. Did you hear it, Addie?" I murmured that I'd finally gone to sleep and must have missed the storm.

"I can't believe you slept through it, there was such a racket!"

"I was mighty tired, I guess. Mama always said I could sleep through most anything."

"Well, you missed a hell of a show. It was really something, that storm. Them lightning bolts was hitting each other in the sky, exploding like they was cannon balls filled with gunpowder. You'd think the earth was comin' to an end, the way that lightning was striking through the sky, like God was fed up with us here on earth. One of the bolts hit so close I got throwed down to the ground; I could see the steam and smoke rising up where it hit. Them lightning strikes kept on comin' and I was sure I was gonna get killed if I stayed out there. I sure as heck didn't want to leave you a widow so soon, so's I crawled on all fours across the field to the barn, which was the closest place to get some shelter. That's where I seen it, Addie. It's your Miss Fern." He shut up again, and the quiet went on so long I finally poked him in the side.

"Is that all you got to say; 'It's your Miss Fern?' Or you got more to tack on to that? 'Cause if you don't, I'm goin' back to bed, Garvus."

"It was pretty dark in there 'cept for the lightning bolts. When they hit, you could see as clear as day in the barn. They lit up everything, and I couldn't help noticing that there was two people in one of the stalls, lying in a pile of hay. It was plain what they was doin', 'cause they didn't have a stitch of clothes on and the man was on top, grunting, and she was moaning and crying out. I was gonna head out of there quick 'cause it ain't none of my business, but before I left, the lightning hit again. Lord almighty, it showed Miss Fern with Mr. Hugo holdin' her in his arms and kissing her all over, both of 'em naked as nesting jaybirds."

"You sure it wasn't some high yeller girl he found in the fields?"

Garvus shook his head. "There was no mistaking; it was Mr. Hugo and Miss Fern and they was kissin' and huggin' and Mr. Hugo tellin' her how much he love her, and she cryin' and laughin' and moanin' so I had to put my hand over my ears. After that, I got out of there quick 'cause I don't need no trouble from watchin' what I ain't supposed to see."

"Did they see you?"

"No. They was too busy tryin' to make a baby."

"We're going to forget this Garvus. Don't tell another soul."

"What, you think I'm crazy? I ain't sayin' nothin' to nobody except you, 'cause Miss Fern is your friend and all."

"Good thinking honey." We were quiet then, just sitting out there on the porch, our sides pressed up to each other, watching the stars peek out from the storm clouds breaking up. "Let's go to bed," I said finally. Garvus nodded and we went back to try to sleep for the couple of hours before the sun rose.

I don't know if Garvus got the idea from watching Mr. Hugo and Fern, but he whispered that he sure wouldn't mind making another baby with me, and for an hour or so we fooled around. I suspect it was that night when our son, Jerome, got his start in the world. It wasn't long before my stomach swelled up as big as a watermelon from that boy child.

Fern and Mr. Hugo didn't make a baby quite so fast. By December that year, I was in my fifth month, and Fern's belly had only started to look a little suspicious. In the meantime, I'd put some distance between her and myself, which I know hurt Fern's feelings. She asked me once what was wrong, and I snapped at her, "Nothin' other than you're a white girl and I'm just a nigger kitchen slave." She looked like I'd stabbed her, and I felt bad after I said it, but I never said sorry. Then, I committed the evil called gossip and told Chemise about what Garvus saw in the barn, so Chemise started given' her the cold shoulder, too.

For the next few weeks Fern stayed away from the kitchen or wherever Chemise and I'd be working. I was as big as a house, feeling that baby boy in every one of my joints, and especially in my back. Chemise would roll her eyes and say I asked for it when I married such a buck as Garvus. "That boy's mama had ten children, bang-bang-bang. You better watch it girl, or you wind up the same way, with a new baby every year or so."

"That ain't gonna happen," I snapped back, rubbing the ache in my lower back with both my fists. We were polishing Mr. Hugo's Mama's silverware, the nice set that only got taken out for special occasions. Bert and Sara were coming for a visit and the usual excitement rose in Miss Lucille. She came out of her sickbed long enough to plan for their visit, mainly by heaping on the chores to Chemise and me. Both of us was polishing away, when Fern came in and sat at the kitchen table.

"Look who the cat dragged in," muttered Chemise, and Fern burst into tears and lay her head down on the table. I felt bad for her all of sudden, 'cause she didn't have nobody in the world and even Chemise and me had given her the air. When I thought about it, Fern never was anything but nice to me, yet I had acted like she was dirt since her and Mr. Hugo's foolin' around. I let her cry for a minute, then I gave her a pat on the back.

"What's wrong, honey?"

Fern raised her head and looked up at me, and she was as white as the fresh sheets we'd put on the beds earlier that morning. "I think I'm going to be sick." I passed her the slop bucket just in time. You could see her shake with the force of those retches. When she finished puking, Chemise handed me a damp cloth and I wiped Fern's face down. "I'm as good as dead, Addie. I think I'm going to have a baby." She started crying again, great big sobs that made her hiccough and gasp for breath. "What am I going to do?" she wailed. "I should drown myself in the pond!"

"You ain't gonna do any such thing while I'm around," I said. "For right now, you gonna pull yourself together, Fern. You better carry on like usual as long as you can, for your and that baby's sake. Now stop cryin', girl. I can hear Miss Lucille calling you."

"Thank-you, Addie." She dried her eyes and straightened her pinafore. Before she left, she threw her arms around me and hugged me real tight.

I hugged her back. "Don't worry yourself sick, honey. Things have a way of working out," I said. Secretly I was thinkin' that maybe she'd lose hers and Mr. Hugo's baby and save herself a whole lot of sorrow and the pain of being disgraced. I felt bad that I thought that way, so I hugged her harder. "I'll be here to help you, Fern."

After she left, Chemise picked up a silver serving spoon and waved it at me as she spoke. "Just be careful Addie, that you don't end up getting into the middle of a big ol' mess by taking too much interest in little Miss Fern who gone and got herself in the fam'ly way by messin' in where she shouldn't have."

"You can't help but feel sorry for her."

"Why sorry? At least she's white and not some sweatin' slave."

I didn't answer. We finished polishing all that silver and the only sound was Chemise muttering under her breath now and then.

Fern Dumond
Sweetbrier Plantation
March 1838

At Mercy House, Sister Judith always warned that I'd come to a bad end unless I suppressed my headstrong ways. "You were stubborn and willful when you arrived. The quiet room changed your behavior for the better. You hated being in there." It is true, I hated the quiet room, and I hated Sister Judith for confining me there as punishment.

My first weeks in the orphanage were plagued with troubles. On top of the misery of being in the awful place, one of the older girls decided to torment me with relentless pinches when no one was looking. Finally, I'd had enough; I set upon her with both fists flying. Sister Catherine tried to restrain me, but anger made me reckless, and I kicked her when she got in the way of my target.

"Tell her to stop pinching me, you old witch," I screamed. I ran outside and climbed up the tree in the courtyard. Sister Amelia, the youngest and most sympathetic of the nuns, coaxed me down when it got dark and cold. The next day, I refused to eat the cabbage stew and overturned a dish of it on the table. "It smells like the outhouse," I announced.

Sister Judith's glare was icy. "It's time you learned a lesson, Fern." For my bad behavior, I spent a week in the quiet room on a diet of water, bread wrapped around a thin slice of cheese, and an occasional bowl of cabbage stew. I was hungry by then, and I ate it.

"Are you ready to cooperate, Fern?" Sister Judith asked after seven long days.

I nodded. "Yes, Ma'am." She led me back to the dining hall and made me apologize in front of everyone.

Afterwards, I was cautious and tried always to exhibit a cooperative demeanor and to keep my opinions, and fists, to myself. The lesson was imprinted by those days of solitude in the quiet room.

Sister Judith suspected that a willful spirit still lurked below the surface, and for the rest of my time at Mercy House she counseled me against it. "God sees everything, Fern. You must always strive to suppress the wickedness in yourself, or it will lead you astray."

I suppose she was right. My weak nature led me to commit sins with Mr. Hugo, and for those misdeeds, God is surely displeased. He couldn't do a better job of punishing me: I have lost all of what I'd gained after leaving Mercy House: my dignity, my position as a lady's companion to Miss Lucille, the love I thought I had, and I've lost my health, for being with child makes me bilious and weak.

Addie, on the other hand, is filled with vigor and vitality. Pregnancy doesn't appear to have any ill effect on her, and she is at least five months farther along than I am.

"Why, girl, it looks to me like you losin' weight everywhere but that belly. You better eat more Fern, 'cause your legs is like sticks, and your arms, too!" Addie and Chemise kept at me with rich custards and fried chicken, but I would most often lose everything I ate afterwards. The only food that stayed down was dry toast and tea with milk, but Addie and Chemise wouldn't stand for a toast diet. "You gotta' eat whether you throw up or not, honey. Your baby is hungry even if you ain't." Regardless of my constant queasiness, the baby grew.

My swelling belly didn't stop Hugo from making love to me in the middle of the night, in the parlor where Miss Lucille and I had read from her Book of Psalms that afternoon. "What will I do when Lucille notices my condition?" I asked. Hugo answered with hot kisses and loved me right there on the couch with my skirts thrown up over my big belly. When I tried to ask again, Hugo put a finger to my lips, to shush me. "I'm sure things will work out," he whispered. "Now, off to bed with us both."

It was the last night I slept in my comfortable rooms down the hall from Miss Lucille. When I set the tea tray on her bedside table the next morning I could feel her eyes rake over me. The contents of my stomach rose, and I bolted from the room to be sick in the washroom across the hall. When I returned to help Miss Lucille dress, I could tell from the steely look in her eyes that something was wrong.

"What gown do you want to wear today?" I asked. "I've guessed the green organdy day dress. Does that suit you, Miss Lucille?"

"Sit down Fern. We need to have a little talk." She waited as I sank into one of the overstuffed easy chairs across from her dressing table. The bodice of my dress pulled tightly across the mound of my stomach. Miss Lucille pointed to it. "How far along is the bastard you're carrying?" she asked in a flat voice.

I did what one might expect in the situation and burst into tears. In anticipation of Miss Lucille eventually discovering my condition, I'd prepared a story about a dance I'd gone to months back. "I walked to Smithfield to get your tonic, because all the boys were out working the fields, planting a new crop of cane. Do you remember that day?" Her silence was stony. "It was so awfully hot. I decided to stay until the sun went down, when it would be cooler." A new wave of sobbing overtook me.

Miss Lucille waited. "Go on," she said.

I continued my story about a hoedown with live fiddlers in the town square and a handsome young man passing through town who asked me to dance. "We drank some whiskey from his flask, and I am not used to spirits. I don't remember anything afterwards, but I woke the next morning in a barn with the stranger next to me." I cried harder, hoping that Miss Lucille would show some pity, but she just looked at me like I was something she scraped off her boot.

"When our conversation is over, I've spoken the last words I'll ever speak about this sordid business. I'm finished with you, Fern. Plead your case before the gates of heaven."

I was shocked at how she turned. Just the day before she'd kissed my cheek while insisting I was the incarnation of the daughter she'd longed for. "You saved me from drowning in sadness, Fern. For that, I'll be forever grateful." Now, her expression showed nothing but disgust. "Your services are no longer needed at Sweetbrier. A lady's companion should be morally fit. Your condition proves you are little better than a common whore. I will arrange for a carriage to take you back to the nuns."

"Please, Miss Lucille, I can't go back to Mercy House. I'd rather die!"

"You should have thought of that before you engaged in wantonness. Do you know you're a sinner, Miss Dumond? You belong in the convent where you can make atonement."

"Miss Lucille, I beg you to let me stay, at least until the baby is born. I've nowhere to go, no family to take me in. I can't give birth on the streets!"

Miss Lucille nodded, a quick, cold inclination of her chin in the manner of a queen dispensing a favor. "Very well. You may stay here until you give birth. After it's born, you'll have to find other means of support."

I drew in a breath and wiped away my tears with the back of my hand. "Thank-you, Miss Lucille. I know you don't have to keep me. I appreciate your kindness, ma'am…"

Miss Lucille froze me with a look. "You'll need to move your things from the upstairs bedroom. You'll sleep in the attic from now on." She dismissed me with a gesture to the door. Her parting words froze me in my tracks. "God always punishes a liar, Fern." I pulled the door open and left as quickly as possible, wondering why she'd called me a liar, wondering if Miss Lucille somehow knew about Hugo and me.

Whatever her suspicions, I am grateful for Miss Lucille's allowing me to stay at Sweetbrier, no matter how grudgingly. I pray for her forgiveness, and I pray for Hugo, me, and our baby every night, that we might achieve salvation despite our sins.

Addie Turner Washington

Sweetbrier Plantation

1838 - 1843

By order of Miss Lucille, Fern came to work with us kitchen darkies. Chemise and I helped her move her pitiful bunch of stuff into the attic room on the back side of the house all the way up three long flights of stairs. Mr. Hugo, I noticed, kept out of the way. He stuck his head outside the office when we was hauling her stuff, and he looked like he wanted to say something, his eyes all red and sorry. Then he went back in the office and closed the door. What he should of done is set up Fern and their baby in a little house somewhere, but Mr. Hugo didn't have much spine when it came to personal things. His way to handle it was to feel guilty and get away from Sweetbrier as much as he possibly could. As for Miss Lucille, once she'd sent Fern to the kitchen, she ignored her like she was dead.

Fern pitched right in, but she was sickly and sad, so we gave her the easy jobs and made her sit at the corner table in the afternoon. She'd perk up when Jerome would wake up from his nap in the hideaway cradle behind the woodstove, gurgling to be picked up. Fern loved the baby and little Sophie too, and the children took to her like she was some special kind of fairy princess. She had a way with them, and I loved that the color of my brown children didn't matter to her one little bit.

Spring came along with beautiful weather, and Fern would sit outside in the kitchen garden while Chemise and I picked peas or whatever was comin' on. Fern sat on a blanket spread over the grass and shucked the peas or trimmed out the bad leaves on a head of lettuce. "I think I'll name the baby Peter, after my father," she said.

"What makes you think that child is a boy?" I asked.

"I'm just sure of it, Addie." Which was one thing she got wrong.

By the end of May, Fern was so sick and droopy that I ordered her to stay in bed. When I told Mr. Hugo that Fern was sick, he had Garvus carry up a feather mattress, and he called me to the office, closing the door after I came in. He handed me a real pretty carved-wood treasure box. "Please give this to Miss Fern. Tell her the contents are hers to use in whatever way she needs." He looked embarrassed. "That's all, Addie. Thank-you," he said. Then Mr. Hugo took off for who knows where. Though he was cowardly, I always felt sorry for Mr. Hugo with his sad-dog eyes. I took the box straight upstairs to Fern, but she was so weak I had to open the clasp. In it lay a silver rosary, a man's gold wedding band, Mr. Hugo's Mama's diamond and emerald pendant with matching earrings, a gold and silver pocket watch and a fist-sized leather sack filled with gold coins.

"This stuff is worth some money, Fern. Maybe you can use it to set yourself up in a new life once the baby is born," I said.

"Perhaps so." Fern's voice was so feeble it was near a whisper. "Tell Mr. Hugo thank you." She handed me the carved box. "Would you put it in my trunk?"

"Of course I will honey." I opened up her scuffed up old trunk and put the box in carefully, under the winter jackets and caps she stored in it. "Now take a few spoonfuls of chicken soup. Chemise made it 'specially for you."

Miss Lucille didn't notice a thing of what was goin' on with Fern's health until the evening in June when Fern's screams rang through that big old house. You couldn't help but know she was having her baby by the hollering. It wasn't Fern's fault. I was by her side the whole time, trying to coax the baby to come out and yelling at the mama to push, for God's sake! Honestly though, that baby did not want to come out of her mama, and in Fern's sickly state she couldn't give the kind of push the baby needed.

Fern's screams got weaker toward the end, and Chemise, who had practice helping babies be born, finally worked both hands around the baby and pulled it out of Fern. There was a gush of blood. I remember thinking it was an awful lot of blood, more than I'd bled giving birth to either Sophie or Jerome. I didn't think about it too long though, 'cause Chemise handed me the baby, and she was blue. "Breathe into her mouth," Chemise yelled. "Go on, Addie! Now!" She leaned back over the bed and did whatever she could to try to stop Fern's bleeding.

I rubbed the baby girl's back, and I pinched her nose shut real gentle and breathed into her sweet little mouth. I kept breathin' and rubbin', and just when I was about to give up she scrunched up her nose and let out a little wail. I screamed, "Halleluiah! "She's alive!" Fern lifted her head from the pillow and held out her arms. I put the baby down on Fern's chest, and you could tell how happy she was from the glow coming off her face. "Her name is Elizabeth, after my mother," she said.

"That's a mighty pretty name. Now, I'll take the baby. You try to get some rest." Fern closed her eyes, and even though she was weak and bleeding, she had a smile on her face. It was still there when she died less than an hour later.

Mr. Hugo came home in time for the tail end of poor Fern's life. When I yelled down the stairs that Fern needed a doctor fast, he rode a horse into town himself and woke Doctor Brisco up from his bed to come and tend to Fern. She'd been dead a couple of hours by the time the doctor checked her vital signs. His lips pressed into a thin line when he pulled the white sheet up, covering her pretty, pale face.

Chemise and I were crying, and the newborn Elizabeth was wailing to the heavens, and even Miss Lucille cried except her reason for crying was because the problem of Fern interrupted her life. Between the tonic she took and her own stormy feelings, she liked things calm, like a cow in a field. Fern's death made a little too much fluster for her. As soon as she could, she went off to her room and shut the door, so she didn't have to bother with it. The doctor told Mr. Hugo that he would file the paper work on Fern's death, and then he hurried off into the night. I'm sure he couldn't wait to crawl back into bed.

Mr. Hugo and I were alone in the hallway by the time all was said and done. I held little Elizabeth in my arms. "She's a pretty little thing," I said.

He looked at me, dazed, like he didn't know who I was talking about, so I lifted the baby up for him to see. Mr. Hugo stared like she was a ghost. "Take care of her, Addie," he said. Then he closed himself in his office. Mr. Hugo was helpless; he knew Elizabeth was his child, but he could hardly put up a fuss without giving himself away. I hoped his whiskey gave him some peace 'cause that poor man was a tortured soul.

The weather turned awfully hot, and only a day or two passed before Fern was buried in one of the weedy plots in the slave cemetery, not very far from where my own Mama was buried. Chemise, my little Sophie, Garvus with Jerome in his arms, and I with Elizabeth in my arms was the only folks there to mourn her, and in the distance, I saw Mr. Hugo standing mostly hidden in the grove of trees on the edge of the graveyard. He left after the first shovel of earth scattered over Fern's pine box.

In the days after Fern's lonesome little funeral, I took charge of the baby, carrying her home at night and coming back to the big house with the rosy pink child in the morning. Sophie, our precious firstborn, was a month or two past three when the baby came to share the cabin with us. Sophie's childhood lisp stopped her from saying Elizabeth; she called the baby Lizzie, and the name stuck. Lizzie was the prettiest baby I ever did see, before or after, and my heart had a soft spot for her right away. Chemise and I moved a crib from the attic next to Jerome's crib in the corner near the pantry, and between our chores I'd breast feed both of them.

After a few months, Jerome was eating some solid mush, and most days I left him and Sophie with Alberna, the neighbor in the cabin across from ours. Alberna was too old to work in the fields, and a couple of the families left their little ones in her care. Lizzie was born a few months behind Jerome, and she still needed to be fed around the clock, so she came every day with me to work. Tucked into her crib, she was as good as gold with no crying or fussing.

It went on like that for five or six months before Miss Lucille wandered into the kitchen and saw me breast feeding the baby. I could tell she'd been sippin' more of her tonic than she should of, 'cause of the confusion in her eyes. "What on earth are you doing with a white child?" she cried.

"This is Elizabeth; do you remember? Fern's baby."

Miss Lucille winced, remembering Fern's fall from Christian grace. "I think it's time to send this pitiful foundling to Mercy House. It is the same orphanage where the child's mother grew up. I'm sure they would take her," she said.

"Why you gonna send this baby away Miss Lucille? I'm takin' care of Lizzie just fine! Why not just leave matters be?"

Miss Lucille's mind was so clouded by the ever-larger doses of Doctor Brisco's tonic that half the time she was in a dream world. Otherwise, she might of put up more of a fuss about Lizzie. Instead, she puckered her forehead like she had a bad headache and didn't say another word to me about the baby. Whenever she happened across

Lizzie, she'd shudder at the bad memory and rush away to rest in her bedroom. So, I kept the baby, and I loved her like my own.

Garvus raised the only real objection. "When did you go crazy enough to bring a white baby into our house? What are you thinking of?"

"Lizzie ain't causing nobody no problem, honey. You just mind your own business about this baby."

"Who wearin' the pants, Addie? You or me?" he grumbled, but he knew when to let me have my way; he shut up and largely ignored the baby. It was easy to do since she was a quiet little thing who didn't cause any trouble. He loved her as much as I did by the time she was taken from us. But Sophie was the one who loved Elizabeth more than all of us combined.

Sophie was a born mother, and she took charge over Lizzie and her brother like they belonged to her. She was just a little kid herself, but she was tall for her age. It was a funny sight to see, her carrying the baby around the cabin on her hip, pulling Jerome by his hand, bossing them both like they were her children. With love shining in her eyes, Lizzie would look up at Sophie and kiss her on the cheek. It was a sweet thing, the bond between the children as they grew up, two little Negroes being sister and brother to a white girl. It made some eyes roll at the slave cabins, but people got used to Lizzie, and we settled into being a family; a happy family for the years we had together.

Mr. Hugo and Miss Lucille ignored Lizzie as long as they could, which was the usual way they handled their troubles. Mr. Hugo had guilt like a monkey on his back. He'd look away whenever he came across Lizzie, the image of her mama, Fern, living like one of his Negroes, Mr. Hugo knowing that he was her daddy.

Miss Lucille had no trouble ignoring the situation; she perched in her room and since there was no more lady's companion, she filled her days embroidering or crocheting, drinking Doctor Brisco's tonic and reading the Bible. My, that woman did take to reading the Bible and quoting scripture whenever she had a hankering! Miss Lucille always needed something to hang on to, but she didn't keep the right balance. It was like she was all or nothing. She started carrying the Bible around with her and reading from it to me or Chemise, and when she couldn't find one of us, she read to herself.

Lizzie was four when Bert, on one of his visits home to Sweetbrier, saw her playing with the children by the slave cabins. "Who is that child, Addie?" he asked.

"That's Lizzie, sir. Her mama was Fern. You remember, the young lady who came to help with Miss Lucille?"

"Why in hell is she playing with the darkies? Does her mama let her do that?"

"Her mama's dead, Mr. Bert. I been taking care of Fern's child."

Bert raised his eyebrows. "You've been taking care of a white child?"

"Yes, I have Mr. Bert. She is healthy and happy, and we all look out for her. There's been no problems with the way things are. Lizzie's no trouble at all."

"I never heard anything like it before. Do my mother and father know about this?"

I nodded. "It was decided when Fern died that I take care of the baby, part because she needed a wet nurse. When she stopped nursing, she just kind of stayed."

"Who is the father?" Bert took a step or two closer to get a better look at Lizzie. I wanted to poke his eyes out to protect her from him.

"You'll have to ask your mama, Mr. Bert. She knows the whole story. Fern told her all about it."

"I'm not interested enough to interview my mother about a bastard child," he said. I was glad when he walked away and even happier when he rode off on his horse a few days later.

Mostly, the first five years of Lizzie's life were good years. She grew, along with Sophie and Jerome, into a healthy, loving child. Honest to God, it was easy to look on her just like I looked on and loved my own two children. Sometimes I felt guilty 'cause I caught myself favoring her, being easier on her. Maybe it was just because she was white, and somewhere in the back of my mind it'd been beaten into all of us that white was just plain better. Besides, she was born as sweet as taffy, was Lizzie. All of us fell under her spell, which is why it was so hard when Miss Lucille took her away a few days before Lizzie turned six years old.

As soon as she could walk, Lizzie followed Sophie's every step. From making mud pies and playing with corncob dolls to doing their chores, they were glued together. Eventually, they started talking in some kind of secret language they made up. No one knew what they was sayin,' but the way those two giggled and carried on was like they was having the finest time in the world. I swear they thought the same thoughts, the way Lizzie would finish Sophie's sentence or Sophie finish Lizzie's.

On harvest days, Garvus took the children to the fields to pick cotton. Lizzie, Sophie and Jerome stayed together as they moved down the rows, seeing who could pick the most. I couldn't fill them up with enough dinner after the days they were out in the fields, they was so hungry from all that walking and bending.

It was on a picking day when Lizzie came across an underground wasp nest. She stepped in some soft soil, and her bare foot broke through to a whole mess of angry wasps. That poor child must've been bit a hundred or more times before Sophie and Jerome dragged her away from the swarm. They both got some bites doing it, but not near what Lizzie had all over her body. I didn't know nothing about it until Garvus ran into the kitchen, carrying her to me. She was swelled up so bad her eyes were puffy lines. The bites all over her body were flaming red, but the rest of her skin was the color of death.

"Wasps," Garvus gasped. Being as he ran so fast, he was out of breath.

Lizzie started to shiver and twitch in my arms, and I knew I had to do something fast. "Chemise, get the jug of cider vinegar from the pantry." I stripped off Lizzie's dress, laid her in the big old sink and poured the vinegar over her like my mama taught me to do when some bee or spider stung me. I used a cup to keep pouring it over those hot, angry stings, hoping the old wives' tale worked. "Go get Doctor Brisco from town and tell him a white child is sick here at Sweetbrier," I said to Garvus.

Chemise brought the kettle filled with warm water from the stove, and I poured it into the sink with the vinegar and let Lizzie soak in it until I thought her color underneath the angry red bites was starting to look better. Chemise brought a towel from the linen closet, which she wrapped around Lizzie as I lifted her from the sink. She was limp, like a rag doll. I put her down on the kitchen table, next to the vegetables Chemise and I was chopping for the chow-chow, and asked Chemise to get a blanket because Lizzie was shivering so bad. Meanwhile, I tore a kitchen towel into strips, soaked them in the vinegar and lay the strips over as many of the bites as I could cover.

It was not common these days for Miss Lucille to come to the kitchen, but she did that morning because she had a hankering for Chemise's famous pecan pie, and she was coming to ask her if she would make one for dessert. "What on earth?" she cried out when she saw Lizzie, wrapped up in one of her good blankets, smelling like a pickle.

"This child was attacked by wasps, and she is mighty sick," I said, peeling back the blankets and applying fresh strips of the vinegar-soaked cloth. Miss Lucille blinked and looked confused.

"Why, the girl is white, for heaven's sake!" I reminded her again that Lizzie was Fern's daughter. "Oh dear!" Miss Lucille proceeded to wring her hands and moan and say 'oh dear' a bunch more times. "She's not going to die, is she?"

"I sure hope not," I said. Then Miss Lucille surprised both Chemise and I by helping us change the old poultices for fresh ones every few minutes and saying prayers for the little girl on the table who she'd ignored for so many years. Miss Lucille was reciting the Lord's Prayer when Doctor Brisco came to the kitchen.

"When did this happen?" Doctor Brisco pushed aside a pile of carrots so he could put down his doctor bag. I told him the details as he examined Lizzie. "What's been done so far?" he asked, sniffing suspiciously at the cloth strips.

"My mama taught me that cider vinegar does something to calm down the poison from a bite," I explained.

Doctor Brisco said "Humph," and went on poking at Lizzie. She was still out cold, and every now and then she'd shiver and make a little moaning sound.

I held her hot little hand. "Oh, my poor sweet baby, you gonna be all right. The Lord ain't takin' you for any little meat wasp bites, even if there was a lot of them nasty things. Nothin' else hurting you honey, I'll make sure."

Doctor Brisco ordered another warm bath. "Not too hot. She already is running a fever. Make a thin paste of soda powder and water," he said. I dried off Lizzie from the sink and laid her back on the table so the doctor could dab the soda paste on the swollen bites. When he finished, he tucked the blanket up around her neck.

"Give her a dose of laudanum tonic by the teaspoon, Lucille. It will help her sleep through the night and give the child's body and the Lord a chance to fight the poison." Miss Lucille nodded. "And have a cot prepared for the girl. You'll need to watch her closely."

"There's no need for a cot. Lizzie got her bed out in the cabin," I said.

"Not tonight," said Doctor Brisco. He lifted Lizzie off the table and followed after Miss Lucille. A chill went down my spine.

"Bring sheets and blankets, Addie," Miss Lucille called down the hall.

I carried the bedding to Miss Lucille's room and made up the wooden cot Chemise had carted in from the old nursery. Lizzie lay motionless on Miss Lucille's big four-poster. The whole time, Doctor Brisco lectured Miss Lucille. "Is this the love child of the woman who died a few years back?" he asked. Miss Lucille nodded. "Who is responsible for the girl?"

Miss Lucille glanced over at me. "Addie has been looking after the child." Her voice trembled, and her eyes darted away like a guilty dog that stole a loaf of bread from where it was cooling.

Doctor Brisco talked as if I wasn't even there, like I wasn't really a person with feelings. "Impossible! I can't believe it or tolerate it, nor should you! The girl is obviously white. Niggers can't raise her, for God's sake. It isn't right." It was all I could do to stop myself from telling him to mind his own damn business, but I remembered my place and bit my tongue to keep quiet.

"I thought it better than sending her to Mercy House, where her mother came from," murmured Miss Lucille, as a tear slipped down her cheek from the shock of it all, I guess.

"The orphanage would be far more suitable," said Doctor Brisco. "A white child should live amongst people of her own color. As it is, she is becoming a freak of nature. You must not allow this situation to continue. God will frown upon you until something is done. I'll find Hugo and tell him the same thing!" Doctor Brisco gave Miss Lucille a stern look and closed the door behind him. There was a long silence as I pressed my cheek against Lizzie's forehead to test for fever. She was still hot, but she wasn't burning up like before. I tucked the blankets in closer and ran my fingers through her curls.

"You want me to take Lizzie back to the cabin and care for her tonight, Miss Lucille?"

"No, Addie. You heard what the doctor said." She patted my shoulder, but she wouldn't meet my eyes. "That will be all for tonight. You go on home. I'll watch after her until we decide…"

"Decide what, Miss Lucille?"

"Like the doctor said, it isn't right, Addie. Something will have to be done with the child."

I hovered by the door, wishing I could grab up my white baby girl and run off with her. "I'll be happy to stay and watch over her tonight. You must be tired, Miss Lucille."

Miss Lucille looked at me with shining eyes, like she seen the light. "I'll look over her, Addie. I'm not tired at all. I haven't felt this well in years. I think this child is a gift to me in some way." Then she smiled and closed the door ever so gently, right in my face.

In the pit of my stomach, I knew Lizzie would never spend another night in our cabin back in the hollow.

I hardly slept that whole endless night, waiting for dawn's light to come so I could rush off to the big house to check on Lizzie. I didn't stop to say nothin' to Chemise, who was in the kitchen mighty early herself, probably just dyin' to see what come of the whole mess. I tied on my apron as I ran up the stairs to Miss Lucille's room. I stopped in front of the door and knocked on it real soft. Miss Lucille opened it a crack and peered out. She shushed me right off, and then stepped out of the room and closed the door behind her. "She's still asleep, and we don't want to wake her, poor little soul. She needs all the sleep she can get, to work the poison out."

"I'll just peek in to see her, Miss Lucille," I said, looking her straight in the eye.

Miss Lucille pursed up her lips, and her forehead wrinkled into a little frown, but she finally nodded. "Just don't wake her."

I stopped myself from taking Miss Lucille by the shoulders and giving her a good shake. I'd been Lizzie's adopted mama for all these years, and suddenly Miss Lucille has a weird gleam in her eyes and she's telling me what to do about my innocent babe. Lord have mercy on me for wishing evil on her; I just couldn't help myself. I pushed past her and opened the door, and she followed me in and stood behind me as I checked Lizzie.

I smoothed the sheets and passed a damp cloth over her forehead. She was still flushed and feverish, but she was breathing deep, regular breaths. I tucked the blanket around her and kissed her cheek. "When she wakes up she'll be as good as new," I whispered. "I've got her bed ready back at the cabin. I thought I'd slip this shift over her head and carry her home. It won't take but a few minutes, and after I've tucked her in, I'll come right back. Me and Chemise gonna finish the chowchow."

Miss Lucille put her finger to her lips again and crooked her neck at me to follow her out of the bedroom. Once the door was shut, Miss Lucille shook her head. "Going back to the cabin is out of the question, Addie. Elizabeth will stay here for a day or two, resting in bed. After she is completely well, she will move into Bert's old nursery."

"What are you talkin' about, Miss Lucille? You know that Lizzie's been with me and Garvus since she was born. She's used to us. You don't want to bother yourself by fussing over Lizzie—"

"That will be all, Addie."

Her tone was firm and sure, and I was taken aback, since I was used to Miss Lucille sounding quavery and soft. "Her voice is always full of them tears that want to pour out," Chemise said once, and she got it right.

"But Miss Lucille, she gonna wake up and not know where she is. It's enough to scare the life out of a little one! Surely you can see that, Miss Lucille." I was pleading, but I knew in my heart it was useless; Lizzie was now the property of Miss Lucille. In a few winks of an eye, Lizzie became a member of the big house, and I lost my adopted daughter.

For a long time, it was like having a leg chopped off. Sophie and Jerome missed their sister, and even Garvus was off his feed and moping around. Sophie was hit hard, 'cause she and Lizzie was like two little peas in their own pod. She flopped around the cabin like a sad-eyed rag doll and got in trouble in the fields for not picking enough. We was all on edge, and I admit, I wasn't much help, taking everything out on them. The loss of Lizzie ripped a piece right out of my heart that I never did get back.

Seems like for Miss Lucille, the very piece that was ripped out of my heart jumped over and put a patch on her heart, and all the sadness and sorrows of the years, all the broken-heart moments, were shoved into the closet of her past. I couldn't believe the change in that woman, and I'm sure Mr. Hugo was mighty surprised too, seein' as he was dealing with a new person in his wife's old body. Miss Lucille was like a butterfly coming out of its cocoon.

Lucille Bellingham Laurent
Sweetbrier
May 1843

Deep in the night I am afflicted with anxious terrors. My heart pounds; I feel as if I am running from the apparitions populating my thoughts; images of Father clutching at his throat, eyes bulging as he chokes on the chicken bone, images of my lips pressed against Sally Ann Tilson's lips; the guilt of unnatural longing for Fern and rage at her betrayal. Over and over Father chokes to death as I sit watching impassively from my seat across from him. I try to chase the demon visions away through prayer and atonement, but I fear Father will dislodge the bone in his throat someday and reach out and strangle me. "See what it feels like to suffocate, Lucille?" Father says, his hands wrapped tightly around my neck.

I sit up and gasp for air. My heart pounds, and though my eyes are shut, a firework display of thoughts plays out on the insides of my closed eyes. The kaleidoscope of lights makes my poor head throb. To stop the pain and the memories, I take more and more of the tonic prescribed by Dr. Brisco.

All those years ago when I pined for Sally Ann, I never thought I'd feel the same sinful way about another woman. Then Fern came to live at Sweetbrier, and love swept over me. It was a feeling beyond the love of friend for friend; I knew it was unnatural and against all the Christian teachings so dear to my heart, yet I couldn't overcome the imaginings of seeing her naked, of lying beside her in the same bed, imaginings that left me trembling with excitement.

I longed for Fern's touch, I adored her arm around me on walks, I lived for her hands arranging my hair, and I often claimed a head-ache just to have her rub my neck and shoulders. These feelings are truly unnatural; thus, I do not blame God for punishing me. The Bible is my solace, for no matter how depraved and disgusting one is, the Good Book promises salvation. The Good Book is my compan-ion, my friend, and ultimately my savior. I've started marking the passages in Scripture that comfort me, and I often read them to Addie or Chemise when one or the other brings my tea tray, but the blank look in their eyes tells me the words don't sink in. Pity for them, poor heathens.

Chemise and Addie believe I am helpless; they think I take no notice; that I am too distracted by misery to realize what is happening around me. I know more than everyone thinks. I know who little Eliz-abeth's father is. I implied as much to Hugo without directly accusing him. I even promised to keep the secret all the way to my grave. I believe this is the better choice for a Christian woman. It is one step toward repentance, for I accept some blame for Hugo's wandering eye; he is a man after all, and he wasn't welcome in my bedroom.

When he took his physical rights, I suffered with my eyes shut tight and my lips whispering the Lord's Prayer while his pounding hardness made me cry out with pain. Fortunately, Hugo finally gave up trying after my nervous collapse, and though I'd clearly violated my Christian duties, I was relieved. I even understood in a primal way the liaison he formed with Fern, but understanding didn't make me hate either of them less.

Fern's betrayal was a knife in my back. When she first came to my lonely rooms at Sweetbrier, I was certain that God had bestowed upon me a miracle. Her arrival raised a bud of hope in the barren field of despair that trapped me. I could have spent eternity with darling Fern, if only she'd loved me instead of Hugo. She filled my empty cup with happiness during those early months, until I discovered her in Hugo's arms.

The day that Hugo and Fern's infidelity was brought to light, we'd spent a pleasant afternoon in the front parlor. Fern read aloud from the Book of Psalms while I crocheted a soft cap and matching gown for Bert and Sarah's newborn. The hours passed in a regular fashion. After each Psalm we discussed the deeper meaning of the holy canon. Later, Fern played the pianoforte and sang while I finished the baby bonnet.

I ate an early dinner before retiring to my rooms, where I read briefly until succumbing to drowsiness. With the help of Doctor Brisco's tonic, I usually slept soundly; that night, however, my sleep was troubled. I woke abruptly to the grandfather clock striking midnight and passed a restless hour plagued by visions of my father consorting with Sally Ann Tilson. Finally, I abandoned all attempts to return to the sleep I prize so dearly.

The very God who sent Fern to save me also led me to the discovery of her treachery. Because of my wakefulness, I lighted the candle by my bedside, intending to read until I was tired enough to resume the night's rest. The Book of Psalms wasn't on my bedside table tucked in its usual place between matching lion's-head bookends. I remembered I'd left it in the parlor, which is a rare occurrence, as I honor and hold dear the sacred texts and keep them close. I pulled a light silk robe over my night garments, took the candle in hand, and padded softly down the stairs, soundless in stocking feet.

The door to the parlor was open far enough to reveal Hugo and Fern pressed together, the flickering light of a single lantern playing over their entwined limbs while Hugo fumbled to undo the buttons on his pants. I quickly stepped into the shadows and pinched out the candle flame, but it didn't matter: they were too caught up in the amorous activity of their lips to see me. He leaned her over the back of the settee in the parlor, where I'd left my Book of Psalms, and when he lifted her skirts I averted my gaze and scuttled away. I felt my way back to my rooms in the dark, one hand forward like a blind beggar.

I stayed awake the rest of the long night, weeping bitterly into my pillow from the humiliation. All my sadness, all my sorrow, all my rage unified in the hate I felt for my husband and Fern. The only comfort I took was in the words of Psalm 13: "Upon the wicked He will rain coal; fire and brimstone and a burning wind...." When Fern died giving birth, I knew God had reached out and punished her; I knew that she'd gotten her due. I ignored the infant left behind; for my own mental peace I deliberately forgot about Fern and the whole sordid affair until the day Elizabeth was attacked by wasps.

God must have felt I'd hated and suffered enough, because He reached out and saved me by opening my eyes to Elizabeth. Deep in my heart I hold dear the knowledge that God gave her to me to heal my pain, to guide my lost soul to salvation. The day that Elizabeth came to live at the big house I'd wakened in a desperately agitated state of mind. Fragments of unpleasant memories paraded mercilessly through my brain. I knelt by the side of my bed and prayed to God to help me, to stop the screaming voices inside my head, to relieve the bonds of sorrow and loneliness tying me to my rooms.

I know it is a mortal sin to take your own life, but as I knelt, I begged God to give me the strength of will to kill myself if he couldn't bring me to drink from the stream of happiness that others sip from. Addie is blessed that way; she is unfailing in her cheer, unstinting in her kindness. Though she is a Negro, her soul, I know, is white. I am truly sorry I had to take Elizabeth away from her, but nothing else could be done.

That morning, after my plea to God, I waited for Addie to bring my breakfast tray. My agitation grew when it didn't arrive at the usual time. An hour passed, and I decided a surprise visit to the kitchen was a wise plan. It isn't prudent to exercise too much tolerance with the Negroes, after all. Without the assistance of Addie or Chemise it was an effort to change from my nightclothes, pull on a presentable gown and arrange my hair, but I managed.

Addie and Chemise's raised voices grew louder as I descended the stairs, and I wondered what on earth could be causing the excitement. The kitchen's open door revealed little Elizabeth, laid out on the table with piles of carrots and slices of celery forming a halo around her. Addie and Chemise were hovering over her, frantically applying compresses to the scarlet bites spotting her otherwise alabaster skin. In a rough voice I didn't recognize, Addie told me about the wasp attack.

Driven by the haunting thought of the victim dying on the table, I joined Addie and Chemise in tending her. Side by side, the three of us nursed Elizabeth until the doctor arrived. I will never know whether Doctor Brisco's ministrations or the folk remedies of Addie and Chemise helped Elizabeth's breathing steady and her color return from cadaver white. We rejoiced when her temperature went down enough to tuck her into bed.

Doctor Brisco insisted that Elizabeth recuperate in the big house. "For God's sake, Lucille, it just isn't right, a white child being raised up in a colored family," he said. I stood accused, for it was I who cast her out to live like a common slave. It was clearly my duty to rectify the wrong that had been committed. Doctor Brisco carried Elizabeth to the cot Chemise prepared in my bedroom, and I set myself to the chore of watching her through the night.

She tossed uneasily, feverishly, and I tried to soothe her by reading from an old book of nursery rhymes. Under the angry, swollen flesh, she was a pretty little girl. Her honey-colored curls fell to her shoulders in a golden tangle, and when her eyes flickered open and shut they were the same shade of cornflower blue as her mother's. Her hot little hand reached out and grasped mine as I bathed her face and arms with a damp cloth I kept wringing out in the pitcher of cool water Addie brought. I couldn't resist kissing her forehead, poor angel.

"You want me to take over for a while?" Addie asked. I shook my head and told her to go on home to bed. That was the first time I saw hate in her eyes. She tried to hide it, but it only grew and festered over the years until she couldn't look at me without letting a little bit of it show.

I intended, when she was recovered sufficiently from the wasp attack, to send Elizabeth to Mercy House to be raised by the same nuns who raised her mother. My intention was abandoned by the time Elizabeth came to her senses. As I cared for the helpless child, my heart softened little by little to let love in. Love and God's direct instructions led me to the resolution to keep her as my own.

Three days passed before Elizabeth was fully conscious. The poison from the wasp bites took its course slowly; working its way out of her system while the patient tossed feverishly and talked gibberish. More than once I guided her back to her bed from a night terror, soothing her until she drifted to the oblivion of twilight sleep. An armchair dragged to her bedside served as my station at night. In the event of her condition worsening, I wanted to be close by to attend her needs. I skipped my evening dose of laudanum in an effort to stay alert.

As a consequence, I felt more energetic and clearheaded than I had in years. A satisfying feeling of happiness filled me as I watched over Elizabeth. She was a delicate elfin angel, sweet and vulnerable. I felt useful while I nursed her back to health; it brought memories of caring for my darling son.

On the morning of the fourth day, a short time before she came out of the stupor she'd lain in, I sponged Elizabeth with a cool cloth and tucked the blanket around her. She seemed to be sleeping peacefully, and I risked closing my eyes to rest them for just a minute or two. The fitful, scant sleep I'd had during my vigil led me to nod off quickly. During that deep and sudden state of insensibility, a curious thing happened that I shall hold dear in my memory until I die; a presence entered my body. It was heavy, spreading from head to toe like warm honey, filling my orifices and veins and pinning me to the chair in which I drowsed.

I couldn't move, but I wasn't frightened. A feeling of peace enveloped me, and I knew without doubt that God was the spirit causing the strange paralysis of my limbs. A few rapturous seconds passed before a heavenly voice spoke. "The child, Elizabeth, shall be your adopted daughter from this day forward," said God's voice.

I answered, without speaking a word aloud, that I would take the child as my own, promising the divine force I would faithfully devote myself to her care. Just as suddenly as the spirit entered my body, it left. I felt degrees of the heavy presence peeling away as it departed, and I wanted to cling to it, to hold it, to trap the God spirit so it would be in me always. My eyes were filled with tears when I awakened and resumed my watch over my new daughter.

An hour later, Elizabeth woke from her coma. She gazed around the room with obvious confusion before fixing her worried blue eyes on my face. "Where am I? Am I dead?" She spoke in a pronounced Negro dialect.

"No, sweetheart," I said, stroking her silky cheek. "You've been bitten by wasps and have been mighty sick." I fed her spoonfuls of lukewarm broth, and it wasn't long until her eyes flickered shut again. I resumed my vigil, reading the Bible and praying for Elizabeth to heal.

She was sitting up in bed when Doctor Brisco checked on her the next day. "How are you feeling, young lady?" he asked.

Elizabeth's eyes filled with tears. "When can I go home?"

"Hush now, child. This is your home for now."

"No sir, this ain't my home. I live in the cabin with Addie and Garvus. Sophie and Jerome's my sister and brother."

"Don't think about that right now. Get some rest," said the doctor. He poured a draught from a slender bottle he'd pulled from his leather satchel. "Drink it all, little one, and you'll feel better." She drank the medicine, and once she'd calmed down, I drew the blankets up to her chin and kissed her forehead.

Doctor Brisco took me by the elbow, and we left Elizabeth looking at an old picture book of Bert's. "Have you decided which orphanage to place the girl in?" he asked as we walked down the hallway.

"I am tempted to keep Elizabeth here; to raise her as if she is my own."

"She is a charming child, but do you understand the responsibility, Lucille? What about your nervous condition?" Doctor Brisco looked at me sternly. "Have you thought through this decision carefully?"

"I feel better than I have in years," I told him, "and I've never been more unquestionably sure about anything, Doctor Brisco."

The doctor shook his head doubtfully. "I hope you know what you're doing, Lucille." We had arrived at the front door where he spent considerable time straightening his cravat and putting on his coat and hat before opening the door and stepping out. "What does Hugo say?"

I shrugged. "He doesn't know yet, but I'm sure he'll go along with my wishes." After all, he is her father, I thought. He couldn't very well turn out his own flesh and blood.

"If you're going to keep her, you'll have to work on the child's elocution, Lucille. She sounds just like a nigger."

"I intend to address Elizabeth's speech abnormalities as soon as she is well enough," I assured him.

The following day, I started Elizabeth's education and the salvation of my damaged soul. Blessed Elizabeth was my savior, my balance. She beamed love into my shriveled heart. I would teach her, mold her, and guide her away from the precipice where she might follow Fern in her fall from Christian grace.

Once I'd embraced the miracle of Elizabeth, my loneliness faded, and the demons from my dreams stopped possessing me. I was filled with purpose; I became a missionary, and my mission was Elizabeth.

Hugo Laurent
Sweetbrier
May 1843

Lucille has been a trial and a burden, but I never stopped loving her. If she had returned my affections, I might not have strayed with Fern, and before Fern, with the pretty little half-breed down at the western settlement. I am a natural man with red-blooded needs; for that, I do not apologize.

The situation was damnably awkward after Lucille discovered Fern's condition. I did what I could to help Fern without giving our secret away, but mostly I stayed away on plantation business. I meant to find a place for Fern to raise the child. Her death did away with my good intentions. Doctor Brisco said nothing could have saved her, yet I wonder. Her death stands as an accusation; I caused it by giving her a baby to call her own. I mourned Fern quietly, but the passage of time and the desire to forget closed a chapter I preferred to remain shut. Our daughter, Elizabeth, was tucked away with Addie and Garvus, and Lucille and I could forget about her until she came under attack by a swarm of field wasps.

The wasps delivered Elizabeth to Lucille, and by doing so, brought my wife from her chrysalis to become a person with spirit and purpose. The first night that Elizabeth stayed in the house, Lucille answered my knock at the door of the sick room. Dr. Briscoe had instructed me to resolve the problem of where to send the child.

When I spoke of the matter to Lucille, she shook her head and stared me right in the eye. "This child was given to me, Hugo. Though she may belong to you by heritage, she is now mine to raise as the daughter I've always longed for. I sincerely hope you will not interfere, Hugo."

"What do you mean?" I asked.

"I am not a fool, Hugo."

"I'm not sure—"

"That you understand? You don't need to. We'll never speak of it again. I only ask your cooperation in my plans to clothe, feed, and educate the child."

"Of course, Lucille."

"She is an orphan of unknown paternity from this day forward, Hugo."

The business was conducted between us easily, and it relieved a burden of guilt that weighed upon me. "I promise to provide whatever you deem necessary for keeping the child, Lucille."

"Her name is Elizabeth."

I nodded. "For keeping Elizabeth, then."

"Very well, Hugo. Thank you for your help."

Elizabeth's homecoming to the big house at Sweetbrier marked a turning point for Lucille as well as a truce in our marriage. I came to accept the fact that I'd never share Lucille's bed, but Elizabeth drew us into a partnership of sorts. The child, who became such a bright spot in our lives, made us allies at last.

Ten Years Later,

Sweetbrier Plantation, Louisiana

Elizabeth Dumond

Sweetbrier Plantation

Ten years later, 1853

Those ten long years ago, soon after I moved into the big house, Mama Lu took action on the matter of my speaking like a "field Negro." She made inquiries and soon found a school in Boston that specialized in speech problems. She convinced Papa Hugo to pay for tuition for the six-month course and to rent an apartment not far from the school. The advertisement they sent was filled with promises written in beautiful script:

Schlegel's School of Elocution:
Help given to Hare Lips,
the Deaf,
the Inveterate Stutterer,
and those unfortunates
with problems of
Pronunciation, Dialect,
and the
Formation of Words.
We train the Actor to speak,
as well as those born with a Cleft Tongue.

I found the advertisement neatly folded in one of the drawers of Mama Lu's teak writing desk. It brought back blurred memories of the trip to Boston by buggy and train and the excitement I felt from the new sights and sounds. Mama Lucille found an apartment located over a flower shop in walking distance of the school. It was furnished with velvet chairs and elegant carved couches with lions and dragons popping from the polished wood. On warm days that autumn the fragrance of roses and heliotrope would rise up and perfume the entire apartment.

Mama Lu went out of her way to spoil me. I was measured for a modest, "ladylike" wardrobe, and every morning she would dress my hair with her gentle fingers. Back home at the cabin Addie was always in a hurry, and most often my hair had ended up tied in a ribbon, tangles and all.

When my studies at Schlegel's were over for the day, Mama Lu and I visited museums or art galleries, and in the evenings, we attended plays and concerts. I'd never been more than a mile or two from our cabin back in the hollow, and the city was a treasure chest full of fascinations. Though I missed Addie and Sophie and the rest, the city captivated me with its variety, and I forgot my troubles. I loved the crowds of people in their fancy clothes, the vendors at the open-air markets, the hustle of carriages rolling down the narrow streets, the stores brimming with beautiful goods and delicacies that made my mouth water.

In the mornings, Mama Lu held my hand as we walked the few blocks to Schlegel's School. She often stayed in the classroom where I spent grueling hours with Mr. Thomas Peacock, a young, earnest teacher who was endless in his patience and praise. When I'd finished the day's lesson, Mama Lu had me practice speaking "proper sounding English" until she was satisfied that my speech was sufficiently clear.

I had grown fond of Mama Lu, and I wanted to please her. Fortunately, I am clever and a quick learner. Mr. Peacock told Mama Lu, "Why she's as good a mimic as any actress I've trained in the vocal arts." Mama Lu smiled and asked Mr. Peacock to recommend a music teacher. Thus began the daily piano and singing lessons I took in the afternoon with Mr. Peacock's sister, Laura.

Because of the unusual nature of my case, Mr. Peacock extended my elocution course to eight months, and at the end of it, he declared me cured of my negro dialect and gave me a parchment certificate for achieving "clear and succinct speech." I had also learned to read and write, and I got a second, smaller parchment certificate for mastering the alphabet. Mama Lu took us out to dinner on the waterfront to celebrate, and we ate crab cakes and creamy lobster bisque.

A few days later we packed our belongings, plus two new dolls and a small library of children's classics, into several big trunks. We boarded a train to New Orleans, where Papa Hugo was waiting in the same black carriage that had taken us to the station eight months before.

I'm ashamed to admit, at some point during the time spent with Mama Lu in Boston, I'd stopped feeling like my heart was yanked out from missing Addie and Sophie and all. I still loved Addie, but I did not call her Mama anymore. By the time we returned home, Mama Lu had transformed me into an adopted daughter that the Laurents of Sweetbrier could be proud of.

After returning from Boston those many years ago, when I stopped thinking of Addie as my Mama, I still longed in my heart for Sophie. Mama Lu allowed me to play with her "as long as you don't start talking like a darky again." I was very careful from then on to speak to Mama Lu in what she considered "proper English," so that I could continue to see Sophie. After my daily lessons, when Sophie finished working in the fields, we met under the giant old willow in the grove halfway between the big house and the cabins.

The branches cascaded down, fashioning a room hidden behind the leaves where we could talk ourselves silly and play make believe. I often carried a picnic of treats that Addie packed for us, and whatever book I was reading with Mama Lu. Sophie listened, eyes closed and head cocked to one side, while I'd read my favorite parts aloud. Sometimes we acted out the scenes I read, with Sophie playing the boy's parts, and me the girl's.

One afternoon, Sophie asked me to teach her how to read and to write her name. "I got a hankering to read books on my own, and maybe write one myself someday." I giggled but stopped when I saw she was dead serious. I brought pencils, paper, and an early primer the next time we met. After that, most of our time under the willow was spent on Sophie's education. She was an eager pupil, and over the years, I taught her everything I learned from Mama Lu's daily lessons.

As the firmly established spoiled daughter of the Laurents, I dared to make the suggestion to Mama Lu that Sophie would make a fine lady's maid. Mama Lu nodded thoughtfully. "I'll consider moving Sophie to service in the house for a trial period, but you must promise not to interfere with her while she is working."

"Of course not, Mama Lu."

Much to my delight, Sophie came to the big house to work the next day. Although I wanted her at Sweetbrier for selfish purposes, knowing that I could spend more time with my dear friend if she worked in the house, I also knew life picking and cultivating the fields was hard. Some of the women were so bent over by the time they were forty that they looked like Thaddeus, the farrier, who was born a hunchback. As an inside maid, Sophie's hardest duty would be housekeeping and putting Mama Lu's hair up however she fancied wearing it that day.

Most mornings, after Sophie had finished helping her dress, Mama Lu sent her to my rooms. I always dressed myself and did my own hair, so I made Sophie sit in my armchair and tell me stories. Her eyes sparkled, and her hands flew when she told the old tales passed down by Addie and Garvus: stories of revenge and spiteful spirits that fascinated me. I dawdled while I dressed in order to prolong our visits and so passed many a pleasant morning. Occasionally, Sophie insisted on doing my hair, and I let her, but only if she let me dress her hair in return. I loved fussing with her tight, wiry coils that were so different from my own soft waves, but she didn't like being "messed with," so she rarely let me arrange it.

My life at Sweetbrier was as near perfect as lives could be until Papa Hugo up and died one day, a few hours after Mama Lucille, he, and I had eaten lunch together. It was an especially fine lunch; Chemise made her famous crawdad fritters, which are even better than Addie's, and Addie shelled the first green peas of the season. She set a big bowl of them, steamed and seasoned with butter and salt and pepper, next to me on the table. Addie knows that baby peas are one of my favorites. She's always doing nice things like that, which is her way of telling me she still loves me, even though she doesn't show it much. There is a wall between us since I moved to Sweetbrier, and I've given up hope of getting back the feeling of being her precious child. Mama Lu told me long ago, in my first few days living in the big house, that I had to stop calling Addie Mama. "Addie is not your mama, Elizabeth. She is black, and she can't be mama to a white girl."

After we'd finished eating the fritters, Papa Hugo said he had indigestion. He was awfully red in the face when he said it. Mama Lu told him he was working too hard. "Why don't you go fishing, Hugo? It always makes you feel better."

"An excellent suggestion, Lucille, my dear." Papa Hugo stood behind my chair and patted my shoulder. "Would you like to come, Liz?" I said I was tired and needed a nap, which was a lie; I had terrible menstrual cramps and needed to lie down with a hot water bottle. Oh, do I ever wish that I'd gone with him. Maybe I could have saved his life. Papa Hugo and I were the best of friends. As soon as I was brave enough to mount a horse, he taught me to ride, seat-ing me on the back of Nance, my gentle piebald mare that followed along behind his roan.

Despite Mama Lou's claims that it would make me unladylike, Papa taught me how to fish and hunt. We spent many a peaceful day with our fishing poles dangling in a creek or sitting in a blind waiting for a family of ducks. Papa and I would check on the cotton fields and the other crops, visiting the overseer's cottages along the way. I always liked it when we'd come to the settlements, where the sounds of children's laughter and the musical voices of the workers reminded me of the years I lived with Addie's family. It was much quieter in the big house with Mama Lu and Papa Hugo.

Garvus found Papa in the shallows of the lily pond, not far from the bank. I know the exact spot, where the lily pads and cattails cover the water. I can imagine Papa Hugo floating face up with all the greenery and flowering surrounding him, adorned like a god of nature. Sophie tells me that I am too morbid, but life isn't meant to be all sterile white sheets and perfection. The gruesome things are as much a part of life as the moments filled with joy.

The days after Papa Hugo died, I could hardly see straight from crying so hard. I missed him terribly. Mama Lu was worse off; she fainted as soon as she heard the news, knocking her sewing box to the floor as she crumpled into a heap. Garvus was fetched to help carry her to her room, and I picked up the spools of thread and sewing materials, packing them away neatly in her box. When she woke, she started crying and kept it up for days. Addie said it reminded her of the old times, when Mama Lu spent most of her time crying up a storm, closed up in her bedroom. "Doctor Brisco called it nervous wisteria," she said.

"I believe wisteria is a type of flowering tree, Addie."

"Well, something that sounded like it."

I never knew Mama Lu when she was so afflicted. Ever since I could remember, she was calm and cheerful. Addie said it wasn't always her nature. "Miss Lucille was mighty sick and tired of life for years. When you came to Sweetbrier she snapped out of her sad ways like a snake shedding its nasty old skin. She always said you saved her, Lizzie."

"How did I save her, Addie?"

"The Lord tell her she needed a project, and it was you. Her precious son was gone and married, and Miss Lucille didn't have nothin' to occupy herself with other than sad feelings. Lizzie, you was the answer."

"What about Papa Hugo all that time when she was sad?"

"The truth is, you brought Miss Lucille and Mr. Hugo back together. For years those two was so far apart that they hardly spoke to each other. When you moved into the big house, it patched up their marriage. Honey, you were the bow that tied them into a nice little family knot. You could see both of 'em was crazy over you. The love jumped out of their eyes, Lizzie. Miss Lucille started having dinner served in the dining room like a normal family, and Mr. Hugo made a habit of eating there most nights. We all was sure happy for Mr. Hugo, 'cause the poor man suffer so with Miss Lucille's nervous condition, and finally she straighten herself out and become a new woman. Yes, indeed, you saved her from her sad self."

I might have saved her life once, but now that Papa Hugo was gone, my power to help Mama Lu disappeared. It was as if the last ten years of happiness were never there. She pulled herself together enough to arrange Papa Hugo's funeral, but after the funeral reception she went right back to her rooms and sat in her armchair, with a quilt thrown over her legs no matter how hot it was, staring into space. There was no doubt that Mama Lu had entered a new state of being. She talked of her childhood, yet in the present she was forgetful and vague, and I worried that she was losing her mind. Doctor Brisco prescribed a different, stronger tonic, and afterwards, it was hard to get Mama Lu interested in anything much.

Without Papa Hugo, someone needed to be in charge of running the plantation. A few weeks after Papa's death, I took old Nance to get some exercise. I was shocked to find several fields unplowed and the weeds growing thick between the crops that were in season. If left to their own whim, many of the field bosses were as lazy and shiftless as the itinerant farmers who were content to raise pigs and steal portions of nearby crops in order to get by.

Unfortunately, Mama Lu had never dealt with financial matters or plantation business during her thirty-year marriage to Papa Hugo. After Papa's death, she rummaged through his office, sobbing helplessly over the accounts, planting schedules and scribbled notes regarding fertilizers and foremen's duties. Though Papa had given his overseers a degree of independence, they needed a tough hand to guide them in the difficult science of farming and ranching. Papa had encouraged my interest in agriculture and the plantation, and I knew as much or more than any overseer around there. Trouble was, at sixteen years old and a female of questionable parentage, none of the men took me seriously.

I tried to get Mama Lu to take charge of what was needed on the plantation. "Mama Lu, I believe it's time to plant the sorghum and to plow some gypsum into the fields to get ready for the summer crops," I said, and her eyes would turn as hazy as a pool of muddy water, and she'd ask me to adjust the quilt or fetch her Bible. It was inevitable that Bert was summoned home to take the reins and put Sweetbrier back in working order. When he came, he brought the devil on his back.

Papa Hugo had been dead for two long months before Bert arrived at Sweetbrier to take charge. With Bert came the dark undercurrent of a person without a conscience. After everything that happened, I've decided it was one of Bert's troubles; he had no soul. If he'd had normal human feelings, he couldn't have done the things he did so callously, without the qualms of guilt most people feel when they do something bad.

Throughout my years growing up in the big house, I dreaded Bert's visits home. I did my best to avoid him; even so, he would always find a way to pinch my arm or twist my wrist when he came across me alone. "You're an uppity little girl, aren't you, Miss Elizabeth?" he'd say, with an unpleasant grin. I felt sorry for his and Sarah's two children; I could tell they were frightened of him.

I never talked to Mama Lu about how mean Bert was; it was obvious that she was crazy over her son and blind to his faults. She raised such a fuss every time he was expected home, you'd have thought the President himself was coming for a visit. Addie and Chemise were put to work making his favorite foods, and Sophie would clean the guest bedroom from top to bottom. I'd help Sophie more often than not, just to spend time with her. Once I found a thumb-sized scorpion that I captured and kept alive in a little box. I intended to put it between the fresh sheets of the bed Sophie and I made up for Bert's upcoming visit, but I thought the better of it in case he blamed Sophie when he discovered the visitor in his bed. I finally let the angry creature go in the garden where it scampered into some dry leaves.

I knew Bert's dislike of me ran equally deep, which he made clear when he arrived to sort out Papa Hugo's affairs. I had the misfortune to meet him in the upstairs hall. "I've been meaning to talk to you privately, Elizabeth." He drew me out of earshot of Mama Lu's bedroom door. "My parents have raised you in their house, as their own child, yet they never adopted you. As far as I am concerned, Miss Dumond, your origins define your place. You would do best to keep in mind that you are the bastard child of a servant. Don't forget who you are," he said. He gripped my arm a little too hard and left me in the hall, shutting the door to Mama Lu's room behind him. That evening, as I undressed for bed, I noticed the small bruise where Bert had squeezed my arm. Once again, the cold feeling of apprehension I'd felt earlier gripped me, clawing and ripping at my blanket of sleep as I passed an uneasy night full of nightmares of Bert torturing little animals.

Bert had been at home running Sweetbrier for a few weeks when he came across Sophie and me discussing Ivanhoe. The door to the schoolroom was open, and Sophie was reading aloud from a passage she thought was particularly good. I listened, proud of the way she read, happy that I'd been such a good teacher. Neither of us saw Bert at the door, watching us with cold eyes.

"What in hell do you think you're doing?"

"We are discussing Ivanhoe," I said.

He turned to Sophie. "Did I hear you reading?" Sophie nodded. "Where in hell did you learn how to read like that?" Sophie looked down and shrugged. "Answer me, girl." He reached over and grasped her chin so she was forced to look him in the eye.

"I taught Sophie how to read." I took a deep breath and glared at him defiantly, showing a braveness I didn't feel inside. "You know, times are changing and lots of Negroes are learning to read and write. Papa Hugo didn't mind at all. In fact, I talked to him about having a little schoolhouse built between the settlements. He thought it was a fine idea."

"Well, my Papa is dead and gone, and I'll tell you flat, you aren't building any damn schoolhouse for niggers on my property. No man, woman or child is going to take time off his or her work to learn how to read." Bert turned back to Sophie. "Now get out of here and make yourself useful," he snarled.

"Yes, Mr. Bert," she said, slipping quietly from the room.

"As for you, Miss Elizabeth, if my mother wasn't so fond of you, I'd feel no obligation to feed or clothe you, or put up with any of your new-fangled, help-the-slaves ideas. Keep in mind your position." He slammed the door behind him, and I hurled the copy of Ivanhoe at the closed door, where Bert's head would have been if he were still standing there. It fell to the floor with a broken spine. I wept tears of anger as I glued it back together, leaving it to dry on the oak desk in the nursery.

The incident in the nursery marked a turning point: an unraveling of life as I knew it. My protector, Papa Hugo, was gone; Mama Lu was a frail remnant of herself. There was a change in the relationship I had with Addie; she seemed cool and withdrawn, and I couldn't fathom why. Sophie never came back to work in the big house. When I asked where Sophie was, Addie just shook her head and muttered that Sophie was helping out in the fields from now on.

"Why?" I asked.

"Just 'cause. It ain't like she got much say in anything that happens or where she gets to go. Sophie just waits her orders, like the rest of us who is owned by that man."

"Are you mad at me, Addie?" I said, "Because you sound like it."

"I ain't mad at you, Miss Elizabeth."

I couldn't fail to miss the overly formal tone of her voice. "Why don't you call me Lizzie, like usual?"

"It boils down to the whole problem between masters and servants; between white folks and a bunch of darkies and mix-breeds. I'm just mighty sick of the way things are, and someday it gonna change, mark my words."

"Addie, you know damn well I'm not like other white people!"

"You're right, Lizzie, this ain't about you other than you were born with the right color of skin, and there lies the line between us." She turned her back on me, and I knew our conversation was over. I wanted to tell her how much I loved her and agreed with her, but she was in no mood, so I picked up Mama Lu's tray and took it to her room.

I was still hopeful that Sophie's job as a fieldworker was only temporary. Every morning I asked Addie about Sophie and when she was coming back. Finally, Addie said, "Sophie's fine, but she ain't comin' back, so you can stop asking." Her voice was flat and stern, like it was her final statement on the matter of Sophie. I stopped asking her, but I was determined to talk to Sophie herself.

In the evenings, when the workers were home from the fields, I visited the cabin in the hollow in search of Sophie. Addie or Garvus usually greeted me nicely enough, but our relationship lacked the ease it once had. Every time I visited, I got a different story. "Sophie's sick in bed with a fever," or "Sophie's still sleeping," and once, "Sophie's fishing with her daddy," which I figured was a lie, because Sophie never liked fishing much, even though she was handy with a fishing pole. I got the feeling Sophie was avoiding me, which wore at my heart because I thought of her as my sister.

I was an avid, although mostly private, abolitionist. Papa Hugo and I had lively arguments over the issues dividing the United States: still a young, green nation that relied on the back-breaking labor of the enslaved to lay down its foundations. Papa was at least open-minded, and even entertained the idea that Negroes would someday be considered equal citizens, but he was in no hurry for it to happen. "It's a battle of beliefs for the future to deal with, and you're the future, Liz. So, what do you propose? What is the solution?"

Papa Hugo loved to stir up a good discussion. He was a slave owner, which is a shameful thing, but he never had the problems other plantation owners had with their workforce, because he was good-natured, fair, and generous to his workers. Bert's style of leadership was opposite of Papa's. He led with fear and left a path of anger and despair behind him.

As the months passed, tensions on the plantation rose. Bert demanded more from the workers and gave them less in return. I heard rumblings about it from Addie and Chemise, but couldn't investigate for myself, because Mama Lu had fallen and broken her hip and now required my full attention. She was in constant discomfort and needed assistance in every matter of living. I longed to see Sophie and take one of my usual rides on old Nance, but I spent my time tending Mama Lu, trying to lift her spirits by reading her favorite poems and Psalms aloud. Doctor Brisco came out and exclaimed

over Mama Lu's extreme thinness; "You're not feeding her enough," he said to Addie.

"She eats only the smallest bites of food, hardly enough for a bird! It isn't Addie's fault at all," I said.

"I just don't have much appetite," said Mama Lu in the weak voice she'd had since Papa Hugo died.

Addie shook her head and rolled her eyes. "If you ask me, Miss Lucille needs more fresh air and less of the tonic you been pourin' down her throat for so long."

"I'm sure Doctor Brisco knows best," said Mama Lu. Addie harrumphed and left with the tray of mostly uneaten tea sandwiches she made specially to tempt Mama to eat.

The Doctor advised Mama Lu to continue taking her dose of laudanum tonic. "Adjust the dose as you see fit, Lucille. If you are feeling nervous or melancholy, or you are in pain, pour a draught and drink it down at once." He also gave her something to stimulate her appetite, but it made her nauseous, and she refused to take it after the first time. "I'll be back to check on her in a week or two," the doctor told Bert. "I expect her hip to start healing by then."

But the hip refused to heal, and Mama Lu resigned herself to being an invalid. "Thank God for you, dear Elizabeth. I'd be in a sorry state without you," she said. I helped her sit up in bed and arranged her so I could brush and dress her long gray hair.

"I'm afraid I'm not half as good a hairdresser as Sophie, but it doesn't look too bad." I held the hand mirror up for her to see herself.

"Very nice, Liz," she said. "Where did you say Sophie was?"

"I told you, Mama Lu. Bert sent her out to work in the fields from now on."

"Why, what a shame! Sophie was becoming a very suitable lady's maid."

"Perhaps you could say something to Bert. We could certainly use her help in the house, and especially since your injury."

Mama Lu sighed. "Bert must need more hands in the fields. He has made it quite clear; he doesn't want the interference of an old lady like me when it comes to plantation matters. I think I'll rest now. I am suddenly sleepy, no doubt from your fine work dressing my hair. It must be quite late."

"No Mama Lu, it is only ten in the morning."

"Whatever time it is, dear, I need a nap." She closed her eyes and lay her head on the pillow; the blue veins etching a delicate map across her cheeks. I drew the curtains over the windows before tucking the blankets around her.

"Do you need anything else, Mama Lu?"

"No dear. Just shut the door when you go." I kissed her on the forehead and she squeezed my hand.

When I left her rooms that morning, I walked straight to the stables. It was another opportunity to go find Sophie, and this time, I had an idea where I'd find her. I knew Bert was seeding the south fields with sugar beets; I'd overheard him talking to one of the foremen who'd stopped by Sweetbrier for business matters. "It's a speculative crop," Bert said, "but one that promises a high profit from the sugar mills."

The stable boy saddled Nance, and I started down the road, passing miles of cotton fields and cane until I came to an expanse of newly plowed soil and the musty scent of fresh dirt in the breeze. From my mount atop Nance I saw a group of workers at the far end of the field. They were spread out between the rows, bobbing up and down as they planted. In the air drifted the distant voices of the women singing as they worked.

It always thrilled me to hear the men and women sing, reminding me of those early years with Addie and Garvus when the folks would gather around the fire pit in the middle of the settlement, talking and laughing and singing the old spirituals accompanied by one or two fiddle players. Though I'd continued my piano lessons with Mama Lu, the music was nothing like the wild, soulful sound of the singers from the Negro cabins.

I tethered Nance to a shade tree on the side of the road before walking down one of the rows toward the distant workers. Their faint, high voices grew more distinct until amongst the harmonies, I could hear the clear notes of Sophie's fine singing voice. I let the sound guide me through the rows until I found her. She was kneeling over the row with her back toward me so that she didn't see my approach. She was startled when I knelt next to her. "Do you want some help, Sophie?" I said softly.

"Lizzie, why you about made me jump out of my skin! I sure didn't expect to see you here!"

It had been going on four months since I'd last seen Sophie and she looked older. There were dark circles under her eyes and her usual joyful spirit was missing. "Has something happened?" I couldn't help blurting out.

"Lizzie honey, a whole bunch of stuff happens every day. That's what you call life."

"Oh, I do miss your company."

"I miss you too, Lizzie."

"I'm working on Mama Lu so that she'll ask Bert to let you come back."

Sophie's expression was pained. "Did you ever think I might want to stay where I am?"

"What on earth are you talking about?"

Sophie looked away from me. "Things are just different now, that's all."

"The fields are no place to be, and you know it. You've got to come back to work in the house with Addie and Chemise."

Sophie's eyes flashed. "Just keep your nose out of it, Lizzie."

"I don't understand you, Sophie. I thought you'd want to come home."

"It might be your home, but it isn't mine. Remember, Lizzie, I am a nigger girl first and last."

I wanted to talk more, to find out why she sounded angry, but she raised her finger to her lips to hush me. "Look Lizzie." She nodded toward a man on horseback riding down the row break, his eyes moving from left to right as he checked on the workers. "This isn't really the place or time to talk. Mr. Boss there doesn't like it when someone isn't doing her work."

"Could you meet me later? Under the willow?"

Sophie looked uncertain for a minute, but she finally nodded. "Tomorrow night. I'll get there as soon after 6:00 as I can," she promised. "Now scoot on out of here before you get me into trouble."

I hugged her. "See you tomorrow." The women started a new song that followed me across the field as I walked back to collect Nance.

The following evening, I was waiting under the willow when Sophie arrived at half past six. I handed her a small package wrapped in brown paper and tied with a nice silk ribbon I'd found in the sewing cabinet. "I brought you *"Tanglewood Tales,"* by Hawthorne. I hope you like it as much as I did."

"I'm sure I will, Lizzie. I always try to read before I go to sleep." Sophie sat next to me on a giant root reaching out from the trunk of the willow like a wrinkled arm. Sophie kissed my cheek and peered at me like she was seeing me for the first time. "You look skinny, girl. Aren't Chemise and Mama feeding you enough?"

"Did you hear that Mama Lu fell and broke her hip?" Sophie nodded. "I've been so busy taking care of her and running up and down those stairs that I wear off everything I eat! Talk about skinny, you should see Mama Lu. Why, I think she's starving herself to death."

"Miss Lucille always did eat like a bird."

"It's worse than ever now, and on top of everything, I think she's losing her wits."

"I'm sorry to hear that." We talked on for an hour more, until it was difficult to see in the velvety dusk. Sophie reached out and squeezed my hand. "I should go. We get to the fields early."

"What time?" I asked.

"Before you've even thought of raising your sleepy head from the pillow." Sophie stood, and when she did, I verified what I thought I'd seen before: a swelling in her lower abdomen. I put my hand on her belly and looked into her eyes with the question clear but unspoken between us. She nodded.

"Which one of your beaus is the papa?" I asked.

"It isn't something I wanted, Lizzie. A man took advantage of me." Her eyes filled with tears.

I put my arms around her. "Oh my God, You poor darling."

"The worst of it is over now." Sophie pulled away gently from my hug.

"Who was it? He should be taken to jail!"

"I don't want to talk about it right now. I've got to go, Lizzie." Sophie gave me a quick hug and slipped through the willow branches.

I vowed to myself that if I found the man who had defiled Sophie, I'd find a way to punish him.

A year after her fall, Mama Lu's hip still refused to knit together, and as the months passed, her pain grew, and her temperament became more unpredictable. She fussed and was angry, often lashing out at me, Addie or Chemise. One morning while I combed out her hair Mama Lu began to rant. "I can see hate in Addie's eyes. That black heathen wants me dead."

"Hush now, Mama Lu. Addie could overhear you, and it would hurt her feelings."

"She means me ill. I don't want her back in my rooms."

"Mama Lu, you're just overexcited. You mustn't think such awful things about Addie. Why, she's worked in this house for years. She's devoted to the family." Unable to soothe her, I poured a larger dose of Doctor Brisco's calming tonic than usual. She slept through the rest of the day. From then on, Addie was banned from the sickroom, and the job of caring for Mama Lu fell to me, with Chemise's help when Mama Lu had to be turned or lifted.

Her pain became intolerable. She had trouble finding a comfortable position in bed, and though Chemise and I lifted her every day to her armchair by the window, she developed a nasty sore on her good hip from favoring it so much. I did my best to clean and disinfect the sore, but Mama Lu's fragile, thin skin became hot and inflamed. I asked Bert to send for Doctor Brisco.

The doctor was openly alarmed by Mama Lu's condition. He prescribed a tincture of opium for pain and called us into the parlor after he'd examined her. "Now Bert, I'm not going to fool you by saying I have good news. Your mother is in sorry shape. At this point, she is very likely to be bedridden until her death. Liz has done a fine job taking care of Lucille, but she can't be expected to tend her around the clock. I advise hiring a trained nurse to care for your mama."

Bert nodded. "It's time my wife Sarah joined me here at Sweetbrier. She has experience in the sickroom from tending her own mother."

"The sooner she comes, the better." The doctor shook Bert's hand and patted me on the back before making his exit.

In two weeks' time Sarah arrived with Susan and Samuel, her and Bert's children. Her arrival was a godsend; I'd been doing my best to help Mama Lu, but I wasn't used to nursing. Since Mama Lu's aversion to Addie and now Chemise and all the Negroes, the entire responsibility fell on my shoulders. I was relieved to have Sarah's expert help and surprised to find in her a kindred spirit. I wondered privately why such a sweet person would marry someone like Bert, whom I found loathsome.

Sarah took charge immediately. She insisted on throwing open the bedroom windows and had the furniture rearranged so it was easier to move Mama Lu to the chamber pot or her armchair. Sarah took over the job of tending to Mama Lu's needs in the mornings; in exchange, I became a sort of nanny to Susan and Samuel, teaching them math and English lessons. The children were fair students and sweet-natured like Sarah. I enjoyed mornings in the schoolroom helping them master the multiplication table and teaching them to make cursive letters with tidy loops. Life fell into a routine that was tolerable enough. Thankfully, Bert was away most of the time on plantation business, and so was easy to avoid.

I met Sophie under the willow as often as a meeting could be arranged. Near the end of her pregnancy her belly was brimming. It was hard to fathom how she still got around as nimbly as she did. It was no surprise when twins were born. "Mama and Chemise delivered one baby at midnight on July the thirty-first, and the next baby popped out an hour later, on August the first. I named them July and August; that way, I'll never forget their birthdays. We're calling them Jules and Augie for short."

Sophie was crazy over the babies. Some of the lightness of spirit that she'd lost came back as she threw herself into caring for and loving her boys. When we met under our willow Sophie carried the twins in a sling of material that fell like a hammock down her back. I would lift one boy and she'd take the other, and we would sit talking companionably while we burped Jules and Augie and fought the mosquitoes.

Sophie's babies grew like sturdy sprouts. They were handsome little boys with a light, chocolate color that made me wonder if one of the overseers had taken advantage of Sophie. I asked her many times who the father was, but Sophie just shook her head and said that she didn't want to remember what happened, much less talk about it. I had to find out for myself before I could take revenge on the monster who violated Sophie.

Sophie Washington
Sweetbrier
October 1854

No one but Mama knows what happened. She was sitting on the porch in the pitch-black night when I limped up, crying and hugging myself. I had some scratches on my arms and legs, and I knew there would be bruises showing by morning. When I drew closer, there was Mama, lit up by the dim glow of the porch lantern. I was never so glad to see her in my life.

When Mr. Bert ordered me out of the schoolroom, after he caught me reading with Lizzie, he was not finished. That evening, on my way home to our cabin in the hollow, he was waiting for me. My heart started hammering as soon as Mr. Bert loomed up out of the dusky shadows by a clump of trees near the horse barn. I tried to run, but he was already within stepping distance and he easily overtook me, clamping an arm around my neck and pressing the other hand tight over my mouth and nose.

Mr. Bert dragged me through the darkness the short distance to the barn. His arm tightened across my throat, and his sweating palm cut off my supply of air. I wondered if he intended to kill me. My head grew light, and I felt my arms and legs go limp. I was losing the fight for air and consciousness when he let me go abruptly. I took a gasping breath, reeling drunkenly from the sudden rush of reviving air. Mr. Bert took advantage of my weakness, and as I bent gasping and clutching my sides, he ripped a strip from a dirty saddle blanket and tied it tightly in my mouth so that I couldn't make a sound. The pain was sharp; the tight binding tore the corners of my mouth, and the rough cloth pressing against my tongue made me gag. The only passage for the bitterness and blood filling my mouth was swallowing it. I suddenly knew that the way to get out of this alive was to give up the fight. I became like a rag doll in his grip, all struggle gone.

"A negress like you, who thinks so highly of herself, needs to come to her senses I think." Mr. Bert shoved me hard, and I fell backwards onto a pile of hay. He wrenched my arms up and tied my wrists together over my head, pulling the rope so tight that my hands throbbed with the blood trapped in them. He pulled his knife from its sheath and sliced my dress down the front, and then my shift and undergarments. "I've been hungry for a piece of black ass," he said. "Spread your legs, girl." When I didn't, he slapped my face and forced my legs open, his knees pressing painfully against mine. His mouth clamped down on my breast and I could feel the sharpness of his teeth biting my nipples and moving down my stomach to my woman's parts. "Are you a virgin?" he asked.

I nodded, hoping that he would take pity on me, but instead, he shoved the handle of his knife into my cunny. The sharp stabbing pain was such that I thought he'd pierced me with the blade of the knife. "I like it nice and wet, with nothing in the way," he said, and he forced his manhood into my throbbing cunny hole. It felt like forever as he savagely thrust with his hot hardness until a great burst of something wet ran down my legs.

Mr. Bert collapsed on top of me then, nearly smothering me with his weight. My legs were spread so wide that I felt like I was being torn apart. The pain made tears spill down my face. When his crushing weight finally rolled off me, I scrambled up and as far away as I could get in the stall where he'd taken me like an animal. I managed to loosen the binding around my wrists and pull the filthy rag from my mouth. I clutched my torn dress, trying to wrap it around me as Mr. Bert pulled a handkerchief from his pocket and wiped himself before buttoning up his pants.

"You won't be working in the house any more, girl. Your reading lessons are over. You'll start in the south fields tomorrow." Mr. Bert grabbed my chin with his big paw of a hand and lifted my face. "I'm going to say this once, girl. You tell any tales to anyone, like your mama or papa or your little friend, Miss Elizabeth, you can be sure I'll visit you again, and next time you won't feel like standing after I have my way with you. You hear me, Miss Sophie? You and your brother Jerome or someone from your family is going to end up hurt if you flap your jaws about this. You hear me?" He tightened his fingers and squeezed both sides of my jaw. I nodded my head once, hoping he'd let go the bruising grip he held me in. He squeezed once more, and then he lifted the latch to the barn door and slipped out into the night.

I stood there for a minute, blood and Mr. Bert's mess running down the insides of my thighs and tears of pain and humiliation dripping from my cheeks. I leaned against the wall as I gathered myself together, wiping his filth from my legs. I pulled on the remnants of my shift, and with both hands, I held together the ripped navy-blue muslin dress I wore when I worked in the house. The night was dark, with a tiny sliver of new moon giving the only light as I groped my way toward our cabin, bent over and hobbling along like an old woman.

Though the distance from the big house to the cabins was usually an easy walk, it seemed to take forever to reach the familiar sight of home. In the dim glow of the porch lantern I could see Mama sitting on the porch in the rocking chair. "Where you been, Sophie?" she asked, her voice floating in the still air of the night. I ran up the steps and threw myself at her feet, burying my face in the soft, warm cushion of her lap as if I could hide from the terror of what had happened. When my shuddering sobs finally stopped and Mama's lap was wet with tears, she lifted up my face, inspecting the bruises Mr. Bert's finger's had made on my cheeks and the bloody bite marks on my lower lip. She rubbed my back and smoothed my hair with her strong, gentle hands. "You're safe now, honey," she said soothingly. "You can tell me what happened. Who hurt you?"

"Mama, he said he was going to kill me."

"Nobody gonna' kill you as long as I'm around. Now tell me all about it."

Mama drew me up like I was a little child and sat me on her lap. With my head on her shoulder and her arms holding me close, I told her the shameful things Mr. Bert had done to me in the barn. She didn't say a word but sat there with an expression on her face I'd never seen before; rage and frustration and sorrow all wrapped up in Mama's sweet face, and it scared me to see it.

Finally, she patted me on the back. "You'll want to get cleaned up. You sit here a minute. I'll be right back." Mama stood, and I could have sworn that she'd shrunk a little. She opened the door slow and quiet, so it wouldn't creak like it usually does, and disappeared into the cabin. A few minutes later she came out carrying a pitcher of water, a bar of soap, a towel and a fresh shift. She made another trip into the cabin for the tin washbasin and a sponge. Mama helped me take off my ruined clothes. She gently sponged all the sore parts and my bruised face. She lifted the clean shift over my head and hugged me fiercely.

"Ouch, Mama," I couldn't help saying, because of the bruises from Mr. Bert.

"If I had the power of God, I'd use it to make sure that Bert Laurent was punished and sentenced to a hell where he is eaten alive by red ants for eternity," she said. "As it is, I'm helpless. It shouldn't be that way, Sophie, but it is."

"I wish I could punish him for all the pain he's caused, not just my own. Maybe someday I'll get my chance."

"Honey, nothin' you can do but stay out of his way. If you see him coming and there's time, you hide. From now on, you practice making yourself invisible. If you can't avoid him, don't be nothin' but agreeable, and get out of there as soon as possible. Out of sight, out of mind. You hear me, Sophie?"

"Yes Mama."

"As for Mr. Bert, he's bound to get it back in full someday. It may be that he's getting his way with everything now, but he's gonna have a bitter end. Mark my words, that man is hexed from this day forward."

"Mama, he said he'd hurt our family if I told anyone, and I believe him."

"I ain't sayin' nothing, most certainly not to your brother or your daddy. No telling what foolhardy thing one of them might do if they get hotheaded. You and me are keeping this between us, honey. And don't tell Lizzie, either. She's got to live in that household. It's safer if she doesn't know." Mama kissed my cheek. "Now go on in and get some rest. Just be real quiet so you don't wake up Jerome or your daddy. A good long sleep will help you feel better in the morning." I crept softly across the cabin, holding my breath as I tiptoed past Jerome and Daddy. I climbed up the ladder to the loft and collapsed on my narrow cot, falling immediately into an exhausted sleep.

Toward dawn, I woke from a dream. I'd been thrown off a horse into a thicket of thorny brush. In my half-conscious state I thought for a minute that the dream was the reason for my sore, stiff body. I shuddered when I remembered what Mr. Bert had done and burrowed further under my blankets, blessedly falling asleep once again. When I woke the second time, Mama was cooking a pot of steaming oat mush for Daddy and Jerome. I lay on my bed up in the loft, listening to my family doing the usual everyday things, and though I was hurt in both body and mind I felt comforted.

Daddy and Jerome were sitting at the table eating huge bowls of mush sprinkled with raisins and hard little lumps of brown sugar. I could hear their spoons clinking against the dishes, but it was mostly quiet. Mama finally broke the silence. "Mr. Bert told our Sophie her services ain't needed anymore in the big house, and that he needs her to work in the fields with you and the boys."

I could see my daddy shake his head and look puzzled. "I thought that Miss Lucille was real happy with Sophie."

"It ain't Miss Lucille who is in charge of things, Garvus. Sophie and all of us are at the mercy of Mr. Bert now. I heard him tell Miss Sarah he's gonna stay put at Sweetbrier for at least a year. 'The Pierce Plantation has your daddy to run it while we're needed here,' he said, 'plus, the southern fields have great possibilities.' He said he wants to put in a thousand more acres of cane."

Daddy shook his head. "That fool'd be better off draining those swampy fields and putting in sweet potatoes if you ask me."

"No one's askin' you, Garvus."

"So where is Sophie?" Daddy raised his voice. "Are you up, sleepyhead?"

"Shush, Garvus. Sophie is gonna' stay in bed today on account of being sick. Make sure to tell the foreman that she'll show up tomorrow."

"Sure thing, honey." Daddy stood, and so did Jerome. I heard them put on their work boots in the little entry room at the front of the cabin, and then Mama and I were alone.

"Are you awake, Sophie?" Mama called softly up the stairs.

"Yes, Mama."

"Well, come on down and eat some breakfast. Then you and I got some business to take care of."

My body ached, and I felt the tenderness of my woman's parts when I stood up from bed and bent to straighten the blankets and pillow. Mama was sitting at the table waiting for me. A dish of mush and a glass of milk was set at my place. I sat down, and immediately fell into crying like a faucet. Nothing would ever be the same, and I knew it; I had lost forever the innocence I'd had just yesterday. Mama let me cry. She brought her chair next to mine and patted me on the back. "It's all right, honey. You cry as much as you want. Get it out of your system and throw the wickedness of Mr. Bert off like he never touched you."

I lifted my head from the table so I could look at Mama's beautiful brown eyes. "How do I do that, Mama?"

"You got to find a place inside yourself that's still pure, that nothin' can ever touch. It's a place you can escape to no matter what happens around you; a place deep in you that can't be hurt."

I thought about what she said, trying hard to find the place in my mind, but I couldn't. When I told Mama I didn't think I had it in me, she said I just got to keep trying to find it. "You eat your breakfast, Sophie, and then you and me will work on you feeling better about everything."

"I'm not hungry, Mama," I said, but she insisted that I take a bite, and before I knew it the bowl was empty.

"Now get yourself ready, 'cause the two of us is gonna' take a nice walk across the fields to the cabins by the river. I got a hankering to pay a visit to Sister Ardeen."

I told Mama I didn't feel like going anywhere, but she shushed me. "A walk gonna' take your mind off things. Now, go on and get dressed while I run over to tell Chemise I'm having a tooth pulled this morning and won't be back to work until afternoon."

"But Mama, I—"

She cut me off in midsentence. "I heard tell that Sister Ardeen can lay her hands on a sick-spirited person and heal them."

"You really believe that, Mama?" I asked.

Mama pursed her lips into a grim little smile. "Sometimes it helps to believe in something even if it ain't true."

Before I got dressed, Mama helped me take another sponge bath to wash off anything remaining from Mr. Bert, and she rubbed some healing ointment into the scratches he made. Near mid-morning, she and I started out for the river edge of the plantation, where swamp grass and cypress trees grew thick and where the crawfish were so big you could feed a family of four if you were lucky enough to catch the granddaddies. Mama carried a dozen eggs and a few big sweet potatoes in a basket. The walking did help my spirits, and it eased some of the ache from my bruised places. Mama and I talked now and then along the way, but mostly we were quiet, thinking our own thoughts. After an hour of walking at a steady pace, we arrived at a cabin as ancient as the woman who came to the door to greet us.

"Hey there, Sister Addie. And is this your Sophie?" She came close, peering at me through eyes with a peculiar milky cast. "What happened to you, honey?" she asked, gently touching my swollen face. My eyes welled up with tears, and she hugged me with her skinny, strong arms. "Don't cry, honey. Why you're still as pretty as a picture once those swelled places go down." Her wrinkles parted in a smile that showed a set of perfect white teeth.

"Thank you, Sister Ardeen." I kissed the old woman's leathery cheek, and she led us into her cabin. Beyond the closet-sized entrance hall, the cabin was one open room. On every wall hung drying herbs and flowers. The fragrance was part medicine and sharp-smelling plants mingled with the sweet smells of wild rose and mint. Sister Ardeen invited us to sit on two upended wooden crates that served as chairs on either side of a plank table. She poured us each a cup of herb tea before perching on an oak stool at one end of the table. She was puffing on a pipe filled with a fragrant blend of tobacco and herbs that she passed to Mama. I hadn't seen Mama smoke before, so I was mighty surprised when she took a deep puff, blowing it out like an expert.

"Something tells me that there be a deeper reason than just a friendly visit you payin' me. What brings you here, Sister Addie?"

"My girl and I need some help from your spirit guides, Sister Ardeen. You got one of them voodoo dolls of yours?"

Sister Ardeen peered at Mama through her hooded, milky eyes. "They carry powerful magic, effigy dolls. You know if you use them, sometimes the magic can turn around and bite you in your own back. You got to make sure your heart be pure in such matters, and it ain't just because someone made you hot-faced."

"No need to worry about that, Sister. My heart is pure, and so is Sophie's; rest assured, the subject of this curse is bad from his inside soul. Not an inch of this man would you or I regret seein' hurt for one second."

The old woman nodded her head and jumped off the stool with the ease of a much younger woman. She rummaged through a trunk and brought out a rag doll about six inches long. It didn't look like much, but Ardeen held it gently, between two fingers, as if it was something she wanted to touch as little as possible. Mama reached out her hand for it.

"Just a minute." Sister Ardeen took a handkerchief-sized cloth from the same trunk from which she'd gotten the doll. She wrapped up the little figure and tied a piece of twine around it. "Now, you gonna have to sew some of that man's hair to your little poppet, or get some of his essence if you can, from a piece of his clothing or his handkerchief, and you'll be ready, Sister. And then every so often, do to this little poppet what you want done to the real flesh and blood man. You can use pins, or embers, or scissors. Whatever you can think of to create torment."

Sister Ardeen began to chant in a mumbo-jumbo language I recognized as the one the old people in our settlement used when they wanted to communicate with the spirit world. I'd never really believed the old people when they talked about the powers of voodoo, but I could feel a strange and mighty energy flowing from Sister Ardeen. It surrounded Mama and me and the little doll Mama had put in the basket, and then suddenly it was gone, like someone blew out a candle. "Now your special doll is ready. It might take some time, but a living hell gonna fall on your subject. Just you wait and see."

"Thank-you kindly, Sister Ardeen," said Mama. She kissed the old woman on the cheek.

"And remember to watch your own back, both of you," she called as we set off down the road toward home.

Elizabeth Dumond
Sweetbrier Plantation
1854-1858

Mama Lu sank a little every day, like a shipwreck descending ever so slowly to its graveyard on the ocean floor. She got so thin, her skin pulled tight and showed all the underworkings of her body: the bones and veins, muscles and tendons. Eventually it was no trouble at all lifting her to and from her bed. Sarah and I worked out a routine of shared duties, and a solid bond of friendship grew between us. "I swear you're like a little sister," she said as we sat side-by-side working on Mama Lu's star pattern quilt that she'd asked us to finish for her.

"I feel kin to you, too," I replied. "I wish you were my sister." What I didn't say was how much I detested and feared her husband. I was happy that Bert wasn't around much. His time was spent between Sweetbrier and the Pierce Plantation, where Sarah's aging father had a growing need for Bert's help. More responsibility for the management of Sweetbrier fell on Sarah's and my shoulders.

Bert was a thorough manager who left instructions about what should be weeded or thinned, or which fields needed a cover crop. "While I am gone, I need your eyes on the men and the niggers, too. They'll take any chance to laze around like paying guests. Any slow-downs in work, you report to Ed Boney. He'll see to it that they do what they're supposed to do," he'd instructed Sarah and me at dinner

on one of his visits home. His eyes narrowed as he stared at me inso-
lently. "My daddy took little Miss Elizabeth with him on plantation
business, and she knows Sweetbrier like the back of her hand. She
will be your eyes and ears, Sarah."

In the afternoons, when Mama Lu was napping, I'd have Nance
saddled and take her on the familiar trails and dusty roads leading
from one part of the plantation to the next. In the evenings it was my
job to report plantation business to Sarah. We became closer than ever
as we worked together. I still couldn't fathom why Sarah had married
Bert, but it was clear that Bert had married Sarah for convenience
and gain.

Sarah was a plain woman, while Bert was handsome enough
to have wooed and married almost any eligible woman in the state
of New Orleans. "He married me for the Pierce Plantation," Sarah
said matter-of-factly. "I don't have any illusions about Bert's motives."
Though Bert didn't love her, he treated her with respect. Sarah Pierce
was a hard worker and an asset on any plantation. With Sarah, Bert
had a reliable partner who could oversee his business duties when he
was away.

Sarah begged me to take charge of the children's lessons. "You
are far more patient than I, and smarter too. And while you are tutor-
ing, I will tend to Lucille." Our days revolved around our duties.
I spent mornings with Susan and Samuel, teaching basic reading,
history, and arithmetic and encouraging them to play. They were less
timid now, but still grew quiet and hid behind their mother whenever
their father appeared. Around noon I took Mama Lu's tray up to her
bedside and relieved Sarah, so she could eat lunch and spend time
with Susan and Samuel.

I was always happy to escape the sickroom in the late afternoon when Mama Lu was in the habit of napping. I'd waste no time
saddling Nance for my inspection rides in the nearby fields. Sarah
and I traded off in the evenings, and I met Sophie as often as the

two of us could manage. Between my duties and Sophie working the fields and caring for Jules and Augie, it wasn't near as often as I would have liked.

Sophie's babies were over a year old and teething when Mama Lu died in her sleep. Doctor Brisco was called in to verify the obvious. "She is finally at peace, the poor woman. You ladies will need to prepare her for the undertaker." I could hardly see from crying so hard as Sarah and I gave Mama Lu a sponge bath and dressed her one last time, in the rose-colored, ruffled dress she wore on special occasions. Now that my adopted mother had gone to join Papa, I was truly orphaned, and I couldn't help feeling a gnawing apprehension about my future.

With both Papa Hugo and Mama Lu dead, I knew my position in the household was no longer protected. Sarah would do her best for me, but Bert was ultimately in charge of my fate. My apprehensions were confirmed when, a week after Mama Lu's funeral, Bert called Sarah and me to the office. After we'd taken a seat, Bert spoke abruptly. "You realize, Elizabeth, my parents took you into their home as a charity case, do you not?"

"Bert—" interrupted Sarah.

"Hush, Sarah. This is Laurent business. You'll listen and keep out of it." Bert's tone was harsh. "You are not mentioned in my parents' estate, Miss Dumond, and you have reached a majority of age, yet you are still dependent. In order for you to stay here, you will perform a regular servant's duties for your keep." I heard Sarah gasp. I merely nodded at him, trying to keep the defiance and hatred I felt from showing in my eyes.

"Elizabeth has been teaching the children—" Sarah murmured, but Bert silenced her with a look.

"As the illegitimate child of my mother's maid, it seems fitting that you follow her footsteps. You may continue as a governess to

Susan and Samuel, assuming other household duties as necessary. You'll earn your board and keep from now on."

I rose from my chair. "Are you finished with all you have to say?" He nodded, his eyes cold and mocking.

"Bert, do you mean to be so harsh? Elizabeth has been a family member for many years now! You can't treat her as if she is merely a servant."

"Elizabeth Dumond is the upstart daughter of a slut, Sarah. You'll not interfere with this or any business I undertake, or decision I make. I'll not tolerate a carping woman." He threw open the door, and it was clear that Sarah and I were to leave the room, which we did.

Later, as we worked together tidying the schoolroom, Sarah said she was frightened of Bert. "But I must resign myself to making the best of things. I am deeply sorry, Liz. He talked to you so unkindly!"

I didn't know what to say, other than it wasn't her fault and I knew it. "I'm sorry, too, that you must live with a man you're frightened of."

"I wish I could make him treat you decently, but I am powerless with my husband."

We hugged affectionately, like sisters would, and finished cleaning the schoolroom.

In September, almost six months after Mama Lu died, when the long stalks of sugar cane were ready to harvest, and the sugar beets burst from the surface of their rows with red, swollen globes, the hurricane season turned ugly. All of us at Sweetbrier had seen storms, but the fury of the wind and the sheets of rain dropping in vertical waves from a deep indigo sky were so formidable that Addie and Chemise had to turn back when they tried to get home. "I ain't never seen nothin' like it," said Chemise, sitting in one of Papa Hugo's old bathrobes as she wrung her sodden dress and stockings into a basin.

Addie was wearing another of Papa's old bathrobes and hanging up her wet clothes. "I remember back when I was a girl; once it flooded so bad we couldn't leave the cabins or we'd have drowned.

Lucky our cabins was up high enough; otherwise a whole peck of us would have floated out to the river and down to the ocean to be some fish's dinner. Do you remember that storm, Chemise?"

"I sure do. Your mama and I couldn't get to the big house that day unless we went swimming. I'm guessing this storm is just about as bad," she said. "It's Our Father in Heaven telling us that he's the one holding the real power."

As Addie and Chemise reminisced about past storms, the wind and sheets of water blew in great gusts, buffeting the walls and pounding the roof until you couldn't hear yourself over the din. Sarah was forever worried about the infamous twisters she'd heard could strike with such force that entire homesteads and even villages were left in piles of rubble. "I don't think twisters strike around here. It's mostly hurricanes," I said, trying to soothe her, but she got more and more riled up. The noise became terrifying, as if a train was on top of Sweetbrier, and Sarah gathered the children, insisting that we all move to the basement where the thick stone and mortar walls would protect us if the house got ripped from its foundations.

I wasn't convinced the basement was the best place to go, but I didn't argue. It was much quieter down there, and a bit clammy. Sarah comforted the terrified children while Addie and I lit the lanterns hanging from the beams. Chemise sang 'Swing Low, Sweet Chariot' and 'There is a Balm in Gilead,' and we spent an hour pleasantly enough, distracting ourselves by singing old spirituals while the wind and weather waged nature's war above us.

The safety of the basement was only temporary. It wasn't long before a creeping puddle of water covered our feet. I took one of the lanterns from its hook and sloshed through the deepening water to find the leak; a substantial volume of water was pouring through a casement window which appeared to have been broken out by a tree limb, an ugly, gnarled thing that stuck through the window. Water gushed through the hole and showed no sign of stopping.

"Heaven help us," wailed Chemise.

Sarah made an effort to sound calm and reassuring. "Hush now. You're frightening the children. We simply need to go upstairs to higher ground."

"That's where I'd have gone in the first place," Addie muttered.

Sarah led the frightened children upstairs to the second floor. Addie, Chemise and I followed, stopping briefly in the kitchen to gather some cheese, pickles, and cold meats since none of us had eaten dinner. Mama Lu's rooms were the most spacious and comfortable for us to set up a roosting station. There, we spent a long evening telling stories and playing guessing games while the storm made sounds like a speeding steam locomotive. Finally, we all fell to sleep from sheer exhaustion.

Fortunately, Sweetbrier was built to withstand nature's excesses. The horrible roaring noise continued through the night and sounds of solid objects banging against the house made us all sleep fitfully. The next morning, when the thunderous wind calmed and sunshine broke the clouds apart, we ventured downstairs. A few inches of dirty brown water covered the floor, and the flood line a foot and a half up the wall showed that the water was receding.

Sandy foam lined the walls to the level where the water had risen, and in the dining room, Mama Lu's prized Aubusson rug was covered with thick mud. But the damage in the house was nothing compared to the fields of cane and sugar beets. Sweetbrier's main house and outbuildings were on a knoll that elevated it above the worst flooding, but over half of the acres and acres of its field land were low lying, and the floodwaters covered the cane stalks. When the waters ebbed, the cane was rotten, and the beets were uprooted and split.

Bert was beside himself with the loss of his crops. In the months following the storm, he divided his time between the Pierce and Laurent plantations, cleaning up storm damage, repairing roads, and rebuilding fencing. His mood was understandably grim, and Sarah did her best to keep the children out of his way and to have meals prepared so he could eat on the run. Between helping Addie, Chemise, and Sarah clean the mud and sandy debris from the house, I served as a courier for Bert while he was away. Nance and I fought the swarms of mosquitos and biting flies that multiplied after the storm to deliver Bert's messages and written orders to the field bosses.

Bert became angrier as he worked tirelessly to repair the damage. His ruthlessness reached extremes, and he charged ahead like a bull, demanding that his overworked slaves shore up levees to protect his future crops, and once the land was dry enough, he made them work from dawn to dusk, preparing the earth to plant more expansive fields of cane and what he hoped would be a high yield crop of cotton. A less ambitious man would have moved more cautiously, but not Bert. The storm had driven some farmers to ruin, forcing them to sell off portions of their land in order to stay solvent. Bert took advantage of the misfortune of some by buying up neighboring acreage near both plantations. Though I hated Bert, I reluctantly acknowledged that he was a canny businessman.

With a natural ease, Sarah and I coordinated household duties. After Mama Lu's death, Sarah joined us in the schoolroom most mornings. She helped the children with math and geography, and I taught short lessons in history and English grammar. Our afternoons passed in pleasant companionship while working on projects Sarah created to keep us busy. It was a pleasure to have Bert away most of the time. I heard plenty about him from Addie and Chemise whenever I went to the kitchen. "Mr. Bert gonna get it in his own back someday if he keep doin' what he doin'. The men hate him more every day," Chemise muttered.

Addie nodded in agreement. "Garvus said Mr. Bert caught two boys fooling around fishing when they was supposed to be working on one of them levees. He had the field boss whip 'em so bad, them boys still have bleeding sores. One of them boys was only twelve years old."

Chemise grunted sympathetically. "I hear tell he been trading some of the old men so's he can get younger fellas who can work harder. I just talked to my sister who lives at the settlement by the river. She say that last week he traded two old men who have been with the Laurents for fifty or more years. One was old Millie's husband, and she ain't stopped cryin' since."

"I'm tellin' everyone to stay out of his way, and don't do nothin' to give Mr. Bert a chance to take out his ugliness on them," said Addie. "You better watch it too, Lizzie. Mr. Bert ain't no friend of yours, either."

"It's lucky I am close to Sarah and the children," I said.

"It ain't gonna protect you in the long run, honey. Be careful around that man." Addie needn't have warned me; I was already wary around Bert, but in the end, caution was not enough.

When most of the physical damage of the storm was erased and the levees were in place to keep future floods out of his fields, Bert turned his energies to saving money wherever he could. He expected longer hours and harder labor from his slaves as well as his hired men. The workers grumbled and cursed, but most of them rose to meet his demands, fearing repercussions from their harsh owner. Bert was a dictator; there was no milk of human kindness to temper his rule. His notoriety grew, and hatred festered among the workers.

It was a year after the hurricane; a year marked by hard work, blood, and punishment that paid off in fields so pregnant with bounty the very smell of fertility lingered in the air for hours after the sun went down. During harvest, Sarah and I took over all the cooking and housekeeping duties; every available hand was needed in the fields. Addie and Chemise were sent to set up one of the camp kitchens that moved along with a crew of cotton pickers.

It was quiet at Sweetbrier without Addie and Chemise making a commotion in the kitchen, breaking now and then into laughter or a few lines of a song, and without the stable workers and dairy girls talking in the yard. I remember the penetrating quiet in the kitchen that afternoon, and how startling it was to have it broken by screaming, angry voices.

I hadn't seen Sophie for a few weeks. Since the beginning of the harvest season, she'd been working at a camp several miles from Sweetbrier. Her crew was picking the acreage on the southwestern edge of the plantation; a place rich with crops, mosquitoes, and poisonous snakes. Just a week before, news came that one of the children in camp got bitten by a cottonhead and died. I was relieved to hear it wasn't Jules or Augie. I missed Sophie and her boys. We had celebrated Jules and Augie's third birthday before they went away to camp with their mama. Addie baked a pecan custard pie for the occasion, and I gave the boys matching cotton vests I'd stitched painstakingly, since I've never been a gifted seamstress. They were sweet little boys, and I hoped they would come home soon.

Sarah and I were in the kitchen making buttermilk potato bread, my special favorite. Samuel and Susan played quietly, hunched over a game of jacks in the sunny alcove by the pantry. The day was peaceful; a sort of placid drowsiness hung in the room until sharp screams punctured it. The four of us froze like statues in Medusa's garden, our ears cocked toward the sound. The shrieks were similar to those I'd heard coming from a mountain lion I'd surprised on a ride through the woods a few years ago, except they were human screams, and I thought I recognized Sophie's voice. My heart beat faster, but I quickly dismissed the possibility; Sophie was far away at the temporary encampment where she was picking. The other voice raised in an angry shout was Bert's.

Sarah pushed open the kitchen door with her floury hand, and we stood, our calm shattered by the screams coming from the side of the house where Bert's office looked out over the beautifully kept lawns. Samuel and Susan, their eyes round with fright, ran to their mother. Susan grasped her mother's arm. "What is that horrible noise, Mama?"

"Stay with the children," I said quietly. "I'll find out."

I closed the door behind me to muffle the sound of those screams, which by that time were mixed with cries of pain and Bert's vile cursing. He's killing whoever it is, I thought. I flew across the grand, polished entry hall and yanked open the office door. Bert dropped a silver candelabrum he held in one hand, and it fell to the floor with a heavy clatter. "Good for nothing black bitch. Next time, count yourself a dead nigger," he said to the heap on the floor. It was Sophie, as I'd feared. Blood poured from a wound on her head, pooling on the floor where she lay. Bert wasn't satisfied with the damage he'd already inflicted, and he drew his foot back to kick the moaning woman.

"Don't!"

I took a violent blow to my side as I threw myself over the injured body of the woman I considered my sister. Bert's face, scratched and bleeding and contorted in an ugly rictus, glared down at me. "That crazy bitch tried to kill me with a damn bowie knife." His eyes were glittering feverishly, and I could see the violence excited him, somehow fulfilling his warped nature. It was clear Bert wasn't just mean; he was insane. "As for you, Miss Elizabeth, you tell your black friend she'll be a worm-eaten corpse if she ever comes near me again."

Without a backward glance, Bert stalked out of the room. Seconds later the front door slammed, and silence returned to the house. A sense of overwhelming relief that he was gone overcame me, and I straightened up from my protective crouch over Sophie's broken, bleeding body. My side throbbed painfully where the stiff toe of Bert's boot had struck, and I wondered how many of Sophie's ribs he'd broken with his heavy boots and his ruthless fury.

Blood seeped from the open gash on Sophie's head, which I suspected was the work of the silver candelabrum lying next to her on the floor. Her right arm was bent unnaturally; I was sure it was broken. But it was Sophie's face that was shocking. Bert must have deliberately aimed for her head. The lids of both eyes were swollen shut, and I couldn't be certain, but what looked like part of Sophie's eye hung from a bloody mass beneath her right eyelid. Blood trickled from her poor, smashed nose, and one cheekbone appeared to be broken into a pulpy sponge. I gasped when I saw the damage, then I bolted up and retched into the leather wastebasket next to Bert's desk.

After collecting myself, I did what I could to straighten Sophie out a little, to make her more comfortable. She was unconscious, and as a dead weight, she was too heavy for me to move alone; Sarah would have to help. "Just stay right here, honey," I said to her soothingly. "I'll get help, and we'll fix you right up." I pulled down the beautiful tapestry with a hunting scene Papa Hugo had hung up on the wall when the office was his and draped it over Sophie's inert form. She was breathing raggedly, and for a moment, I wondered whether or not she would live. "You'll get through this, if I have anything to do with it." I said, fiercely. Then I left to fetch Sarah. She would know what to do.

Sophie Washington
Sweetbrier
Early fall 1858

After Mr. Bert beat me to near death, Sarah's nursing, Lizzie's encouragement, and most of all, Mama's love, put me back together like I was Humpty Dumpty; someone they could glue up and heal by force, and they did heal me by their will alone 'cause for a long time I surely didn't care if I lived or died. Bert Laurent, my master—a word I hate—destroyed my life. He raped me, he stole my children, and finally, he disfigured me so that I couldn't stand to see myself in the mirror. It is lucky that I never wanted a husband, because after Mr. Bert was finished, I was too ugly to attract one. What I regret more than anything is that I didn't succeed in my intention, which was to kill Mr. Bert. It would have saved a peck of trouble and heartache if he'd been dead sooner rather than later, may his evil soul be plagued by Hell's never-ending torments.

When I was lying in bed in the cabin recovering from my injuries, Mama and Lizzie were forever trying to convince me to do something they thought I should do, like eat or talk or comb my hair. I wished they'd just shut up and go away to leave me in peace, but they never gave up, and as the months went by, I came back slowly from a place of being numb and empty. They don't know the truth though; the day I tried to kill Mr. Bert was the last day I was the old Sophie. Since then, a person who is not Sophie has gotten inside my body, and it is that possessor who controls my legs and arms, and once in a while speaks from my mouth. If it were up to me alone, I'd never talk again.

Picking cotton is hot, hard work, particularly when you got a mean field boss nearby ready to whip anyone who hasn't brought in enough fluff. I liked working in the fields though, where I could be with other folks just like me; who aren't their own person but belong to someone who tells us poor dumbass niggers what to do and how to do it. At least in the fields I felt safe; Mr. Bert left the crews to the field bosses, and I hardly ever saw him. When he did show up I took Mama's advice and tried to make myself invisible if I couldn't go off and hide in the bushes.

Life wasn't too bad. We were in a moving camp, setting up for a few weeks in one spot until the surrounding fields were picked, and then moving the whole camp to the next spot needing our labor to tend it or pick it. It was hard work, but I enjoyed the change of scenery and meeting workers from other settlements. Jules and Augie were three years old and too young to pick or work the fields, but everyone from our settlement, even Mama, was on a job somewhere, so the boys had to come to camp.

At first, I woke them early in the morning and half dragged one boy while his brother rode piggyback to the field, but it was miserable for Augie and Jules having to be good little boys in the hot beating sun for hours at a time. I made arrangements with Tillie, an old grandmother of one of the families in the camp, to keep an eye on Jules and Augie when I was out working.

Tillie was ancient and bent over like a wind-battered tree trunk, with about as many wrinkles as weathered bark. At mealtimes she helped in the camp kitchen. Otherwise, she sat smoking her pipe, stitching aprons and vests out of the sacks our flour, beans, and rice came in. I was glad when she'd offered to watch over the boys. It relieved my mind since there were so many possible dangers that haunted me: snakes, white men, and the big water where children and sorry drunks drown every year.

It scared me to the bottom of my soul when I saw Tillie come barreling toward the field where we were working. She was moving fast for Tillie, and even at a distance I could tell she was in a panic. In my gut, I knew immediately that something had happened to the boys. Leaving my basket in the dirt, I ran to meet her. She burst into sobs when I reached her. "Oh Lord, oh Lord," she said, again and again, shaking her head from side to side, her hands clapped to her cheeks.

I took her by the shoulders and shook her, hoping she'd come to her senses. "For God's sake, what's wrong, Tillie?"

"He's taken them. They're gone," she wailed.

"Who's gone? Speak plain so I can understand you." I tightened my grip on her shoulders.

"Mr. Bert took Jules and Augie. He be trading them for a field-worker he say, and he grab up both boys, and they rode off with them."

I dug my fingers into her shoulders. "You let him take my babies?" I shook her again. Tillie gave a shriek of pain, and I let her go abruptly.

"There wasn't nothin' I could do, Sophie. I told him there was surely some older boys to trade, that Augie and Jules was too young and they needed their mama, and he say it none of my business, it was Jules and Augie who he was after, then he pushed me out of the way. He grab up the twins like they was sacks of potatoes and carry them one under each arm, them poor little boys cryin' and snifflin' and screamin', and he handed them up to another man on a horse, and that was it. Then Mr. Bert got up on his horse, and off they rode."

The grits I'd eaten for breakfast rose to my throat. "When?"

"It took me half hour to walk here. It was right before that."

I ran, leaving her behind in the field, past the other workers who looked at me curiously with my arms swinging and my face like a madwoman's. I ran faster than I ever have run in my life before or since, so fast I thought my heart might pop through the skin it was pumping so hard. As fast as I ran, it was an hour or more before I got to Sweetbrier, since the camp where I was working was some miles away. I knew that no one would be home at our cabin when I stopped to get my brother Jerome's knife from where he kept it hidden under his mattress. I would beg Mr. Bert to tell me where my boys were, and if words were not enough, I'd use the knife.

I walked the rest of the way from the cabin to the big house, hiding the long knife in the folds of my skirt. From the backyard, I saw Lizzie and Miss Sarah in the kitchen, so I avoided the kitchen door and went around to the front door, a forbidden entrance for all of us of color. No one witnessed me opening the door and slipping into the wide entry hall with its polished floors and high ceiling. It was flooded with a warm hue from the rose-tinted glass window in the south-facing wall. It reminded me suddenly of the color of blood. I shuddered violently, thinking of my babes in the hands of strangers, and the horrors of what they might be subjected to made my stomach cramp. My heart was in my throat, pulsing so hard I could hardly breathe when I reached the door to Mr. Bert's office. Without knocking, I pushed the door open.

"Where are my boys? I want my sons back." I didn't recognize the voice as my own, nor did I have control over myself as I rushed at him with the knife raised.

I don't remember much after that; a whole lot of hurting places told the story later. The broken bones hurt like the fires of hell, but losing my eye was the worst of the damage. I was pleased when Lizzie said I'd cut him pretty bad, across his cheek and down his neck, and left him with a real ugly red scar. It is one of my few triumphs.

Mama said that for weeks she didn't know whether I'd live or die. "Your poor self lay there, and your eyes would open now and then, and your good eye would roll back in the socket and scare the living daylights out of me! I was glad when you closed your eyes again! And, finally one day, you opened your good eye and looked right at me. 'Mama?' you said, and I knew you was gonna be all right."

But I wasn't all right, though I didn't tell her so. I just listened to Mama talk and nodded now and again. Somehow, in losing my children, my eye, my reason to live, I'd also lost my voice. I became silent Sophie, who listens. I suppose that's why people tell me stories and secrets about themselves. I can talk when I need to, but I keep quiet most of the time.

Mama sat with me at night while I was healing, wiping away the rivers of tears from my good eye and bloody pus from the missing one as only a mama can do; tenderly, without disgust or squeamish hesitation. She bolstered me with her wisdom and her determination that I get well. "Don't give up, or Mr. Bert wins. You simply handin' yourself over to that wicked man if you stay on layin' there like a tub of butter." The next day I got up from my bed and made the motions of being a real person.

I'd like to say I am a good person, but I can't say it with much truth. I have good parts to me: I am mostly kind to others, I was a loving daughter, sister, and a good mother, I thought. But a good person doesn't have a voice in their head that tells them they've got to kill someone. The voice told me I must someday put an end to Mr. Bert's mortal life; only then would I be a free woman.

Elizabeth Dumond
Sweetbrier
March-April 1859

There was a question when Sophie was unconscious about whether she might come back crippled or simpleminded. It seemed unlikely that she would come back whole as she lingered for days in a nether world of insensibility, somewhere between sleep and death. Sarah sent for Doctor Spivens, the half-dead old fellow who reeked of stale whiskey and doctored just about anybody, even a man's horses or his darkies, in order to get money to pay off his gambling debts. Sophie's swollen face, with pus and eye tissue spilling from the empty socket, gashes in her forehead, places where the skin was raw, like a beefsteak, was something to behold, even to the doctor. "What in the name of God happened?" he asked, as he stitched a jagged wound to the best of his abilities.

When he heard whom the perpetrator was, he shook his head and said nothing until he paused on the porch, bag in hand, and money in his pocket. "If she wakes up with her wits about her, tell that girl to learn her place. She should know better than to talk back to the man who owns her sorry hide. You tell her that Doctor Spivens said so." I was glad to see the old broken-down hack going down the stairs.

Sarah, Addie and I devoted ourselves to caring for Sophie. Gradually, the swelling subsided, and Sophie's face became more recognizable, but it was ten days before she opened her eyes, and over a month before she could stand on her own. The interior healing took years, and I'm not sure if Sophie will ever knit together her broken heart.

Because of her frail state it wasn't hard to keep Sophie close to the cabin and out of Bert's way. I visited her every day and tried, desperately, to cheer her somehow. Aside from wearing a patch over her missing eye and her nose sitting slightly askew, she'd healed better than I'd anticipated. For a long time she didn't speak, not even to Addie. A few words came out finally, and it was a relief knowing she wasn't a permanent mute, and she still had all her wits about her. One of her most notable full sentences, spoken without prompting, was to me. She said, "It is a good thing we did, Lizzie, even if we fry in hell for doing it." At the time, we were dragging Bert's lifeless body to the basement of the manor house at Sweetbrier. I question whether or not committing a mortal sin could ever be qualified as good, but Sophie's comments were comforting, and I wanted to believe her.

Sarah was increasingly homesick for Pierce Place. When Sophie was finally up and walking a few months after her tangle with Bert, Sarah confided that she didn't feel safe at Sweetbrier anymore. "I never witnessed any violence in my childhood. Papa is a gentle person. He wouldn't harm a soul. I fear Bert's tempers, and that he might turn against me or the children." There wasn't anything I could offer to comfort her; Bert was a vicious monster in my opinion. "I'm going to take the children back home. I want you to come with me, Liz, to help with the education of Samuel and Susan." Sarah squeezed my hand. "We'll be safer from Bert at home. Papa wouldn't tolerate for one minute the meanness we've seen from him. I know Bert respects Papa's wishes, and he doesn't want to jeopardize his future at the Pierce Plantation by displeasing him."

What Sarah said made sense. It would be safer for us to be as far from Bert as possible, yet I loved Sweetbrier. My early roots twined around Addie and Garvus, Sophie and Jerome, and later, Mama Lu and Papa Hugo. I couldn't abide the thought of leaving Sophie. I'd made up my mind to protect her as part of my life's purpose. She had suffered too much at the hands of a man who treated his Negroes worse than his animals.

"Sarah, I'll come with you and the children as long as I can bring Sophie with me. I can't bear to leave her here, where Bert is sure to cross paths with her someday. His threat to kill Sophie if he sees her is not an idle one, I'm sure."

Sarah patted my hand. "I knew you'd want Sophie to come with you. I think it would be a happier place for her. She has too many memories here. The question is, will she agree to leave her family?"

"I'll make her come."

"Tell Sophie she is always welcome to live at Pierce Place. It would be a new start for her, and maybe she could forget a little of what Bert's done to her." We left it at that, for Bert had entered the dining room where Sarah and I were setting the dinner table. I could feel his eyes on me, and my back stiffened.

"Did I hear my name?"

"We were wondering if you'd be at the supper table tonight, Bert. Shall I set a place for you?" asked Sarah. Bert nodded and left the room as abruptly as he'd entered it. Sarah waited until the door of his office banged shut. "I'll mention my plans to Bert over dinner, Liz. Hopefully, we'll be at home with Papa before the month is up."

Chemise was serving sweet potato pie for dessert when Sarah spoke to Bert about her intended return to Pierce Place. It had been a quiet dinner, with the children excusing themselves as soon as they'd eaten, probably to escape being around their father. Bert had a grim presence that invariably made for an uneasy dinner table.

Sarah took a sip of the sweet port that always accompanied dessert in the Laurent household. "I've been meaning to talk to you,

Bert. I think it's time for the children and me to go home, to Pierce Place," she said. Bert grunted, and she rushed on. "Papa isn't getting younger. I am certain he could use my help to run things at home. Now that Mama Lu is gone, I am not needed here. I never really planned to stay at Sweetbrier as long as I have."

Bert took his last bite of pie and chewed thoughtfully. "It would certainly save money if you and the children joined your father."

"I hadn't thought of it, but yes, combining households would be more economical," said Sarah.

Bert took his pipe and tobacco pouch from his pocket. "It's not a bad idea. I need to stay near Sweetbrier until it can stand on its own, without as much nannying as it needs now. If you're holding up our end at Pierce Place, we keep an eye on all our holdings."

"It is a prudent plan, I think," said Sarah, softly, and I knew she was pleased with the way her proposal had gone over.

Bert narrowed his eyes speculatively. "When are you planning to go?"

"Before the month is up if it's possible." Sarah took a sip of port and dabbed her lips with her napkin. "Liz will join the children and me. She has agreed to be a sort of governess, which is a godsend. She is a much better teacher than I." Sarah smiled encouragingly at me, while Bert glared from the opposite side of the table.

"That is tolerable as long as it is understood that Miss Elizabeth is expected to earn her keep. She is not Mother and Father's little princess anymore. If she fails to perform her work adequately, she will have to find another position. Is that clear?"

Sarah bobbed her head while I sat with my hands clinched tightly in my lap and my eyes cast down, so Bert couldn't see the hate in them. Bert wiped his mustache with the linen napkin and threw it onto the dirtied plate. "How much time do you need to prepare yourself and the children for the move?" he asked.

"Not much. A few days to pack the luggage and tie up any loose ends," said Sarah. Though she tried to disguise it, I could hear the relief in her voice that Bert had agreed.

"It's settled then; next Saturday I'll have a wagon made ready to drive you and the children to Pierce Place."

"And Liz, too," said Sarah.

Bert swallowed his last sip of wine. "Sweetbrier will be near empty without you and the children. I will be here infrequently, and except for my bedroom and the office, it makes no sense to keep the house open. Elizabeth will stay with Addie and Chemise to pack Mother's and Father's valuables and to close up the house. Only the necessities should remain. Elizabeth can keep an eye on the niggers, so nothing gets stolen." Bert rose from the dinner table.

Sarah was about to protest, but I met her eye and warned her with a look to keep quiet. "I suppose Liz can stay for a short time, as long as it doesn't interrupt the children's lessons, so they forget what Liz is teaching them," she said.

"It shouldn't take more than a week or two of steady work to close up Sweetbrier. You can send a carriage to pick Elizabeth up after that," said Bert.

"Do you think that is a sound plan, Liz?" Sarah looked worried.

"I don't mind. It will give me time to say goodbye to Sweetbrier."

Bert stood up and threw his napkin on the table. "It's decided then."

"Very well. Liz and I will start packing our trunks tomorrow."

"I have some business to take care of with the old man. I'll drive you and the children up myself," said Bert.

I often wonder what my life would be like if I'd left that Saturday with Sarah and the children. Where would my path have led? In daydreams, I picture a life quite the opposite from the way things turned out.

Sarah's upcoming move set in motion a whirlwind of activity. We sorted and packed the Laurent linens and kitchenware that Sarah wanted and did the same with Susan and Samuel's clothing. I carried a basketful of the clothes the children had outgrown to the settlement, and while I was in the neighborhood, I took the opportunity to drop in on Sophie. She listened to me talk and nodded now and then. She was stirring a bowl of muffin batter, and she held out the spoon, so I could have a taste. Sophie is a good cook, which she inherited from her mother. I told her she should start getting ready because she and I were moving to Pierce Place in a few days, when Sarah sent a carriage for us. Sophie just smiled and said, "Humph," which was about the extent of what Sophie said those days.

I got back in time to help Sarah pack the elegant blue willow china Mama Lu had bequeathed to her before she died. "You are very dear to me, Sarah, and I want you to have something special, to remember me by," Mama Lu said. A few days later, Mama Lu announced that she wanted me to have her silver-backed mirror with matching comb and brush, but Bert said Mama Lu's wish wasn't in writing, so it didn't mean a thing. "Frankly speaking, Miss Elizabeth, you don't have a right to a single item in this household," he said.

At dawn on Saturday morning, four matching quarter horses pulled a spacious, serviceable wagon up to the front steps, where Sarah's and the children's boxes and trunks waited to be picked up. Bert supervised the stable hands who had followed on foot. The men packed as much luggage as they could fit into the boot and tied the rest to the top of the carriage. Sarah settled Susan and Samuel, still half asleep, on opposite seats in the enclosed sedan, and climbed back down to say goodbye. Bert mounted the driver's seat, and Malcolm, one of the stable boys, climbed up to sit in the seat beside him. Sarah gave me a hug and kissed me on the cheek.

"We're waiting, Sarah." Bert's voice was impatient.

Sarah bent close to my ear. "It won't be long before I see you again, dear Liz. I'll send a carriage from Pierce Place for you and Sophie a week from today. Mark your calendar and be ready when it comes."

I handed her valise up after she'd settled herself in the carriage. "I love you, Sarah," I said.

"I love you, too, Elizabeth."

Bert gave rein to the horses, and they clattered down the drive-way. Sarah waved her blue handkerchief out the coach window, and I waved back until the little blue flag faded into the distance.

It was the last time I saw Sarah, one of my truest and dearest friends.

The house was stripped down, and though it was an especially warm day for April, its barrenness made it seem chilly inside. Addie, Chemise, and I were packing what seemed like endless china bowls and plates, fancy tea sets, and Mama Lu's collections of spoons and glass figurines she'd brought to Sweetbrier as a newlywed. Bert's instructions were to box everything frivolous, unnecessary, or too valuable to leave lying around, and to store it in the third-floor attic.

"I ain't been in here for years," said Chemise, huffing from the climb up the stairs with a box in her arms. We were all carrying boxes I'd labeled neatly with the contents, so it would be easy to find the candlesticks or the silver tea set if someone was looking for it.

"Lizzie and I better stack these boxes and make room for more," said Addie. "Why don't you go down where it's cooler, Chemise, and start packing the good silverware."

Chemise wiped her sleeve across the top of her sweaty lip. "Fine with me," and off she went, clumping down the stairs.

Straightening the boxes didn't take long. After we'd lined them up in neat rows with the labels facing out, Addie took my hand in hers and squeezed it. "Come over here, Lizzie. There's somethin' I want to talk to you about." I followed her across the room to a sunny alcove where the eaves came together in a peak and formed one of the dormer windows that gave character to the beautiful old house. There was a narrow bed tucked to one side, and next to it was an old trunk serving as a bedside table.

It was obvious from the dust that nothing had been moved in a long time. Addie sat on the bed and patted the spot next to her. "Sit with me for a minute, Lizzie. There's a few things I think you ought to know." Addie took my hand in hers. "This here bed we're sittin' on is the very spot you was born, and where your poor, sweet mama died." Addie stopped to wipe away a tear. "I never told you much about Fern; you got a right to hear the truth, honey." I listened spellbound as Addie told me about my mother. "She had to live most of her life in a nasty old orphanage, and when she got to Sweetbrier, she was like a silly, happy little butterfly."

Addie said how pretty and lively my mama was when she came to Sweetbrier to be Mama Lu's companion. "But things took a turn for the worse when she got herself in the family way. Fern wanted a baby so bad, but she was miserable sick the whole time you was in her stomach. She kept saying no matter how sick she got, it was worth it 'cause in the end she'd be a mama. At least she got to hold you in her arms and kiss your pretty little face before she went off to meet the maker." When Addie got to the part about Fern bleeding to death, tears ran down both of our faces.

"There's something in this here trunk that belongs to you," she said, after drying her eyes with a corner of her apron. The cot creaked when Addie stood up. "Fern brought this old trunk with her when she came to Sweetbrier from the orphanage. It was as light as a feather when I hauled it up the stairs for her, like there wasn't much in it. She was so sweet and eager to please after all that suffering when she was growing up." Addie lifted the lid of the trunk and slipped her hand under the stacks of neatly folded clothes. "Here's what I was lookin' for." She held an intricately carved wooden box, about ten inches long and two inches deep. "This was given to Fern by your own papa," she said.

I gasped. There had been little mention of my father when I was growing up. Mama Lu told me both my parents were dead, and she didn't know much about either. "The best thing you can do is forget about them. Papa Hugo and I are your parents now, and we love you very much." I was too young to dwell on people I'd never known, and I'd only wondered fleetingly about my dead folks.

Before living in the big house, when Addie and Garvus were my adopted parents, I asked one day why my skin was a different color than the rest of the family. Addie told me my mama was a beautiful lady named Fern, but she never said a word about my father. When I asked, she just shrugged her shoulders and said she didn't know anything about him.

"You know who my father was?" I took the carved box and held it on my lap.

Addie nodded and sat next to me on the bed. "It's time for you to hear about who your papa is," she said. "You must promise not to judge your mama, Lizzie, for being weak." Addie explained how Fern and Papa Hugo fell in love and committed the sin of adultery. "Mister Hugo was practically out of his mind with Miss Lucille's nervous condition. When Fern came into the picture, he couldn't stop himself from falling in love with her." Addie patted my knee. "Your papa was a good man in his heart, Lizzie."

I clasped the pretty and surprisingly heavy box to my breast, which was beating hard from the startling news about my father. A sudden wave of sorrow swept over me that Papa Hugo was dead. "Now I know why I always felt so close to Papa," I said. "Why didn't you tell me before, Addie?"

"Don't fret none about why I didn't say nothin' before. I'm tellin' you now, and that's what matters. Now, ain't you gonna open up this here box and see what's in it?"

I undid the clasp and lifted the lid, but I didn't have time for more than a glance. "Where in God's good acre did you all disappear to?" Chemise came through the attic door with a box balanced on each hip. She paused to stare at us. "You actually sittin' on the job?" Her voice was incredulous. I closed the box and tucked it under the folds of my skirt.

"We're just taking a load off our feet, talkin' about old times and Lizzie's mama, Fern," said Addie. She stood up from the cot.

"Well, come on, you twos," Chemise grumbled, "there's a whole heck of a bunch more boxes to drag up them stairs."

"We're comin', we're comin', Chemise. Just hold your horses." Addie bent down and gave me a quick hug. "Hide your treasure box somewhere safe in your room," she whispered as she went past to join Chemise on the stairs.

On my way downstairs, I took a quick side trip to my bedroom where I slipped the carved box under my mattress. I could hardly wait until later that evening, when I had time to inspect the contents of the box and to think about the secrets I'd learned from Addie.

Sophie Washington
Sweetbrier
Mid-April 1859

Sometimes, in the dead of night, the images of Augie and Jules pass through my head like those little books you can buy for a penny; when you fan the pages real fast it looks like the picture is moving. That's what my brain sees: Jules and Augie changing before my eyes from babies to grown boys, their faces filled with fear and confusion, always crying out, raising their arms pleadingly. The wounded look in their scared-animal eyes grips my heart so strong that it pounds and flutters in my chest. There is no chance of sleep after these frightful imaginings, which is why, to this day, I get up and walk. It calms me to walk; afterwards I can usually get some rest. It was moving pictures of Jules and Augie that sent me walking the night in April when Lizzie and I left Sweetbrier for good.

It was around eight when I left the cabin for a walk. Earlier in the evening, at suppertime, Mama told me everything in the big house was packed and the furniture covered up with sheets to protect it from dust. "That big ol' house look like it's haunted. You ought to see it," said Mama. I shrugged indifferently and kept eating my soup. I had no desire to see the inside of the big house. I hoped never to enter it again, holding Sweetbrier itself partially responsible for the wicked nature of Mr. Bert; yet that night, haunted by the moving images of my sons, my feet moved as if I was being pulled by puppet strings toward the very place I hated.

Lizzie was leaving Sweetbrier any day now, as soon as Miss Sarah sent a carriage from Pierce Plantation. She begged me to go with her. "Sophie, you can't stay here. It just doesn't make sense! I can take care of you if you come with me. If you stay here, who knows what might happen!" I didn't say anything either way, just nodded my head to show I'd heard her. Those were times when I didn't say much of anything to anyone, preferring to keep my thoughts private.

Truth is, I had no intention of going with Lizzie, even though Mama urged me to. "Get out and away from that man who say he gonna kill you. I'd sleep a lot more peaceful if I thought you was out of harm's way." No matter how practical it was, I couldn't fathom starting somewhere else; a beaten down, one-eyed darky by herself in a new place, away from Mama and my daddy and brother, forever hoping to hear the whereabouts of my lost boys. And there was the matter of the voice in my head that kept telling me I had to stay and finish what I'd started the day I tried to kill Mr. Bert. Someone had to stop that wicked man from causing more havoc and hate, and I knew I was the person.

The darkness wasn't too thick that night; a half moon lit the path and threw a greenish light. My mind was jumping like a frog from Jules to Augie, to imagining Mr. Bert tied up on some godforsaken train tracks with a big train about to squish him, while my puppet legs carried me to the side of the house where Lizzie's second story bedroom window faced an immense lawn that had been Mr. Hugo's pride. I came out of my visions and ponderings to realize where I stood. I lifted my eyes to Lizzie's window.

When we were younger, I'd throw a few pebbles against her window. She'd stick her head out, and I'd bird whistle or hoot like an owl, which was the signal for her to sneak out of the house and meet me. On hot nights we'd swim in the pond, naked and giggling until our skin pruned up, and we were too tired to dogpaddle any more. I always walked her back home to Sweetbrier, where she'd sneak in through the kitchen door with nobody the wiser.

I gazed up at the window, thinking wistfully of those happy days. On impulse, I picked up a few pebbles to toss in our old signal. As I readied my hand for the throw, Lizzie's silhouette appeared, framed behind the partly open window, softened by the billowy eyelet curtains. *Of the same mind* I thought, taking it as proof that Lizzie and I were connected by something deeper than friendship. As girls, we always read each other's mind. I whistled a soft imitation of a lark's song, but it was drowned out by a strangled scream coming from Lizzie's bedroom.

"Let go of me!"

"Shut up, you little bitch," snarled the unmistakable voice of Mr. Bert. Frozen in place as if my feet were nailed to the ground, I watched the shadowy struggle of two figures behind the window until the sharp sound of glass breaking and another scream prodded me into action. I ran past the woodpile and nearly broke my leg tripping over the handle of a splitting maul that someone had thrown down carelessly. I grabbed it and carried it with me as I ran to the back of the house and up the steps to the mudroom adjoining the kitchen.

The door was locked, and all the windows closed. Time was flying. My mind flooded with memories of Mr. Bert and what he did to me in the barn. *Hurry,* I told myself, and ran quickly to the coal scuttle door where a couple of times a year the delivery man spills brimming bucket-loads of coal down a chute into the basement. The scuttle door was not fastened on the inside, and though it was a tight squeeze, I managed to wiggle in, feet first. I slid the rest of the way down the dirty coal funnel into the basement, landing on my knees on the pile of coal remaining from the last delivery. I didn't notice that my knees were bleeding until much later.

Lizzie and I had spent hot days playing tag and hopscotch in the coolness of the big basement, thus I knew it well enough to grope my way through the darkness and up the steep stone stairs to the main floor. A noise startled me when I opened the door at the top of the steps until I realized it was the sound of my own gasping breath. I ran swiftly and quietly across the house to the central staircase. I crept up the stairs, heavy maul in hand, and turned down the corridor. At the end, the door to Lizzie's room was partially open, and from it spilled a faint light.

As I came closer I heard sounds; an animal grunt, a muffled cry, the rhythm of the bed pounding against the wall, a moan of pain. A single candle burned on the night table, illuminating Mr. Bert's naked ass moving up and down like a battering ram between Lizzie's pale white legs. Neither of them noticed me until I was standing right up by the head of the bed. Lizzie saw me first; I knew because her eyes got wide. Mr. Bert had put a gag in Lizzie's mouth and tied her hands together over her head, just like he'd done when he raped me. Tears were running down her cheeks; blood oozed from her nose. I paused for a minute, thinking about how to hit only him and not Lizzie.

Though I was as quiet as the bayou in the fog, Mr. Bert must have sensed me standing there at the side of the bed. He twisted around to look over his shoulder, and he saw me in the flickering light. "What in the hell? Are you back for more, you crazy nigger she-devil?" He rolled off Lizzie, and as he straightened up to come at me, murder in his eyes, I lifted the maul high and brought it down as hard as I could on Mr. Bert's sleek head. It was a sharp maul, and my aim was true. There was a thud, and Mr. Bert's head split open like a coconut. He fell face first, hit the side of the bed and slid to the floor where he lay sprawled on his stomach.

I waited a minute, holding the splitting maul ready in case I needed to use it again, but he was as still as a side of beef. I left him bleeding while I went to the other side of the bed to release Lizzie from the ropes that tied her. Her eyes were wide with fear and pain. "It's going to be all right. Everything's going to be just fine," I said. Those few words were the most I'd spoken in the six months since Mr. Bert had tried to beat the life right out of me.

Elizabeth Dumond
Sweetbrier Plantation
Mid-April 1859

Sophie untied my hands and loosened the knotted cloth in my mouth that half suffocated me. I was blubbering like a baby. She helped me from the bed. "It feels like the end of the world, but you're going to be fine, Lizzie." She held me in her arms until my sobs subsided. "Let's get you cleaned up. You'll feel better afterwards. I'll get your clothes together while you sponge yourself off." Sophie helped me dress and it did make me feel better; though I was scratched and bruised and though my woman's part felt like it was on fire, I knew I'd survive the physical damage of Bert's violation. The phantom of him would not be as easy to overcome.

On the other side of the bed, Bert Laurent moaned. Sophie and I looked at each other in horror. She picked up the heavy maul where she'd leaned it against the foot of the bed, and we went cautiously to where he lay on the floor, half expecting him to jump up and attack us. We needn't have worried; Bert was unconscious, his breathing labored. "Give me that, Sophie." I took the maul from her before she could resist and slammed it once more into Bert's open, bleeding skull. He gave a little twitch, and his gasping attempts to breathe stopped altogether. In the following silence, Sophie and I stood dazed as blood splattered, waiting for God to strike us dead. He must have decided against an immediate execution; we were still alive by all the usual measures when Sophie and I dragged my bully of a half-brother down the stairs to the basement below.

Bert was not a small man. He measured over six feet tall and was solidly built like one of those greased wrestlers who put on fights at travelling shows. Sophie and I strained as we pulled him by his legs down the long corridor to the stairs. Sophie had the foresight to fetch one of several hall runners that carpeted the elegant catwalk overlooking the atrium at the center of the house. We rolled Bert onto the rug, and with both of us pulling we bumped unceremoniously down the stairs to the floor below. We didn't talk much, grunting as we were from the effort of dragging the dead man to the basement door.

The steep stone steps leading to the basement were tricky. Sweating with the effort, we pulled Bert's body on the now bloodstained Persian carpet, descending backward into the dark cellar. Halfway down, the rug with its heavy burden slid abruptly, then stopped. It wouldn't budge, and no amount of tugging would loosen our bier with its grisly cargo. "We're stuck somewhere," I said. Bert's arm had wedged between two side railings, and Sophie had to crawl over him to wrestle the arm from where it was pinned. In death as in life, Bert didn't want to cooperate.

A wave of exhaustion swept over me when Bert's body finally rested on the flagstone floor. A shaft of moonlight from one of the casement windows fell on his open, glassy eyes. They seemed to stare accusingly right at me. "Oh my God, what have we done?" I cried, hearing the hysteria in my own voice from a numb, detached part of my brain. "We've committed the mortal sin of murder. What's going to happen to us?"

Sophie took me into her arms again while I sobbed in the clammy basement, comforting me with the assurance that we'd gotten rid of a piece of the Devil's work. "It's a good thing we did, Lizzie, even if we fry in hell for it." Her simple words hit me like I'd taken a draught of Mama Lu's soothing tonic. I drew a deep breath and stopped crying as suddenly as I'd started.

It was too dark to see in the basement, so Sophie ran upstairs to fetch a lantern and a flint. I waited in the dark, trying not to think about the dead man keeping me company. Sophie returned, carrying one of the hall lanterns. It illuminated the body on the carpet, playing ghoulishly across Bert's bloody skull. I shivered. "We can't just leave him here."

"There's a pile of loose coal I fell on when I came through the scuttle door," Sophie said. "Heaping the coal over him would be a whole lot easier than trying to bury him under the flagstones."

Sophie hung the lantern on a hook near the center of the basement and used a taper to light another lantern on the side near the coal bin. She walked back in the dim light to where I waited with the body. "You ready, Lizzie?" I nodded. Sophie took her place at the end of the carpet and grasped a corner. I took the other corner. Making slow, steady progress, we pulled the rug that carried Bert.

It took what seemed like an eternity to drag Bert's dead body from my bedroom to the pile of dusty black coal at the far side of the basement, but we finally arrived. "This here is the end of your magic carpet ride, Mr. Bert," Sophie said. We grabbed the long side of the rug, tilting it up so that Bert's body rolled off, ending face down next to the lumps of coal. "Good, now we don't have to look at his wicked face," she said. I found a couple of buckets and a coal shovel, and working side by side, we covered Bert with a good-sized heap of coal. It took a while, and when we were done there wasn't hide or hair of him showing.

Sophie put the buckets back and picked up the lantern. She peered at me through the dim light. "You look like a true African! Your face is just as black as mine from the coal dust." She let out the first laugh I'd heard from her since she'd lost Jules and Augie. I was shocked for a second, but her giggle was infectious. Soon we were rocking with laughter, both of us clutching our sides, laughing and crying at the same time in the manner hysteria sometimes brings on. It was crazy laughter that I'll never forget. I can only think it relieved a mental distress built up in both of us.

As suddenly as we'd started the peculiar, infectious laughter, we both stopped. "What are we going to do now, Lizzie?" Sophie's voice was worried. I'd been contemplating the same question and had come up with the only course of action that seemed the likeliest for insuring both Sophie's and my future.

"We're going as far away from Sweetbrier as we can. You must go collect the things you'll need for a long journey. And, of course you'll want to tell your mama."

"Tell Mama what?"

"That you and I murdered Bert, and we'll be hanged by the neck if they catch us. Tell her the truth Sophie, then pack your things and be ready when I come for you."

"I can't leave Mama and Daddy and Jerome. They're all I have..."

I took her face between my hands and made her look me in the eye. "You can't stay here, and neither can I. If we don't get away from Sweetbrier, Bert and his memory will haunt us to the death. I, for one, am not going to let this hang like an anchor around my neck. I'm leaving tonight, and I'm taking you with me." Sophie's good eye gazed into mine, and she nodded once. I gave a silent prayer of thanks for her decision to join me on our flight away from Sweetbrier, on our flight to freedom.

I caught a glimpse of myself as I passed the mirrors hanging in the gallery upstairs. Sophie hadn't exaggerated; I was filthy with coal dust. I didn't take the time to do more than wipe my face; I wanted to leave Sweetbrier as quickly as possible. I took a large leather satchel from the closet in Mama Lu's room and packed it with the bare necessities; leaving behind my pretty dresses and shoes and choosing a couple of serviceable gowns and the boots I wore when I rode Nance around Sweetbrier. In a smaller bag I packed gloves, a cashmere shawl that Mama Lu wore whenever she took a chill, and a few personal things. I took some warm blankets from the hall closet and stuffed them in a canvas sack along with a box of flints and a handful of candles.

I stopped in the kitchen to fill another sack with provisions; a bag of flour, some sugar, a tin of walnuts and jars of preserves and pickles. I dragged the sack to the door and went back to collect the other items. Halfway down the hall, I remembered the carved box Papa Hugo had given Fern, my real mama. It was under the mattress where Bert had raped me a few hours before. I ran back, stepping gingerly over the coagulating pool of blood marking the spot where Bert's head had lain on the floor. I fished out the box and opened it to see if the contents were intact. The gold coins and the jewelry were valuable, and I felt fortunate to have assets to cover travel expenses, wherever we were going. With the box safely away, tucked in the bottom of the smaller satchel, I was almost ready. There was one last stop to make before the stables: Papa Hugo's office.

The stained-glass front of the gun cabinet was easy enough to break, though I regretted doing it, as it was a very pretty hunting scene I'd always admired. I selected my favorite rifle and Papa Hugo's silver-handled revolver that he'd taught me to shoot when I was a little girl. "Always carry a pistol Liz, for protection against snakes and if, god forbid, the Negroes ever decide to rebel."

I filled two leather ammunition bags with bullets and found holsters for the guns. In the top drawer of the desk, hidden toward the back, was a canvas sack of coins: Bert's petty cash. I took it, too. I didn't want to deplete my treasure box too quickly; we would, after all, require food and lodging and money for the journey.

The accumulated gear was too much to carry to the barn. I would have to drive the carriage around to pick it up. My heart raced with the passing minutes, and I ran to the stables. Nance whinnied when she saw me. "I can't take you, Nance. You're too old for a trip like this. It might kill you." I kissed her on the nose. "I love you, girl."

I wiped away my tears and hitched a team of four strong horses, led by Midnight, a glossy chestnut bay, to Papa Hugo's pride and joy: a sturdy carriage that seated two on the driving platform and had a spacious black sedan, a good-sized trunk and luggage racks on the top. I loaded the trunk with Papa Hugo's camp kit containing everything you might need for cooking over a campfire, and I tied a saddle onto the luggage rack.

I made a quick stop at the barn for fishing poles and a tack basket and stopped at the well house long enough to fill two kegs with water. Next, I pulled the buggy around to the kitchen porch and loaded up the gear and food I'd piled there. It was probably an hour past midnight when I drove the rig toward the settlement. I hoped that by the time the sun rose, Sophie and I'd be miles away from Sweetbrier. The question was, where we would go.

Suddenly, I knew our destination; we would go west, to the new frontier, where Sophie and I could lose ourselves and live as free women.

Addie Turner Washington

Sweetbrier

Mid-April 1859

After the babies were stolen, Sophie had trouble sleeping. Mind you, this was the girl who, just like her daddy, could sleep through a storm from hell. That ended after Jules and Augie got taken. She started wandering at night, God knows where. I am usually a light sleeper, and her rustling around never failed to wake me on the nights she tiptoed down the stairs and out the door. As for me, I wanted to follow Sophie, to protect her on her midnight walks, but I didn't 'cause I knew she must be thinkin' about Augie and Jules, or maybe her missing eye, and above all, she want time to be alone to think and to grieve. So, I stayed put in bed and worried until I heard my girl come back. Some nights it was hours before she opened the door real quiet and soft-footed across the cabin to the stairs. I was always relieved; I could finally doze off again knowing she was safe in her bed.

That night, after Sophie slipped out of the cabin, I lay there staring into the dark, a circus of thoughts crowding my mind. It was my time to think and grieve about them two darling little caramel grandsons being ripped out and thrown away like they was a couple of weeds in a vegetable patch, and about our Sophie losing her eye and her spirit. Then I had to stop thinking, 'cause my inside hate wanted to boil up and destroy Mr. Bert and Sweetbrier and everything they stood for. I imagined myself killing Mr. Bert, and my heart pounded so hard I had to sit up in bed and take deep breaths to calm down. I thought about putting my shoes on and going out after Sophie, but I just lay next to Garvus and listened to the little whistle he was making every time he let out a breath of air.

A person being owned by another person ain't ever right. Jesus talks against it in the Bible after all, and I do hold Him to be, at the very least, a prophet. Day will come, mark my words, when Negroes will be protected by the law instead of being helpless in the face of it; living in a hopeless world where the wrongs done to you ain't ever addressed, but accepted by the victims themselves. Those were some of the thoughts I was thinking when, a few hours later, Sophie came creeping back into the cabin. She was real quiet climbing the ladder up to the loft where she sleeps and keeps her things. She lit a candle up there, and I heard her rummaging around. Pretty soon she came down the ladder backwards, and the moonlight was just enough so that I seen she was carrying a big bundle under her free arm.

At the bottom of the ladder, she stopped. "Mama," she whispered ever so quietly. I got up quick, but careful so as not to wake up Garvus.

"I'm right here," I whispered. She put her finger to her lips, and I followed her out to the front porch. She led the way down the porch steps, stopping a few paces away from the cabin, where we could talk without waking Garvus and Jerome. Setting her bundle down, she turned and took my hands. Moonlight lit up her face and I could see fear in her good eye. "What's wrong, Sophie?"

"Oh Mama!" she cried, crumpling up like a rag doll when I put my arms around her. I held her tight until she calmed down enough to talk.

"What's goin' on? Why you carryin' this big bundle, Honey?"

"Something terrible has happened, and I'm going away with Lizzie."

Sophie spilled out the story about Mr. Bert raping Lizzie, and her and Lizzie killing Mr. Bert with a splitting maul and burying him under a pile of coal in the basement. I 'bout had heart failure then and there. It isn't every day your child tells you they committed murder, and particularly not a slave girl killing her master. I tried not to let on that I was sick with fright and worry to the bottom of my feet. I just held my girl in my arms, and we both hugged and cried.

"I hate to leave you, Mama, but Lizzie and I might be caught and hanged for murder if we stay around here."

"It's surely better for you to go away, but I'm gonna miss you somethin' fierce, Sophie," I whispered, and the two of us cried some more.

Lizzie walked up real quiet and startled us out of our weeping fit. She dimmed the lantern she carried and put it down so it shined up and lit all our faces, her's so white and pale. "I tied the buggy past the settlement, so I wouldn't wake anyone," she said. Then she hugged me tight, and her and I and Sophie stood there together, our arms around each other, crying and whispering. Lizzie finally broke us apart. "It's time for Sophie and me to get going. The longer we stay, the more chance of getting caught."

Her and Sophie got busy stashing the contents of Sophie's bundle into the flour sacks, saddlebags and a valise Lizzie had brought. While they packed, I slipped into the cabin to gather a half a dozen boiled eggs and the biscuits and ham we'd had for supper. I wrapped the ham in a piece of oiled paper and tied it with some twine. In a flour sack I packed a fry pan, a bunch of potatoes and a few onions so's they could fry up somethin' to eat when they had to stop who knows where. "Here's some vittles," I said.

Sophie took the food and kissed me on the cheek. "I love you, Mama. I can't tell you how much I'll miss you." I practically smothered her in a bear hug. "Tell Daddy and Jerome that I love them, too." I let go of her and nodded.

Lizzie took her place for a last hug. "You'll always be my true Mama," she said, clutching me so tight around the middle that it was hard to get a breath in for a minute or two.

"I feel the same way about you, Lizzie. Even though you're a different color and all, I think of you as my own flesh and blood." By that time all three of us was crying up a storm again. We could probably have filled a goldfish bowl with tears, the way we were carrying on.

Lizzie put an end to our crying when she picked up the lantern. "It's time for us to go." The three of us carried the bundles and saddlebags past the settlement, where Lizzie had tethered the horses. The girls stowed Sophie's bags in the sedan. "Addie, I left the kitchen door unlocked. Be sure to go and take any supplies you need from the pantry. Bert certainly won't be needing them." Lizzie smiled, but there wasn't no happiness in her face.

"Where you gonna take my girl, Lizzie?" I asked.

"We're heading west. I've heard an awful lot about California and the city of San Francisco. We'll aim in that direction. Of course, there's no telling if we'll actually get there."

"Promise that you'll be careful. I'll be worryin' and thinkin' about you every minute."

"I'll take all the back roads, Addie, and we'll try to travel when there isn't much traffic going our way. Plus, I've got a gun if we run into trouble."

"God forbid that you should have to use it!" I clasped her hands in mine. "I have a feeling you two will end up safe. Now, go on, mount up and get free of this damned plantation." I kissed them both goodbye one last time, before they climbed the metal steps to the driving platform. Lizzie took the reins, and the carriage started off with a little jerk forward. Sophie craned herself around so she was leaning over the edge, and she called out, her voice faint against the noise of the wheels. "I'll come back someday, Mama." I hoped she would, but I wasn't sure I'd ever see her again.

I crawled into bed with Garvus just to warm up from being in the night air in my sleepin' dress. He was snoring up a storm by this time, but it didn't bother me for once; I couldn't have slept even if I wanted to. My mind was too busy thinking about Sophie and Lizzie rolling down the road in Mr. Hugo's fancy black carriage, running away from their memories and a whole lot of pain and sorrow. My mind jumped like a grasshopper back and forth from the carriage to fearful, worried imaginings of the girls alone on the trail. Every danger that could befall them marched through my thoughts; the worst was the possibility of getting caught and hanged for the murder of Mr. Bert. Pictures of that cruel man's face bounced and bobbed from one side of my mind to the other, and I thanked God he couldn't hurt another soul.

The torture of thoughts ended suddenly when a voice in my pounding head told me exactly what to do. It was still a couple of hours before dawn when I got up, pulled on my work dress and fumbled in the dark for my shoes. The air outside the cabin was refreshing, and I breathed deep draughts of it before setting off for Sweetbrier, through the darkness of the early morning, feeling my way over the fields to the back of the big house. I went in through the door that Lizzie left unlocked, my heart bumping so hard I half expected it to burst, but the kitchen was quiet and empty.

Since it was as familiar to me as my own kitchen, I knew my way in the dark. I felt in the drawer of the big oak sideboard for a flint and some candles, which I put in my apron pocket. I lighted the small lantern that we keep in the pantry and passed down the hall to the broom closet. In the broom closet were three big cans of kerosene; one was half empty but the other two was full. I carried them out, setting one can next to the basement door for the second part of my mission, and the half- empty one in the kitchen. The other, I saved to set aflame the big house, starting in Miss Lucille's bedroom.

I climbed them polished stairs one last time, lugging the big old five-gallon can. Miss Lucille's room smelled musty, 'cause it hadn't been used since she died. I thought it was only right to start in her room; after all, she was the woman who caused a lot of upset in the world, as well as giving birth to a monster. I splashed some kerosene across the floor and gave the canopy bed a good dousing. Working backward, I poured a little stream of it down the stairs and over the rugs in the entry hall. The bottoms of the linen draperies touched the floor, and I made a kerosene trail to them, splashing a bit at the bottom of the drapes. Finally, I dribbled the rest of the can down the hallway to the kitchen. I emptied the can I'd left in the kitchen across the floor, ending with a generous pour of the stuff around the legs and over the top of the oak table where I'd sat a million times.

I needed to hurry, now, to beat the sunrise. From the kitchen hall to the basement door, I splashed the second can of kerosene, not too much though; I saved most of it to pour over the grave of coal in the basement. The can was heavy and carrying it down the steep stairs with a lantern in one hand was awkward. At the bottom I hung my little lantern on a post and carried the can back up to douse the stairs by feel more than sight, a splash here, a splash there.

The dim lantern threw patterns of shadow and light across the dark basement, and one of them shadows startled me something terrible 'cause it looked like a man. I was so tired out and jittery by then, I almost turned and ran, thinking that Mr. Bert had risen up from the coal like those folks that mistakenly get buried alive. It wasn't nothin' though, and I took a deep breath to steady myself and kept going until I got to the pile of coal. I hung the lantern on a hook and poured the rest of the kerosene on the coal, splashing most of it where I imagined Mr. Bert's body had its final home.

When the can was empty, I took a stubby candle from my apron pocket, lighted it with the lantern, and let hot wax drip so's I could stick the candle upright, next to a little puddle of kerosene. It had about two inches to burn before it reached the puddle, which gave me enough time to finish my preparations. I rushed across the basement and up the stairs to the big old quiet kitchen where I cooked so many meals, washed so many dishes. From the pantry I took a bag of rice, a sack of brown sugar and a jar of honey, which I set outside the kitchen door on the back porch.

I returned to the kitchen where the candle I'd set on the counter flickered cheerfully. Except for the smell of kerosene, everything looked normal. I cupped the flame of the candle as I carried it up the stairs to Miss Lucille's bedroom. From my pocket, I took another candle from several that I carried and lighted it with the other flame. Once again, I dripped a little pool of wax from the wick end of the candle onto the floor and stuck the candle into the wax so that it stood upright next to a pool of lamp oil. I set up six candles along the trail of kerosene, where they was sure to set off the oil and climb up the thick linen drapes to the hardwood paneled ceiling.

I done it all pretty quick, 'cause I wanted to be home when the first curls of black smoke rose from Sweetbrier. I figured that as soon as we could smell smoke at the slave cabins, the pile of coal and the little voodoo doll I'd placed on top of it would be burning like hellfire. Black magic had made devil's work of Mr. Bert, but the cost had been more than I'd expected to pay.

LOUISIANA WEEKLY OBSERVER

May 12, 1859

Sadly, we report that the Laurent plantation home in Western Louisiana, near the town of Smithfield, burned to the ground last month. The pile of rubble was still smoking when lawmakers convened on the locale three days after the fire. Arson is suspected, with a possible motive pointing to horse thievery, as an unspecified number of horses were reported missing from the premises the following day.

Arnold Snelling, Federal Marshall for the region, investigated speculation about a Negro uprising on the plantation. The investigation has found no evidence that the Laurent Negroes collaborated to set the fire, however, Ed Boney, overseer, identified one Negress, Sophie Washington, as a runaway slave. A reward bulletin has been posted for her arrest.

Sarah Laurent, wife of the plantation owner, reported that her husband, Hugo Laurent III, and the family governess, Elizabeth Dumond, are missing and believed to be victims of the fire. Although the remains are not yet recovered, funeral services were held on March 22 to commemorate the deceased.

Owned and operated by three generations of the Laurent family, the fallen mansion reflects the crumbling state of affairs in our nation, which, if the country allows these misguided notions of freedom for the work force to continue, will result in the entire country lying in ruins.

PART II

The Southern Trail

Elizabeth Dumond
The Southern Trail

Late Spring–Summer, 1859

During my years as a treasured child at Sweetbrier, Papa Hugo encouraged my interest in geography, partly because of his own enthusiasm for the subject. The two of us would sit together, poring over his map collection. He'd quiz me after our study sessions, awarding me a penny for naming the location of a river, a nickel for naming the Great Lakes, and a dime for calling out a state's capital city. If I named the thirty-two states from top to bottom, Papa Hugo would fish two bits out of his pocket and hand it over. "Put it in your piggy bank, Liz." He patted me on the head.

Papa Hugo was fascinated by the rush to the West, devouring every article or news story he could find and listening to anyone with tales of the gold fields. "Why there are cities and towns thrown up in a matter of days!" he marveled. He spread the big map open on the library table. "Look here, Liz." He used a red pencil and traced three light lines across the map. "These are the main overland trails that people take, depending on what part of the country they are leaving behind and where they're bound. There are some variations along the way, but the basic routes are the most traveled."

"If we were to leave Sweetbrier and go to the gold fields in California, which trail would we take?"

"You tell me, Liz." He pointed to an "x" penciled lightly on the map. "Sweetbrier is right about here. Now what route makes the most sense?"

I studied the map carefully and pointed to one of the trails Papa had traced out. "We're closest to the trail that goes through Texas."

"Exactly right, Liz. We'd take the southern route across Texas and Arizona through some beautiful country and a formidable stretch of desert. We'd make a beeline to the Pacific Ocean." He tapped a spot on the coastline. "Right here to San Diego where we'd board a boat for San Francisco. It would be the journey of a lifetime!" His eyes looked dreamy as he imagined the trip.

"Maybe we'll go there someday, Papa Hugo."

"We just might, Liz! We'll have to convince Mama Lou first."

It wasn't more than a week after our conversation that Garvus found Papa Hugo floating in the lily pond, and everything fell apart. I still thought of Papa every day, and as I studied the map of the states that I'd taken from the office at Sweetbrier, I silently thanked him for being such a thorough geography teacher. The route was clearly drawn, and I could hear his voice telling me about the rivers, towns and forts along the way.

It is silly and superstitious, I know, but I prayed that Papa, like a guardian angel, was watching over Sophie and me. We needed all the help we could get. "Lord God and Papa keep us safe from harm," I muttered softly as I drove the carriage down the muddy, pitted road.

"What did you say?" asked Sophie.

"Just a little prayer. Now you better tie your bonnet on tight, because we're going to make some time. By my calculations, we've got a mere fifteen hundred miles to go, give or take a few."

Sophie gasped. "Oh my! That's an awfully long way. Do you think we can make it that far, just the two of us?"

"I don't know Sophie, but we are sure going to try." I gave the reins a shake, and the horses started forward. We settled into the swaying, bouncy rhythm of our carriage rolling steadily down the long road ahead.

I adjusted to life on the run more easily than poor Sophie. She is edgy by nature, and it doesn't help that her vision is limited by the singularity of her eye. She couldn't help herself from imagining all manner of frightening incidents. Any slight obstacle threw her into panic. I did my best to comfort and soothe her, but a mere twenty-four hours after our run for freedom I was forced to assume an unaccustomed sternness in demeanor in order to straighten her out. She was fussing something terrible about sleeping on the ground. "Why, there are scorpions and snakes, and who knows what else!"

"It's not like we have a passel of alternatives, Sophie. Your complaining isn't helping matters. We can't be particular like we're staying in a fine hotel. This bedroll and blankets are what we've got. Now, you sleep first, and I'll keep watch. After a few hours, we'll trade."

"Why don't we empty the cab and sleep inside? I'd feel a whole lot better if I could curl up on one of the benches or even the floor."

"The cab is packed so tight with necessaries that it would be an hour ordeal to take all our gear out, and then repack it before the sun rises. We don't have the time, Sophie. Something might come up where we have to leave in a hurry. Besides, we don't want to put our food out where a bear or a wolf can get at it."

"You think bears and wolves are around?"

"Without a doubt, and panthers, too. We'll be going through some rough country. It's the Indians we need to worry about more than wild animals."

"You're scaring me, Lizzie."

"We've already survived an ample share of tribulations together, and we're going to get through this, too, don't you worry."

"We might get through it, but I doubt I'll sleep much until we end up wherever it is we're going!"

She crossed her arms across her chest and watched me untie and roll out one of the bedrolls. "It's been a long day. Why don't you lie down and rest for a while, even if you can't sleep," I said. "I'll wake you in a couple of hours when it's your turn to keep watch." She grumbled, but she settled down on the bedroll and pulled a blanket up to her chin. A soft snore a few minutes later let me know she'd fallen asleep despite her fears. When the time came, I didn't have the heart to wake her. I spent the night feeding a small campfire from a pile of sticks left behind by another traveler and pacing back and forth in order to stay awake.

My goal was to cover as many miles as possible during the early hours of the morning. I woke Sophie before the sun rose. "We should travel as far as we can before noon, Sophie. I don't trust broad daylight. Morning is safer." We hitched up the horses and ate some of the biscuits and ham Addie had given us back at the settlement. "Pull your shawl up close around your neck and keep your bonnet tight. We want to avoid attention as much as we can."

"Mama used to tell us kids to imagine ourselves invisible, and that would help protect us from the evil eye. It's an old wives' tale but it's worth a try," said Sophie.

"I'm going to imagine that we're birds having a lovely, effortless flight to San Francisco." Sophie gave a weak smile. I adjusted my broad-brimmed riding hat so that it covered my hair, and I tied a bandana around my neck. I hoped that the hat, along with Papa Hugo's hunting jacket, gave the impression of a man driving the rig. The only drawback was my long skirt. I made a mental note to look for a pair of trousers.

We traveled about fifteen miles down a fair road, eventually stopping for lunch at a waterhole where the horses could drink their fill and graze on a small expanse of green grass while Sophie and I ate the last of the biscuits and ham. "We'll stock up on food at the next town," I said. "And we're going to have to coordinate what we say if people ask us nosy questions. We'll figure out a story so that we're prepared."

"You've always had a good imagination, Lizzie. I'm sure you can come up with more than one story. I'll go along with whatever you decide."

"I'll put my mind to it soon." I hadn't slept since we left Sweetbrier, and I felt lightheaded. "I need a nap, Sophie, but you must wake me around four or so. Keep your eye on the pocket watch, and even if I put up a fuss, don't let me go back to sleep. We'll start out at sunset and travel by moonlight. And from now on, you're going to have to pull your weight as night watchman."

Sophie sputtered indignantly. "You let me sleep through the night and you know it! It's you to blame, not me!"

"If you weren't so jumpy and nervous all the time, I'd be more inclined to wake you up!"

"Just hush, Lizzie. I am doing my best!"

I hugged her. "I'm sorry Sophie. I'm just a little tired and it's made me cranky."

"Well lie down and get some rest, for goodness sake!"

I stretched out on the grass and fell into a deep slumber until Sophie shook me awake at four that afternoon.

Sophie didn't know how to shoot a gun, and I knew it was essential to educate her as soon as possible in case she needed to use it. "But I'll get arrested if a soldier or a lawman sees a darky shooting a firearm!"

"We're going where no one can see us, Sophie. Besides, I'm not afraid of defending us if I'm forced to."

"Whatever you say, Lizzie."

Fortune took us to a dried streambed with a narrow, overgrown wagon road running parallel to it. I turned our carriage onto the rutted path. We rattled down the rough road, searching for the perfect spot for Sophie's training. Eventually, a straight section flanked by banks on either side presented itself. We tied the horses and walked down to the stream bottom. I showed her how to load the barrel and cock the trigger on Papa Hugo's silver-handled pistol and gave the same tutorial with the shotgun.

A pile of rusted cans at a campsite on the bank of the creek provided ample targets for practice. I set them up, coaching Sophie on how to line up the target in the site and to hold the barrel steady. Sophie caught on quickly and proved to be a good marksman, despite the limitations of her eyesight.

"Why you're a crack shot! Will wonders never cease!"

"Not such a wonder! After all, even a person with two eyes can only use one eye to aim." Sophie reloaded the rifle, hoisted it up to her shoulder, and a rusty can flew off its perch with a resounding ping.

"You are a born gunfighter, Sophie," I teased.

"I hope to heaven and earth that I don't ever have to pull the trigger on this infernal thing again," she said.

Sophie never had to shoot either gun for anything but target practice. I can't say the same. I used Papa Hugo's silver-handled pistol more than once. I love that gun. Without it, we wouldn't have made it across Arizona.

A pattern emerged in our daily schedule. We rose early, filled the kegs with water if we were near a good spring or waterhole, fed the horses feed corn or oats purchased at stage stops and settlements along the way. We ate a cold breakfast of whatever was left over from our dinner meal, which was eaten during our siesta time from noon to four. After hitching up the horses, we usually commenced travel by dawn.

The provisions of Mother Nature determined when and where we stopped in the afternoon, as we were always on the lookout for water to fill our kegs and barrels, grass for the horses, and the possibility of fish in a stream or creek. Sophie rose to the occasion and became an expert fisherman; we fried up trout or catfish a few days a week.

We ran into fellow travelers who told horror stories about murderous Indians and thieves along the trail, but our passage through Texas was uneventful and monotonous. The roads were mostly tolerable to good, and afternoon showers kept the dust down. The landscape was beautiful at times, and occasionally so ugly it was a wonder why there was a cabin or two thrown up in such places.

Sophie kept a tally of the number of miles we traveled every day in a blank journal she found in a little store at a stage station. "We left home sixty-eight days ago. How many more days do you guess we'll be on this endless highway, Lizzie?"

"Depending on the weather, the condition of the roads, and how the buggy holds up, there's no way of knowing the exact number of days it will take. I would guess at least two more months, or possibly three."

"Lord have mercy!" Sophie grumbled.

Almost daily we passed by groups of migrants who'd set up camp for lunch. Eventually, we grew bold enough to stop when it was apparent that a wagon train had women and children among the travelers. It was reassuring to develop some fellowship with the groups going in the same direction and to know that there was help should an axle or a wheel break in the middle of a forty-mile trek to the next station or fort.

Fortunately, our carriage was of excellent quality, valiantly holding together in one piece as we crossed Texas. Other travelers didn't have such reliable conveyances; every few miles the rusty, twisted remains of abandoned wagons and carriages appeared by the roadside. The wooden parts of the older wrecks had been pried off and carried away to make campfires. Only the metal parts that no one wanted were left behind.

"Look." Sophie pointed to a wagon that was partially hidden by a thicket of brush bordering the road. "It's obviously abandoned but it's still in one piece. It must not have been here very long. Let's look inside, Lizzie."

I reined in the horses and pulled the carriage to a stop just off the trail. "It's time to stretch our legs anyway."

The wagon floor was strewn with belongings. Sophie found a pair of men's pants in a battered suitcase and held them up. "You've been looking for some trousers. I think these will fit if you cinch them with a tight belt."

I climbed down from the wagon and circled the area to see if anything useful was left behind. My search led me to the side of the wagon that faced the chaparral growing in thick, grayish clumps. One area had been cleared of the brush and shrubs, and I wondered why. I crossed to the little grotto and peered in. "Here's the reason this rig got left behind. Come on out, Sophie," I called. She joined me, and we gazed down at the piles of stones that marked three graves. A single cross stood at the head of the burial site. Sophie stepped closer and squinted her eye at it.

"Someone etched some writing into it, Lizzie."

"What does it say?"

" 'Billie Montrose, aged 3 years, Margery Montrose, 32, and Delbert Montrose, 42, all died of the cholera. May their souls rest in everlasting peace.' The date reads June 1859. Why, that's just last month!" Sophie shuddered. "I've heard about the cholera being a nasty way to die. Let's get out of here, Lizzie."

Later that afternoon, Sophie and I gave the pants she'd found a good wash at a nice stream where we'd stopped. We spread them over a bush in the hot sun to dry in time for our departure at dusk. I put the trousers on when it was time to go, and from then on, the pants became an essential part of my wardrobe. "Every woman should try a pair in order to feel the freedom from skirts and petticoats!" I said. "Pants are perfect for travel, Sophie."

"I'll take your word for it," she replied.

The number of adobe houses and structures increased as we traveled west. We passed little villages where Mexican families came out offering eggs, potatoes and onions to sell to travelers. I was surprised how decent and clean they were, having heard that they were a dirty, ignorant race. The women were gracious and friendly, and quite attractive with their shiny dark hair and big brown eyes.

In El Paso we stopped at a bodega to buy groceries. We were stocking up before crossing the Rio Grande and entering rough territory where mountain ranges, deserts, and Indians made travel unpredictable. I bought twenty-five pounds of flour and twenty of cornmeal along with sacks of rice, beans, sugar and oatmeal, a tin of baking powder, slabs of bacon and salt pork, a tub of butter, a dozen corn tortillas and two-dozen eggs. Sophie added a spool of thread, some darning wool and a package of needles she found on the dry goods aisle. "It's high time to mend our clothes."

As Sophie and I secured the supplies in the carriage, a man on a brown and white pinto bearing outsized saddlebags stopped next to us and dismounted. He looked at us with frank curiosity, pausing to eye our purchases piled up on the clapboard sidewalk. "Looks like you're stocking up. You got a long way to go?" he asked.

"We've got a fair distance ahead of us," I said.

He looked at me more closely. "We'll I'll be! I thought you was a boy."

"I'm dressed for the trail, sir. Now if you don't mind, we've got to pack our gear." I turned my back to let him know the conversation was over. He moved away slowly, stopping to lean against the wall of the store where he watched us finish stowing our purchases in the carriage. I sensed his eyes fixed like a leech on our buggy as we left town, heading west toward the river. "I hope we don't run into him again," I said. "He gives me the chills."

"He sure was kind of nosy," said Sophie.

We drove through town and found the river crossing just as

the grocer had directed us. A train of wagons and their herd of cattle were crossing the river and keeping two large ferry rafts busy. "We'll get this crew across by late afternoon, and if it ain't too late, we'll take you and your rig over then," shouted one of the bargemen. We tethered the horses in a nearby meadow shaded by a few stunted scrub oaks. Sophie started a small campfire banked in an old fire ring left by other travelers. I cracked four eggs into the skillet and fried them with a pinch of salt and some pepper. I gave Sophie her share and put the rest on my plate.

We had barely started eating when the man who'd watched us with such interest rode up on his horse. He dismounted and doffed his hat. "Good afternoon, ladies."

"Same to you." I set my plate down. "How can we help you?"

"I saw you a while ago, didn't I? At the little Mexican store?"

"That's where we got these eggs," I said. "If I knew company was coming I'd have cooked a couple extra."

"Thanks, but I already ate. I take it that you ladies are waiting to cross the river?"

"We are."

"I'm crossing over myself after I tie up some business matters in town."

"What is your business?" I asked.

"I'm a bounty hunter." He leered at me, and the disgusting smell of rot brought on by chewing tobacco wafted across the space between us. "My name's Phineas Snipe. Howdy do." He paused, waiting for us to volunteer our names, but I just stared at him with a blank face. He broke the uncomfortable pause. "There's been a rash of slave escapes in Louisiana and Texas. I'm down here to catch anyone who might of thought to take the low road." He leafed through some papers he'd pulled from his saddlebag. "I find it helpful to look over the wanted posters. It keeps my memory fresh for recognizing a face when I see it." He held one out to us. "Have you seen any of these men in your travels?"

Under the pictures of three black men were the words: ESCAPED SLAVES. CONSIDERED ARMED AND DANGEROUS. NOTIFY LOCAL LAWMEN IMMEDIATELY UPON DETECTION!

"There's a bounty on these boys, dead or alive," said the man.

"What a pity for them. And what's your interest in our business. Mr. Snipe?" My voice had a sharp edge, and Sophie's good eye shot me a warning.

"I wanted to make sure you were safe. Women traveling alone don't fare too well, particularly in Indian country."

"We've been very fortunate so far." I took a last bite of the now cold eggs and tossed the rest into the fire, then busied myself by wiping our skillet and tin plates, hoping he would leave. He moved around to face me.

"You wouldn't mind telling me your name and the name of the Negress with you?"

"Not at all," I said. "My name is Mary Harper, and this is my personal maid, Jojo Jefferson."

"What's your destination? It isn't often I see women traveling unescorted."

"You're very direct, sir. It happens that we are on our way to San Francisco, where my father is waiting for us."

"How did you come to be parted from him?"

"Papa is in the dry goods business. He and his brother, my Uncle Ben, heard of a need for such stores in the west. He left our store in Houston in care of my uncle and took a shipment of goods with him around the horn. I was horribly worried! I've heard gruesome stories about shipwrecks and people getting murdered by pirates on the high seas. Imagine my relief when I heard from Papa. He found a satisfactory storefront for the business, and he sent for me to come join him. I am his only child, and we can't bear to be apart, Papa and I."

"It would seem more prudent for a young woman of means to have, at the very least, a boy to drive her rig."

"We had a young man with us until just last week. Poor fellow got kicked in the head by a horse. Afterwards, he couldn't move. We had to leave him at a doctor's clinic in San Antonio with instructions to send him home as soon as possible."

The bounty hunter spit a sticky brown wad in the dirt. He pulled a pouch from inside his vest and took a bite of his foul chewing tobacco, stuffing it in his open mouth filled with black, rotting teeth. "I'm curious why you would keep a one-eyed darky," he said.

"Why, Jojo has been with me since I was a child. I wouldn't think of having anyone but her. No one else has ever been able to handle my hair." Sophie widened her good eye at me behind the man's back, and I winked at her when he wasn't looking.

"Well, I wish you luck in your travels, ladies." The bounty hunter mounted his brown and white pinto and picked up the reins. "Who knows, we might meet again on the road."

"I hope not," I said under my breath as he trotted away.

Sophie's eyebrows were raised up so high it was comical. When he was out of sight, she giggled. "Jojo? How in God's heaven did you come up with Jojo?"

"It's all I could think of at the moment."

"That's the best story you've made up yet, and you've had some other good ones! Honestly, those lying words came out of your mouth as smooth as buttermilk, Lizzie. Maybe you should work as an actress with one of those traveling troupes that move from town to town."

"Maybe you should hush," I retorted, but I was proud of the way I'd handled the bounty hunter and of my ability to tell a tale with ease.

It was near sunset when the raft delivered us to the opposite side of the river. "If we keep going for a couple more hours we just might cross into New Mexico by late tomorrow morning. Las Cruces is only 45 miles or so."

"You're the driver, Lizzie. I'm just along for the ride," Sophie said.

The horses were slowed down by thick, powdery dust that settled over everything and made us tie bandanas over our nose to keep from breathing it. "Let's pull over for the night, Lizzie. I've had enough of this infernal dust," Sophie said. I steered the carriage off the road into a flat area next to a wash with a skimpy stream running down the middle. We got busy and made a small fire. I put our kettle over for a hot cup of tea before we took turns sleeping. Sophie was unusually quiet. Finally, I asked her if something was wrong.

"It's that Phineas Snipe creature. He set me off to thinking about the law catching us for Bert's murder and throwing us in jail. Do you think they're looking for us, Lizzie?"

"It's possible."

"What would happen if we were arrested for killing Bert?"

"I guess we'd hang if they could prove it. On the bright side, if anyone is after us, they'd probably have already caught us."

"That's some comfort, I suppose." Sophie finished her cup of tea and stood up. "Why don't you go ahead and sleep, Lizzie. I'll take the first watch."

"Thanks, Sophie. I need a nap; I am awfully tired." I spread out the bedroll and settled into an uneasy sleep troubled by dreams of Sophie and I standing side by side, each with a hangman's noose around our neck.

It was fortune that led us to share an afternoon resting site with a wagon train from Missouri traveling in the same general direction. The people were open and friendly, and we immediately accepted their invitation to trail along with them through New Mexico. The territory was notorious for Indian raids, often resulting in the loss of lives of migrants, and it was advised by the soldiers we spoke to at forts along the way to seek security in numbers whenever we could.

The wagon train had several families and was protected by a

brigade of armed men. They were driving a good-sized herd of cattle that were to be split up among the families at the finish of their journey. "We started with four hundred and twenty beeves; now we're down to barely three hundred. Some banditos around El Paso rustled a bunch of 'em, and we lost several weak ones that couldn't hold out for water and grass along the way. I'm sure we'll lose a few more when we cross the desert," one of the men said.

We stayed with the wagon train for three weeks until it parted at the border of Arizona and New Mexico to take a detour via a different trail heading towards the Los Angeles area in California. Sophie and I were sad to part with the nice folks from Missouri, as it meant an end to a pleasant interlude of safe and secure passage. Now, we were once more alone in our carriage and back to taking turns sleeping while the other stood watch. It was not restful sleep, but we both touched the chord of steel inside that keeps you going even when you are exhausted.

Our buggy pulled us faithfully through the red rock mesas rippling across the vista. We could see for miles; it looked as if a giant being had squeezed out layers of rust-colored clay that centuries of baking sun, wind and weather sculpted into gargoyles and church spires. Strange cactus plants thrust up from the infertile, sandy soil, and the sun blazed down hot enough to bake eggs at midday. Our consistent luck in finding water and grass held, despite the harshness of the terrain, and made for good camping along the way.

"We've been on this everlasting trail for 108 days and six hours," Sophie announced. "I'll sure be happy when we don't have to jounce up and down in this darn carriage! It's starting to shake my bones apart!"

"Nonsense, Sophie. You are still in one piece as far as I can tell, and you look healthier and happier than you did when we left Sweetbrier. You are thinner, however. You need to eat more." On the other hand, though we ate the exact same fare, I had gained weight, and no longer had to cinch the trousers so tightly.

"No matter what you say, my bones are aching something fierce. Let's find a campsite early and take the whole afternoon and evening to rest."

An hour later Sophie pointed out a green patch nestled in a crevice at the foot of the mesa we'd been approaching. "Look, Lizzie, trees and grass way down there at the bottom. Do you see?"

"Yes. Let's try it." I drove the carriage a mile or two over a rough side trail to the area we'd seen. A small grove of ancient, gnarled scrub oaks formed a ring around a flat camping area, and a good spring bubbled up in a rock-lined pool. The camp had served other travelers; a blackened fire pit and a crude bench made of a plank held up by two boulders were the remains. "This looks presentable," I said.

"It's a fine camp," she replied. "I'm more than ready to set here a spell."

"We'll eat an early dinner and rest. Don't get too comfortable, because we're hitching up in the early morning, when the stars are still out, to make up for lost time today."

"You're already talking about leaving and we haven't even had a chance to put our feet up! You're like a field boss, Lizzie!"

"Someone's got to take charge, honey."

I unhitched the horses so they could graze. "I'm going to try to scare up a jackrabbit or some partridges for dinner. I don't know about you, but I'm awfully tired of corn meal mush and salt pork. It's starting to make me nauseous every time I take a bite."

"Something different sounds mighty fine, Lizzie. I'll just sit right here on this nice bench someone made and do our mending. We've still got a dozen potatoes. I'll peel them and put them over to boil for supper. I'll make a light potato bread for the road, and we can use the leftovers for pancakes tomorrow."

"Since you're doing chores, would you mind filling the carriage lanterns? We'll need to light them when we leave in the morning."

"Sure. I'll get the kerosene." She climbed up the steps to our carriage full of supplies. "Oh, Lizzie, take a fishing pole in case you come across a nice creek." She handed me the fishing pole and Papa Hugo's old canvas and wicker fishing basket. Sophie helped lift the saddle down from the gear rack, and I saddled up Midnight, the black roan. I took the silver-handled pistol from the saddlebag I always had in reach and tucked it into the tackle basket. "I'll be back in an hour or so, hopefully with some dinner."

I pointed Midnight toward a weathered bluff I could see in the distance and let him take the lead across the wind-sculpted landscape while I scouted for dinner. A bevy of quail broke the silence as they rushed from a thicket of mesquite. I took aim, but something spooked them, and off they flew in a fluster of whirring wings. A descent into a draw presented a slash of greenery in the middle of which gushed a narrow little stream. It spilled over the rocks, forming bathtub-sized pools that spilled into more pools.

I dug into a soft, damp bank for worms and uncovered several grubs that would do. I threaded a couple of the bugs onto the hook and dropped my line into the first pool. The response was almost immediate; I pulled a wiggling ten-inch trout from the pool. I worked my way downstream, through the pools, and caught four more fish. I sat on a sandy ledge and gutted them immediately, as Papa Hugo had always instructed. "Wrap them up in some wet leaves so they stay cool," he'd said. There weren't any suitable leaves, but there was a patch of grass that would do. I moved the pistol to the outside pouch to keep it away from the fish and cut some grass to line the bottom of the basket. I sprinkled a little cool water over the trout like Papa Hugo had shown me.

With dinner settled, I got back on Midnight to make the return trip to the campsite. It was farther than I'd realized, and the long shadows fell across the mesa by the time our carriage came into view. The campfire was burning cozily, but Sophie was nowhere to be seen.

I slid off Midnight and tethered him to the branch of a scrub oak. "Where'd you disappear to, Sophie?" I called. "Yoo hoo, Sophie! We're having trout for supper!"

Out of the dark shadows behind our carriage stepped a frightful image I will carry to my grave. It was Phineas Snipe, the bounty hunter. His left cheek was bleeding from a nasty looking scratch. He had bound Sophie's wrists and was dragging her by a lasso around her neck. He jerked it violently, and she screamed with pain. "This one's a real mountain lion. She's sure got the claws." He drew his pistol, aimed it at Sophie's head and mimed pulling the trigger. "You're worth more alive. Otherwise you'd be one dead she-cat."

"Let go of her," I cried.

"Well, hello there, young lady. I can see you're still playing at being a boy in those pants. I'll take those trousers off later and inspect your equipment, but for now, I can wait until dessert for a delightful taste of vanilla followed by chocolate. Did I hear you say we're having trout for dinner?"

"What do you want from us?"

"Ever since I seen you at that store I thought there was something fishy about you two. It's my bet there's a bounty on your heads, and I aim to follow through and collect on it."

"You're wrong!"

"And you're a liar. You told me her name was Jojo, but I heard you call her Sophie. Whatever you're hiding, I'm going to get to the bottom of it. But for right now, you're going to cook up a nice dinner. Now, don't do anything funny or I'll blow this bitch's head into the state of Texas." He led Sophie to the carriage and tied her to a back wheel.

I could see in his eyes that he meant business, and I knew I'd have to take unusual measures. What the measures were, I wasn't quite sure of. "Just calm down," I said. "I'll fry up this fish. We can talk things over when you've had something to eat. Maybe we can come up with a reasonable solution."

"By all means, put dinner over," he said. I set the fishing basket down on the bench next to the fire ring. "What's that?" he asked.

"The fish are in there," I said.

I fed the fire; building up the wood so flames leapt up directly under the pot of potatoes that Sophie, true to her word, had put on the fire. I poured some oil into the skillet and put it on a cooler part of the grill to heat up. Phineas Snipe watched every move. "I need salt for the fish," I said.

"Where is it?"

"There's a sack of salt in a big tea tin, just inside the carriage."

He got up and crossed to the carriage door. "I've got my eye on you," he called, framed inside the open doorway.

"The tin is on the floor under the bench on the right," I said.

He bent down to rummage for the tin. This was my chance. With deliberate calm I opened up the fishing basket and quickly removed the pistol, tucking it partly under the bag where it was concealed. I took out the trout, placing them side-by-side in the heated pan. While they sizzled, I used our long wooden spoon to poke at the potatoes, breaking them up in the now vigorously boiling water.

"Here's the salt." The bounty hunter handed me the sack of salt and returned to his seat on the bench.

I turned the fish over and sprinkled the finished side with salt. They crackled in the oil, sending up a mouthwatering aroma. "Everything's just about ready. Come and get your plate."

He crossed to the fire, took one of our tin plates from the end of the bench and stood with it held out. "Pile it up little lady. I'm hungry enough to eat all them trout."

In one smooth movement I grasped the pot of potatoes with both hands and threw the contents in his face. "Hell's whore!" he screamed, clawing the potatoes out of his eyes. I lunged for the silver-handled pistol hidden by Papa's fishing basket, leveled the barrel, aimed at his head and pulled the trigger. The gun resounded; there was a sound a pumpkin might make if it exploded. The top half of Phineas Snipe's skull burst into a spray of bone and blood. Like a chicken with its head cut off, his body moved convulsively; he swayed backwards then wheeled forward on rubbery legs, took a step and crumpled face first into the fire pit, upsetting the skillet of trout sizzling on the grill.

"There goes dinner," I muttered. I ran to cut the tight knot from Sophie's chafed and bleeding wrists and free her from the wagon wheel. We clung to each other and rocked back and forth, breasts heaving and hearts pounding. Both of us were spattered with blood and gooey bits of Phineas Snipe's brain. I staggered a few steps to the bushes and vomited.

Sophie handed me her handkerchief to wipe my face. "What will we do now, Lizzie?"

"Come and help pull him out of the fire. He's sharing the embers with the trout I caught this afternoon and making a terrible stink."

It took considerable effort, but we managed to roll the bounty hunter free of the fire pit. Sophie stared down at the crumpled form of Phineas Snipe illuminated in the flickering light of our camp lanterns. "We'll be hanged by the neck before this trip is over!" she said.

"Not if I can help it. Plain and simple, we need him to disappear forever without a trace."

"And how are we going to do that?"

"Leave it to me. I know just the spot to dump him, not far from where I caught the fish. It's a place where he'll turn to dust before anyone ever comes across his lousy, verminous bones. I need you to help load him onto his horse."

I removed the man's belt and slipped off the knife he wore in a sheath. In his pockets were a few coins, a wad of paper bills, and a ticking timepiece, which I removed. Another pocket carried his foul chew, which I tucked back in gingerly. I debated about keeping his gun; it was a fine pistol, but I decided that we couldn't risk it in case it could be identified. I shoved it back in his holster.

Sophie and I removed the saddlebags and the saddle from the bounty hunter's brown and white pinto so that it would be easier to drape the body over the barebacked horse. Phineas Snipe weighed a good 250 pounds, and as a dead weight he did not cooperate. The two of us struggled mightily but we couldn't lift him. Finally, we rolled him onto the canvas tarp we used for a ground cloth and dragged him under the nearest of the ancient scrub oaks that formed a ring around the campsite. "This makes me think of burying Hugh under the coals," Sophie said.

"Remembering Hugh and the way he ended doesn't do a darn bit of good right now. Now, heave-ho, Sophie. We've got to get him on the horse."

We propped him in a sitting position, his back leaning against a boulder. I loosened the lasso he'd looped around Sophie's neck and slipped it under his arms. "Sophie, could you bring a long coil of rope from the trunk?" She took one of the lanterns and went to search for the rope, while I threw the other end of the lasso over a sturdy oak branch directly above Phineas Snipe's body.

"Here." Sophie handed me the thick hemp cord.

"Help me tie this around his knees."

As soon as he was securely trussed, Sophie and I saddled Midnight. We looped the rope ends dangling from the oak branch around Midnight's strong chest. "Pass your rope this way, Sophie, and we'll tie everything to the saddle horn."

I patted Midnight on the nose and gave him a cube of our precious sugar to reward him for his cooperation. "This is going to be tricky, but I know we can do it," I said. "You'll need to hold the pinto steady while I urge Midnight forward. Our aim is to raise the body high enough, then lower it over the pinto's back."

I cracked the reins. "Come on boy, you can do it." Midnight

pulled mightily, raising Phineas Snipe inch by inch until his dangling body was finally in position.

Sophie coaxed the reluctant pinto to the spot directly under the body. "Hurry up, Lizzie. This horse is not happy about these shenanigans."

"Hold him as still as you can," I said. "We'll go backwards now and lower him down." After several attempts, we finally planted the bounty hunter face first on the pinto, his head drooping over one flank and his legs over the other.

Sophie and I tied the rope around the body and under the horse's belly, fastening it so it would be less likely for the man to slide off. The pinto was skittish and wanted nothing to do with his dead passenger. Sophie fetched more rope from the trunk and we tied the pinto tightly between two sturdy young oaks. "We'll move this repulsive load as soon as it's light enough to navigate," I said. "In the meantime, why don't you get some sleep? I'll take watch."

"I couldn't sleep a wink. I'm too wound up." Sophie threw some wood on the fire while I fetched another lantern from the carriage.

We did the best we could to sweep earth and dried leaves over the bounty hunter's blood. When signs of the struggle were sufficiently erased, Sophie made a pot of tea, and we sat together on the crude plank bench. I emptied the contents of Phineas Snipe's oversized saddlebags. A tangle of clothing and camp gear tumbled out. Sophie poked at the items with a stick. "Nothing much here," she said.

I ran my hand inside both saddlebags and found, at the bottom of an inner compartment, a leather pouch heavy with coins. "Look Sophie. A pot of gold at the end of a mighty ugly rainbow." I set it aside to add to our assets. "Thank-you, Mr. Snipe," I murmured. As for the rest of his possessions, we fed the things that could burn to the fire. The remaining items we stuffed back into the saddlebag, which would accompany the body to its final resting place.

It wasn't until the first light of morning that my hands began to throb unbearably from the burns I got when I grabbed the overheated pot of potatoes. "My hands are hurting something awful. I think they might need to be bandaged." I held them out for Sophie to see.

"Oh Lizzie, honey, why didn't you say something before? Those hands look nasty!" Sophie wrapped them in gauze for cushioning and helped me pull on Papa Hugo's leather driving gloves to protect them.

"You're going to have to lead the pinto, Sophie. My hands are on fire."

We set off on foot with Sophie tugging the pinto's reins and my hands dangling uselessly at my sides. It took an hour to find the spot I'd seen the day before. It was a perfect final resting place for Phineas Snipe down a deep, narrow gorge at the edge of a ridge overlooking a rugged and wild landscape. It took both of us to pull him off the horse and move him to the edge of the plunging precipice. Then it was simple; we rolled his body over the edge and watched it tumble into the black, rock-lined fissure. His saddlebags followed him down the hole. "Goodbye and good luck in hell," I said.

"What about his horse?" Sophie asked.

"I don't have the heart to shoot it, and I'm not sure I could even pull the trigger anyway. You'd have to do it."

"There's no way in hell and damnation that I'm going to shoot some poor innocent horse just because his master was evil and monstrous. Let's turn him loose."

"Go ahead," I said.

Sophie unfastened the halter. "Go on, boy. Get!" She slapped his flank with the reins. "Go on, horse!!" The horse looked confused, then wandered to a patch of grass and began to graze.

"Now let's leave this place of trouble and put it behind us forever," I said, but it wasn't that easy to forget Phineas Snipe. For a long time, my sleep was troubled by visions of blood pouring from the gaping hole in his head.

Sophie Washington

The Southern Trail

Late Summer 1859

The burns on Lizzie's hands were deep where she'd grasped the red-hot pan with her bare palms. Some of the skin had cooked to the point that a layer of it stayed attached to the pan when she let it fly. The wounds were red and oozed pus and they throbbed something terrible. Lizzie can't abide being helpless; she is a person who likes to take charge, and her injured hands were a vexation.

Until the burns healed, it was too painful for her to drive the carriage. We switched seats on the driving mount, and she became the bossiest passenger you could imagine. "There's a rut, Sophie! Steer to the left! LEFT!" . . . "Watch out for the boulder!" . . . "Slow down or we'll have a runaway carriage!" and so forth.

Finally, I told her we could just sit in some camp until her hands healed enough to take the reins. "Otherwise, you can just hush up and stop being Miss Bossy Britches!" She tried, but she couldn't help sticking her two cents in.

A lack of water plagued us for a few days; it was a blessing when we came across a campsite with a good well and an iron basin. I washed Lizzie's hands as gently as I could; her pain was so much that I poured her a shot of whiskey, which we kept for emergencies.

I made a poultice of cold oatmeal mixed with a few drops of opiated laudanum we'd acquired for a sore tooth of mine. I packed it around her hands and wrapped them in soft rags.

The only benefit of her helpless state was that she got to watch while I washed our blood-splattered clothes. I scrubbed and scrubbed the stubborn stains, and though they faded, the spots were still visible if you looked carefully. "I sure would like to burn this spotty dress in the fire," I said.

"We don't have that luxury, Sophie. Pretty soon your other dress is going to fall to pieces it has so many holes and mends." It was true; travel had been hard on the few clothes we'd started out with. The day was hot, and my dress and Lizzie's trousers and blouse dried quickly. "You're going to have to help me put these on, Sophie," she said.

I helped her step into the pants and drew them over her hips to her waist. "Why the top buttons won't close all the way! Either these pants shrank or you're getting fat, girl," I teased. She looked stricken, like I'd offended her, so I shut up and put my own dress on.

"When we get to San Francisco we'll find a store with ready-made dresses," she said. "Then we will burn these grim reminders of Phineas Snipe."

"I hope we have money for new boots. I've got so many holes in this pair, it'll be like walking barefoot soon."

"Boots and dresses, and whatever else we need. We can't go galli-vanting around in San Francisco looking desperate."

"What about money?"

"With Mr. Snipe's coins added to our original bank, we have enough to get by for a few months if we're careful."

"Well at least something good came out of a bad situation," I said.

Lizzie gave a grim smile. "Killing someone is not a way I want to acquire money in the future, that's for certain."

After a couple of days of my driving, Lizzie couldn't stand it. She insisted on taking the reins. "Are you sure your hands are healed enough?" I asked.

"I am sure only of the fact that your driving is dangerous. No offense, Sophie."

I handed the driving duties over gladly. Now I was free to gaze at the ever-changing view of mountain ranges, canyons, gorges and mesas. It was harsh, beautiful country. Temperatures in the higher elevations made for tolerable passage; when we descended to the desert floor the temperature soared. It was impossible to travel in the heat of the day; we traveled in the evening as soon as the sun sank, stopping at midnight for a few hours' rest.

Mornings were cool enough until around eleven, at which time we holed up in the shadiest spot available. Other travelers followed similar schedules. It was the only way to survive the dreadful heat. Fortunately, the miracle of a spring or a well broke the miles of desert now and then; otherwise even more travelers would die on the unforgiving trail. Roadside graves marked with makeshift wooden crosses were a common sight.

Lizzie's hands became infected. She'd forced using them too soon, and the wounds cracked open. The deepest burns had an unhealthy greenish tinge. I cleaned them as best I could in the only water we'd found in a couple of days and wrapped them once more in the soft rags, but the wounds oozed and did not improve.

I insisted on stopping at a doctor's office in Tucson. The doctor took a look at Lizzie's hands and brought over a basin and a slender bottle. "Put your hands over the basin,' he said. "You're going to feel this." He poured the liquid over Lizzie's hands.

"Mother Mary and Jesus!" she squeaked, tears leaking from the corners of her eyes. 'Feel' doesn't begin to describe the sensation! My hands are burning up!"

"The pain will stop in a few minutes," the doctor said. He

wrapped her hands in gauze bandages. "Unwrap them at night to let the air circulate around your hands. You want the infection to dry out. Here's some linseed oil to rub into those palms. And you absolutely can't use them. It's obvious that you've re-opened the wounds more than once. If you're not careful, you could get gangrene. It's quite common for wounds occurring on the trail."

We stayed in Tucson for three days to give Lizzie's hands a chance to heal in a civilized place with clean water and bathing facilities. She was once again stuck with me helping her do the simplest things: tying her boots, pinning her hair or helping with buttons. I noticed from the last time I'd buttoned her trousers that the gap at the top was widening. I threaded a rope through the belt loops and tied it in order to keep them up. "Honey, if you gain any more weight we'll have to find you a new pair of pants!" I laughed and gave her stomach a pat.

"It isn't funny, Sophie." She began to weep piteously, which took me aback as Lizzie is not the crying type.

"What's the trouble, Lizzie?"

"I'm fairly certain that I'm pregnant. Bert has reached out from the grave to ruin my life even further!" She wailed and beat at her stomach.

I caught her arms. "Lizzie honey, stop! Don't hurt yourself! You're taking this awfully hard. Just keep in mind that it isn't the end of the world!"

"I wish I would lose this baby!"

"Don't say that, Lizzie! You'll put a curse on the child. I'd be happy if I was going to have a little one to love. I know from my own boys that babies are a joy." Thinking about the twins made my good eye tear up.

"I hate this baby, Sophie. I don't need it or want it, and I certainly don't love it!"

"Talking this way is no good. You'd better find a happier attitude toward the innocent child you're carrying."

She glared at me with blazing eyes. "I am entitled to my feelings, Sophie!"

"All I'm saying is—"

"Let's not discuss it anymore, please." For the remainder of our journey, that was the end of the conversation about the growing being in Lizzie.

Elizabeth Dumond
The Southern Trail
August–September 1859

Sophie is by far the worst driver alive! She has almost killed us more than once. I try to keep from pointing out every rock and rut in the road because it makes her so mad, but I have our lives to consider. I've decided that she is nearsighted, which compounds the limitation of her having only one working eye. I intend to look into a pair of spectacles for her as soon as we settle in San Francisco.

We are closer to our destination by the day though the going is slower because we've joined a wagon train heading in the same direction. The people we've joined plan to farm in San Diego and are driving three hundred cows and fifty-eight horses, and one of the wagons is carrying over a hundred chickens. The train travels at a considerably slower pace, but it is worth going slower because Sophie is no longer behind the reins! One of the young men offered to drive the carriage, and now I don't have to fear for our lives.

The last straw of Sophie's bad driving happened when we'd been forced to take a detour because of a rockslide across Cooke's Road. We came to a stop and scanned the area for a way around the slide. On one side, the river had cut a narrow, rocky gorge, on the other was the lofty mountain slope from which the slide had tumbled. "It looks like our only choice is to go back the same way we came," I said. "There must be a trail that goes over the hill and connects with the road on the other side of the slide."

Sophie turned the carriage around, and we doubled back in search of a passable trail up the mountainside. "Look." Sophie stopped the carriage and pointed to a wagon coming down a steep dusty road.

"Let's see if those folks have any pertinent information." As always, when we approached strangers on the road, I made sure that my silver-handled pistol was within reach. Burned hands or not, I could still defend us if I had to. The wagon driver, a white-haired man with a gaunt, bony face, pulled up next to us. "Do you know a way to get around the rockslide on the main road?" I asked.

He pointed over his shoulder to the trail he had come down. "You'll have to go up this trail and over the top of the mountain. It's a good ten miles until you get to the road that takes you back into the river canyon. It is a rough, bumpy trail, but it's the only way. Good luck." He clucked to his team, and they disappeared into the dust cloud trailing the wagon.

Sophie inched the carriage up the switchbacks to a high plateau above the canyon. The road was uneven, littered with boulders and potholes that made passage slow and tedious. It took over an hour to reach the other side of the promontory. We stopped where the road split into two forks. "I'm inclined to take the trail off to the left." Sophie said.

"But Sophie, you can see by the ruts in the road that this other way has been traveled far more."

"I have a feeling that it might be a shortcut, and you know me, any way to shorten up this everlasting trip, I'm for it. Besides, I'm driving, Lizzie." She turned the horses down the less traveled fork in the trail. It proved to be a nightmarish route. In the middle of our descent, the road narrowed to little more than a ledge hugging the rocky mountain on one side; the other side plunged hundreds of feet to the canyon floor. We inched forward, creeping at a snail's pace with Sophie screeching at the horses to slow down.

A bear-sized boulder in the road was our undoing; Sophie tried her best to squeeze around it but the back wheel on the driver's side slipped down over the ledge, and we came to an abrupt and precarious stop. The carriage teetered as Sophie and I clambered down from the driving platform. "God almighty and all the guardian angels, what did we do to be punished this way?" cried Sophie.

"I knew you shouldn't have taken this fork," I said.

"Now is not the time to bring that up, Lizzie!" she sputtered.

"Hello up there!" A voice rose from the flat plain still considerably below our present location on the craggy road with its sharp slope. I squinted my eyes and located the voice coming from a man seated on a horse. "It looks as if you are in distress. Stay there. I'll get some strong men. We'll help you down," he yelled.

An hour later, eight men, all wearing round black hats with broad brims and thick canvas trousers held up by suspenders, drove their horses up the dangerous trail from the canyon floor. "Thank God you're here!" cried Sophie. "I was worried sick that we'd have to abandon the carriage after I almost drove it over the edge!"

"Don't worry, Miss. I've seen worse. It's nothing that some strong arms and horsepower can't fix." Soon, the carriage was lifted, and all four wheels were back on the rocky ledge. "Follow us," said one of the men. "There's a washout on the trail and we might have to take some of your load out, tie your wheels, and use some muscle to get it across. You ladies will need to traverse it on foot. Jeb will drive the buggy." Jeb took the driver's seat and guided our distressed team down the trail. The men tied the wheels at the particularly sharp drop off, and the other men held the ropes to keep the carriage from rolling down the washout. I thought the carriage would break apart, but through their combined strength we made it safely down the dangerous trail.

It was a relief to be on level ground. "Thank you," I said to the man who had first seen our troubles. "We would never have made it down in one piece if you hadn't come to the rescue."

"It is God's teaching to help our fellow men and women when they are in need. I consider it my duty," said the man. He shook hands with me and Sophie. "I am Noah Smith. We are part of a wagon train camped down the road a piece. After such an ordeal, you ladies must be exhausted. Please join us for the night. You can park the carriage in our wagon circle and share a meal with us."

We gladly accepted, and the men escorted our rig a few miles down the road to the camp. "You can park the buggy here," Noah said. He and one of the other men helped unharness the horses. "We'll take your horses over to the feed wagon and let the boys tend to them. You two can dust yourselves off. When you're settled, I'll introduce you to my wife, Martha, and the other women. They are preparing dinner at the chow wagon."

Noah came back after a half hour or so, and we followed him across the circle formed by the wagons. "The chow wagon carries our camp gear and most of the food supplies. It's our traveling kitchen." In front of the wagon were several women and children. The women all wore shapeless dresses cut from printed gingham with big aprons tied over the gowns. Close fitting caps with no adornment completed the outfit. The children wore child-sized versions of the same clothing as their parents. Noah stopped and gestured to a slender, sweet-faced woman. "This is my wife, Martha." Sophie and I introduced ourselves and shook hands.

"Please make yourselves comfortable," she said. "We'll have supper ready soon. I pray that you will join us."

"Only if there is enough to share," I said.

"There is always enough to share in God's kitchen," she replied.

Noah disappeared to help drive the cattle to a pond the men had scouted, and Sophie and I joined the women and girls preparing dinner on a makeshift table propped up on sawhorses. Sophie offered her help; I held up my bandaged hands. "I am afraid I am useless. I had an accident and injured my hands. It's been a burden for Sophie; she's had to do all the work."

"What happened?" Martha asked.

"I caught an Indian trying to rustle our horses. I ran after him with my pistol, but in the excitement of the chase, I tripped and fell face forward right into our fire pit. Thankfully, the gun got knocked out of my hand when I fell. I put my hands in front to break my fall, and they landed on red-hot embers. Lucky for me, the hands were the only place I got burned."

"How awful!" Martha said. "You must never feel safe after someone tries to rob you in the night!"

"You've got that right," Sophie said. "I haven't felt safe the whole time we've been on the road!"

We spent a pleasant evening with the women and children, who sang hymns in harmony as they prepared the evening meal. Several men came for a hasty supper, after which they returned to their posts guarding the herd. Next, the women and children took places at the table. Martha led a blessing, and we all tucked into a tasty beef and potato stew with light bread to sop up the gravy. After supper, there was much good-natured conversation and more singing until the sky filled with stars and folks began to drift away to bed down for the night.

Sophie and I unrolled the bedrolls and spread them under our carriage. We snuggled in side by side. "What kind of clothes are these nice folks wearing?" Sophie whispered. "I've never seen plainer looking dresses, and the caps are even worse!"

"It is unusual garb. We'll ask tomorrow. Good night, Sophie." I was asleep before I heard her reply.

Martha told us the next morning that they belonged to the Mennonite church. "We left Kentucky at the end of March. Noah intends to farm the land just up the coast from San Diego. We'll sell our cheese and produce in the towns that are springing up. Of course, we also plan to establish a church and a school for our flock." Martha beamed. "What about you two ladies? Why are you heading west?'

I had become an expert liar, bending and embellishing a basic story depending on whom I was telling it to. "My husband heard about the need for doctors in California. He left Louisiana a month ahead of us with the intention of finding a home in San Francisco and setting up his medical practice. As you can see, he left me in the family way." I paused as Martha and the other women scrutinized my belly. "I am determined to arrive in San Francisco in time for him to deliver his own child."

"We will pray for you to arrive in time," said Martha. The other women murmured and nodded in agreement.

"Thank you," I said.

"I hope I don't offend you, Miss Lizzie, but I must ask why you're wearing men's trousers?"

"Besides the fact that my skirt is in ruins, the trousers are extremely practical to travel in," I replied. "I've told Sophie every woman should have a pair, but she refuses to try them."

Martha gave a gentle smile. "Noah and I talked last night, and we would like to offer you the chance to travel with us in the train. It would be much safer to cross the Apache lands with armed company than two women alone and vulnerable. Noah says the desert lands that we cross on the final push to San Diego are only fifty or sixty miles distant, and many travelers lose their lives in the unforgiving climate."

Sophie gave a little nod. "I'd rather have company than go on our own. What do you say, Lizzie?"

"I was hoping we'd find a train to join. Considering the territory we cross next, it would be a godsend," I said.

Martha clapped her hands. "Good. I'll tell Noah." She turned to go, then turned back again. "There is one small thing I must ask of you, Miss Lizzie. I do not mean to insult you, but I must request that you take off the trousers and don proper female garments. We prefer our girls to wear modest, decent clothes meant for woman, and your outfit might influence them to do otherwise."

"Of course, Miss Martha. I'd be happy to comply with your concerns. Perhaps it would be even better if Sophie and I donned your very garb. We would certainly draw less attention if we blended in with the other women."

Martha nodded thoughtfully. "I think it is a wonderful idea, Miss Lizzie. We have a trunk of clothing belonging to Mrs. Grimes. She was swept downstream when we forded the Pecos River. The men searched for hours but didn't find her body. I'm sure her dresses will fit you and your maid. God welcomes all people, whatever the color of their skin."

She returned later with a valise full of clothing. "We're preparing the train to leave early this evening. I've brought the clothing we talked about for you to select. That way you can be dressed modestly for the journey." Martha put the valise down. "I'll check with you before we start moving," she said.

Sophie and I shook the wrinkles from the shapeless dresses, petticoats, and aprons inside the valise. Sophie chose a print in subdued blues and grays and I picked a dress of the exact same cut in dull green. Once we'd put on aprons and tied the bonnets under our chins, we couldn't be distinguished from the Mennonite women. "What a great piece of luck," I said. "Now we can travel all the way to San Francisco in the perfect disguise!"

Caravanning with the Mennonite train took us across the deadly deserts and perilous canyons that made up the last leg of the route to San Diego. In spite of the rigors and hardships of the trail, the spirit of the train was peaceful and calm; I could almost forget Phineas Snipe except for his reappearance in my dreams. It wasn't long before my hands healed enough to join in with meal preparations and daily chores, and I resumed the reins of our carriage.

Days of steady travel passed with relatively minor mishaps; several cows perished during a particularly arduous stretch of desert, and a rattlesnake bit a horse in the infamous Box Canyon and had to be shot. Sophie and I, however, had some blessed relief from our troubles and the added benefit of the Mennonite's fine singing.

We parted ways with the pleasant, generous folks when we finally arrived in San Diego at the end of August. I gave Noah and Martha two of our horses in payment for their hospitality, and he offered to buy the other two ponies and our trusty carriage that had held together so admirably during the long, bumpy ride. I accepted, as the expense of ferrying a carriage would eat too big a hole in our sack of coins and miscellaneous valuables. Sophie and I packed our few personal belongings into a large valise and a small trunk that we would take with us on the boat ride to our new life in San Francisco.

Only one detail marred the perfection of our achievement and the excitement of starting a new life; it was the baby inside me growing larger by the day.

San Francisco

Sophie Washington
San Francisco
Late September 1859

Worse things could have happened than ending up on this hillside overlooking the bay. We could have landed in one of the crammed-together row houses next to the marsh flats south of the wharf where you can smell it every time the neighbors' bowels move. We looked at a cold, dirty room in one of those houses. Lizzie brought her handkerchief to her nose when we stepped into the stale air left by the last tenant. "We have another room to look at before we decide," she told the landlord. Next, she made me walk up a steep old hill like nothing I was used to back in the flatlands. "We need to find cheaper lodging, Sophie, but I don't want to take a room where we catch a disease," she said. "Perhaps this next place will be up to snuff."

We huffed and puffed up the hill, and though it was a cool day, sweat was pouring off me. "Why on earth do you want to be stuck up here?" I asked her. She didn't answer, so I shut my trap and took in the scenery. That woman reminds me of an army sergeant, the way she runs me ragged. The hill flattened out, bless it, and we turned down a road that ran the same direction as the bay. After all our travels my shoes were mighty worn out, and my feet were hurting something fierce.

I was getting ready to throw a fit and put an end to the hunt when Lizzie stopped. "This must be it." Lizzie pointed to a rambling, weather-beaten house sitting by itself at the end of the road. A canvas sign hung from the porch railing. Its faded lettering told us we'd arrived at *Wayside Inn and Lodging House*. We climbed the steps to a broad veranda. "Wait here while I ask about rooms," Lizzie said. I understood; it was better to inquire about rooms without a patch-eyed black woman at her side.

I'd never seen a prettier view than the one from the porch; late afternoon sun shimmered across the purple and green hills, and the trees just about touched the cotton-ball clouds. We're going to live here, I thought to myself. Soon, Lizzie came back with a key in her hand. "Come and see the room." The house was shabby inside, but it was clean and tidy and surprisingly warm compared to the chilly lodgings we'd seen so far. A weathered woman, her back frozen into a permanent bend, greeted us in the entryway. She smiled stiffly.

"I'm Verna McCurdle, the landlady, and I don't allow any smoking in the rooms nor shenanigans that ain't appropriate." She gave us the once over through squinted eyes. Apparently we passed her inspection; she gestured for us to follow her. "The room is this way." We followed her up the stairs and down a long hall. She stopped in front of one of the closed doors. "Number six is empty. The outhouse is down the back stairs." She waved her hand to indicate a place farther down the hall. "You got the option of two meals a day, but that's extra." She paused and glanced at me again. "Who's your friend?" she asked. "We don't want no trouble with the law here."

"This is Sophie Washington. She's my traveling companion and assistant, and I am Liza Laurent," said Lizzie. "I can assure you that we are law abiding women. I have the papers for Sophie if you need to see them." Having papers on me was a pure lie and another example of how good Lizzie had gotten at bluffing. Verna McCurdle just nodded her head and seemed satisfied with the explanation.

"Pleased to meetcha'," she said. "I'll let you see the room yourself, and if you're interested, come and find me in the kitchen. I just oiled the lock, so it should open real easy."

"Thanks, Mrs. McCurdle."

"Take your time, ladies." She waddled off down the hall.

"Since when's your name Liza?" I whispered, raising my eyebrows at Lizzie. "And when the heck did you get papers on me?"

"Shush," she said, fitting the iron key into the lock. The door opened to a large, airy room. A screen with Chinese painting separated the two beds, which I thought was a nice touch. Lizzie pushed up one of the windows and a fresh breeze blew in. There was a large bureau, a washbasin and dressing table in an alcove, and a couple of chairs that had seen better days. I tried one; it was comfortable enough after our march up and down the hills. "What do you think?" asked Lizzie.

"I think that sitting here taking a rest in the chair is real relaxing for a change, the way you've been running us around like field darkies and all. That's what I think."

"About the room, Sophie. What do you think?"

I shrugged my shoulders. "It seems clean and homey and not such close quarters as we'd be stepping on each other's apron strings. It's the best place we've seen so far."

"I'll go tell Mrs. McCurdle that we'll take it," said Lizzie.

The next day, after we'd collected our few possessions and Lizzie had paid the hotel bill, a cab pulled us up the steep hill we'd walked the day before. I was terrified. If the carriage unhitched and rolled backwards, we would surely die. I said so to Lizzie, and she just laughed. "We've come too far to end up dying now. You worry overly much, Sophie." The driver unloaded our bundles and helped carry them to our new room at Wayside Inn. Since we weren't heavy with belongings, it didn't take long to settle in.

A feeling of safety and peace came over me as I sat in the room in one of the shabby chairs with my feet propped on a stool. It was comforting to be in a place where we didn't have to hide, where nobody could hurt us or boss us around or treat us like we were cow dung. My spirits lifted, and I felt better than I had in a long time. Looking back on our travels across the lower states, we were always making a beeline to the house on the hill. It was as if fate had picked out a home for us.

On our first night as tenants at Wayside Inn, Lizzie announced that she was renaming herself. "I'm going to start out fresh in this town, Sophie. If anyone comes searching for Elizabeth Dumond, they won't find her. That girl is dead." Lizzie's voice was fierce. "From now on I'm going by Liza Laurent."

I yawned, tired from our busy day. "Whatever you want, Lizzie."

"Sophie, even you can't call me Lizzie anymore. You'll have to remember; it's Liza from now on." I could tell she meant business; her voice turns steely and mean and it's no good going against her. From then on, whenever I slipped up and called her Lizzie she'd give me the dagger-eye. "What'd you call me?" she'd say. After a while I got used to calling her Liza.

Elizabeth, Lizzie, Liza, Liz, whatever she goes by or used to go by, she is not the same person I grew up with. And I am not the same person she grew up with, though I have managed to hold on to my tender side a whole lot more than Liza. She took on a harsh edge, a roughness. Her new name transformed her. Her inside anger is pent up, and like a sidewinder it can strike all of a sudden, particularly at poor Rose. I don't admire Liza's changed temperament, but I will always be her faithful friend; we are sisters of the soul.

My memories of Jules and Augie are what prey on my mind; I worry they might fade away forever until I won't remember the treasured faces of my darling boys. Liza is plagued by the memories of our last night at Sweetbrier, when her innocence was lost. She sees it reflecting back to her in her daughter, who is also her niece. It isn't Rose's fault that she looks like her daddy. Bert was a handsome devil of a man, and Rose takes after him with her dark, glossy curls and indigo eyes. She is a lovely girl, but not to her mother. "Every time I see her I think of Bert," she said. "I can't help it."

Liza's solution was to hand Rose over to me. Maybe I should have raised more of a fuss and forced Liza to care for own daughter, but I was filled with joy to have a child in my life, especially a half-sister to my lost boys. Having a child to care for and love filled a little corner of my empty heart.

Though I don't admire the way she is toward Rose, I will never stop loving Liza. She and I have been through the fires of hell, and we climbed out of there on our own feet, up a rickety ladder to what might lead to redemption someday. The times I was ready to give up, Liza's steely grit and determination made me keep going. When we were crossing the Colorado and the current swept me downstream, she yelled out something like, "You're not dying on me now!" Then she jumped in and dragged me out by the hair.

That's Liza in a nutshell; whatever's in her path, she's just got to conquer it, tame it, handle it. She's brave and bold, and in dangerous circumstances she's as tough as any man. The trip west sharpened her ability to fib her way out of any predicament or tricky situation, which came in handy in Liza's new career.

Liza Laurent

San Francisco

1860

I became notorious out of necessity. There really wasn't any other way to survive and live decently, without working my fingers to the bone like poor old Verna, our landlady at Wayside Inn. If I'd only had myself to take care of, it might have been different, but I had Sophie. And along came Rose. Her arrival was the rock around my neck that dragged me under, drowning any chance of a more carefree future. Rose made me worry and fret about our state of poverty, adding to the growing pile of vexations caused by that child.

A week or so after we rented a room at the Inn, I tried to fix my problem with a crochet hook. Besides wanting to avoid the expense and the responsibility of a child, I was desperate to rid myself of the reminder of my half-brother. Sophie found me bleeding on the floor of our room. "Have you lost your mind, Liza? Did you ever think you might die along with the innocent creature you're trying to kill?"

In my low state, I didn't really care. "I've already made it plain that I don't want this child! If we both died there'd be an end to a lot of misery and pain."

Sophie clutched me to her chest in an embrace that reminded me of Addie and Mama Lu and everything motherly. "You snap out of this right now! You're going to have a baby. Now show some gumption, Liza, and try to forgive this baby for being inside you. Do you hear me?" Sophie helped me into bed and propped a pillow behind my back. She brought tea and made me eat a bowl of barley soup. "Now you sleep through the night and get some sense into your head." I slept soundly and woke late the next morning, weak and sore and resigned to my condition.

A few days later I walked all the way to the pawnshop in the Italian section of town. After a tense round of dickering, the jaded shopkeeper, his nose a mass of broken red veins, gave me seventy-five dollars for Papa Hugo's gold wedding band with matching cuff links and watch fob. Our funds were diminished more than I liked, though I still had a handful of double eagle gold coins and a few remaining pieces of jewelry Papa Hugo had given my mother. Phineas Snipe's coins were long gone. In a matter of a few months we would run out of money, and in spite of myself, I began to worry about how we would survive.

When the midwife put the baby in my arms, I saw her uncanny resemblance to Bert. Even with the pinched features of a newborn she was his spitting image. I turned to the wall and refused to hold the child. Sophie had to lift the baby from where it mewled on the bed, its arms waving helplessly. "Take her away, please," I cried. "I can't bear the sight of her."

"She's just dazed after the birth," the midwife said softly. "I've seen more than one new mother fall into melancholy after her child is finally born. Liza will get over it, don't worry." She straightened the sheets and tucked the blanket tightly around my legs. "She needs rest is all."

But I didn't get over it.

Sophie was in seventh heaven at having a baby to tend. She cooed endearments to the little bundle of Bert's and my flesh, cuddling her close when the newborn cried. A few hours after Rose's birth, Sophie came to my bedside and held out the baby with her head of wispy dark ringlets.

"You keep her, Sophie." I pulled the blankets over my head, but Sophie peeled them back off.

"What are you going to name this little angel?" she asked.

I shrugged. "You choose a name for her."

Sparks flew from Sophie's good eye. "Don't be ridiculous, Liza. You're acting like you've got a screw loose. This beautiful creation is your daughter, for God's sake. Now give her a name!"

"My real mother's name was Fern. It seems fitting to name her granddaughter after a flower or a plant of some kind: Willow or Jasmine or Daisy, I don't much care which. You decide, Sophie." I burrowed under the blankets.

"All right, if that's the way you want it, this child's name is Rose."

"Fine. Rose suits her. I'm awfully tired, Sophie. Could you pull the curtains? It's much too bright in here to sleep."

Sophie nestled the baby in one arm and drew the curtains across both windows in our room. She opened the door and paused like she wanted to say something. I peeked out of the blankets. She and Rose were framed in the doorway, frozen in position like a new-fangled photograph. Sophie's back was turned, and Rose's bright little face was perched up over Sophie's shoulder. She looked straight into my eyes, and even then, her stare felt accusing. The door closed on the two of them, and I promptly went to sleep, a blessed state in which I could forget I had an unwanted child.

I knew Rose was an innocent babe, and I tried to love her, but I could not let her into my heart. I felt suffocated by the baby, and resentful she'd forced her way into my life and burdened me with motherhood. I was deeply guilty that I didn't want her, and knew I was an unnatural mother. The baby's needy suckling was a chore I endured with grim resolution. It didn't surprise me when, a few days after Rose's birth, my breasts went dry.

The baby cried and fussed and grew weak from lack of nourishment until Sophie fetched goat milk from a little Mexican store on the south side of town. Sophie took over feeding Rose with a bottle. I was secretly relieved. Though I felt terribly guilty for my feelings, I comforted myself with the fact that Sophie loved the baby and was happier than I'd seen her since she'd lost Jules and Augie. I left her to coo over Rose while I gratefully escaped to help Mrs. McCurdle with her chores.

Sophie took on all the duties of motherhood, and the baby became a permanent appendage on her hip. Meanwhile, a friendship blossomed between Mrs. McCurdle and me. She accepted my offer of help in exchange for a small reduction in our rent, and we began working together, preparing meals for Wayside Inn's tenants, keeping the shabby furniture dusted and the linens clean. "Call me Verna," she said one day while we hung sheets to dry in the afternoon sun.

Verna was around sixty years old, give or take a couple of years. "I don't know my actual age because I lost track of counting a while ago." She grew up in Illinois on a dairy farm and was a confirmed old maid when, at twenty-seven, she surprised everyone by marrying Stuart McCurdle, the boy next door. "Why, he was ten years younger! Can you imagine the gossip around town? The tongues were waggin'!"

"Gossip can be very hurtful," I murmured.

"It didn't bother us none; we were happy together, plus we were too busy runnin' ourselves into the ground tryin' to keep up with work on the farm." Verna handed me a basket of laundry to hang. "My parent's farm was bigger, so Stuart moved in with us and took over some of the hard work from my father. Over time, him and I milked what seemed like a million cows. It's why I got so bent over, from sitting on a little bitty stool and pulling some mama cow's teat."

"Do you and Stuart have children?"

Verna shook her head. "One of the sore spots in my heart! Though we tried and tried, no baby ever took. It might 'a been on account of Stuart having a shrunken testicle, but who knows. Whatever the reason, we didn't have the children we wanted and needed. The saying 'many hands make light work' is especially true in the farming life."

"How did you and Stuart end up here in San Francisco?"

"Well, like I was sayin', no one came along to help with the chores. Dairy work ain't easy by any stretch of the imagination, but we managed until a bad influenza took my mother and father. Suddenly, half the workforce was gone, and Stuart and I couldn't keep up with everything."

"It sounds like things were tough." I gave her hand a little squeeze of sympathy.

"You'd think losin' my folks was bad enough, but things got worse. That same winter was the coldest one anyone had ever felt. The freeze went on for months and it ended up killing half our dairy cows. Stuart was beside himself."

"Back home in Louisiana, I witnessed a hurricane destroying years of hard work. I know how you feel, Verna."

She nodded. "Nature isn't fair, just like life isn't. Poor Stuart lost the end joint of his ring finger and most of an earlobe to frostbite when he was out trying to save the rest of our cows. It was so cold it hurt to breathe. Before the spring weather had a chance to melt the drifts, we decided to sell and move west."

Verna was forty-eight when she and her husband arrived in San Francisco. The city was bustling. "You should have seen it! New stores opened every other day, and the whole city was noisy with carpenters building houses and such. Why, they pounded nails from dawn to dusk when they built City Hall. It was something to behold!"

Stuart found a room for them, and Verna stayed in San Francisco while he went off to the gold fields. "I lived in a boarding house by the wharf and worked in a hash house for six or seven months, until Stuart hit a nice pocket of gold in the hills north of Sacramento. He was one of the lucky ones, let me tell you. Most prospectors never found much of anything, but Stuart came back to San Francisco with enough stake to buy the Inn and fix it up."

Stuart hired a crew of Mexicans, and they put up real walls instead of the canvas panels separating the rooms. Next, he replaced the poorly built front porch, and he added an apartment onto the back of the house, so Verna and Stuart could live separate from the tenants. "Stuart could build anything!" Verna sighed and shook her head. "It took us a couple of years, and in the end, everything was real nice with new paint and curtains, but as soon as the first tenants moved in, Stuart left for the hills to do some more prospecting. Nothing I said could stop him. My dear husband was truly bitten by gold fever." Verna was quiet for a minute. "I never saw him again."

"What happened to him?"

"Nobody knows for sure. There were a couple of stories going around: one fella said he heard Stuart went sleepwalking and fell off the side of a cliff. Another man swore he died in a brawl over a mining claim. He wasn't much of a fighter, Stuart, so I like to think it was the sleepwalking. It seems more peaceful than dying in a gunfight."

"I'm sorry you lost him, Verna."

She shrugged and kept on washing the breakfast dishes. "Whatever happened to him, he never came back home. Nothing I could do but accept it. At least he left me with a way to make an income. I've been renting rooms at the Inn ever since. It hasn't made me rich, but I get by all right, and I even have a little bit put aside." I squeezed her hand sympathetically, and she smiled.

As we worked and talked Verna and I grew closer, and Sophie became Rose's mother. Really, everything turned out for the best. I hope Rose will someday come to that conclusion herself.

Verna McCurdle decided to move home to Illinois around the same time as Rose's first birthday. "I got a letter from Alice, my sister in Chicago. Her husband died, and she's alone in the house. She asked me to come and live with her. To tell the truth, I'm homesick, so I'm going to take her up on it."

I was shocked. It came out of the blue, and it brought to mind the true flimsiness of our situation. I immediately wondered where we'd have to move and how I would manage to pay for it. There wasn't much left of our stake; the only valuables left in the carved box were Papa Hugo's pocket watch, an emerald and diamond pendant and two Double Eagles. The laundry that Sophie and I took in once a week from the boarding house down the street had supplemented our shrinking budget, but it was hardly enough for three people to live on.

Worry must have shown on my face. Verna reached out and took my hand. "Come and sit down with me," she said. "I have an idea that might suit us both." I poured two cups of tea, and as we sipped them, Verna proposed a plan that proved to be a stroke of fortune. The business arrangements we made that day certainly shaped my future and allowed me to become a woman of means.

"I've come to know you well, Liza, and I've worried about leaving you and your little family without a home."

I started to reply, but she held up her hand to indicate she wasn't done speaking, so I sat with my hands folded in my lap and listened.

"You need a home, and I need an income. I was hoping you could run the boarding house and send me some money every couple of months, so as I have my own little nest egg. My sister ain't poor, but she tends to pinch the pennies, and I don't want to be beholden to her in any way."

I blurted out what I feared and suspected she would do. "You could just sell the Inn, Verna. Then you'd have some money to buy your own place if you wanted."

She shook her head. "Look, I never had children, and the truth is, Liza, you feel like family. I want to help you and Sophie, and Rosie, too. You can help me at the same time. Besides, it might not work out with my sister. Alice is a bossy one. I think it would be wise to keep the option of coming back to San Francisco."

Our plan went forward; Verna had an agreement written up and signed by both of us before a notary; Sophie, Rose, and I could stay in the back apartment rent free, and every quarter I was to send her half the monies I'd collected from the tenants. The other half was to be divided into funds for maintaining the Inn, and a small income for us as innkeepers. It was nothing short of a miracle, and I couldn't thank Verna enough for her generosity.

"I promise to do my best for the Inn, and to make every payment on time."

"I trust you, Liza." We hugged as Verna's luggage was stowed away on the coach that would carry her on the first leg of her journey toward Chicago. "You've been a mighty good friend, Liza." She kissed Rose and shook Sophie's hand. "Wish me luck," she cried from the top step of the sedan. We waved until the carriage descended the crest of the hill.

With Verna gone, I was now the mistress of the house. A feeling came over me when I stepped out of the morning fog into Wayside Inn that day. I knew I'd been given a chance in life, and I decided from then on, I'd be in charge of my own destiny. A new era began, and during it, I would become a woman of means.

Only three of the Inn's ten bedrooms were occupied when Mrs. McCurdle left Wayside. "Having more mouths to feed and rooms to clean would be too much for these old bones! I sure ain't getting any younger," said Verna, when I'd asked her a couple of months earlier why she didn't rent more rooms. "For years I rented all the rooms out, and I worked myself silly. One day when I was cleaning up the parlor, I saw my reflection in the big mirror that hangs over the settee. Honest to God, I didn't recognize myself, a tired old lady with skinny, wrinkled-up arms sticking out of a sack of a dress, staring straight at me! Can you imagine? I thought it was a stranger until I saw her knuckles were bloody from scrubbing the sheets, same as mine. That's when I decided to let a few of the rooms go empty. Afterwards, when a tenant died or moved, I didn't replace him. It worked out; I don't have the extra coins to put in the strongbox each month like I used to, but I get by. It ain't much but it suits me just fine, and at least I'm not dead from overwork."

There were three elderly tenants besides Sophie, the baby and me. Twins Albert and Joseph Swenson shared two adjoining rooms overlooking the back garden, with a view of the bay from their own little balcony. The Swensons were at least seventy, and both were afflicted with rotten teeth and needed soft food from the kitchen of Wayside. Sophie made pot roast and egg custards so the brothers could have something they didn't have to chew too hard. Mr. Tinker, the oldest tenant at eighty-five, left his room each day for a constitutional walk in the early morning, after which he retired to the front parlor to read and smoke his pipe. Each of the tenants paid twelve dollars a month for his board and twelve more for two meals a day.

Verna trained me well; I knew how to run a tidy, well-organized Inn, and I threw myself earnestly into the job of innkeeper. Sophie and I did our best to keep the big house clean and to serve adequate meals to the funny old men who lived at Wayside. Our laundry business, which we conducted on weekends, had expanded to several tenants from two boarding houses in walking distance from Wayside. Our hands became roughened from washing men's overalls and long johns, along with Wayside's dirty laundry. The extra job kept us fed, and we were able to buy shoes to replace the holey ones that had come with us across the lower states.

A shock came with the first quarter after sending Verna her half of the collected rent money and paying taxes to the newly formed San Francisco Bureau of Revenue Collection. With little money left, all we could afford to put on the table was porridge or potatoes covered with a thin gravy made from one tough cut or another. The tenants grumbled, and even Sophie complained about the poor fare. "Can't we do any better than this?" she asked.

"We could advertise rooms for rent on the billboards down by the wharf," I said, but I wasn't thrilled about the idea and neither was Sophie. "Or, we can take in more laundry."

It was Sophie who encouraged me to seek employment. "I can do the work at the Inn and take care of Rose at the same time," she assured me. "If we bring in more tenants, we have more mouths to feed and bedrooms to clean. And, about taking in more laundry, to tell the truth, I've done so much laundry in my life I wouldn't be sorry if I never had to crank a washboard again!"

"Well, aren't you getting spoiled?" I grinned at her, so she would know I was kidding. "You're right, Sophie. An outside job would help." That afternoon I started the process of looking for employment in a city where jobs for women were few and often less than desirable. A week later I was hired as a barmaid at the ill-reputed El Dorado, a gambling parlor in one of the rougher parts of town.

Though dangerous, the El Dorado excited me. I felt alive, noticed, admired. I could forget myself as I served up shots of whiskey and bottles of tequila to the clientele. All walks of life, mostly male, filled the place around the clock. When the stakes got too high, tempers turned violent, and the fights that resulted often drew blood and brought the crooked city police who were notorious for taking bribes. "If a fight breaks out, seek cover behind the nearest table or counter," said the woman who trained me. "The girl you're replacing got caught in a gun fight." She pointed to a dark stain on the wood floor. "That's where she died." I heeded her warning, and though I moved boldly through the throngs of drinking, gambling men, I was always vigilant.

The pay for a barmaid was stingy, but I was popular and earned decent tips serving drinks to the players crowded around faro and blackjack tables. Waves of gamblers and party-goers floated in all night, requiring the barmaids to be on our feet for hours. I often came home in the early morning and collapsed into bed still wearing the dress I'd worn to work. In the daylight hours, Sophie ran the Inn while I slept.

At noon, I joined her in the kitchen. With Rose perched on one hip, Sophie would pour my coffee and put a plate of toast and eggs in front of me. It was one of our few chances to talk and feel like the old Lizzie and Sophie. The cozy times in the kitchen reminded me of the good days at Sweetbrier, when Addie and Chemise waited on Sophie and me like we were the queens of Sheba. So much had changed.

At work, I struck up a friendship with Max Steiner, a blackjack dealer at a table in my section. After a few weeks of observing the way I handled the rowdy customers, he took me aside during a quiet moment. "I've watched you, Liza, and your way with the men." His voice got soft. "Some of the guys have been asking me whether you're available or not." I shrugged. "Well, I don't know if you're interested in making some money under the table, but if you are, you can earn an extra fifty dollars or more on a good week. I could set you up on an appointment any time you say you're ready."

"You're talking about going on a social call for money?" I asked, surprised in spite of myself.

"It's a little deeper than going on a social call. A girl's got to satisfy what's always on a man's mind. That's why he's paying her." I must have looked shocked. Max laughed and patted the back of my hand with his hairy paw. "It isn't so bad if you're choosy about your clientele, Liza honey. Like I said, I'll help you get set up if you're interested." The pit boss walked toward us, and Max shut up.

The next day he motioned me over to his table. "Have you thought about what we discussed?" I nodded. "Do you see the man wearing a gray duster at the faro table on your right?" He indicated a tall, slim man wearing a stylish fedora and a pair of expensive snakeskin boots. "That gentleman has requested a night of companionship, and he pointed you out, specifically. Said he's had his eye on you for a while now."

I glanced at him; the man looked familiar with angular features that were somehow pleasing. "Yes, I've seen him around."

"I can vouch that he is a gentleman through and through, and he's willing to pay sixty dollars. After my tip, it leaves you with fifty, free and clear. I'd say that's an unusually good wage for an hour or two of work."

I'd been thinking about Max's proposal ever since he'd presented it the night before. It was tempting. Fifty dollars would help toward our continuing financial troubles, but I shook my head. "I'm not sure it's my cup of tea, Max."

"Don't worry, Liza honey. Whatever you decide," said Max. "If you change your mind I'll set you up with a decent guy, and a rich one."

I did change my mind a few weeks later. It was Sophie's bad eye that led me to my first encounter with sex for hire. I'd taken her to a special doctor to see if there was anything he could do for Sophie's ugly missing eye under the leather patch that hid half her face. "I can tighten up the empty eye socket with a few stitches, so it could hold a glass eye," said the Doctor. "I'd have to put her under at the clinic and make a few incisions, but the whole procedure could be done for somewhere around seventy-five dollars. She'd have to wear a bandage for a while, but when it comes off, it would certainly be an improvement to her appearance." I left the clinic determined to fill Sophie's empty socket and fix her face back to the face I grew up seeing. At work the next day, I told Max I was ready.

"Sure thing, Liza. I'll see what I can do."

Max arranged a meeting with my first client, a wealthy gentleman, fair in looks, and clean. He was the perfect client, and from him, my new career was launched. I'd been apprehensive, but when the paid event took place, my detachment surprised me; I'd prepared myself for the worst, but it wasn't as bad as I'd imagined. The man had the right balance of passion and gentlemanliness, and he was not selfish in his pursuit of pleasure. Since my entire sexual experience so far was a brutal, incestuous rape, having sex with a civilized stranger was an improvement. I found the work tolerable enough, and the money I earned improved our circumstances enormously. In a matter of weeks, Sophie looked out at the world with a new glass eye in addition to her good one.

Max made sure my first customers were decent men, free from the less wholesome desires a lady of the night is certain to encounter in the course of her career. He took ten percent of whatever I made, which I knew was fair, since many fancy men took half. "I'm just a fool for a pretty face, Liza," he'd say. "Besides, you're the one doing the actual work." Our arrangement went on that way until circumstances came together, and I established a new line of business at the Inn.

It really happened of its own accord, as if Wayside was always meant to be a house of joy. First, the Swenson brothers complained of the cool summer and announced they were moving to the Southern part of the state where it's always warm. A few days later they loaded a carriage with a few boxes and a steamer trunk, leaving their empty rooms behind for Sophie and me to clean. Mr. Tinker, the other old fellow, died in his sleep, which is the nicest way to go if you ask me. The undertaker carted him off the next day. Now, all the rooms were empty except for the one I slept in, chosen because it was the quietest for sleeping during the day and out of Sophie's hair in the back apartment. As I sat down to compose an advertisement for potential tenants, I had an idea that ended our financial worries for once and for all.

There were thousands of single women who migrated west, most of them seeking husbands. Some were successful, but many of these yearning souls floundered once they arrived in the wild city of San Francisco. Some fell prey to white slavers who sought out single women. I knew several girls from my work at the El Dorado; young women in jobs that wore their fingers to the bone and paid so little they could barely get by. I recognized an unmet need. The girls needed safe lodging and an income until they were able to land a husband or a job that paid a livable wage. Wayside Inn, with its abundant rooms, was the perfect place for shelter.

I started a careful recruitment of promising candidates, and in a few months, I became the Madam of Wayside Inn for Gentlewomen. The quantities of single women in need of a home and an income gave me the opportunity to be selective with the ladies I hired. I wanted girls who would appeal to a wide variety of clients, and I wanted a clean house with an excellent reputation. I had the canvas sign hanging from the front porch re-lettered, and once the girls were established in their rooms, men came in steady numbers. Max helped develop the clientele at first, but soon word of mouth brought more clients than we could handle.

It might seem wicked, but it was a source of pride that Wayside Inn for Gentlewomen became the top house of joy in San Francisco, with customers who returned again and again. Almost two years after Verna left San Francisco, business was so good that I could afford to hire Max as Wayside's bouncer and bartender. The following year, when Verna wrote that she wanted to sell the Inn, I was able to pay her off in three installments. We did not want for money ever after.

I regret that over time I became an absent friend to Sophie. The business at Wayside demanded my attention, drawing me away from the apartment in back where she lived with Rose. I am sorry I became so hard during those years. A woman in a business like mine has to be tough, and I regret the loss of a softer nature I once owned. And I regret my miserable failure as a loving mother.

Though I can never go back to do things over, I hope for a shred of understanding and forgiveness from Rose some day; forgiveness for exposing her to a life of sin she couldn't help being tainted by; forgiveness for my despicable lack of love; forgiveness for being absent from most of Rose's life. I live in the hopes that she will let me make it up to her.

Ten Years Later

Rose Laurent

San Francisco

1870-1871

I knew from a young age that my mother didn't want me. She gave me to Sophie as if I were a kitten someone had abandoned on the doorstep. She never held me in her arms or said she loved me or volunteered the least bit of affection. I sensed that I was a nuisance to Mama. I interfered with the elegant life she preferred as Mistress of the Inn. Sophie's love and mothering tried to make up for what was missing from Mama, but though I adored Sophie I still longed for my mother to show me the slightest bit of love.

Sophie did everything in her power to give me a good life, and a happy one. We were an inseparable pair until my mother decided to send me to Madame Pritchard's Youth Academy. I was ten when Mama enrolled me at the school, which was the beginning of my troubles. I'd give anything to go back to the almost perfect life I had before Mama made me go to Madam Pritchard's.

Sophie said I was a precocious child. "You were always asking a million questions and chasing after the bees and the butterflies. Sometimes, it about wore me out!" According to Sophie, I practically taught myself numbers and the alphabet. "You could read when you were barely four years old!" she bragged. When I was five, the matter of my education was discussed. Sophie suggested that Mama find someone to teach the subjects I'd learn if I attended school. The outcome was Miss Smithson, a young woman newly arrived from the British Isles, who Mama hired to tutor me during the morning hours. In the evenings, Miss Smithson worked for Mama at Wayside Inn.

Miss Smithson was an enthusiastic teacher, and I enjoyed the praise she heaped on me for my achievements. I loved reading, and I devoured books as if I were starving for them. Every week or so, Sophie and I came off our hill and walked to the lending library through the neighborhoods and busy streets lined with shops of every kind. The librarian was a large, grandmotherly woman who smelled of cinnamon and mothballs. Every week, I'd take home the stack of books she'd set aside for me and spend hours reading in the sunny window nook at the end of our hallway.

I enjoyed a fairly well-rounded education between Miss Smithson's efforts and the piano and art lessons I took twice a week from Franny Brant, another of Mama's tenants. Life followed a comfortable, pleasant routine, until Franny Brant had to go to the sanatorium because of the wasting disease, and Miss Smithson quit in order to get married, and my mother decided to send me to school.

It was a rare occasion that my mother ate breakfast in our apartment at Wayside Inn, so when she joined Sophie and me for breakfast one morning I was thrilled. My excitement turned to dread when she spoke of her plan for me to start school the next week. "Rose is ten years old, and she is too much like a little old lady," she said to Sophie. "It is time for her to be around other children."

I was of a different mind. There was nothing I enjoyed more than spending my days tagging around the neighborhood with Sophie, or throwing a ball for Gus, the dog that adopted us, and then curling up somewhere to read. I was horrified by Mama's plans. When I said so, Mama fixed an icy gaze on me and said I wasn't to argue with her but to obey, and that I would go to school starting the next Monday. Mama walked down the hill that morning in a modest, proper gown with a high neck, to enroll me in Madam Pritchard's Youth Academy.

"I won't go," I said to Sophie.

"I'm afraid you don't have a choice, honey. When Liza decides something, there isn't much hope for arguing."

"She hates me, Sophie."

"Your mama wants the best for you, Rose."

I went to my room and slammed the door, spending the next few days moping around in anticipation of going to school, and dwelling on the fact that my mother wasn't affectionate like other mothers with their daughters. Sophie tried to cheer me up, but I was inconsolable.

"Rosie, learning is a wonderful thing! Why, I'd give anything for the opportunity to go to school!

"Then you can go instead of me!"

Sophie's good eye blinked. "I would go in a heartbeat, if I could." The passion in her voice surprised me. "Now, it is considered a privilege to learn, but some day it will be seen as a right."

"I already know how to read. I don't need to go to school. Mama could hire another tutor!"

"You're going to have to accept it, Rose. The decision is made."

"I just won't go!"

"Indeed you will go to school on Monday, young lady. Now stop making yourself and everyone else miserable." She softened her words by patting my shoulder. "It won't be so bad, Rose. Besides, you'll meet some young people your own age. Liza's right about you being in the company of too many old people." It was no use arguing, so I sulked in my bedroom for the rest of the weekend.

At breakfast on the dreaded Monday morning I couldn't stop crying. I felt sorry for myself for losing my carefree life, but worst of all, I was disappointed in my secret hope that Mama would walk me to school on the first day instead of Sophie. I cried harder because I felt I was being disloyal to Sophie, who loved and cared for me so unselfishly.

I could scarcely see because of my tragic weeping. My dear faithful Sophie held my elbow to guide me down the steep hills. After several minutes of tears, Sophie heaved a big sigh and stopped in the middle of the sidewalk. "For heaven's sake, Rose, you better stop crying. We're not more than a few minutes to Madam Pritchard's." Sophie handed me her handkerchief and led me to a low brick wall bordering an empty lot. We sat on it for a few minutes while I finished sobbing. She patted me on the back, and when my tears were dry, she took a package from her handbag and gave it to me. "This is a little something for you, Rosie." I untied the twine and tore off the brown paper wrapping. In my hand was a simple wooden box, narrow and fairly long. "Open it, honey."

I unlatched and raised the lid. Inside was a tidy row of pencils, an ink pen and nibs, a ruler, an eraser, a sharpener, and small box of colored chalk. "Your mama wanted me to give you this pencil box on your way to school. She said, 'Rose is so smart that she'll need the best pencil box in the class.'"

"Really?" I forgot my tears in my astonishment and pleasure over Mama giving me the pencil box. I could picture her beautiful, slender fingers laying the pencils in a tidy row and organizing the contents just so.

"Yes, indeed. Liza knows you'll be the top of your class."

I clutched the box close to my chest, imagining I could feel Mama's love when my fingers touched the smooth wood. It helped me through those first days of school, when I was as shy as my rabbit, Mr. Whiskers, around the other children. Two years before, I'd saved Mr. Whiskers from becoming rabbit stew by throwing a huge tantrum when Sophie was going to chop his head off. Sophie had sighed and ended up killing one of the chickens instead.

On the first day of school I vowed to make Mama proud of me. I threw myself into my studies and excelled in the daily exercises. Every time I used a pen or one of the pencils or the colored chalk for my lessons, I thought of how proud Mama would be. All through the first season I earned high marks in every subject. The tiny French lady who taught art praised my work and used my creations as examples to show the other students. I was dazzled by my success, and I imagined that Mama would be pleased and surprised.

My academic skills were good, but my social skills were lacking. I'd kept company mainly with adults, and the children in my class seemed silly and rough. I longed for a friend but was shy, disappearing to an obscure corner of the playground to read while the others were playing. Mostly everyone left me alone, and I felt lucky to escape the notice of Bobby McPherson, the school bully, and the boys who were in his pack.

A couple of weeks before term reports were to be carried home to parents, I decided to decorate the pencil box in honor of Mama and to show her my handiwork. I practiced writing my name for several days before I inscribed it in my most careful handwriting on the upper right corner of the box, using a special bottle of green ink that Sophie found for me. It smudged a little, but overall, the effect was nice.

More time was spent on finding the perfect cutout pictures showing mother and daughter pairs in matching bonnets, holding hands as they walked or prepared a meal together. There were endless pictures to choose from in the castoff magazines and newspapers of Mama's tenants. I spent a long time considering the possible selections before choosing a few that were best at showing love between mothers and daughters. I glued them on carefully; coordinating the colors of the pictures I'd cut out. It was pretty when it was done, but I worried that the paper cutouts would eventually become smudged. I showed it to the gardener, Shamus, to ask his opinion.

"Why, it needs a coat of clear lacquer over it, and then you've really got something, lass." I let him take it home over the weekend, so he could paint the shiny topcoat on. The following Monday he brought it back, and I thought it was a lovely thing to behold. When it was completely dry and the pens and pencils were back in their neat rows, I showed Sophie. "Why it's just beautiful, Rosie." She gave me a kiss on top of my head before she went back to forming dinner rolls and the long loaves of French bread that were served to the tenants and their guests in the main house. The tenants of Wayside Inn for Gentlewomen had their own cook and kitchen, but Sophie baked all the bread and pastries for both our side and the Inn.

"Do you think I could show it to Mama?"

"Not right now, honey. Liza is busy entertaining some important gentlemen. I'll tell her how pretty you decorated the box. How about that? Then someday, when she isn't quite so busy, you can show her."

I nodded, but when Sophie went off to feed the chickens in our coop out back, I took the key for the connecting door from the drawer where Mama and Sophie always kept it, and I let myself through to the forbidden side of the big house. I was halfway down the long, dimly lit hallway when a door opened. A sweet, flowery fragrance followed a woman in a red silk robe stepping into the hall. I recognized Flora, one of the tenants who always spoke gently to me when we met. She stopped dead in her tracks and said something softly to someone in the room before she closed the door real quick. "Why, if it ain't little Rose! What are you doing here, child?" she asked, pursing her bright colored lips into a cupid's bow.

"I came to show Mama the pencil box she got me when I started school," I said.

Flora bent down and admired my work. "It's real pretty. You're quite the artist, Rosie. Let's find your mama and show her." I followed Flora down the hall to another door that opened into a small parlor, one of several throughout the house. "Wait here, sweet pea, and I'll get Liza," she said, closing the door firmly behind her. I sat on the edge of one of the cushiony armchairs and waited, the little box balanced across my knees.

It wasn't long before Mama swept in. She looked beautiful as always, but I could tell she was angry. "What on earth are you doing here, Rose?"

"Why Mama, I just wanted to show you how I decorated the pencil box you gave me." I held it up for her to see. From her blank, puzzled look, I knew she hadn't set eyes on the box before. Sophie had made up the story about Mama's special gift. My heart sank, and part of my spirit died from the sorrow of the truth.

"That's very pretty work, child. You say you decorated it yourself?" Mama looked it over and handed it back to me. "You spent a lot of time working on it. You'd be better off studying your books. It's a pretty thing, though." I turned away so she wouldn't see the tears running down the sides of my nose. I brushed them away quickly with the back of my hand. "All right, Rose, it's time for you to go home. You know you're not supposed to come to this side of the house unless you're given permission."

"Yes, Mama."

"Well, run along now."

I could feel Mama watching me as I retraced my steps down the hallway to the connecting door. Sophie had returned from feeding the chickens. She was surprised when I came through the door. "What in the heck are you doing, Rose? You know better than to go over there," she said. Without a word I put the key back in the drawer, laid the pencil box on the countertop, and went straight to my bedroom. I didn't want to talk to Sophie; she was the cause of my unreasonable hopes from the lie she'd told about Mama giving me the pencil box. When Sophie came to check on me, I told her to stay out. I went to bed without any supper and cried myself to sleep.

In the morning, Sophie woke me for school. "Rose, I'm sorry about tellin' you your mama got you that pencil box. I been thinking about it, and it was the wrong thing to do. I just wanted you to be happy on your first day of school. Can you ever forgive me, Rosebud?"

I hugged Sophie and told her I forgave her. It was impossible to hold a grudge against Sophie, but my heart did harden more against Mama; we were like two fortresses, remote and defensive. Sophie fed me an egg and toast and sent me on my way to school. The handsome satchel Sophie had made for my school things bumped against my leg. It was heavy with a bag lunch, a jar of milk, my notebook and the pencil box that had broken my heart. I walked slowly, dawdling because of my melancholy thoughts. I stopped at the same low wall where Sophie had given me the pencil box. I sat on the wall, and from the satchel I pulled the pencil box to look at the contents I'd foolishly believed were placed there by my mother. Finally, I shut it and slid the little latch closed.

A tear fell from my eye, and I impatiently brushed it away. I will not cry about Mama ever again, I thought. I stood up, intending to throw the pencil box into the bushes. From the higher vantage point gained by stepping up on the low wall, I saw in the corner of the empty lot two quite dirty children; a girl around my age and a little boy whose resemblance to the girl made it clear he was her younger brother. They were sitting on a flat stoop that was the only standing part of what appeared to have been a cabin. The rest of it lay in a few piles of rotting boards that hadn't been worth hauling off. When the children saw me, they waved and gestured for me to come over. I collected my satchel and stepped over the debris to join them.

The girl rose from the stoop and stared at me through crisp blue eyes older than her years. "Excuse me, Miss. Do you have anything to eat in your handbag? My brother and I haven't eaten since Saturday afternoon." I set the pencil box down and rooted through the carryall to find the paper lunch sack Sophie always packed for me. In it were ham salad sandwiches and oatmeal cookies. I wondered if Sophie really thought I would eat two large sandwiches and half a dozen cookies. She knew I had a peckish appetite, but today I was glad Sophie packed a lot because the girl and her brother looked hungry. I handed over the sack, which they tore at eagerly, reminding me of a pair of hungry dogs. I gave them the jar of milk to wash everything down, and when they were done the girl laid a grubby hand on my arm and thanked me.

"God bless you, Miss. We were awfully hungry."

"Where are your parents? They should feed you enough so you aren't hungry."

"This was our house until it fell down a couple of years ago." The girl indicated it with a sweep of her thin arm. "Our daddy died of the drink, and Ma works as a live-in maid to get by. She's renting a room for us down the street, over the Chinese laundry. Ma comes by to check on us as much as she can."

I couldn't think of anything to say, so I just nodded.

"My name is Kitty, and my brother is Joseph."

I introduced myself, and said I had to go to school or I'd be late. They both thanked me again for the sandwiches, and I started down the hill. When I realized I was still carrying the pencil box, I ran back and gave it to Kitty, along with my exercise book full of blank paper. Her mouth fell open. "We couldn't take this. It's too pretty," she said, but I insisted. I glanced over my shoulder as I resumed my trek down the hill; they were bent over the notebook, each with a piece of colored chalk. Kitty looked up and waved, and I felt the warmth of friendship from a girl of my own age, which, as a solitary child, had eluded me.

At school I was scolded for being late on the first day of the new term. We had switched teachers, and Miss Russell, a stern woman with thin lips and a ramrod-straight spine, made me sit at the desk in front of class that was usually reserved for the bad boys who threw spitballs and interrupted lessons. Since I'd given away my pencil box and exercise book, I had nothing to write with. Miss Russell, eagle-eyed, soon noticed I was empty-handed. "Why aren't you doing your work, Miss Laurent?" she asked.

"I lost my pencil box," I said.

Miss Russell's eyes widened. "No pencil you say?" I shook my head, and a wave of apprehension moved down my spine.

"Come to my desk right now. Children, your attention please." Miss Russell made me stand at the front of the class as she whacked my hand three times with her wooden ruler. It hurt but I didn't show it; I clenched my teeth and stared straight ahead. "Take this as a lesson in preparation, children," said Miss Russell. "Miss Laurent will sit here all day where others can observe, with disdain, her idleness. To arrive without a student's tools is pure folly."

At lunchtime, I was finally allowed to leave my seat and go out to the schoolyard with my classmates. I sat by myself at one of the picnic tables in a shady corner. The other girls and boys whispered and pointed at me. Bobby McPherson, an older, brutish boy and a notorious bully, accosted me as I sat alone, my stomach growling for one of the ham salad sandwiches I'd given away to Kitty and Joseph.

"My pop says your ma is nothing but a lady of the night in a cat house. I heard she's too busy humpin' to give her kid a pencil to take to school."

"That isn't true," I said. At the time, I didn't know what a cat house was or what humping meant. Sophie told me later.

"It is too true," he said loudly. "Instead of Rose Laurent, you should be called Rose Low Rent." He broke into a loud guffaw and yelled out "Rose Low Rent, Rose Low Rent. Her mama gotta run a cat house to pay the rent." I stared straight ahead with the blank gaze I'd used when Miss Russell punished me. Two other boys, followers of Bobby, joined him as he stood taunting me. "Rose isn't a girl, she's a cat from a cat house," Bobby announced. "Go on, Rose Low Rent, give a meow." I pretended they were invisible while he and the other boys meowed and hissed.

The yowls grew in volume and soon drew the attention of my classmates. A few of the girls looked at me sympathetically, but most of the boys and girls joined in, meowing and hissing like a big cat fight was going on. I was suffering from terrible humiliation and rage. I bit my tongue to stop from screaming that the whole bunch of them were hateful halfwits. Instead, I stared straight ahead with that same expressionless stare, until my lack of reaction became boring to those who taunted me. Though I didn't show it, I was relieved when Miss Russell summoned us to our afternoon lessons. For the rest of the day I sat at the dunce's desk and prayed for the final bell to ring.

The next morning, I walked towards Madam Pritchard's Academy, but instead of going to school, I joined Kitty and Joseph and spent the day talking and playing jacks with them in the empty lot. Going to school after that was out of the question. I spent school hours with Kitty and Joseph, exploring the parts of the city that we could walk to. We had a carefree time the three of us, sharing a hot cinnamon bun or a dozen fresh shrimp bought with the coins I'd stolen from the coin jar in the kitchen. I told Sophie I was especially hungry and could eat three sandwiches. She raised her eyebrows and muttered about me having a hollow leg for such a short person, but she packed the lunch sack full every morning. While it lasted, Kitty and Joseph could depend on at least one good meal a day.

After nearly six weeks of truancy, Miss Russell came looking for me. It was late in the afternoon; at least two hours since the dismissal bell had rung at Madam Pritchard's Youth Academy. I was in the kitchen visiting with Sophie. I about jumped out of my chair when I looked up and saw Miss Russell's face pressed against the window. Her eyes latched on mine, and I could see their mean glitter through the glass. I knew I was in trouble, and while Sophie was letting her in, I ran up the stairs to my bedroom and locked the door.

A half an hour later, Sophie called me from the bottom of the stairs. "She's gone. Now, young lady, you come on out of your room this minute! Get yourself downstairs, because we need to talk, you and me."

I don't know what got into me. Instead of obeying Sophie as

I usually did, I opened the door and yelled down, "You can't make me come out! You're not my mother!" I slammed the door shut for punctuation and locked it just in case she came up the stairs to try the knob, which she didn't. The better part of an hour passed; I grew increasingly apprehensive. Finally, a firm knock on my bedroom door made my heart race. It was Liza herself.

There is something commanding about Mama's voice. "Rose, I need you to come out please, and no dilly-dallying. Do you hear me?"

I knew I'd better open the door or I'd be in bigger trouble yet. When I emerged, Mama turned without a word, and I followed her down the stairs and into the kitchen. Sophie had her back towards us, and she didn't even glance over her shoulder when we came in. A surge of love for Sophie came over me, and I suddenly regretted my angry words, but I remained silent.

"Sit down, Rose," said Mama. "You have some explaining to do, about why you've been lying and pretending to go to school."

"What does it matter? Since when do you care about anything I do?" My voice was insolent, but inside I wanted to throw my arms around her, and for once have the warmth of her arms around me. Instead, Mama slapped me across the face. I jumped up and stormed out of the kitchen, right up the stairs to my room. "I hate you!" I screamed from the top of the stairs. I locked my door, and leaned against it, rubbing the cheek that burned where Mama slapped me. Mama and Sophie were still talking in the kitchen, but I couldn't quite make out what they were saying. Using my old trick, I pressed my ear against the heating vent, and I could hear them perfectly, though their voices sounded a little tinny.

"Why in hell did you slap that child, Liza?" I could tell that Sophie was mad because of how she gets gravel in her voice when she's hopped up.

"It's none of your business, Sophie. You aren't her mother, after all!"

"That's the second time I heard that tonight, once from Rose, and now from you. Well, maybe it's a hint for me that I'm not needed here. Maybe I should just disappear and let you step up and be a mother for a change!"

"Maybe you should!" Mama's tone of voice was shrill, and I could picture her, red in the face with her eyebrows knit together like they do when she is in a foul temper.

"Don't you see, Liza? Rose is hurting inside from the way you act toward her. You're set on your own reasons, and you've gotten too selfish to realize that she's just a little girl who wants her ma to love her. And you hit the poor girl across the cheek and make her feel worse!"

"I tell you, that's enough, Sophie."

"And I'll tell you, it sure isn't enough! You better take note of yourself. You've gotten so hard you're ready to break ice! This Liza Laurent you invented when we got here all those years ago isn't the same Lizzie that I grew up with, and I miss her. I'm not so sure if I always like you anymore!" Mama said something softly that I couldn't hear even though I pressed my ear closer to the grate. After a few minutes I heard the connecting door close. Mama had gone back to her side of the house.

I waited for a long time before creeping down the stairs and into the kitchen. Sophie was sitting in the rocking chair. Without a word, she lifted her arms to me, and I went to her. She pulled me down onto her lap. I burst into tears and threw my arms around her, burying my face in her soft bosom. "I'm so sorry, Sophie, for what I said."

"It's all right, Rosebud. You know I'll always love you, no matter what."

That made me cry harder. Sophie patted my back soothingly, as if she were burping a baby. "I love you, too," I said, finally.

Sophie kissed my cheek. "Let's get you some supper, seeing as how you missed yours tonight."

I climbed from her lap and sat at the table while she heated up a saucepan of soup. "Sophie, why does Mama hate me?"

"Liza loves you honey. She just has a hard time showing it. I know it makes you suffer, Rose. Your mama has had some troubles that have made her tough, but down deep she loves you more than any other living being. Be patient, Rose. Someday she'll soften up."

I've been waiting for Mama's softening my whole life.

At the end of breakfast the next morning, Mama fetched me from the kitchen. She'd decided to escort me to Madam Pritchard's Academy. "It's obvious that you can pull the wool over Sophie's eyes, but you're not getting a chance to skip school today." Sophie harrumphed in the background. Mama didn't even glance in her direction. "Now get your things, and let's go. Don't dawdle, child. We have an appointment with Miss Russell before school begins."

I collected my satchel and an umbrella for the misty morning fog, and Mama and I walked down the hill, with me trailing behind. She looked elegant in her purple wool duster. I admired her willowy figure, swaying gently from side to side. Every so often she would stop to lecture me, and though she was cross sounding, I was thrilled in a deep part of my heart that Mama was paying attention to me.

"You will attend every day from now on, and if I hear of bad behavior you will be punished, Rose. Is that clear?"

"Yes Ma'am." We walked on in silence until we came to the sidewalk in front of Kitty and Joseph's empty lot. They were waiting for me on the steps of the ruined cabin, as they'd done every day for the last few weeks.

"Wait a minute, Mama. I have to speak to some friends." Before she could protest, I jumped onto the low wall and ran across the lot. From my satchel, I pulled the package of sandwiches Sophie had packed for my lunch. I handed it to Kitty. "I was caught for ditching school, and now my mother is making me go back. I might not be able to see you for a while."

Kitty's face fell. "Joseph and I won't have near as much fun without you." She squeezed my hand. "I'll miss you, Rose." Her face brightened. "Maybe we can meet you here after your school lets out."

"I'll see if Mama will let me." I squeezed her hand back.

Mama, tapping her foot impatiently, called from where she stood on the sidewalk. "Hurry Rose. We're nearly late already!"

I said goodbye to my friends and joined her. "Who are those children?" she asked.

"Some friends I play with."

"Why aren't they in school?"

I explained about Kitty and Joseph's mother working her fingers to the bone, so they could stay in their cramped apartment over the Chinese Laundry. "She doesn't have enough money to send them to school."

"I'm sure there are more appropriate children at your school than these beggars you choose to befriend."

"There isn't a soul at school who is nice like Kitty and Joseph," I said to Mama's back. She didn't reply, and we walked the rest of the way to Madam Pritchard's Academy without speaking.

Miss Russell was waiting for us in her classroom. She ushered us in, and we sat down in the desks she'd drawn together for our interview. "Now Rose, what do you have to say for yourself?" she asked.

"Nothing, Ma'am," I replied.

"Rose has shown her defiance and disobedience by her actions at school," said my mother to Miss Russell. "I apologize for her behavior. I fear that Rose takes after her father, who, I am sorry to say, was a wicked man."

Mama's words felt like a fist hitting me, and I shrank into my chair, mortified. Miss Russell hadn't warmed to me before. She nodded enthusiastically, and her lips curled in a mean little smile. "I will keep a tight rein on Rose." My mother and Miss Russell shook hands, and Mama walked out as my classmates came in to take their seats. I saw Bobby McPherson, my tormentor, nudge one of his friends to point out my elegant mother in her long purple coat. They stared at her boldly as she passed them in the doorway, but Mama didn't notice. A few minutes later, Bobby meowed softly as he passed my seat. I sighed. Nothing had changed at Madam Pritchard's.

While my classmates were mostly neutral before, Bobby had spread the news about the type of business Mama conducted at Wayside Inn, and the girls whispered behind their hands and held their hankies to their noses when they passed by. Out on the grounds, when none of the teachers were in attendance, Bobby and his gang taunted me. It was the same meowing and catcalls, which I mostly ignored. I lived for the moment when the final bell rang, and I could go visit Kitty and Joseph and play jacks with them on the stoop. I saved something from my lunch every day, and I asked Sophie to pack extra, so my friends had something to eat.

The rains fell heavily that winter and I saw Kitty and Joseph less often. When they could venture out, I'd find them on the stoop under a big, shabby umbrella, waiting. My two friends were the reason I lasted at Madam Pritchard's as long as I did. The thought of seeing them after school was the only happiness in my day. I had come to hate school with all of my being.

Though I was polite and always had the correct answer when she called on me, I knew that Miss Russell, who disliked and distrusted all children, particularly disliked me. She often accused me of making some sort of mischief and sent me to sit in the desk reserved for troublemakers, though I was never guilty of whatever she accused me of. My classmates stayed clear of me like I had a disease, giggling and whispering whenever I was near, wrinkling up their noses. "Do I smell cat piss?" Bobby said loudly at every chance, and the others would giggle in appreciation of Bobby's high good humor. My humiliation and rage deepened.

At night, thoughts of Bobby and my classmates tortured me. I woke tired from the battles I had in my dreams, and consequently I faced each school day with weary trepidation. I pleaded with Sophie that I was ill and needed to stay home, but Mama wouldn't budge. "Unless she has a fever, Rose will go to school like all the other children. I expect you to follow my wishes in this matter, Sophie." And Sophie did obey Mama, seeing through my pretend colds and ignoring the real apprehension that caused my stomach to cramp every morning.

From my troubles, a bitter spirit grew. I'd been a tender-natured child, inclined to be quiet and well behaved; now, however, the force of hatred for Bobby and his friends built a fortress inside me. My dreams turned to shadowy scenes in which I punished my tormentors until they begged for mercy. In those dreams, the seeds of revenge were sown, and I resolved to somehow put an end to Bobby's bullying.

Kitty and Joseph were on the stoop when I passed by on my way home from school. It was a warm afternoon, surprising for so early in the spring, and Kitty suggested that we walk to China Town. "I found two bits in the gutter." She held up a coin. "I'll buy us some egg rolls."

Both Sophie and Mama had forbidden me to go to China Town alone because of all the gambling houses and saloons along the way. Newspapers reported stories about gunfire and murders in the barrooms and gambling dens. The most violent brawls happened when the moon was full, when the men were crazy with moon-sickness. "There's always someone getting shot in that part of town," said Sophie. "I've heard they kidnap girls and do who knows what to them. You must not go near that area. It's best to avoid it, Rose." I thought of Sophie's advice, but I didn't want to disappoint my friends.

"Eggrolls would sure taste good," I said, and we headed down the hill toward the south side of town. It was twelve long blocks before we reached our shortcut: the turn leading past a long row of drinking establishments and Faro parlors. The roughness and lively vigor of the gambling section was fascinating. It was bursting with humanity, mostly men of all shapes and colors, and sometimes a woman in cheap finery would walk by on the elbow of a freshly shaved gentleman ready to make or break the bank. Excitement rippled through the air. In the rumble of voices, I could hear guffaws of boisterous laughter. Outside, men smoked on the street, lingering over conversations spoken in many different languages.

We were near the entrance to one of the gambling houses when the door burst open. A sharp smell of stale alcohol blew out, followed by a man who rubbed his eyes and blinked as if blinded by the daylight after hours in the dark saloon. He paused for a moment, long enough for two men to tackle him from behind. I trailed after Kitty as she pulled Joseph across the street to an empty storefront where we watched the three men fighting fiercely on the sidewalk in front of the bar. More men poured out of the saloon doors, and soon the sidewalk writhed with arms and legs throwing punches and kicks. A shiny object flew from the center of the battle and landed in a dusty corner where the steps to the bar met the sidewalk.

It wasn't long before a pair of policemen showed up on foot, followed by two mounted deputies and the carriage used to take people to jail. Many of the fighters fled, leaving only those who were too beaten up or too drunk to run. The police loaded the few men remaining into the paddy wagon and drove off. The bartender, a hefty man in a fancy silk shirt and a brocade vest stretched tightly across his stomach, threw a bucket of water on the sidewalk to wash off the blood in front of the door. It was clear that our entertainment was over.

Kitty and Joseph followed as I dashed across the street. I kneeled on the sidewalk and drew my fingers through the dust where I'd seen the shiny object land. My hand came in contact with something hard, and I pulled up a knife opened to a sharp blade. Joseph showed me how to push a button, so I could fold the blade into its sheath.

"That's what they call a switch blade. You can kill somebody with it 'cause it doesn't fold up like a regular pocketknife," the little boy said. I wondered how he came by his information, but I didn't ask. Joseph handed the knife back to me. "What are you going to do with it?"

I considered taking the knife into the bar to give to the bartender in case the owner turned up looking for his lost property, but after a moment I slipped it into my school satchel. "I'm sure Shamus, our gardener, could use a knife like this," I told Joseph, and I forgot about it until the following day.

After the usual morning studies Miss Russell announced lunch hour, dismissing class by ringing a little hand bell. I gathered my satchel and coat from the hat room and went directly to a picnic table off by itself around the side of the school grounds where the younger classes played. I'd started eating my lunch there a few days ago and had so far been left alone by Bobby and his gang. I was relieved and hoped that being out of sight translated into being out of mind. Maybe my chief tormentor would forget about me.

My relief was fleeting, for no sooner had I sat down and opened my satchel when Bobby and two of his rough-mannered friends sauntered around the side of the school building and over to the table where I sat. Apprehension rose in my stomach, sending a sour taste to my mouth. The isolation of the picnic table, which had been a haven until now, was suddenly terrifying. The younger children's lunch period was held before ours, leaving the yard on that side abandoned. I was alone with Bobby and his friends.

I rose from the table, gripping my school bag in front of me. I tried to leave but was prevented by the boys who surrounded me in a half circle. Bobby faced me in the middle. "Where do you think you're going, Rose Low Rent?" Bobby pushed me roughly so that I sat back on the picnic table bench. "We was just coming over to visit with you."

"Why don't you go pick on someone your own size!" I said, struggling up to my feet and trying to break through the barrier created by the three boys, but Bobby was tall and strong, and he held me fast.

"I been wanting to see what goes on in a cat house. My uncle told me that all the women up there who work for your mama, they let men stick their peckers into their pussies. My uncle said that pussy stinks. What does your pussy smell like, Rose?"

Bobbie's friends grabbed my arms and held me as Bobby lifted me up and pushed me back on the top of the picnic table. Though I screamed and kicked, no one came to stop the boys as my skirt was pulled above my waist. Bobby grasped my girl's undergarment and wiggled it down until it was around my thighs. While the boys pinioned me, Bobby thrust one of his fingers into my private part. The pain was fierce, and I screamed again.

The boys let me go suddenly, and I jumped up and did as best I could to tug up my undergarments. Bobby made an elaborate show of sniffing the finger he'd stuck in me. "Now I know what pussy smells like." He laughed and turned his back on me, holding the finger out to his two friends. "Do you want to smell it?"

A force beyond conscious choice possessed me to reach into my satchel and grab the knife I'd found the day before. The blade sprang into place when I pressed the button Joseph had pointed out. With a rage that surprised me as much as it startled the three boys, I lunged after Bobby and stabbed the knife into his back as hard as I could, not once but twice. Splotches of blood blossomed against the white shirt, growing larger as the wounds oozed. "Jesus, I'm bleeding to death. The crazy little bitch tried to kill me!" he cried. With his friends at his side Bobby hobbled away, disappearing around the corner to the large playground where the voices of our classmates tinkled faintly.

I straightened my undergarments, pulled my skirts down and gathered my satchel. I wondered what would happen when Miss

Russell heard I'd stabbed Bobby. I decided I wouldn't wait to find out. I picked up the switch knife, closed it and threw it into the thorny patch of blackberries growing alongside the fence. I let myself out the back gate and walked away, vowing to never again set foot on the grounds of Madam Pritchard's Academy. In that vow, my wishes were fulfilled. The cost, though, was my banishment from everything and everyone I loved.

Mother has decided to send me off to Most Holy Name School, which is run by Catholic nuns. I have to board there during the term, except for holidays, because it's far away from San Francisco and Wayside Inn for Gentlewomen and my best and only friends, Kitty and Joseph, and dearest Sophie. I will miss Kitty and Sophie terribly. I might even miss Mama a little, but I wouldn't say so for the world. I suspect that letting her know how much I love her and crave her attention makes her draw away even more, until someday I fear she won't be there at all. It stands to reason that I am mostly like a rock around Mama, stony and quiet.

I learned from eavesdropping on a fight between Sophie and Mama that I was being sent away. It was a couple of days after Miss Russell told Mama that I'd stabbed Bobbie. Mama and Sophie were in the kitchen of our apartment, and I could hear them yelling up a storm through the heat vent in my bedroom.

"Rose has really done it this time! I can't afford the gossip that I'm sure is being spread by her troubles at school. Attacking the boy is the last straw!"

"Will you for once in your life stick up for Rose? Why don't you ask for her side of the story? The way you act, you're no better than a hanging judge!"

"I've decided to send her away to a convent school. Maybe the nuns can civilize her. As it stands now, the child is obviously a savage."

Sophie begged my mother to let me stay at home, but she

refused to budge. "I don't care what you say, Sophie! You're to blame for spoiling Rose. What she needs is a firm hand." I heard the connecting door from the kitchen to the Inn slammed shut and I knew that Mama's say was final. My days of living peacefully with Sophie in the back apartment at Wayside were over.

Sophie Washington
San Francisco
April 1871

Rose's troubles were like a bad toothache that keeps getting worse until the sufferer is practically begging to have the damn tooth pulled. When she stabbed the boy at school, I was shocked. It hit me over the head like a hammer, seeing as Rose didn't tell me until later what had been going on at Madam Pritchard's Youth Academy. It was really my fault, because I hadn't been listening to Rose, nor encouraging her to talk about school and her problems. Liza warned me not to let Rose complain. "It just gives her encouragement, Sophie. Rose must learn to fit in. You mollycoddle her too much."

There's nothing to excuse my neglect. In failing to realize the torments Rose faced at that awful school, I am to blame. I turned a deaf ear on Rose's pain. I was sick and tired of listening to Liza tell me how to raise her child, and what I should and shouldn't do. I longed for my own sons who would be young men soon, with faces I might not recognize as much as I swore to myself I'd never forget them. Though I never abandoned her, I took a step away from Rose. If I hadn't, things might have turned out differently.

Months before the stabbing incident, when Rose was caught skipping school, Liza laid down the law. "You've been deceiving us,

Rose, by pretending to go to school. From now on I expect you to be where you are supposed to be."

The next morning, Liza surprised us all by walking Rose down the hill to Madam Pritchard's. Being the center of Liza's attention was a rare thrill; it didn't matter to Rose that it was because she was in hot water with her mother. When Liza didn't show up to escort her to school the following morning, Rose was obviously crushed. It was one of her many disappointments. After that, I followed Liza's orders, walking Rose directly to the door of her classroom. "Whether she complains that the fires of hell are burning her feet, she is going to attend school!" said Liza. I felt sorry for poor Rose, but I couldn't get around it: Liza was the real mama, so I glossed over Rose's troubles when she came home and tried to tell me about her day. Finally, she just stopped talking.

A few months after Rose was born, Liza marched me down to the city offices to fill out all the proper legal papers for my emancipation. Liza got a bug under her bonnet to declare me a free woman after she read Uncle Tom's Cabin aloud in the evenings while Verna and I sewed or ironed the endless laundry. The three of us had tears in our eyes practically every time she read, it was so sad. When it got to the part about Cassy killing a third child, so she wouldn't be sold into slavery like her other two children, I nearly collapsed from crying. It made me think of Jules and Augie, and I could feel every terrible thing Cassy went through.

When Tom got beaten to death, Verna, Liza, and I sobbed with our arms around each other. "Slavery should never have happened in the first place," said Verna. "It ain't right for any human being to have such power over other folks!"

"It's past time for an ugly practice to die," Liza declared. "We're going to the courthouse tomorrow, Sophie. It's time for you to get rid of the name 'slave.' "

True to her word we took a Hansom cab across town to the court, and a week later I was declared a free woman in front of the civil court judge. To celebrate, Liza poured champagne for Verna, me, and the tenants, and she made shrimp gumbo served over rice. Though the gumbo was missing an ingredient or two, it was darn tasty. It reminded me of home. Rosie put an end to the celebration when she woke up from her nap and started crying. Life went back to normal; I was a free woman doing exactly what I'd done before, except now I didn't have the demeaning title of slave staining my good name.

Mr. Lincoln's war started not long after my freedom was granted. Fortunately for us, the war pretty much stayed out of San Francisco. Articles and editorials against slavery appeared in the local newspapers, and a couple of days a week an abolitionist group handed out anti-slavery pamphlets on busy street corners, but no battles were fought in California.

The foreigners who came to seek their fortunes in the gold fields brought ideas from far and wide. All those opinions and the mixing between cultures made San Francisco a whole lot more open in its thinking than folks back home. Most everyone in the city sympathized with the North and favored the abolition of slavery. It was refreshing to be in a place where most of the folks are for your cause, rather than against it.

Over the course of the war, hundreds of men from San Francisco joined the army or navy and left to fight on the Eastern battlefields. California was so far away from the fighting we could almost forget there was a war at all, except when one of the soldiers came home dead. That always meant a big hullaballoo with a parade and a 21-gun salute.

I followed every bit of news on the war that I could find. Liza kept newspapers for her clientele, and she'd drop them off in the apartment kitchen for me to read. The news was always old by the time we got it; nevertheless, I kept a map for marking the battles and the number of casualties. I looked anxiously for anything that might be a danger to my family back home. The letters I sent to Mama and Daddy and Jerome were never answered, and I wondered if they were alive and well. I missed my mother something fierce and would often hear her wise voice in my mind. It comforted me.

It was a victory to be declared a free person; however, nothing much changed. I'd been free in everything but name since we'd left Sweetbrier. Liza never treated me like a slave; we'd grown up as sisters and friends. Liza and I were a team. She needed me to be her confessor and the mother to her little girl; Liza's part was paying the bills and providing us with a home. She didn't mind using that point whenever our arguments jumped the line into real fights, when I'd threaten to go off on my own and take Rose with me. "Don't forget where your groceries and your nice, cozy apartment come from, Sophie."

"And you don't forget that I'm a full-time nanny to your daughter. I earn my living, and you know it."

"You're spoiling Rose, and it isn't improving her character! She needs a firm hand. She's got her father in her, mark my words!"

"She isn't one bit like him, and you're crazy to suggest it!" We'd end these arguments by giving each other dirty looks, and then Liza would sweep out like a queen, her fancy skirts leaving little trails where the floor was dusty, banging shut the connecting door to mark her exit.

After Rose was born, and Liza's personality got so bitter, there was a lot more bickering between us. Sometimes our fights were bad enough that we wouldn't talk to each other for days, but pretty soon Liza'd come around with a tin of my favorite tea and a bar of sweet chocolate, and we'd make up and be friends again until the next battle.

We had a humdinger of a fight over Rose stabbing that terrible boy. Though I hadn't yet heard the story from her own mouth, I knew in my gut she had merely taken justice into her own hands.

To Liza, the stabbing was proof that Rose was the resurrection of her father. "Rose's wicked nature must be tamed once and for all," she said, and there was no argument or proof I offered that convinced her otherwise. Something in Liza was determined to find fault with her daughter, there was no getting around it, just like there was no way to stop her from sending Rose away. Stabbing the boy was the last straw, even if Rose did it to defend herself.

I can picture the day clearly; the fog burned off early for a change, and folks were out in the fresh air when I took my walk in the morning. The neighbor down the block, a sweet white-haired woman, gave me extra seedlings that had come up in her garden. "The smaller ones are marigolds," she said, "and the others are petunias." I took the pots of seedlings and thanked her.

The day passed with my usual chores and the afternoon nap I was in the habit of taking. Rose wasn't home when I woke up around four, but I suspected she was visiting her friend Kitty and didn't think much of it. The seedlings I'd been given were on the porch waiting to be planted. I put on my gloves and took a trowel and the seedlings to the front of the Inn.

The trees in the yard were full of songbirds, and the day had warmed up enough so I was comfortable in my shirtsleeves. I got busy planting and was lost in my thoughts when, out of the corner of my good eye, I saw Rose's teacher, Miss Russell, approaching like a storm cloud. She was perspiring from the climb up the hill, and she had a mean look on her face. No wonder Rose dislikes her, I thought.

My intuition told me there was trouble coming. I stood up and nodded to her as she passed. Though I was in plain view, Miss Russell walked right by, pretending she didn't see me. She dabbed the perspiration off her face with a handkerchief before she clip-clopped in her dainty heeled boots up the stairs to the front door of Wayside Inn. The sharp sound of the doorknocker brought one of Liza's girls to the door. She stuck her head out.

"We aren't taking any new tenants right now." The girl started to shut the door, but Miss Russell held onto the knob and spoke sternly.

"I'm here to speak to Mrs. Laurent about an important matter."

"Just a minute, please. I'll see if she is available." The door closed.

"Is there something I can help you with?" I asked.

"I must speak directly with Rose's mother." She tapped her foot impatiently until Liza, gowned in one of her fancy lounging costumes, came out onto the porch.

"Why hello, Miss Russell. What a surprise to see you."

Miss Russell spoke abruptly. "As before, it is your daughter who brings me here. During lunch today, Rose used a weapon to attack one of the other students. Afterwards, she ran off from school." Miss Russell pulled a knife from her handbag and held it up for inspection. "One of the children found this in the berry patch. It still has blood on it."

My mouth dropped open so wide a bumblebee could have flown in. Rose was a gentle child, and I couldn't imagine her raising a hand to hurt another person.

I stood up from the garden with my trowel in hand. "Rose did what?"

Miss Russell ignored me. "Mrs. Laurent, is Rose here? I'd like to speak to her."

"Rose hasn't come home yet," I said.

She frowned at me before directing her gaze back to Liza. "I must speak frankly; Rose is not welcome back at Madam Pritchard's Academy. It isn't often that we expel a student, but committing physical violence cannot be ignored."

I waited for Liza to defend Rose, but she was still and silent, like a rock. That describes Liza's attitude toward Rose perfectly: cold as a stone toward her own flesh and blood. At times it makes me want to slap her.

"What exactly happened that made Rose mad enough to do what you say she did?" I couldn't stop myself from blurting out.

Miss Russell ignored me as if I hadn't spoken. "The boy was bleeding badly enough that he was taken to a doctor's clinic for stitches. His father is very angry and says he expects you to pay the bill, Mrs. Laurent." Miss Russell took an envelope from her bag. "Whatever harmless teasing took place on the school grounds does not in any way justify stabbing a classmate with a knife. Such violence in a child indicates an evil streak, or perhaps bad blood."

Miss Russell handed Liza the envelope. "I've prepared a short list of boarding schools within a hundred-mile range of San Francisco. I thought you might want to explore the option of enrolling Rose in an institution that provides an environment designed to tame the wickedness of an out-of-control child." Liza took the envelope and nodded. My heart jumped in my chest. *"How dare you suggest sending my darling Rose away!"* I thought, but I kept my mouth closed because I knew whatever I had to say didn't matter. We had entered a new stage in our lives, and from that day on, Rose's path was out of my control.

Rose never came home that night. By morning I was frantic, pacing the kitchen until I wore a worry path from end to end. Liza came through the connecting door around eight in the morning, which was early for her. In spite of the dark circles under her eyes, Liza looked elegant in a white silk dressing gown. The Inn was often host to parties that went on when most folks are tucked in bed. The girls burned the candle at both ends, and the men and the money kept rolling in. Wayside girls were loyal; they respected Liza. She paid well, was fair, and she had a knack for making life at the Inn entertaining to all.

"Where is Rose?" she demanded without so much as a hello.

"I'd like to know the answer to the same question," I said. "She didn't come home last night. I'm worried to death!"

A flicker of concern crossed Liza's pretty face, but it was immediately replaced by a look of irritation. "Oh my heavens! What next?" She sighed and shook her head. "I'll have the girls go door to door to ask if anyone has seen her. If nothing turns up, I'll send someone to notify the police." Liza's toe got busy tapping, which is a habit of hers when she's rubbed the wrong way. "This is just one more reason to send Rose to boarding school. She is proving to be unmanageable!"

"The way you talk about Rosie tells me you don't know her for the wonderful person she is! You act like she's something to get rid of. Someday you're going to regret what you're doing to your only child! And now she's gone off to who knows where! Anything could happen to her!"

Liza's face flushed red as a beet, and I knew I'd gotten to her, but all she said was I'd better get going looking for Rose if I was so worried. "I certainly have no idea where she went. Maybe she slept on a bench. You might try the new park across from the cathedral."

Suddenly a light went on in my memory, and I knew where to find Rose. Several weeks ago, on a shopping trip to buy candied gingerroot, I remembered seeing Rose in Chinatown with her friends, Kitty and Joseph. They were stepping onto the sidewalk from a door tucked in the middle of a row of storefronts, next door to a laundry service. I waved from across the street, but they didn't see me. The three of them walked off in a hurry and were quickly out of sight. When I asked Rose about it, she said her friends lived in an apartment above the laundry.

"I think I know where she is, Liza. Don't send for the police quite yet." I pulled on a coat to keep off the misty fog. "You ought to do some deep thinking about why you're treating Rose so poorly. It's a crying shame!" I closed the door softly, leaving Liza with a stricken look. Good, I thought. Maybe she's finally feeling guilty about the way she acts.

My heart was heavy, and you'd think it would slow me down, but I was so mad at Liza, I walked all the way to Chinatown in half the time it usually took. Once there, I threaded my way through the maze of streets and alleyways, hoping and praying to find the door where I'd seen Rose and her friends.

Rose Laurent
San Francisco
April 1871

Sophie found me with Kitty and Joseph, sleeping on the floor of their single room above Mi Ling's Laundry. I would never have come home on my own if it hadn't been for Sophie swallowing me in a hug, her good eye tearing up from happiness that I was alive and well. "Oh Rosie, honey! I'm so glad you didn't come to harm! They've been capturing girls and selling them to be used by wicked men. There are stories in the news every week! Don't you ever, ever disappear again! Do you hear me?" She hugged me tight. I hugged her back, forgetting for a minute my anger at her for not understanding the depths of my troubles at Madame Pritchard's Academy.

Sophie made me change my clothes the minute we got home. "And bring what you're wearing now downstairs for me to wash. Who knows what kind of bugs and diseases are hiding in that closet of an apartment your friends are living in."

"Their room is actually very clean. It's the fish market on one side and the laundry on the other that make it smell so bad," I said. "Kitty says you get used to it after a while."

"Nevertheless, go on now; change your clothes and wash up. There's a fresh basin of water in the washroom."

I dragged myself up the stairs, and after I'd washed my face and hands I changed into a dark gray dress suitable for church or funerals; the color of it matched my grim mood. Sophie set the table while I was changing, and a bowl of chicken soup steamed invitingly. The delicious smell of it made my mouth water. I took one spoonful and followed it with a second when Mama burst through the connecting door. I could see she was on the warpath by her eyes; they glittered anger like a diamond throws sparks of light when the sun shines through it.

"Where have you been, young lady?"

"What do you care?" My voice sounded insolent even to me.

"How dare you speak to me like that!"

"I'm just telling the truth. If I got kicked in the head by a horse, I bet you wouldn't blink an eye."

Mama hauled off and slapped me hard on the cheek.

Sophie took Mama by the shoulders and gave her a little shake. "What on earth do you think you're doing, Liza? Get a hold of yourself before I go after you with a broom." The two of them glared at each other like a pair of fighting cats. I rubbed my cheek where it smarted from Mama's slap.

Mama stood up straighter and threw her shoulders back. "It would be best if you don't interfere, Sophie. After all, I am Rose's mother." Mama pulled her shawl closer together and cleared her throat. "I've made a decision to send Rose to boarding school. Rose has shown that she needs an environment that teaches proper behavior and encourages discipline. Miss Russell gave me a list of schools, and I've chosen a Catholic academy across the bay."

"But I don't want to go away—" I stood abruptly from my place at our kitchen table, accidentally jostling it so that my water glass fell, spilling water across the embroidered tablecloth.

"Now look what you've done!"

"It's nothing, Liza. It's only water," said Sophie. She mopped up the spill with a kitchen towel.

"Tomorrow morning, I am taking the ferry to meet with the headmistress in order to enroll you at Most Holy Name. Sophie, you must start packing a trunk with the belongings Rose will need at school."

"I'm not going!" I stormed out of the kitchen and up the stairs to my bedroom. I took the key from the brass lock and locked the door from the inside. It was the only key to my bedroom. I stayed in there for the rest of the day and most of the next day before Mama had the locksmith disable the lock and open the door. Mama was waiting for me when he unlocked the door, her arms crossed tight across her chest and an angry look on her face.

"You will cooperate from now on, Rose," Mama said in her iciest voice.

As I followed her downstairs, trailing behind as far as I could, I suddenly realized that my feelings for my mother had undergone a transformation; I felt hate for Mama, and it was replacing the hope I had kindled in my heart ever since I could remember. I know Mama saw the look of hate in my eyes because she looked startled, and her eyes darted away, glinting with the tiniest flash of guilt. "I trust that you will talk some sense into Rose," Mama said to Sophie before sweeping through the connecting door without a backward glance.

Sophie put a bowl of beans and a plate of cornbread in front of me, and despite my wounded spirit, I was hungry after being locked in my room for two days. I ate the beans quickly, and Sophie ladled another helping into the bowl. I crumbled the rest of the cornbread into the beans. Sophie sat down heavily in the chair opposite mine and watched me eat. "We've got to get your things packed up today, Rose," she said when I'd finished. "Tomorrow you go to your new school."

"I don't want to go." My voice was accusing, my glare hateful.

"Don't look at me that way, honey. It isn't my idea. I'd rather you stay right here, but it isn't my decision. It's your Mama's."

"Can't you say something to her, Sophie? I promise that I'll be good from now on."

"I already tried, Rose. There isn't a thing I can do to change her mind."

"Why can't she hire a tutor to come in like she did before?"

"I told Liza she should hire a teacher for you, but she is set on sending you to a convent school. She says that San Francisco is too dangerous for children, and that you're going to the Most Holy Name School for Young Ladies no matter what. You know how Liza is when she fixes on something. She's like a bulldog. You're the same way yourself. Something you get from your Mama, I guess."

"Don't say that Sophie. I'm not like her at all." I angrily swept the china bowl to the floor. "In fact, I hate her with all my heart!" Sophie stepped over the shattered pieces of the bowl, and for a minute I wondered if she meant to shake some sense into me, but she just held me in a bear hug while I sobbed into her ample bosom.

"I know, Rosie, I know," she crooned. "Just go ahead and cry yourself out, honey."

We sat at the table and talked until I was finally dry-eyed. It was past noon when Sophie and I climbed the stairs to my room to pack my clothes and essential items I would need at my new school. Later in the afternoon, after the last pinafore was neatly folded and stacked in the trunk, Sophie coaxed me to walk the steep hills to the Italian neighborhood for a plate of my favorite spaghetti. She undoubtedly hoped to cheer me up, but my gloomy mood refused to lift despite the festive atmosphere at Russo's Family Diner. I couldn't help thinking about my departure the following morning to Most Holy Name School.

When bedtime came, Sophie came up to say goodnight as she usually did. She kissed me and tucked the blankets closer. "Sleep well, Rosie." She paused at the door. "Your mama made me promise to lock you into your room. She's afraid you'll sneak off in the night." I turned my back to her, my anger keeping me quiet. "If you need anything in the night, you can ring this bell." Sophie took a brass hand bell from her pocket and put it on my bedside table. "I love you, honey." Sophie closed the door and turned the key in the lock. I heard the bolt slide into place and realized I was trapped.

I threw off the blankets and stood up, thinking recklessly that I'd escape through one of my bedroom windows. Unfortunately, the absence of a ladder or a conveniently placed tree ruled out a safe descent from either window. Jumping would definitely end with broken bones. I gazed at the moonlit backyard I knew so well, at the tidy flower beds I'd helped Sophie plant and the chicken coop where I'd gathered eggs; at the giant oak where Seamus hung a rope ladder so I could climb to the platform he'd built. "It's your very own tree fort, Rose. You can take a book up there and read," he'd said.

My tears fell on the windowpane, gathering in the moonlight in little glistening drops. Finally, exhausted from my sorrows, I crept back to bed and slept soundly until Sophie awakened me early in the morning for our departure to Most Holy Name.

Mama had hired a carriage to transport me to school and agreed to let Sophie accompany me on the thirty-five-mile trip. I was relieved to have Sophie's companionship, yet I was too glum and downhearted to be good company. Benicia, a port town at the northeastern end of the San Francisco Bay, was home to Most Holy Name School. Our route required us to board a ferry, carriage and all, and chug across the gray expanse of water to the fast-growing town that was to become my home in exile.

Mama flew out the front door of Wayside as Sophie and the driver of the carriage loaded my trunk. "I expect to hear good things of you, Rose," she called from the porch. I didn't even glance her way or wave when the carriage lurched forward for the descent across town to the ferry. We drove past the empty lot where I usually met Kitty and Joseph, but it was early in the morning, and they were not on the concrete steps.

My heart sank; I couldn't say goodbye to my friends, and they would wonder why I'd disappeared. Sophie noticed my distress and patted my knee. "Don't worry, Rose. I'll tell Kitty and Joseph you've gone away to school for a while, and you'll come visit them when you're home for the holidays and school breaks." I nodded, not trusting myself to speak, sunk as I was in wretched misery.

The northbound ferry was late. "By golly, I can't even see her yet." The landing attendant squinted in the direction "she'd" be coming from. "It'll be at least an hour, I can tell you that. She's got to unload and be made ready for the return trip. You ladies can entertain yourselves until then. You'll hear three short blasts on the whistle when she's ten minutes off from departure." Sophie, doing her best to cheer me, bought a nickel bag of stale buns to feed the birds that frequented the piers. I usually enjoyed the seabirds and pigeons in their amusing efforts to outmaneuver and steal from each other, but today I remained grim and unsmiling.

Sophie patted my shoulder. "It's going to work out, Rosie. Going away to school isn't the end of the world. As much as I hate to see you go, we can't let it ruin our lives." I moved away to feed the next group of birds and didn't respond.

By midmorning, nearly two hours behind schedule, the ferry whistle blew. Boarding took another half an hour; a supply wagon carrying a load of goods broke a wheel, and several men had to move it out of the way of the other carriages. When we were finally underway I stood at the railing on the top deck watching the city disappear from sight.

Weeping quietly as the vessel chugged slowly across the turbulent bay, I imagined what it would be like to mount the railing and disappear over the side into the murky gray water. I wondered if Mama would mourn me and thought that she would probably be relieved.

"You'll be back, Rosebud." Sophie put her arm around my shoulders and drew me close. "Like I said, you'll come home for the holidays, and during the summer break. I'll get the schedule from the headmistress, and Liza will send a carriage to pick you up."

I nodded in reply, not trusting myself to speak. Though I would come home, I knew that nothing would ever be the same.

Sophie Washington
San Francisco
1871-1872

It's funny how patterns repeat themselves. My mama, Addie, was a stand-in mother to Liza when she was a little girl. She loved Liza just like she was her own flesh and blood, and I feel the same way about Rose; she is as much a family member to me as my own lost sons. When Liza sent Rose away to live with the nuns, I felt like a rubber balloon caught in a patch of thorns. The small, cautious store of happy air got let out of me in a hurry.

Rose and I kept each other company in our shotgun apartment for too long not to feel an aching loss, which I was already familiar with. The first few months after Rose got banished to Most Holy Name were the worst; I missed her terribly, and when she came home on break, I was so overjoyed that I reminded myself of Miss Lucille when Bert visited. That picture scared me, and I forced myself to get some gumption and try to fill up the emptiness inside me.

I joined The Freedom Society, a Negro club that met downtown once a week, and I made friends with Cherie Poineux, a pretty half-breed who'd gone to work for Liza and ended up marrying Max, the bartender. Cherie became the main cook for the busy kitchen at Wayside Inn. I helped her when Liza threw big shindigs or when the pantry boy was recovering from a drunken binge. A few days a week I baked bread for the Wayside Inn ladies, and every Friday night I helped out at Liza's new saloon in the front parlor. It was a comfort that most of the men who frequented the bar treated me like I was a regular person, not some low-grade insect because of my color and my scarred-up face.

Though I'd never say so to Rose, her going off to school wasn't all bad. I loved Rose in every pore of my body, but I hadn't asked to be her mother. After Rose was born, I thought Liza would come to her senses and be a decent parent. When it didn't happen, I stepped in to fill the hole left by Liza shunning her own flesh and blood.

For ten years, Rose was the joy and the center of my world. When Liza sent her to Most Holy Name, Rose's absence spurred me to go out and get a life of my own, which wouldn't have happened if my precious girl was home to care for and mother. For the first time, I was my own person with no one tugging on my apron strings or my heartstrings. As for Rose herself, being away protected her from the black cloud of gossip about Liza's business, and she wasn't faced every day of her life with Liza's lack of love for her.

On the one hand it felt like I was truly free for the first time, yet no matter how busy I got, I felt a gnawing emptiness for my absent and missing children: Jules, Augie, and Rose. I knew Rose was safe with the nuns, and that I'd see her on the longer holidays. Jules and Augie were a different story. My dreams were haunted by frightening visions of what had happened to the twins, and I'd weep myself back to sleep, my good eye crying double the tears to make up for the missing one.

I felt guilty about this new-found feeling of freedom, but the joy that flooded over me when Rosie came home from school reassured me that my heart was in the right place.

Rose Laurent

Most Holy Name School
Benicia, California
1872

I was angry when I arrived at Most Holy Name. The circumstances of my banishment from Wayside stung my sense of honor and filled me with sorrow and fury. I had been unfairly and unkindly treated at school and judged guilty by my own mother. Princess Liza's decision to send me to boarding school was a prison sentence. I was prepared for the worst.

Most Holy Name was staffed by gentle, patient nuns, fortunately opposite in nature to Miss Russell. Sister Margaret, the headmistress, a saintly woman dedicated to educating and nurturing children in her charge, was unfailing in her tender concern when I refused to speak for several weeks after arriving at Most Holy Name. "When you choose to speak, Rose, I am sure you will be a benefit to any conversation," she said. Sister Margaret patiently continued to ask questions all through that silent period.

I don't remember that my first words spoken at Most Holy Name were particularly notable; speaking them, however, marked my acceptance of life there, with its predictable and ultimately comforting routine. I found it suited me. The other girls received me kindly, a welcome change from the shunning I'd been the target of at Madame Pritchard's Academy.

I formed a few friendships, though none compared to my friendship with Kitty and Joseph. Mainly, I preferred my own company to the chattering clusters of girls. My classmates didn't taunt me for my reserved nature, which was in line with the school's philosophy: *"Love, tolerance, acceptance, kindness."* The words were prominently displayed in a framed needlepoint over the chapel where special services were held. Sister Margaret often referred to it when addressing the body of students and staff in the inspiring sermons she gave most Sundays.

I give credit and thanks to Sister Margaret for helping me manage my nagging sorrow over Mama. Sister Margaret has the knack of saying the right thing. Confiding to her about my troubles with Mama was a relief. "Someday, Rose, I am certain that you and your mother will mend your torn relationship," she said, during our last talk. "You must keep your heart open to that end." Sister Margaret understands that underneath my anger, I secretly harbor hope for a day when Mama and I make peace.

It is Mama who must offer the olive branch; my heart is cold stone until then.

Liza Laurent
San Francisco
1874

Antipathy toward your own child isn't a sympathetic position in the eyes of greater society, yet in spite of the disapproval of my peers, I couldn't overcome my feelings toward Rose. She was a thorn in my side from the day she was conceived. And though it was a relief to have her gone, my decision to send her to boarding school was for her own good as well as mine.

Rose was languishing in the back apartment, getting in trouble at the Pritchard Academy, becoming more noticeable, becoming an embarrassment. My business at the Inn didn't need any untoward attention spawned by the tongues of gossips. I've maintained discretion at Wayside; it is one of the Inn's attractions. Men of good reputation come and go without the worry of their characters being dragged through the mud.

Managing the Inn suited me. My girls were my family, and I became the housemother who solved problems big and small and paid a generous wage compared to the prevailing pay at other means of employment available to women. My business endeavors at Wayside evolved and expanded as the city of San Francisco grew as fast as a patch of weeds in spring. Our offerings included a gentleman's lounge run by Max and a high-stakes game room where the richer clientele played poker. I hired additional help for

Cherie, our cook, and every Friday and Saturday night we served dinner to a crowded dining room of gentlemen seated next to ladies dressed in flimsy, figure-hugging outfits that made a man hungry to remove them.

The Wayside girls were skilled in the arts of seduction and renowned for their good looks. If a man fancied a redhead or a blond, or preferred a dark beauty, he had his choice. A man could start his evening eating a fine dinner, follow it with drinks and entertainment in the bar, and end with an erotic adventure. Clients flocked to Wayside. Eventually, I had to turn men away.

Because demand was so high, I doubled the number of live-in girls from seven to fourteen and hired a crew of carpenters to erect dividing walls in several rooms. After the construction was finished, there were bedrooms for all the girls as well as four specialty rooms furnished with props and a variety of equipment for acting out a man's fantasies. I expanded the staff by adding a carefully selected crew of party girls who came for special occasions, and soon, we were operating around the clock.

Max and I screened prospective customers carefully. Our clients had to be clean and able to pay for the finest services available. The Gentleman's Lounge was a stroke of genius, allowing Max and me to screen new clients before they were entered into the schedule of delights we provided at Wayside. The Inn became a refuge for single men who ran businesses in the city, or were passing through on their way to whatever Mecca beckoned, and married men who needed some erotic enhancement. Whatever the men wanted, the girls performed. My only rules forbade inflicting bruises, shedding blood, or destroying the furniture.

We were remarkably lucky in the orderliness and cooperation of our clients. The few occasions when matters got out of hand, Max intervened as only Max can. The man has a golden tongue and can usually calm an unruly fellow with a few soft words. Because of Max,

I've only had to use the silver-handled pistol I took from Sweetbrier twice. Fortunately, I didn't have to pull the trigger either time.

Rose came home from school for most holidays, but I rarely saw her unless I made a special visit to the apartment. Rose knew she was forbidden to come to the Inn without my permission. There was far too much for her to stumble upon should she choose to wander. On the occasions when I came face to face with her, she was cool. She no longer reminded me of a puppy craving attention.

Sophie went into a frenzy when Rose was due home, combing the newspapers and billboards for activities that she and Rose could do together. I'd see the two of them walking, elbows linked and deep in conversation, to town or toward the wharf. They obviously enjoyed each other's company. The two had always been close; now, the intimacy of their relationship caused an odd and unexpected flush of envy. I shook off the feeling fast. I was too busy overseeing my business to waste time and energy on envy.

Rose was home on summer recess when she broke the rules and came uninvited to the Inn. She'd knocked on the front door, and one of the girls brought her to my office. I was taken aback by her appearance; she was three or four inches taller than I'd seen her last, and she was on the verge of growing a chest. Rose was fetching, I realized; she'd overcome the gangly awkwardness that had always reminded me of a young colt.

"Rose. What brings you here? You're not supposed to come over without permission. You know that."

"It's important. I need to make some money, and I can't ask Sophie."

"What's this about?"

"A surprise for Sophie's birthday. I want to buy her a locket she's admired for a long time."

I considered giving Rose the amount she needed, yet my instincts told me it was best to make her earn the money. She was spoiled enough. It was good for her to know what it took to earn one's keep. "I had a serving girl quit this morning. You can serve breakfast until I find another girl to replace her. It isn't glamorous, but it's available if you want the job."

Rose nodded. "When do I start?"

"Tomorrow morning. Come to the kitchen by 6:00 to help Cook get ready. You'll serve and help wash the dishes after breakfast. You should be finished around 9:30 or 10:00."

"Thank-you, Mama."

"And don't call me mama in front of any guests who are breakfasting with us.

"What should I call you?"

"Call me Ma'am."

"Why, yes, Ma'am." I glanced up, detecting a subtle note of mockery in her voice. I chose to ignore the exaggerated curtsey she made on her way out the door. Someday Rose will understand how hard it is to make a living, I thought.

"And don't forget, it's only temporary," I called after her.

Rose got glowing reviews from the staff. Cherie, our cook, spoke earnestly and enthusiastically. "Your Rosie's a hard worker, Liza. Most of the servers who worked here have been as slow as turtles. I'd hire her any day of the week!"

Cherie's comment caused an unexpected surge of pride in Rose instead of my usual irritation at her. "I'm glad to hear the child's not lazy and useless."

A week passed smoothly with Rose serving breakfast to the girls and their morning company. "Rose is a gem. All the girls love her, Liza," reported my head girl, Essie Vaughn. It was working out well for everyone until one of the men decided he fancied Rose.

Max took me aside in the Wayside Gentleman's Lounge. "Do you see the man sitting at the end of the bar?"

I nodded. "Of course. That's Charles Sturtevant."

"Yes, old Charlie. He asked after Rose. Said he saw her serving breakfast in the dining room. Wants to know how much you'll charge for a night with her."

"Did you tell him she's not available?"

"I did. He said he'd pay triple for young flesh like hers. I thought you should know Liza."

"For God's sake! She's only a child! Please inform him that he's no longer welcome here. I don't care how good a client he's been; I won't tolerate perverted liaisons between grown men and little girls. Get rid of him, Max."

Charlie's attraction to Rose put an end to her table service career. Early in the afternoon, I took it upon myself to walk two miles to the women's hostel in the Mission District. The rooms there had bunk beds in rows that barely allowed a heavy girl to pass through, and one room was shared by up to ten girls. It was easy to hire a new worker from a place where there was often little hope of escaping squalor. Cherie was already training the new girl when Rose arrived to work the next morning. She followed my instructions and sent Rose to see me in my office.

Rose had tears in her eyes. "I thought I was doing a good job," she cried.

"I told you in the beginning it was temporary."

"What about Sophie's present?"

I handed her an envelope containing twenty-five dollars. "This should be sufficient. I think you'll find it a generous wage for a week's work."

Rose opened the envelope and gasped. "Why, that's a lot. Thank you."

I picked up my pen and resumed making entries in the account book for the month's expenses. There was a pause, and I could feel her eyes fixed on me. "Is there something else?"

"No, Ma'am." The door shut behind her. A ripple of unease crossed over me. I knew by the tone of her voice that Rose was losing love for me, and though I'd detached myself from motherhood there was some perversity of pleasure knowing the child adored me. I shook off the unpleasant feeling quickly. Rose would go back to school next week, where she'd be safely out of sight and out of mind. In a few short years Rose would complete her courses at Most Holy Name. I'd have to think of a suitable solution to the problem of Rose before she came home for good.

Sister Margaret Kirkpatrick
Most Holy Name School
Benicia, California
1878

Rose Laurent refused to speak for her first nine weeks at Most Holy Name. She was prone to night terrors, and her screaming woke the other boarders. Soon after her arrival, necessity required relocating her from the dormitory to a single room. She was not conscious during the nocturnal fits and appeared to be unaware of the events the next day. Since she wouldn't say a word in those early days, I relied on my intuition to guide me in the best way to help her.

Like most good sisters of the cloth I am ultimately a healer and a servant of the Holy Spirit to whom I have sworn allegiance. I joined the convent when I was sixteen, which started the long process of healing from the wounds of my own unhappy upbringing. Life with a drunken father and witch of a stepmother drove me from the nest as soon as I could get free.

As a girl I read over and over again the tale of Cinderella; a tattered volume of fairy tales was one of the few books in our threadbare household. I pictured a savior prince who'd rescue me from the dull entrapment of my life. My stepmother dashed my hopes when she told me that with looks like mine, I'd better not count on a husband. She held the back of my head with one hand and a hand mirror in the other, forcing me to observe the reflected image. "Look at yourself, Mags. Your face is enough to scare a newborn half to death! Best stop putting on airs and complaining about your chores." She pinched the back of my neck hard before releasing her hold. "The floor needs mopping again. You'll mop it until it's clean enough to eat off of, do you hear?"

I mopped the floor with tears streaming down my cheeks. From that day forward, I accepted the disharmony of my face, resigning myself to live without the advantages of prettiness.

The unrelenting dreariness of life at home drove me to seek relief through the nunnery. I'd been raised in the Catholic faith, and in church found escape from my troubles. The choice to enter the Lord's service was an easy one. Besides the qualities of security and serenity, there is something equalizing about wearing the cloth. A habit makes the ugly less ugly and the beautiful less beautiful. It frees the wearer from her appearance.

Years of contemplation, study and prayer prepared me for my position as headmistress of Most Holy Name. The Mother Superior in our denomination in St. Louis chose me for my ability to work with children. "You are genuinely kind, Sister Margaret," she said. "I couldn't think of a better person to administer a good Christian education." She sent me to help establish a Western branch of our convent's school.

After the usual fits and starts, Most Holy Name settled in Benicia. Our reputation was superb, and the small student body expanded quickly. It was the fourth anniversary of the school's existence when Rose came to us. I recognized a kindred spirit in her immediately. I'd felt sympathy for her from the day her mother enrolled Rose at school. It was rare to encounter a parent so willing to label their child as a troublemaker. I didn't believe it then, and when her nanny delivered Rose a day or so later, I knew immediately that she was an exceptional child with a broken heart.

Rose became my special project. I began to care about her as if she was my own daughter. She eventually broke her silence in my counseling chambers. Meeting individually with each of the students was a tried and true method of learning personalities and preventing problems before they happened. I'd initiated the practice in my first year as headmistress. It was a part of the position that I cherished and where I felt I could help the most.

I'd had no success in the first two sessions with Rose. I talked during the meetings, trying to draw her out to no avail. Persistence paid off; during our third interview, Rose broke her reserve and began to speak. It was a passionate confessional of her young life thus far. She spoke of her mother's abandonment of her, and the unpleasant experiences at her former school. Her story moved me, and I made it a mission to surround Rose with whatever she needed to heal her inner sorrows.

Rose blossomed at Most Holy Name. She was a model student, excelling in athletics as well as academics. She became the lead player on the Most Holy Name tennis team, and her participation in the glee club and the debating society made her a frequent performer in the pageants and theatrical events put on at Most Holy Name. No matter what Rose accomplished, her mother, Liza Laurent, never attended any of the school doings. Sophie Washington, the Negro woman with a glass eye, came instead.

It was obvious that Rose and Sophie were crazy over each other; it was also obvious that each time her mother didn't show up was another blow to Rose. When Rose was due to graduate from Most Holy Name, I found myself impelled to meet once again with the famous Liza Laurent who had been so conspicuously absent from Rose's years at school. I hoped I could make the woman see what a true flower her Rose was, a bud of humanity to be treasured.

Banking business required a trip to San Francisco and provided a perfect opportunity to visit Wayside Inn for Gentlewomen. I'd heard years ago about the true nature of Liza Laurent's business, yet the place looked stately and gracious; nothing like the bordello I pictured in my mind's eye. The woman who answered the door looked at me in surprise. "Mrs. Laurent doesn't allow preaching on the premises," she said.

"I am headmistress at Most Holy Name, the school her daughter attends. Is Mrs. Laurent at home?"

"Wait here. I'll see if she's available." The sound of men laughing and a smell of alcohol wafted out on a blast of warm air as she closed the door. I crossed myself and gave thanks that Rose had been with us at Most Holy Name instead of in proximity to the debauchery of the Wayside Inn. No matter how elegant it was in appearance and fittings, the place was a house of sin unworthy of an angelic innocent like Rose.

A few minutes passed before the door opened, and Liza Laurent stepped out to meet me. She was as striking in appearance as I remembered. There was something regal in her bearing that made me think of Rose's nickname for her mother: Princess Liza. It suited her. "Hello, Sister Margaret," she said, extending a hand for a limp shake. She offered tea, and I accepted. "Shall we sit on the porch? It's such a pleasant day." I followed her to a small table where we chatted about the weather and made small talk until one of the wanton souls employed at the brothel carried out a tray. Liza cut our chat short. "It's been years since a teacher came around about Rose. The last time it was because she stabbed a classmate. I hope she hasn't caused more trouble."

"On the contrary, Mrs. Laurent, I came to tell you that Rose is an exceptional member of Holy Name's student body. You should be proud of her."

Liza's expression was sour. "I take offense at people telling me how I should feel about my own daughter. It really isn't your business, is it?"

The tea commenced awkwardly. None of the glowing commendations I made about Rose made a dent in the woman's armor. It became immediately clear through her cold and flippant demeanor that my mission was fruitless. My intention of reconciling precious, dear Rose with her mother had failed. We parted with my offer of counsel if she ever felt in need. In response, she smiled like the sphinx.

Even though it was done with her best interests at heart, I betrayed Rose's confidentiality. Mrs. Laurent assured me that she would keep our visit between the two of us, and I hope I can trust her to do so. The last thing I'd intended was to add to the poor girl's sorrows about her mother. As I walked the long, hilly blocks to the pier where the ferry was moored, I prayed that dear Rose would remain ignorant of my attempted interference, and I prayed for the misguided Liza Laurent who didn't recognize the treasure from her own womb.

LIZA LAURENT
San Francisco
1878

One afternoon in early May, Sister Margaret Kirkpatrick from Most Holy Name School paid Wayside Inn a surprise visit. Jade, one of the newer girls, fetched me from the card room where I was in the middle of my once-a-month indulgence at the poker table. I often won, but this time I was losing badly when Jade tapped me on the shoulder. "A nun is here to see you, Liza." She eyed my low-cut gown and scandalously bare shoulders. She untied her silk shawl and handed it to me. "In case you want to cover up or something."

"Thank-you, Jade." I wrapped the shawl around my shoulders.

Sister Margaret was waiting on the veranda. She offered a hand to shake. "I don't know if you remember me, Mrs. Laurent. It's going on seven years ago when you enrolled Rose at Most Holy Name."

I recognized the sister immediately from our only meeting in the convent office, when I'd taken a ferry across the bay to enroll Rose as a boarding student. We'd spoken about the details of tuition and boarding fees for the year, and I'd written her a check, handing it to her across a desk covered with neat stacks of papers and books. "I must warn you that Rose is troubled," I said, drawing on my gloves in preparation for the chilly walk to catch the afternoon ferry. "She needs a firm hand to drive out her wicked streak."

Sister Margaret's gaze was penetrating. I felt it measuring me, reading me, and it was uncomfortable. "I have yet to come across a truly wicked child. Usually, when they act out, there are underlying reasons. Perhaps something is bothering her. Sometimes it relates to family matters."

"I hope you're not implying—"

"I'm not implying anything. Mrs. Laurent. I will wait to meet Rose before forming an opinion."

"Very well, then. I will send Rose on the Thursday morning ferry."

"Will you accompany her on the ferry? Sometimes it helps if a parent is present to ease the effects of homesickness."

"I am hosting a chess tournament at my Inn on Thursday. It's quite impossible for me to leave. Rose's nanny will ride over with her."

"I understand, Mrs. Laurent. You must be hard pressed for time with your business obligations." Sister Margaret drew a watch from one of the pockets hidden in the folds of her habit. "I must go to mass, Mrs. Laurent. We lost a dear friend and fellow sister last week to pneumonia, and the service is about to commence."

I paused at the door. "Let me know as soon as possible if Rose misbehaves."

"The sisters who make up the staff at Most Holy Name are trained to work with troubled children when they come our way. You needn't worry, Mrs. Laurent. Have a safe journey home."

Until she showed up on the porch, it was the only dealing I had with Sister Margaret. For the rest of Rose's school years, I sent the checks by post, and if the school put on a pageant or a recital, Sophie made the trip across the bay to attend the doings. Now, the woman had come unbidden to the Inn and I couldn't fathom why unless Rose had caused some kind of mischief.

"Is something wrong, Sister Margaret?"

"No, nothing is wrong, Mrs. Laurent. I'm here to talk to you about Rose. Is there a place we can speak in private?"

"I'll send for a pot of tea if you'll drink a cup with me. There's a table and chairs around the corner."

"That would be lovely."

I popped in the front door, called for Jade to organize a pot of tea, and rejoined the nun on the porch. She followed me to a set of wicker furniture tucked into a corner where two walls of the Inn met and formed an alcove that buffered the breeze on a windy day. Sister Margaret settled into a chair, and we chatted politely until Jade appeared with a silver tray laden with tea and a plate of shortbread.

I poured a cup of tea for both of us and passed a bowl of sugar cubes to the nun. "You said you wished to talk about Rose."

"May I speak frankly, Mrs. Laurent?"

"By all means," I said, hoping that the interview wouldn't drag on much longer.

"I sense a deep hurt that Rose carries. I can see the sadness in her eyes sometimes, as if a dark cloud chases away her sunshine. I've asked her what makes her so melancholy, and she mentioned that the two of you don't get along."

I put down my teacup. "My relationship with Rose really isn't anyone's business. It is, after all, strictly a family affair."

"I'm here as Rose's advocate and friend. I wish I had a daughter like her to cherish and to watch develop into a splendid specimen of womankind. My fondness and high regard for her has brought me to you in the hopes that I can aid her in a happy future. Rose has no idea about our visit today, and I'd prefer it to remain between the two of us."

"What is the need for secrecy?"

"Rose has told me that you don't love her and never have. She divulged it in confidence. I am breaching her trust in the hope of helping her." Sister Margaret took my hand in hers. "I am of the belief that you can heal your relationship with Rose if you try."

I withdrew my hand. "Isn't it a tad presumptuous to advise me on how to be a parent when you're not one yourself? Or is there a skeleton in your closet?"

Sister Margaret shook her head and clasped her hands together. "I am sorry to upset you, Mrs. Laurent." She fixed her penetrating gaze on me. "Please think about Rose. Reach into the depths of your conscience and recognize her for the treasure she is. Otherwise, you will both lose in the end. I don't want Rose to lose."

"You obviously care a great deal about Rose, but I'll thank you not to meddle."

Sister Margaret drew her cloak around her shoulders and stood. "Rose is finishing her studies at Most Holy Name at the end of this term. Her future is a bright one, and you will miss out most of all if you remain as uninvolved as you've been."

"Rose is loved and mothered plenty by Sophie. She doesn't need me."

"No matter how devoted, no surrogate can make up for the rejection of a child by his or her mother. Though Miss Washington is a saint with Rose, your daughter longs for your approval and love above all others."

I collected both teacups and put them on the silver tray. "You'll have to excuse me, Sister Margaret. I have something I must take care of." I picked up the tray and took a step away from the table.

Sister Margaret nodded. "I'll pray for you and Rose." She peered at me with her earnest, penetrating eyes. "If you ever feel the need of a friendly ear, you know where to find me, Mrs. Laurent. I welcome all souls, especially those that are lost."

"Thank you, Sister Margaret, but I assure you that my soul is anything but lost."

"The offer still stands." She was at the steps leading from the porch when she paused. "I hope you attend Rose's graduation. It takes place on Saturday the sixteenth of May. The parents of all our graduates are encouraged to come to the ceremony."

"I'll be sure to keep it in mind."

But I didn't keep it in mind. Sophie attended the festivities, and the next day she helped Rose pack her things for the move back home to the apartment adjoining the Wayside Inn.

Rose Laurent

San Francisco
1878

I am home now, for good, not just visiting on holidays or harvest break. My upstairs bedroom in Sophie's and my apartment is cozy. The walls are painted a soft shade of lavender, which coordinates with the new quilt and matching pillows on the bed. I'm sure the decorating is Sophie's work. Mama wouldn't for a minute do anything nice for my homecoming. I'm convinced that she thinks of me as little as possible. It's been her record so far; there's not much chance of changing her ways. She is Princess Liza of Wayside, and she grows more beautiful and more indifferent every year.

I never thought that I'd miss Most Holy Name for one minute, but I do miss it: especially Sister Margaret, who was kind and loving in a motherly way. I long for the same caring spirit in my own mother. Someday, I hope to turn my insides to steel, so that Mama's indifference towards me can't pierce the center of my lonely heart the way it does every time I see her or think of her. "Keep love foremost in your heart, Rose. Bitterness and anger lead to loneliness and despair," said Sister Margaret as I wept in the chair opposite her desk in the Most Holy Name office.

Sister Margaret counseled me that love would surround me if I invited those who have caused pain into my heart and offered the gift of forgiveness. Though I am not an especially fervent believer, I find the ideas comforting, and I do try to keep love and forgiveness as beacons to light life's path. Still, I have not found it in myself to excuse my mother for her stony-hearted attitude.

Near the end of May, having completed the full course of study at Most Holy Name, I was presented with a certificate verifying my graduation in good standing from the school. Another certificate qualified me to teach the primary grades. Sister Margaret and the other nuns organized a party to celebrate the coinciding dates of my graduation and seventeenth birthday. I had no inkling of the festivities, so it was a lovely surprise. The cook prepared my favorite applesauce cake and my friend Maud presented a very pretty hand-made card signed by all the girls. The sisters gave me a leather-bound memory book with thick, gilt-edged paper. I was so overwhelmed by the fondness I felt from them all that I had to hold back tears.

As I boarded the ferry for San Francisco a few days after gradu-ation, Sister Margaret clasped my hands between hers and made me promise to stay in correspondence. "You will always be a favorite of mine, dear Rose. I hope for regular visits from you," she said. I was pleased and honored. Sister Margaret had patiently and lovingly brought me from being a hate-filled child to a young woman with a willing, open heart, for which I will be eternally grateful.

Due to a strong headwind, the ferry from Benicia to San Fran-cisco was slower than usual. After the first miserable passage to school six years ago, the ferry ride had always been enjoyable and something that I relished. A wave of bittersweet feelings filled me as I feasted my eyes on the familiar landscape disappearing as we churned across the bay. From the top deck, one of the mates pointed out a pod of dolphins and lent me a pair of binoculars to watch the sleek grey swimmers.

A sudden jolt announcing that we'd landed filled me with a sense of urgency to hurry home as fast as I could. I was the first passenger off the boat when we docked, waiting impatiently for the buggy carrying my trunk to roll out of the lower deck. "Hurry up," I whispered under my breath. I practically jumped aboard when the driver stopped at the bottom of the ramp. I could hardly wait to get home and complained of the leisurely pace of the horses pulling the buggy. "Can't you make them go faster?" I asked.

"Naw, can't do any better than we're doin'. Howie and Jimbo is jus' too dang old to rush around." He leaned out and spit a stream of molasses-colored tobacco juice into the street. I resigned myself to the slow gait as we passed through the busy city streets, eventually starting a slow assent up the steep hills to Wayside Inn. As we approached the Inn my heart beat faster with the anticipation of seeing Sophie and being home. And, in my secret chest of hopes, I longed to see my mother, though I would never acknowledge it to a soul. I promptly suppressed the sentimental desire as it arose. "She doesn't care a whit, and neither should you," said the voice in my mind.

The driver carried my luggage around the side of the house and down the steps to Sophie's and my apartment, which faced the back yard and had a bird's eye view of the bay. "You can go ahead and set it down. I'll get someone to help carry it in." I withdrew a nickel from my purse and handed it to him. He scowled angrily before pocketing the coin and walking away, grumbling in an offended tone. On another day, I'd have run after him and added to his tip, but I was eager to see Sophie. I wanted to surprise her, and I let myself in quietly.

I tiptoed down the hall, following the delicious smells of Sophie's good cooking. The kitchen's open door framed the back view of my dearest friend in the world, bending over the stove as she stirred the contents of a large saucepan. Without a sound I moved to her, slipping my arms around her waist that had grown wider with the passing years. She gave a start of surprise until she realized it was me, upon which she put down her spoon and wrapped me in her familiar bear hug. Sophie's arms are sheltering. I find her embrace one of the warmest and most comforting places in the world.

"My God, girl, you're a prettier picture than any I've seen at the newfangled art gallery they just opened up town," she said, relaxing her grip and holding me at arm's length. "Oh, Rose, honey, you're really and truly home!"

"Yes, Sophie, I am home forever! You have no idea how happy it makes me."

"It couldn't make you happier than it makes me, Rosie."

Mama didn't make an appearance until the next day. When I asked Sophie where Mama was, she shrugged and told me not to worry. "Liza is looking forward to seeing you something fierce, but she's throwing a party for some important clients. Knowing Liza, she probably won't have a free moment until tomorrow."

"I don't doubt that she is wrapped up in her business obligations, but the part about her looking forward to seeing me isn't true, and you know it. You shouldn't lie, Sophie," I said.

"Oh, hush now, Rosie. Let's not get started on your mama. Why don't you tell me about school?"

"I'm tired as can be, Sophie. I'll tell you about everything after I rest for a while," I said, doing my best to hide the disappointment I felt. Though I was accustomed to Mama being aloof, it didn't make it hurt less.

"I'll have Shamus take your trunk upstairs a little later, and after your nap, I'll help you unpack."

I nodded and climbed the stairs to my freshly painted room. As I sat on the edge of the bed I was suddenly tired, not just pretending so that I could be alone in my melancholy. I lay down and went to sleep immediately. Preoccupying thoughts about my mother undoubtedly caused the peculiar dream I had as I napped. In the dream I was six or seven years old. Mama sat opposite me at the breakfast table and lifted her arms out to me. Surprised at this show of affection, I sat frozen for a minute, before running to her and climbing into her lap.

As we hugged, an iridescent bubble surrounded us, lifting us from the sturdy oak table where Sophie and I ate our meals. Trembling and shimmering, the bubble ascended while Mama and I cuddled. It was blissful until the bubble collided with the kitchen ceiling and abruptly popped. I plummeted toward the hard plank floor and was about to hit when Sophie wakened me. "What are you yelling about Rose? You're safe here at home in your bedroom. You must have had a bad dream."

Sophie and I unpacked my trunk, and I made an effort to be cheerful and entertaining with tales about school. Much later, at bedtime, Sister Margaret's words went through my head, about keeping my heart open. I had tried hard to be open-hearted, and now I was finished; my dream told me beyond doubt that there was no hope for Mama and me.

At noon the next day, Liza decided to pay a visit to the apartment. Sophie and I had spent the morning making soup and preparing dough for Sophie's cinnamon buns. Sophie still made all the bread and desserts for Wayside Inn, which kept her busy since Mama had a full house with all the girls and a steady stream of clientele.

Sophie told me about the hardships that befell poor Shamus, our kindhearted gardener, whose wife had contracted the wasting disease and was sent to a sanatorium. Shamus was left caring for his brood of five children, the youngest of whom was three. "He said it was mighty lucky that his sister decided to visit from Ireland when she did. Otherwise, he doesn't know what he would have done," Sophie was saying when the connecting door pushed open and Mama stepped in.

"Hello Rose," she said. "I see you've arrived home safe and sound."

"Yes, Mama. I got home yesterday afternoon." Mama nodded and asked Sophie where she was keeping the tea.

"Sit down, Liza," said Sophie. "I'll make us all a cup."

The kitchen was quiet except for the sounds of Sophie pouring hot water into the white porcelain pot, and after it steeped, into matching teacups. I was temporarily lulled by the seeming companionability of sharing a cup of tea with Mama when she cleared her throat and doused my momentary glow of contentment. "I've received a letter from the Brinsley Finishing School in New York accepting you into their program, Rose. It is a very exclusive school, and it comes with high recommendations."

"But Mama, I just got home. I'm not ready to go off to some other school," I said, trying to keep the disappointment out of my voice.

"The term for first-year girls starts in August, so you have time to be home for several weeks." Her voice was cool and flat.

"And what if I don't want to go?"

"Until you reach the age of adulthood, Rose, you will do what I say."

"I am an adult! I'm almost eighteen years old!"

"Do you pay your own way, Rose? Buy your own food? Put clothes on your back?" I shook my head. "Then you can't call yourself an adult."

"As usual, Mama, you are determined to get rid of me, aren't you?" I stood quickly. "I am going for a walk, Sophie." I swept by Mama without another word. The escalating sound of their voices followed me up the stairs to my bedroom. "You're colder than a block of ice with that child. What in the hell is wrong with you, Liza?" said Sophie. I heard the connecting door slam and knew that Mama had gone back to her side of the house.

I took a blue serge jacket from the closet and retraced my steps down the stairs to our entryway. "I'll be back by suppertime," I called to Sophie, and let myself out into the brisk spring air. The sun had burned the fog away, and the city glittered like a sparkling jewel rising from the white-capped bay. I walked several blocks down the hill, hoping to pay Kitty and Joseph a visit, but the burned-out lot where we'd played had a makeshift cabin built on top of the old foundation. I knocked on the door and asked if the residents knew anything about Kitty and Joseph.

The frumpy woman who answered shook her head. "Never seen hide nor hair of the folks you're describing. Sorry, Miss."

Next, I tried the dingy, cramped apartment above the Chinese laundry where Kitty and Joseph still lived when I visited them in December. I climbed the rickety flight of stairs and knocked on the door. After a few seconds, a Chinese woman poked her head out. When I inquired about Kitty and Joseph, she pantomimed that she didn't speak English and quickly shut the door. The Chinaman running the laundry on the ground floor grunted in broken English when I asked him about my friends. "They move. Mother die, and they not pay rent," he said.

"Do you know where they went?"

"Girl say she and brother go to work for mining camp in mountains. They gone for few months now."

"Did they say where the camp was?"

The man shook his head. "No. They just go. Sorry." The door closed behind him. I asked around the neighborhood, but no one knew where Kitty and Joseph had moved. It was near six in the evening when I gave up, saddened over my failure to find my friends.

Our apartment was empty when I returned home; Sophie had written a note that she was helping at the Inn, and to serve myself soup because she wouldn't be done working in time to eat supper with me. In addition to her regular line of business, Mama had opened a gentlemen's lounge in the front parlor, serving drinks and comestibles a few evenings a week. Sophie said it was against the law to run a bar in a neighborhood, but Mama paid off the town police, and the chief of police was one of her best customers. The lounge was popular; a steady stream of well-dressed gentlemen came for the whiskey and a game of dice with Max. Sophie helped Max behind the bar and served platters of oysters prepared by the cook.

The soup was still warm, and I ate a bowl sitting alone in the kitchen feeling sorry for myself. My old friends had disappeared without leaving a trace as to their whereabouts, and my mother had devastated me with her intention to send me away again. Even Sophie was too busy to keep me company. I was at wit's end and unused to idle time. At Most Holy Name the sisters organized a schedule of extracurricular activities each night of the week: evening walks, games, study hall, dramatic readings or musical recitals. I'd become quite proficient at playing the flute and thought briefly of digging it out of my partially unpacked trunks to alleviate the boredom and loneliness that overcame me.

I wandered our apartment, stopping in the parlor to play the piano. It was badly out of tune, and before long I rose from the bench and moved on to browse the titles in the hall bookcase, searching for something interesting to read. A quick inspection verified that I'd read almost every book on the shelves more than once, and I impulsively decided to defy Mama's rules and visit the library at the Inn. Mama and her girls had built up a decent collection of novels and biographies in a sunny room with thick-cushioned chairs and carved teak bookcases bought in Chinatown for cheap. I rummaged through the sideboard drawer until I found the key that unlocked the door to Mama's side of the house.

The long central hallway was dark and deserted. At the far end of the hall where it meets a spacious foyer, the door to Mama's gentlemen's lounge was wide open, spilling out sounds of laughter and revelry. "Throw the dice again, Max, you tricky son of a bitch," said a man's gravelly voice. I was about to turn back when someone pulled the door shut. I seized the opportunity to dash swiftly down the hall and across the foyer to the library. I entered, closing the door behind me. My relief at arriving undetected was fleeting; I was not alone in the room. A tall man sat in one of the cushioned armchairs. He was reading a newspaper, his long legs stretched in front of him, his heels resting on a footstool. When he saw me, he uncrossed his ankles and stood up. "Good evening." He inclined his head graciously.

My first instinct was to flee, and I stepped toward the door with that purpose in mind. "Please, don't go." He intercepted my hand as I reached for the doorknob. His touch made my hand tingle with a strange electricity. The gentleman looked startled, and I wondered if he'd felt the same sensation. He cleared his throat. "I'm sorry if I frightened you." I pulled my hand from his, suddenly embarrassed and alarmed at the feeling that swept over me.

"I am not supposed to be here. If my mother finds out, I'll catch hell."

"Judging that I've been here for over an hour and no one has intruded, I'd say you're safe from detection."

"All the same, I'd better go."

"What's your hurry? Why not stay and visit for a while? I'd enjoy some company." He returned to his chair, and after a moment of hesitation I sat on the edge of the settee across from him. "You look as though you are ready at any minute to run. Am I that intimidating?" I shook my head. "Good then. I'd hate to think I was frightening such a beautiful woman."

"Thank-you for the compliment, but I am afraid beautiful is a gross exaggeration."

"You shortchange yourself." He looked at me directly and smiled, revealing a set of white, even teeth.

I was flustered and confused at the sensations in my inner regions. I blushed and rose from the couch. "I should go. Mama would kill me if she knew I was here."

"Who is your Mother?" He had a subtle lilt to his speech that was charming, and I wondered where he came from.

"Liza Laurent. She owns the Inn." His eyebrows raised a fraction at hearing my parentage. "I am Rose, her daughter."

"A pleasure to meet you." The man smiled and gave a slight bow. "My name is Nolan MacDonald."

"I was bored and wanted a book to read. I'd better go back before I'm caught."

"Get your book. I won't give the alarm." He chuckled softly, and settled into his seat, picking up the newspaper he'd been reading when I entered.

I crossed to the bookcase, pretending to look at the books while taking the opportunity to observe his appearance without staring. He was a sandy-haired man of sun-browned complexion, clean-shaven except for a neatly trimmed moustache. His face was chiseled in a pleasing way, creating an overall effect of handsomeness without the touch of prettiness that ruins some men's appearance. He glanced up and noticed my gaze, upon which I turned my attention back to the bookcase, looking hurriedly for an appealing title that I hadn't read.

"Have you read *The Scarlet Letter*?"

"No, but I've heard of it."

He joined me at the bookcase. "I spotted it on the shelves earlier this evening. He pulled a volume out. "It's a fine story. I believe you would enjoy it. The Puritan ethic comes under harsh scrutiny with works like *The Scarlet Letter.*" I reached out to take the book, and he held my hand for the briefest moment. The same strange tingle between our fingers proved that I hadn't imagined the sensation of our first touch. I withdrew my hand from his and turned toward the door.

"Thank you for the recommendation, sir."

"Don't run off quite yet. You said you were bored; perhaps we could entertain each other. Surely there's no harm in friendly conversation," he said, and though I thought of Mama's anger should she discover me, I sat again on the settee.

There was a comfortable harmony between Nolan MacDonald

and me; I felt as if I'd known him for years. We discussed the books we'd read and our favorite authors. "I just bought a copy of Gulliver's Travels, by Jonathan Swift. He's devilishly clever. You are welcome to borrow it when I'm finished," he said.

"I'd like that."

Nolan stood and leaned against the bookcase nearest me, pulling a tobacco pouch from his pocket and carefully filling his pipe. "Do you mind if I smoke?" I shook my head, and he lit the polished wooden pipe. "Please tell me about yourself." A cloud of sweet-smelling smoke billowed up as he puffed. I told him I'd just come home from Most Holy Name. "What do you plan to do now that you're done with school?"

I shrugged. "My mother intends to send me to a finishing school in New York, but I don't want to go. I earned a teaching certificate from Most Holy Name. I might stand up to Mama for once and find a job. Sister Margaret said there are dozens of schools opening across the state."

He nodded. "Perhaps you will find a husband instead."

The look in his eyes made my heart flutter, and I quickly changed the subject. "What brings you to San Francisco?"

"My brother and I run a shipping business we inherited from my father. We transport milled timbers down the coast from Canada as well as smoked salmon, whale and dogfish oil, coal, you name it. Our boats carry whatever commodity a company needs to ship. I skipper the boat that delivers to northern ports down to San Francisco. My brother, Martin, takes his loads further south, to Panama and beyond, and my cousin sails around the Horn to Boston Harbor. He's away from home much of the year, poor lad." I listened to him talk of the excitement of storms at sea and his love of his home. "Vancouver Island is wild and beautiful. I'd like to show it to you someday."

"Since I live in San Francisco that's not likely to happen." The glass-domed gold clock on the mantle chimed ten. I realized that I'd spent hours talking to Nolan MacDonald. They'd been lovely hours, but it was time to go back to the apartment before Sophie started worrying. "I'm breaking my mother's rules." I stood and extended my hand to him for a parting handshake. "I must go now."

"It was a pleasure to meet you, Miss Rose." His sea-green eyes burned into mine, setting off a confusing undertow of feelings. He ignored the hand I offered, instead taking my chin and kissing me gently on the lips. I kissed him back, my lips obeying something primitive. As quickly as he surprised me by the sudden kiss, he stepped away. "I am sure we'll meet again, and soon, I hope." He smiled and left the library, closing the door softly behind him.

I pressed my fingers to my lips and took a deep steadying breath before dashing down the hall to the safety of our apartment. My heart was beating wildly, and I was aware of desires surging in my body that I had never experienced before I met Nolan MacDonald. At Most Holy Name the only men were the priests who led Sunday Service and the Mexican gardeners who manicured the grounds. Romance was new to me, and it conducted a symphony in my dreams that night.

Mama came to the kitchen the next morning. Sophie and I were eating biscuits and eggs and we were both surprised to see her; it was unusually early for Mama to visit the apartment. Her work kept her up late and most mornings she slept until noon. She sat at the table and selected a warm biscuit from the plate. Sophie got up to fetch an extra teacup. "Do you want eggs, Liza?" she asked.

Mama shook her head and buttered her biscuit carefully. "I hear that Rose entertained a visitor in the library last night," Mama said, at last. She peered at me as if I was a specimen under inspection, and my heart sank.

"What are you talking about, Liza?"

"Let's let Rose tell," said Mama.

Sophie gazed questioningly at me, but I couldn't answer; I was speechless and sat woodenly, expecting a scolding from Mama followed by a list of punishments, but her demeanor was surprisingly mild. "Mr. MacDonald was smitten with you, Rose. He asked if he may call on you, with the intention of courtship. I have given my permission." She sipped her tea. "He would be a quite suitable mate."

My heart leapt to fury at Mama. Though I'd been entranced by Nolan MacDonald, the idea that my mother was suddenly giving a man permission to woo me was unbearable. Who did she think she was, suddenly playing the matchmaker? All the good counsel of Sister Margaret flew from my mind; I hated my cold, heartless mother. I opened my mouth to speak but nothing came forth.

"Close your mouth, Rose," said Mama. "You have food in it." She raised the red-checkered napkin and blotted her lips daintily. "You would be wise to consider Mr. MacDonald as a serious suitor, Rose. He is decent man and he has the benefit of wealth."

"I don't intend to follow any of your orders, Mama. From now on, I will make all my own choices and decisions." I rose, leaving my plate of half-eaten eggs on the table. "And, I refuse to go to finishing school or marry someone just because you want to get rid of me!" I slammed the door to punctuate my exit. Something changed forever that day; my soft spot for Mama was cemented shut.

In spite of declaring a war of independence against Mama, I couldn't stop my heart from racing when Nolan MacDonald appeared at the door to our apartment the next day. I was tucked into the cozy window nook in our parlor reading *The Scarlet Letter* when I observed his approach. I leaned into the folds of the curtain, so he wouldn't see me watching.

Sophie answered the door, and he introduced himself. They murmured a few pleasantries, and then Nolan spoke clearly. "Mrs.

Laurent has given me permission to visit her daughter, Rose. Is it possible to see her on such short notice?"

Sophie took the monocle she kept in her pocket and held it up to her good eye, peering at him suspiciously. "I'll see if Rose is taking company or not. Wait here, Mr. MacDonald." She closed the door firmly.

"Rose," she called up the stairs, assuming that I was in my bedroom.

"I'm right here."

"Goodness sakes, you scared me sneaking up like that."

"I didn't sneak up at all! I was reading in the window seat."

"You have company. He introduced himself as Nolan something-or-other, and my guess is he's the fellow you met in your mama's library."

I nodded my head. "I believe Nolan was his name. May I invite him for tea?"

Sophie harrumphed. "I suppose, but you be careful, Rosebud. Your company is a man, not a boy."

"Don't worry, Sophie. I'll be very careful."

She nodded. "You've always been a good girl, honey. I don't know why I said that. I'll just shut up now and put a pot of water over to boil." I kissed her cheek, and off she went to the kitchen while I let Nolan in.

We shook hands. "Hello Rose. I see you're even prettier than I remember from last night."

"You must have spent considerable time practicing the art of flattery, Mr. MacDonald. It isn't common for a person to become prettier overnight but thank you. Please come in for tea."

Sophie had set the table with two teacups and I insisted she bring a third cup for herself. Nolan also urged her to join us. I could see that she was pleased. Sophie got chatty right away and asked him a million questions while I listened and poured the tea. Soon, they were laughing and exchanging stories like old friends. By the end of our tea, I could see that Sophie liked Nolan; he treated her with respect, not like she was some background servant. My own feelings for Nolan MacDonald grew warmer. I walked him to the door afterwards, wondering when I'd see him next.

"May I call on you again, Rose?"

"That would be nice."

"Is the day after tomorrow too soon? I thought we could take a walk over the hills to the ocean if you enjoy that type of activity."

"I am a devoted bird watcher, Mr. MacDonald. I would very much enjoy a walk. The weather is perfect for a brisk stroll."

"I hope you feel comfortable enough to call me Nolan. Mr. MacDonald is far too formal."

"All right, then, Nolan. What time shall I expect you?"

"I thought we could set out by mid-morning, say around nine? If we pack a lunch, we could have a picnic when we get to the beach."

I volunteered to put together a basket lunch and lingered in conversation with him while he donned his hat and coat. When the door closed, I danced down the hallway, bursting into the kitchen to tell Sophie about Nolan's invitation for a walk to the ocean. "Slow down, child. You're about as giddy as a gadfly," said Sophie. "I've got to say that your Nolan seems like a real gentleman. Otherwise, a body could worry about a man's actions alone with a young woman. Do you think you should ask your mama's permission?"

"I am my own person from now on, Sophie. Mama can say whatever she wants, and I'll do exactly what I choose to do. And I intend to take a lovely hike with Nolan MacDonald on Thursday."

Sophie nodded, and was quiet for a minute. "If you want, I'll help you fix a nice lunch."

"That would be wonderful, dearest, darlingest Sophie." I threw my arms around her. "Have I said lately how much I love you?"

"Just yesterday you mentioned it. Same goes for you, Rosie. Now why don't you help me make some oat muffins? The ladies have been begging for them for a couple weeks now."

Sophie and I prepared the batter and spooned it into muffin tins, and though we talked, I don't remember a word; my mind was on Nolan MacDonald.

On Thursday morning at a quarter to ten, Nolan arrived with a leather knapsack and an enormous bouquet of flowers that he presented to Sophie.

"Why, no one has ever brought me flowers before. This is a beautiful assortment. Where on earth did you get them?"

"One of the guests at the hotel where I'm staying told me about a Chinese hothouse on the south side of the city. I borrowed the hotel driver and he took me over. It didn't look like much from the outside; just a big canvas tent, but inside you should see the flowers. The fragrance was like the finest perfume. None of the workers spoke a word of English, so I just pointed to the flowers I wanted, and a gal put them together. I'm glad you like it."

"Why there are enough flowers here to fill two vases! I'll arrange them after you two go off on your adventure."

Nolan handed me the knapsack. "I thought we could pack the lunch in here, and I'll carry it on my back."

Nolan filled two large canteens with water while Sophie and I packed the knapsack with egg-salad sandwiches, pickles, oranges, and a half dozen of Sophie's applesauce cookies that she'd baked especially for our picnic. When we finished our preparations, Sophie walked us to the door. "When should I expect you back?"

"Early evening, I estimate. The trail we're following goes along the bay all the way to the sea. Which reminds me, I hope you're wearing your best walking shoes, Rose."

"I am, Mr. MacDonald."

"Nolan, remember?"

"Nolan, yes. Shall we go?"

A coach and driver were waiting for us in front of the Inn. At my confused expression, Nolan explained that he'd hired the cab to drop us off at the starting point of the trail leading over the rocky cliffs to the ocean. "I walked the same trail a couple of years ago on a stopover. You've never seen such beautiful views, Rose. I think you'll like it very much."

"I'm sure I will. At Most Holy Name we often took long hikes on the weekends."

"My idea is to walk to the beach and eat our picnic lunch facing the sea. How does that suit you?"

"Very well indeed," I replied.

"From the trailhead, it's five or six miles to seaside. Once we're there we can spend a few hours exploring. I've hired the coach to meet us near the beach in the early evening. The driver will arrive by 5:00 and will wait for us."

"How does he know where to meet us?"

"We drove out yesterday, and I showed him where the trail meets the Coastal Road. Don't worry Rose, you'll be safely home by seven at the latest."

"I'm not in the least bit worried, Nolan," I said. And I wasn't.

Though my walking boots weren't pretty or ladylike, I was glad of their sturdiness as we traversed across cliffs and rocky gulches. The trail crumbled away in places; we had to blaze a new path when it disappeared entirely from a slide that made a deep gouge down the side of a steep hill. "I imagine that kind of earth movement is caused by torrential rains," said Nolan. "It looks like it wasn't too long ago, either." It was a challenging detour, and when we reconnected with the trail on the other side, Nolan handed me the canteen. "Drink as much as you'd like. There's another canteen in the pack, and we can always refill when we come to a stream or a spring."

The day was perfect. Nolan brought strong binoculars, and we watched eagles, hawks and seabirds of all types soar through the brilliant blue sky, the monotony of which was broken by decorative clouds puffing across and transforming into misty gargoyles and bunnies. Spring's fragrant bouquets of blue lupine and wild roses perfumed the air. A picture-book view of the bay, peppered with little sailboats and an occasional freighter chugging into port, entertained us with its changing scenery. We ate the oranges as we rested in a wildflower meadow, playing the cloud game and pointing out all the queer creatures and shapes forming in the sky.

We hiked steadily after our rest, not stopping until the majestic Pacific Ocean came into view. The trail began a slow, winding descent to the rocky beach below. I've daydreamed about that day ever since. A brisk wind blew at the beach, and after walking along the margin where cliff met sand, we came across a shallow depression carved by nature into the cliff face. Someone before us had built an additional barrier of driftwood on each side, creating a dry, wind-free shelter. "This looks like a prize spot for a picnic. What is your opinion, Rose?" I agreed. We spread the blanket he'd carried in a roll attached to his knapsack. With hearty appetites from the exertions of our walk, we devoured four of the sandwiches and all of pickles, ending the feast with applesauce cookies washed down by gulps of water from Nolan's canteen.

After lunch, we took off our shoes and socks. Nolan rolled up the legs of his pants and I held my skirts above the waves as we waded in the shallows and up and down the lagoons, looking for starfish and the brightly colored crustaceans that fixed themselves to the sides of rocky tide pools. On the shoreline we laughed at the silly little sand crabs that scuttled when a shadow fell over them.

The hours passed, and the late afternoon sun plunged closer to the sea, signaling the time for us to start our homeward trip. We returned to the little cave for our things. When our boots were on and the picnic gear was stowed neatly away in the knapsack, we stood in the rocky archway savoring the view before starting down the beach. As we lingered, Nolan put his arms around me and we kissed. It was intoxicating; every inch of my flesh desired his touch and the feel of his body against mine. He sank back on the sand and pulled me to him, although I didn't need any pulling. I couldn't have been more willing.

Nolan stopped before passion took us too far. He stood abruptly and held out his hand to help me up. "I shouldn't have kissed you like that, Rose. I just couldn't resist. Can you forgive me?"

I brushed the sand from the folds of my skirt. "If I forgive you, you'll have to forgive me, too. I kissed you back."

"I absolutely forgive you. I wouldn't trade your kiss for a gold nugget the size of my fist."

"What if it were the size of a cannonball?"

He pointed to a large rock shaped like a porpoise. "If it was a nugget as big as that boulder, I'd still choose a kiss with you." He took my hand, and as we crossed the beach to the trail that met the Coastal Road, I knew with certainty I was in love with Nolan MacDonald.

Sophie Washington
San Francisco
1878

When Liza suggested Nolan MacDonald as a suitable marriage prospect for Rose, I had to stop myself from pouring the contents of the honey jar over the top of her selfish head. Liza said all she wanted was to have Rose safely married, and maybe, in a deep-down buried particle of Liza that loved her daughter, it was true. I suspect the other reasons she wanted Rose to marry Nolan MacDonald were more self-serving.

Liza told me more than once, the very sight of Rose triggered visions of Bert; "She's the spitting image of him." I stopped myself from pointing out that Liza herself had the same daddy as Bert, and the family resemblance touched her as well as Rose. The Laurents were all good looking; even Bert had been a fine figure of a man, though his outside looks disguised the deformed devil that lay beneath his skin.

When Rose got home from Most Holy Name she'd become a beautiful peach of a woman. In my heart of hearts, I reckoned Liza was a little jealous of Rose's good looks, plus Liza didn't want a grown-up daughter showing everyone she was older than she looked. Liza got more and more vain over the years; I suppose she needed to be vain in order to stay in her line of work. The truth is, Rose was only seventeen years old, and the very idea of her getting married to someone so quick and moving so far away from home made me mad as hell. I didn't have anything against Nolan. He was a gentleman from the start, but I selfishly hoped they would wait a year or so before they tied themselves into a family knot.

I told Liza as much one night after Nolan MacDonald came courting and took Rose to the music hall to see a travelling troupe perform a minstrel. Nolan had personally invited me to go with them, but I wasn't interested in seeing a bunch of white people in black face, so I stayed behind. That night, Liza and I got in a terrible, mean fight. I almost stopped loving her, but our ties are just too strong to break over a fight, even a nasty one. It's hard to disown someone so close to you in the tangle of life, even if she's become every bit the uppity white bitch who acts like she's a queen.

I said she should tell Rose to take her time before jumping into being a wife. "Why are you so hell bent to marry that child? Why not make them wait a year before they get hitched?"

Liza's laugh was a brittle as broken glass. "Mind your own business, Sophie. You are not in charge of what happens to Rose. After all she is my daughter." Liza crossed her arms across her chest, which is her sign that the conversation is over.

"Years ago you sent the poor child away and broke her heart, and it's as clear as ice you'd like to get rid of her now. Have you ever considered Rose? Have you ever taken the time to know your own child? You haven't, Liza. You're nothing but a sorry excuse for a mother." She slapped me then, hard across the cheek. I slapped her back, and it stunned us both. We froze opposite each other, face to face, vibrating with anger.

"How dare you touch me!"

"What, because I'm a Negro and you're a white woman who secretly thinks she still owns a slave?"

"You're talking craziness, Sophie!"

"Am I? Keep in mind you slapped me first."

Liza's face turned white. The only color was the red patch where my palm had crossed her cheek. In our years together, neither of us had ever raised a hand in violence against the other. Through quarrels and disagreements, mostly over Rose, I still considered Liza to be my sister. I knew she felt the same about me. That evening a hurt opened in the sisterhood we'd shared, and it wasn't easy or quick to mend.

Because of the doldrums in the horse latitudes, Nolan MacDonald was in town an extra ten weeks as he waited for a shipment of dry goods and hardware traveling around the Horn from Boston Harbor on the freighter *Northern Star*. He'd rented a room at Seagull's Nest, a rooming house close to the piers that put up sailors and merchant marines when they had to hold over in town, but he didn't spend much time there; the day after he'd met Rose, those two were practically glued together. When they weren't gallivanting around on an adventure, Nolan was a regular visitor to our apartment.

In spite of Rose's rebellion against Liza, she couldn't help falling in love with Nolan. I could see why; if I'd been a young white girl, I'd have gone for him as fast as a shark goes after a hunk of raw meat. He made points in my book right away by treating me with respect: like I was a real person, not some hanging-around servant ready to fetch tea or do the boss's bidding.

Nolan was generous and thoughtful. He brought with him armfuls of flowers from the Chinese hot houses on the outskirts of the city or arrived carrying fresh-caught crabs wrapped in butcher paper, one for each of us. He presented Rose and me with beautifully carved ivory fans and brought fat beef tamales to steam for supper. It wasn't long before any reservations I had about him disappeared. Rose couldn't have met a nicer man. She was giddy with happiness, and I found myself liking him more every day. Not only was he good humored; he was handy; I put him to work fixing whatever was broken or needed improvement in the apartment.

When Rose told me Nolan had asked her to marry him, I was delighted. Their love for each other was beyond question, and everyone commented that they made the perfect couple, yet I still secretly wished their marriage could be postponed so I could have Rose to myself a little longer. Nolan took the question to Liza since there was no daddy in the picture. After Liza gave her blessings, marriage plans went ahead with the speed of a jackrabbit running for its life.

Liza rose to the occasion and paid Lee Wong, the haberdasher, a small fortune to fashion a suitable wardrobe for a newlywed. "I'll tip you an extra gold piece to have it ready in six weeks." Liza took a large gold coin from her purse and held it up as an example of what she was willing to tip. Lee Wong nodded, and soon the shop whirred with the sounds of treadles operated by the tiny pumping feet of Lee Wong's female relations. Rose and I visited the shop several times while her gowns, coats, and undergarments underwent the transformation from raw material into fancy ruffled dresses trimmed with lace, serviceable day gowns, and wool overcoats ordered by Nolan as necessary for the climate on Vancouver Island.

Liza even showed up for the first fitting and inspected the material and drape carefully before giving Lee Wong final approval. It was one time an outsider might imagine Liza as the proud mama of a bride-to-be, but relations between the two of them were frosty, especially now Rose had stopped trying. She'd truly closed the door on Liza by then. I didn't blame Rose at all. I understood how she felt; her mama treating her like a troublesome stranger most of the time. Her distrust of Liza was only natural, but I can't help wondering if that fitting session could have been a time to open up and try to heal things between them.

The wedding, a simple ceremony led by a client of Liza's who was also a Justice of the Peace for the county courthouse, was held in the back garden of the Inn on a warm afternoon in August. The wedding party of forty-six included Sister Margaret, a few schoolmates from Most Holy Name, the Wayside Inn ladies and a dozen neighbors. I wasn't the only one sniffling; Liza's girls raised dainty handkerchiefs to blot their tears, and Sister Margaret removed her glasses to wipe her streaming eyes.

Nolan and Rose beamed like twin lighthouses, and their happiness was infectious. Even Liza stepped out of her usual aloofness. Though she tried to hide it, I could see that she was proud of Rose for once. Over the years she had become preoccupied with herself and her business, and not much else was important to her. On the wedding day she showed a spark of her old self, and I knew there was hope for her yet.

For their honeymoon, Nolan rented a suite of rooms at the Palace Hotel and a fancy touring buggy to carry them in grand style into the drive-in carriage court. No one saw them for the next couple of days. When they came out, they were blissful. It was enough to make some people jealous. Rooms at the Palace Hotel were expensive, and after a few days, they moved into Rose's upstairs room until Nolan's cargo arrived for the trip north.

It was pleasant to have a houseful of merry company. Rose and I cooked up a storm, both of us taking pleasure in feeding Nolan's appreciative and seemingly endless appetite. I delighted in their company; at the same time, the apprehension of Rose leaving began to gnaw at me like a sneaky little mouse pecking away at a wedge of cheese.

When *Northern Star* finally arrived from its long delay in the calms, the reality of Rose's departure for Canada hit home. Thankfully, it took several days for Nolan to get the freighter *Good Hope* loaded and provisioned. The ship was further delayed while Nolan rounded up stray seamen to replace the missing crew. During the long layover, several of his crew had lost their wages in the gambling or opium dens and couldn't afford to wait for the return voyage. I secretly prayed for delays; it meant I had Rose longer.

The three of us were finishing biscuits and gravy that Rose helped me prepare. She'd asked the night before if I would teach her the recipe. "Biscuits and gravy is Nolan's favorite breakfast. I wonder if he has southern ancestors," she said. True to her word, she'd arrived in the kitchen promptly at 6:00 a.m. and set to work. I gave instructions; Rose mixed the batter and cut out rounds of buttery dough. The biscuits turned out especially light and flaky, and the three of us devoured an entire dozen, with Nolan eating half.

"You've got a magic touch with biscuits, Rose. These are some of the best I've ever tasted," I said. Nolan nodded agreement as he ate, with obvious appreciation, an enormous serving of gravy-covered biscuits. He swallowed his last gulp of tea and shook his head when I offered to pour him another cup.

"We'll be making headway for the island by the end of next week, Rose. It's time to pack the things you want to bring home to Victoria. I've arranged for a couple of extra steamer trunks to be delivered this afternoon. Hopefully, between those and your own cases, there will be plenty of room to pack everything you need." He stood and pulled on his hat, pausing behind Rose's chair to kiss the top of her head. "I'll be back late tonight. The skipper of *Northern Star* and I are settling business over dinner. Some of the other merchants are joining us; I hope they'll become future clients."

"I'll stay up reading until you get home." Rose rested her hands on his shoulders and stood on tiptoe to kiss him. I busied myself clearing the table and fussing around the sink with the intention of giving them some privacy for what proved to be a good long kiss. "I'll walk you to the front door," she murmured, and they left holding hands. She was dreamy-eyed when she came back to the kitchen a few minutes later. "I'll wash the dishes, Sophie, and dry them too, if you will please write out your recipe for biscuits and gravy."

"Sure thing, honey. It's the recipe that my mama used when she made biscuits in the kitchen at Sweetbrier. I've never written it down before, but I have it memorized, so it shouldn't be hard."

"Tell me about Sweetbrier, Sophie."

I grunted. "That's where both your Mama and I were born and raised. It's a plantation in the southern states, about a million miles from here."

"You've never said much about you and Mama when you were girls growing up, Sophie. I'd like to know all about it."

What parts of Liza's and my girlhood could I tell without doing damage to Rose, I wondered? The forbidden territory in Liza's and my history was dangerous even to think about, much less try to explain to an innocent like Rose. What she doesn't know can't hurt her, I thought. Rose looked at me expectantly, and I shrugged. "Truth is there isn't much to tell."

"I don't believe it for one second. There must be reasons for Mama being the way she is. I'd like to know why. Maybe I could understand her better." Rose placed her hand gently over my scarred eye. "And, you never told me about how this happened to your poor eye."

"Some things are better off left alone. You start talking about the past, and it can make those demons rise up to pull you down and smother you with bad memories. Better they lie dead."

"Sister Margaret would disagree. She believes facing bad memories makes them less painful." Rose shook her head. "I'm not sure who's right: you or Sister Margaret." We were silent for a few minutes, both of us caught up in our own thoughts as I wrote down Mama's recipe. It sparked my memory of the last time I had her biscuits and gravy, and I thought about my family so far away, and my poor lost boys.

"What are you sighing about, Sophie?"

"Sometimes I wonder how my family is," I finally said, and before I knew it a few tears leaked out.

Rose wiped her soapy hands on the apron she was wearing and hugged me tight. "I love you Sophie. I know I can't replace your real family, but you've always been a mother and a friend to me. I am blessed that you are in my life." She paused, loosening her hug enough to lean back and gaze earnestly into my good eye. "Sophie, Nolan and I have been talking, and we would like very much if you came with us to Victoria." I gasped. Rose rushed on, talking a mile a minute "Nolan said he'd be relieved if you were there to keep me company during the months when he's gone to sea. You would have your own apartment, Nolan says. The house is split in two. Until they died, Nolan's parents lived in one half, and he lived in the other. Now they're gone, an entire side of the house is empty. Nolan says it is yours if you want it."

"This is sure out of the blue, Rose. I don't know what to say."

"Say yes, Sophie." Rose threw her arms around me and squeezed like she didn't want to let go. "The truth is, I need you."

I didn't answer right away, but when I woke the next morning I knew I'd join Nolan and Rose on their journey to Vancouver Island.

Liza Laurent

San Francisco

Summer 1878

Sinners such as myself must either cut the cord on guilt or suffer through life hating ourselves. We must develop techniques if we hope to survive our ghosts. The way I tamed guilt and stifled unwanted thoughts was developed long ago. Through repeated practice I trained my mind to enter a neutral ground. Nothing hurts or disturbs me when I am there. I am free to live in the present. All my baggage, shelved and secure, can't fall on me. This is handy in my line of work; I enter the neutral zone during sex; detaching whenever necessary; enjoying the moment when pleasurable.

The numb mind of the neutral zone demotes guilt to a place of insignificance, allowing the guilty to live a full life. But sooner or later, unless you are the kind of cold-blooded murderer who simply doesn't feel remorse for what he or she has done, the unease of one's sins, failures, wrongdoings, and indiscretions rub a sore spot, scratching and tearing away peace of mind, etching a hole in tranquility, allowing guilt to visit. When the long-held belief that Rose was a thorn in my side began to unravel like a favorite sweater coming apart, my guilt swallowed me and spat out a naked and vulnerable loving mother. Hidden carefully under layers of indifference was a kernel of love all along. It just did not come to light in time to save my relationship with Rose.

I could ignore Rose more often than not, but after her graduation from Most Holy Name she was no longer a malleable little girl who I could safely hide in the back apartment. The last thing I needed or wanted in my life was a daughter verging on adulthood. I realized it would be impossible to keep her sequestered with Sophie; she'd developed a mind of her own, helped by the meddling interference of the headmistress, Sister Margaret. Rose had grown bold and defiant, which proved out when she disobeyed our rules and entered the library at Wayside. As a result, I lost a fine client to her.

Like a dark twist in a Dickens' novel, Nolan MacDonald was my personal customer before he met Rose. This secret will follow me, come hell or high water, to the grave. Fortunately, my ladies are fiercely loyal. They have to be, or I'll let them go. San Francisco is rough on single women; the girls I hire generally want to stay put where they are safe and well fed. I trust they will keep my secret, as I keep theirs.

I am ashamed to admit that pure lust led me to Nolan. I didn't need the money; I'd reached a state of financial comfort. Careful management and the expansion of the business paid the bills with plenty left over to stash in the safe. Besides managing the day-to-day business matters, my main functions were to dress exquisitely and to entertain the clientele in our lounge.

Max and I took turns dealing cards at the discreet table tucked away behind velvet curtains in an alcove next to the bar, where stakes were high and men deadly serious. That's where I met Nolan. He won the table that night, tipping me generously for dealing winning hands, kissing me full on the lips. It captivated me, that kiss.

I couldn't resist him. Instead of sending one of the girls, I slipped into the darkened room where he waited and gave him the deluxe service, though he'd paid for something more straightforward. The seduction of Nolan was a glorious romp of the flesh, and though I was old enough to be his mother, our lust was mutual. After our first encounter, he paid generously for a week of companionship while he waited for his shipment to arrive from around the Horn. We spent nearly all of it in bed. Good fortune made him one of a handful of lovers who know how to pleasure a woman. It was an extraordinary week.

When it came time for him to skipper his boat back to Canada, I was sorry he was going. We had an especially stimulating and intimate last fling in the bedroom before he left. "I don't say this often, but I'll miss you, Nolan MacDonald."

"I'll be back in four or five months," he said. "I hope I can see you again."

"Perhaps by then, your tastes might have changed."

"Not a chance." He kissed my hand on his way out of the bedroom.

We had two more dalliances, with several months between visits because of Nolan's shipping schedule. They were equally memorable times, and I looked forward to his layovers in San Francisco. It was mutually beneficial until he met Rose. Then Nolan charted a course that was out of my control.

"I met your daughter in the library, Liza." Nolan paced nervously in front of the overstuffed armchair in the lounge where I sat. "I must be honest and take the risk of being too blunt; I am asking your permission to call on her, as a serious suitor." I stifled a gasp of surprise and worked at making my face expressionless – a skill learned years ago, when I had to hide my feelings and thoughts. "I hope you'll understand and forgive me, Liza; I believe I've fallen in love."

"Aren't you being a little hasty, Nolan?"

"I know it's sudden, but I wish very much to marry Rose if she will have me." He looked at me with earnest concern. "I hope you're not angry, Liza."

"I'm surprised mostly. I didn't think you were the marrying kind."

"I didn't think so either, until I met Rose. May I court her?"

"Rose is almost eighteen and at the age when she can make her own decisions." My tone sounded icy, even to me. "If you choose to call on her, you have my permission. I promise I won't shoot you through the back window."

Nolan looked me straight in the eye and spoke softly. "I will never forget our time together. It will remain between us of course. Rose must never know." He held out his hand and gave mine a formal little shake, as if we were sealing a business deal.

I managed a nod and crossed to the door to indicate that our interview was over. I spent the rest of the afternoon on my bed with a sick headache. The next morning, I rose with a clear resolution to forget Nolan MacDonald had ever made love to me.

Nolan's marriage proposal to Rose came a mere two weeks after he asked for my permission to court her. Cherie announced the news at breakfast one morning. "Sophie said he brought two dozen red roses and a diamond ring with a stone as big as a pea! Rose said yes right away, and now she's acting like she's drunk with love. Sophie says the two of them are floating along on their own little cloud." Since we weren't speaking, Cherie was Sophie's and my chief mouthpiece. She was obviously thrilled by the young couple's love affair. "Sophie said to tell you that Nolan wants a wedding soon, before he has to go back to Canada. She says you should think about a trousseau for Rose."

"Tell Sophie I already arranged an appointment for Rose to be fitted at Lee Wong's Haberdashery tomorrow, at ten in the morning. Will you let Sophie and Rose know that Shamus will bring the buggy around at 9:30?"

"Sure thing, Liza. I'm going over there later tonight to play a game of Hearts with Sophie. I'll let her know about Shamus."

"Will you also tell her I'll be helping with the selection of clothes for Rose?"

"I'm sure they'll be real happy to see you at Lee Wong's, Liza." I didn't respond, and Cherie bustled off to the kitchen to finish cooking a pot of baked beans.

Nolan and Rose's happiness was like a fever. Sophie, Rose and all the ladies at Wayside were infected by the romance, bitten by the wedding bug. Sophie strutted around looking so proud I itched to slap her again; mostly because she was everything that I was not: a doting mother helping her daughter plan a wedding, a beaming beacon of love, a bonded friend to Rose. I was left out: in the background for the first time in my life, and I didn't much care for it. The fitting session at Lee Wong's amplified my feelings of unworthiness; Rose couldn't have been less interested in my presence in the staging room, much less in my opinions. I was pleased when Sophie stood up for me at one point. "Your mama is right about that color on you, Rose. The peach shade is far more becoming." Sophie shot the tiniest smile in my direction, and I curved my lips in return.

"While you finish fitting, I'll go over the fabric choices for a stout winter coat. I imagine you'll need something warm so far north," I said. "I am thinking a fine wool tweed in warm brown tones. How does that sound, Rose?"

She shrugged indifferently. "I prefer black or dark blue for a coat, but I might consider brown. I'll decide after I look at the fabrics Mr. Wong has in stock." Rose lifted her arms so that Lee Wong's seamstresses could pin the sleeves of a scarlet silk gown to the bodice. I watched as Sophie called out opinions to the tiny women swarming around Rose with measuring tapes and mouthfuls of pins. No one paid the slightest bit of attention to me except Lee Wong; he knew the hand that buttered his bread. I followed him to the shop's cavernous front room where he led the way down narrow aisles formed by hundreds of bolts of fabric.

I was curiously distressed by my status as an inconsequential outsider, and my distracted state made it doubly hard to understand Lee Wong's announcements in broken English of prices per yard. Finally, after inspecting the weight and drape of several wool fabrics, I instructed him to take samples of the fabrics I chose to the fitting room. "Mrs. Washington and my daughter, Rose, can make the final selection," I murmured. I paid Lee Wong double to have Rose's wardrobe finished in six weeks' time and went home to lie down with another sick headache.

The fitting session at Lee Wong's was the start of my unraveling shroud of indifference. Though I knew it was illogical to expect any kind of affection from Rose after years of motherly neglect, I suddenly longed to be part of the happy preparations. Sophie, Rose and the Wayside ladies made enthusiastic plans for a simple outdoor wedding followed by a five-course dinner, the menu of which was under spirited debate. I was accustomed to being the center of things; now I was the odd man out. My only contribution was to pay the bills.

In an attempt to avoid the discomfort of my feelings, I steered clear of everything to do with the wedding. Even so, bits and pieces came to me through the Wayside ladies, and feelings of loss were percolating in my depths. A lingering melancholy caught me more than once, and a recurring dream broke my usually sound sleep. In it, Rose is a little girl. She is running down a dark hallway. I am in pursuit, trying to save her from an unknown danger, pleading with her to stop, but she doesn't listen to me. Instead she runs faster. At the end of the hall she disintegrates into thin air. I wake screaming.

On the wedding day, I was surprised by the emotions raging beneath what I hoped passed as a calm exterior. Under the bower Shamus had constructed for the ceremony, Rose and Nolan stood against a background of trumpet vine and cheerful yellow sunflowers.

The ice-pink ruffles on Rose's dress shimmered and rippled in a gentle breeze; the color, chosen by Sophie, was the perfect complement to Rose's auburn curls and ivory complexion. Nolan stood at her side, a golden-haired warrior straight from the Norse myths. They were both beautiful, but my eyes were fixed on Rose. It was as if I was seeing her for the first time.

I began to weep, and quickly raised my handkerchief to dab away the evidence. It is fortunate that I was sitting with most of the assembled guests in back of me. It spared from scrutiny a floodgate of love for Rose, pushing its way past long- established barriers. It took a couple of minutes to stop the flow of tears, but a madam and business woman must maintain her composure without fail, must keep any chink in her armor a secret close to her chest.

In the face of San Francisco's unpredictable summer weather, luck provided a perfect, warm August evening for an outdoor dinner following the ceremony. Sophie and the girls had formed two long tables by stringing every card table in the neighborhood together. They were set with white tablecloths, candles, and vases of red roses sent by one of the Inn's most prominent clients who I still entertained once a month. Max popped the champagne bottles, and everyone toasted the bride and groom.

I don't remember much about dinner that night; my appetite was missing, and I only picked at each course. I am sure it was delicious; Cherie is an excellent cook. The dog under the table at my feet was well fed by the end of the evening. It was past seven when Sophie and Cherie carried out a splendid three-story wedding cake and a bowl of freshly whipped cream to spoon on top. Despite my lack of hunger, even I couldn't resist Sophie's special wedding cake, from an old recipe made in the kitchens of plantation homes across Louisiana. I hope she will write the recipe down someday. Who knows, there might be another wedding in the future: perhaps a granddaughter, if fortune shines.

After it grew difficult to see in the dark, the wedding party retired to the lounge at the front of the Inn for some entertainment. A pair of fiddlers hired by Max warmed up with "Camp Town Races," and the rug was rolled back for dancers. Rose and Nolan took the floor, and the wedding party clapped and whistled as they danced a fast mazurka. When a circle formed to do a traditional folk wedding dance, I stepped in next to Rose. The highlight of the evening was holding her hand during the dance, though it didn't appear to mean much to Rose. What could I expect, after all?

In the weeks after the wedding, I made tentative efforts to mend our relations, but it was too late; Rose had shut and locked the doors of her heart against me by then. I don't blame her; I only wish I'd come to my senses long before she married Nolan, so I had more time to work at winning her heart. As it was, I lost Rose and Sophie at the same time, and my awakening love for Rose moved into the category of unfinished business.

Sophie Washington
San Francisco
August 1878

Once the decision was made to go with Rose, the days remaining were filled with a flurry of packing. I helped Rose first. We folded her new dresses, skirts, blouses and coats in layers of tissue paper, keeping separate the traveling clothes she selected. Those were left out to pack in a large valise for carrying onto the freighter. The big trunks would not be within easy reach once we were underway, as they would be stowed in the hold below deck with the rest of the cargo *Good Hope* carried. "When we land at Victoria Harbor, yours and Sophie's trunks are first in line to be delivered to our house. It is wise to pack enough to tide you over for at least a couple of weeks in case the men can't get to it for a while. The hold is off limits to passengers, even for the captain's wife." Nolan smiled, and off he went to oversee preparations for our departure.

Nolan said that both sides of the house in Victoria were complete with essential cooking equipment as well as linens and bedding. "There are feather quilts and a houseful of furnishings. If you find something lacking, we'll replace it in Victoria, or on the mainland in the city. Vancouver is quite modern and not the rural backwater folks in the states would have you believe." Still, I packed a small trunk with my most handy kitchen items; a favorite cast-iron skillet, my sharpest paring knife, a set of spoons carved from olivewood that Mr. Pinelli, the old Italian grocer, had made for me a few years back.

I'd spread sheets of newsprint from the California Chronicle over the table and was preparing to wrap the owl teapot and matching cups I am especially fond of when I felt a pair of eyes on me. "Surely, you'll need a teapot when you come back, Sophie." Normally, Liza's tone was sassy; that evening it was unusually soft. "And I hope you come back someday. This is your home, you know. The apartment is waiting for you whenever you get homesick." She set a slender bottle on the table. "Will you take a break from packing, Sophie? I hoped you'd share some wine with me. It's blackberry. Isn't that your favorite?"

I nodded. "I'd love a glass."

Relations between Liza and I were frosty since the fight we'd had weeks ago. I hadn't forgiven her for slapping me, and the sting of the return slap had shocked her as well. We kept clear of each other ever since, except when forced by circumstances to be in close contact. Even during the wedding preparations and ceremony, we didn't communicate beyond a slight inclination of the head to acknowledge the other. If either of us needed to talk to the other, we sent a message through a third party. A few days earlier, I asked Cherie, the cook at Wayside, to tell Liza the news about my decision to leave with Rose.

I was glad to see Liza when she showed up that night; otherwise the bad feelings between us might have carried on. As it was, we took the first step toward forgiveness. We drank the whole bottle of wine and ended the evening crying like a pair of rainclouds, with Liza kissing me and telling me she has always loved me like a sister. Both of us were tipsy, but Liza was worse off from drinking the lion's share of the bottle. She wept and flung her arms around me. "Mark my words, Sophie: Someday you'll be back, I know." I didn't say anything, just nodded my head and burped her like a baby.

That night we broke our unspoken agreement to forget the past and talked about everything: Sweetbrier and Mama Lucille, Addie and Chemise, Jules and Augie, Phineas Snipe and his messy brains, and Bert under the pile of coal in the basement. "I dream that he's coming toward me with an axe sticking from his head, and right when he is about to catch me, I wake up." Liza shuddered. "I'm always drenched in sweat. I am afraid he's going to catch me some day. His hands are going to wrap around my throat, and he'll take me with him under the pile of coal."

"Honey, I'm sorry you have such bad nightmares." I knew all about the torment of terrible dreams.

"Oh Sophie, I'll miss you. I am comforted knowing you're here in the apartment. I don't know what I'll do without you."

"You'll manage, Liza. You've always been able to land on your feet. Now, you better climb into bed; otherwise I suspect you're going to lay your head on the table and start snoring."

"You're right, Sophie. I'm bone tired." Liza rose unsteadily to her feet, swaying slightly like dry grass in a breeze. Fortunately, Liza is usually a teetotaler; she makes a sloppy drunk. She needed an arm to lean on, so I walked her through the connecting door and down the hall to her bedroom. "Remember what I said, Sophie. Your home is here, and we are sisters."

"I'll remember, Liza. Don't you worry." I helped her put on her nightgown, and she stuck her skinny arms out obediently like a little child. She got in bed and gazed at me with damp eyes. "You might find it out of character, but I'll miss Rose, too." She let out a gasping sob and laid her head on the thick feather pillow. I bit my tongue from commenting that she was a little too late on the motherly love end of things. I couldn't have gotten a word out anyway; Liza fell asleep almost instantly. I tucked the blankets tighter around her and blew out the lamp.

It was late, and though I was almost as tired as Liza, I needed to finish packing; a wagon would arrive early tomorrow to carry our largest trunks, and a few pieces of furniture Rose had decided she couldn't live without, to the hold of *Good Hope*. Back in the apartment, I wrapped and boxed the owl teapot and cups that Liza had encouraged me to leave behind. I decided the familiarity of my tea set would comfort me in my new home, and though I'd never tell Liza, I wasn't certain I would return to the Wayside Inn for Gentlewomen.

PART III

A Parting of Ways

Liza Laurent

San Francisco

September 1878

A gnawing, sick feeling overtook me when Rose and Sophie climbed into the smart black and silver-trimmed carriage hired by Nolan to take them to his ship. The morning fog was thick, and the small crowd who'd come to say goodbye to the travelers huddled together for warmth. Rose and Sophie, bedecked with fancy new hats and carrying travel satchels, were last to emerge from the house. Our little crowd surged toward them for final farewells. I stepped forward to hug Rose, but she forestalled my embrace by extending her hand and shaking mine as if we were polite strangers.

"Good bye, Mama. I'll write when we arrive, so you'll know we've gotten there safe and sound."

She turned before I could get a word out of my tongue-tied mouth, ascended the steps to the open door and was swallowed from sight by the sedan's dark interior. The slender package I intended to give her was still in my hand.

"Well, Liza, I guess it's time to say goodbye for once and for all." Sophie put down her satchel and threw her arms around me in a tight hug.

"For once, but not for all," I countered and hugged her back. "My sixth sense tells me that you'll be home someday. As I've said before, your apartment will be waiting for you, dear friend and sister."

"Thank-you, Liza. It's a comfort to know."

"Come with me for a minute," I whispered. "There's something I need you to do." I led her out of earshot of the farewell party. "I know I've been a poor mother. You're the one who raised Rose and tended to her needs, and I thank you for it. I admit that I am selfish and shallow. I left it all in your lap, Sophie. I apologize, and I hope that you will understand and forgive me someday."

"No need to apologize, Liza. I love Rose like she's my own flesh and blood. Being a mama to her has been one hundred percent pleasure for me." Sophie paused for a minute and considered her next words carefully. "I'm not the person you need to mend fences with; Rose is the one who's been hurting all these years, hoping for her real mother to show her some love. And Liza, you are the real mother I could never be."

"I am afraid it's too late. Rose is hardened against me, and I don't blame her. My behavior towards her has been unforgivable; I see that so plainly. Now she'll be so far away, undoing the damage seems impossible."

"Rose might not show it on the outside, but in her gut she still loves you, I'd bet all the tea in China."

"I'd be happily surprised if that were true. I'm not so sure it is. I fear she's nailed shut the door just when I'm ready to knock on it." I held out the package I'd intended to give Rose. "Will you give her this? It's a few items of jewelry that I'd like her to have."

Sophie nodded and put the box in her carryall. "Now I better stop holding up the carriage, Liza. Nolan wants us to board the ship and be ready to go by noon."

I kissed her on the cheek and watched her climb up the grill-work steps to the carriage. Though the assembled group of well-wishers surrounded me, for the first time in my life I felt truly alone.

The look on Liza's face was like she was getting a tooth pulled. I felt a tug in my heart too, but not near what her face told the world that morning. Right before we left, I'd leaned from the carriage window and held out my hand. She reached up, but only the tips of our fingers touched.

"Don't worry, Liza. Everything is going to work out fine. You're strong and smart, and you've handled a lot worse than me and Rose going off." She nodded and tried to hide her tears, but she couldn't. I lowered my voice. "I'll make sure Rose gets your package and appreciates the contents."

"Thank-you, Sophie."

"You've been a good mother these last few months. Be patient, and someday Rose will let you back into her heart. Just keep the love going."

"How? Rose will be hundreds of miles away. What if I never see her again?"

"You'll see the both of us before our lives have been paid up. With all the trains going in, soon it won't take more than a few days to get back and forth. Until then, you can write letters. I expect a long one from you at least once a month."

Liza hiccoughed out a little sob and dabbed her eyes with a hanky she pulled from her shirtwaist. "You better promise you'll write back."

"Sure thing, Liza."

"I'll miss you, Sophie. You're my inspiration." She stood on tiptoe, and we squeezed our intertwined fingers one last time before the carriage driver gave the signal for the horses to move. I kept my gaze fixed on Liza with that pained expression on her face until she faded from view.

"What did Princess Liza ask you to do, Sophie?"

"I'll tell you all about it once we're on the water, Rose." We had a lot to talk about on the voyage to Vancouver Island, and it wasn't time to start a long story.

Nagging thoughts entered my mind as the coach clattered down the narrow streets; a sharp pang of worry swept in like a tide. I couldn't help wondering if I was doing a wise thing, moving more than eight hundred miles away. Liza and I had been in San Francisco going on twenty years, and I was used to the place. The thought of starting over in new territory was suddenly overwhelming.

Rose, with her uncanny ability to read my thoughts, patted me on the knee. "I know it's a little scary to move so far away, but it's also sort of exciting, don't you think? Why, Sophie, in a few weeks we will inhabit an unknown place and create the life we want! You and I are pioneers setting forth on the adventure of our lives, and I know it will be grand. I am so happy you decided to join me on this journey."

"I wouldn't have missed it for all the candy in heaven, Rose." I forced myself to sound enthusiastic for her sake. "I've been itching to travel for a while now. This is going to open up a whole new world."

It ended up that Vancouver Island was just one leg in my travels.

At the wharf, the coachman parked the carriage as close as he could to the pier where *Good Hope* was preparing for departure.

Carts and wagons waiting to unload or pick up cargo from the busy harbor jammed the streets so passage through was impossible. "This is as close as we're likely to get unless we want to wait an hour for the traffic to move." He unfolded the steps from under the carriage and helped us down. My legs were a bit shaky from the excitement and fear of the upcoming sea voyage, and I appreciated his steadying hand. I also appreciated the fact that he didn't snatch it away because of my skin color.

"I'll get a handcart for the luggage and a mate from *Good Hope* to help. I should be back in under an hour. One or both of you must stay and watch over the buggy. Around here, if you blink your eyes, they'll rob you blind."

Rose chose to go with the coachman in hopes that she would see Nolan. Their time together had been scarce; Nolan had been preparing *Good Hope* for departure all week. He came home to the apartment late and left early. "You go ahead, Rose. I'll stay and keep an eye on things," I said, plopping myself down on the wooden box the coachman unloaded for me to sit on while I waited.

People bustled back and forth along the clapboard sidewalk. I daydreamed as I watched them from under the awning that shaded the sidewalk in front of Miller's Dry Goods Emporium. Besides Mexicans and Chinese, I saw several people of my own color, as well as specimens from who knows what other nations, some strolling as if they hadn't a care in the world, others rushing past on the wide walkway stretching along the waterfront. A slender Negro man passing by reminded me in looks of my brother Jerome. My mind returned to nagging thoughts about the past.

Though I'd sent letters to Sweetbrier, nothing came back except a tattered envelope I'd put in the mail six months before. Someone had printed *Undeliverable* across the back. I hadn't written a letter since, but the night before departing I couldn't sleep; I wrote to my mother, telling the news about my move to Vancouver Island. "I pray one day

I'll come back to Sweetbrier and see Daddy's and your sweet, dear faces. Your forever loving daughter, Sophie." I sealed the envelope and asked Liza to post it for me. Maybe this time the mail carrier would find my folks.

I sat patiently by our pile of luggage, watching the fishermen and sailors go about their business. An hour or so later, around midmorning, I was glad to see Rose approaching with a weather-beaten man whose skin looked like he'd been stuffed into a drawer wet and dried into a million wrinkles. He introduced himself as Tim. "I'm jack-of-all-trades on *Good Hope*. You ladies stand aside, please. I'll load your gear in a jiffy." Tim stacked our bags onto the handcart he was pulling. We set off down the harbor promenade to a long wooden pier where a dozen ships were moored in the big slips.

I kept thinking that the next ship would be ours, but we passed them all. At the end of the pier, Tim stopped. He gestured to the vessel in front of us. "This is *Good Hope*. She's a dandy craft and she'll get you safe and sound to the island." I wasn't expecting such a large ship. It was twice as long and double the width of most of the other boats we'd passed. Nolan must be doing very well for himself, I thought. All the better for Rose.

A short man with bowlegs and sailor blues came down the gangplank to meet us. "Welcome ladies. I'm Abe Harper. *Good Hope* is primarily a cargo ship, but I serve as the purser when we board passengers. Mr. MacDonald asked me to show you to your quarters." He made a little bow and shook both our hands. "If you'll follow me, I'll take you to your rooms, so you can get settled before we embark. Right this way, ladies."

We followed Abe up the plank and along the deck. Tim abandoned the handcart and followed behind with an impressive array of our luggage piled on every arm, shoulder, and all convenient balancing points including his head. Abe stopped at the last door we came to in a row of highly polished mahogany doors. He opened it and ushered us into a well-appointed cabin with a dozen red roses in a china vase on the table. "This is your home away from home, ladies. The stateroom suite has a sitting room, a bedroom, and a water closet for your exclusive use."

"Why, it's very attractive! Everything is so clean and shiny, I can practically see my reflection," said Rose.

"This suite is usually Captain MacDonald's. It's the most comfortable cabin on ship, and he wanted you ladies to have it. For this trip he's bunking in the first mate's quarters below deck." Abe paused in the doorway. "I'll send around a cabin boy to help stow your gear."

"That won't be necessary, Mr. Harper. Sophie and I can manage."

"Very well. I'll leave you to it. Pleasure meeting both of you." He bobbed his head in the same little bow. "Don't hesitate to come to me should you need anything. I can solve most problems having to do with your comfort and safety aboard ship."

"Thank-you. We'll keep that in mind."

Rose and I unpacked the belongings we needed for the next week and stowed the rest under the bottom bunk in the bedroom. Abe Harper came knocking on the door after an hour or so. "Captain MacDonald wishes he could join you ladies on a tour of the ship, but he is overseeing ship business. He asked me to show you around, if you'd like."

"Of course! We'd love a tour," said Rose.

"Follow me, ladies. After I show you the fine points of *Good Hope*, I'll introduce you to Albert, our cook. He puts on a great tea. We'll have worked up a thirst by then, and perhaps an appetite, too."

Rose pulled a watch from her reticule. "I thought we'd be on the open seas by now. When do we set sail?"

"If you're around ships much, you'll find out that no matter how good the skipper or how new and modern the cargo ship, the time of departure is always hours later than intended. There was a delay in the coal delivery, but it's supposed to be here soon." Abe led us up a narrow set of stairs to the upper deck. "This deck is called the bridge. The cabin in the front is where the business of steering the boat and navigating its course takes place." Abe gave a quick lesson about the bow and the stern. "That's the foresail," he said. "If our steam fails, God forbid, we hoist the sails. It's a lot slower going when that happens, depending on the wind patterns."

"What would make the steam fail?" I asked.

Abe struck a match and lighted his tobacco pipe. "Well, there are a few things that can go wrong with the machinery. Boilers can blow up in the worst case." My expression must have been alarmed, because he quickly assured me that it was rare for a boiler to explode. "Don't worry your head, Miss Washington. If such a thing happened, the boiler rooms are built to contain an explosion. These days, it's rare that a boiler explosion actually sinks a ship."

"Very comforting to hear, I'm sure." The words came out smoothly, but my imagination pictured the gray waters closing over my head. What had possessed me to leave my comfortable apartment at Wayside, I wondered? Fortunately, the thoughts didn't linger.

We finished our tour of *Good Hope* around three that afternoon. Abe had planned it so tea was waiting for us in the dining hall. The cook was serving hot scones with butter and jam when a surprise visit from Nolan sent a smile sailing across Rose's face. She jumped up from the table to hug him. "I wondered when I'd see you, Nolan."

"I'm sorry I couldn't show you around the ship myself."

"Your duties as captain come first. There will be plenty of time for tours on the island. I expect you to show us all over."

"I promise you will see the island and all its secret nooks and crannies. I have a canoe trip in mind for one of our first adventures."

"I can hardly wait." The glow in their eyes was a dead giveaway for how they felt about one another. To tell the truth, I was a little envious.

We spent our first night on *Good Hope* docked in the harbor. At the last minute, Nolan agreed to take on a shipment of pre-made trousers and work shirts, but a broken wheel on the wagon carrying the load of goods made the transport impossible until early the next morning. "We'll have to wiggle things around to make room in the hold. We're carrying a full load already." Nolan used a crust of bread to mop up the last bit of gravy on his dinner plate. "I expect we'll be seaward by midmorning."

He estimated correctly; at 10:15 in the morning, *Good Hope* was finally ready to set out for Vancouver Island. A tugboat dragged us slowly through the foggy mist to the mouth of the bay. The sun was directly overhead, promising to break through the clouds, when we reached the open sea and started north toward Canada.

On the voyage of knowing myself, I've determined I am not a sailor. Traveling over waves of any size makes my stomach churn and fight until the contents end in a bedpan or spittoon. Rose has stayed by my side during the day, leaving me only to visit with Nolan when the first mate sends him to take some rest. She insists that I stand up and walk the deck every few hours. "Come on, Sophie. The fresh air will do you good." The outside air does relieve me somewhat, but never for long. The bunk in my room is where I want to lie most of the time. Thank heavens this trip is fairly short. I'd never make it around the Horn, or even down to Panama.

Rose brings tea every morning. I partake of it gingerly, as my poor insides are sore. A cup of tea and a dry scone are all I can manage most days. After breakfast, Rose reads a chapter from *Great Expectations*. Pip and Miss Havisham keep my mind off my continually jumpy stomach. Estella, Miss Havisham's pet, reminds me just the littlest bit of Liza. I don't share my thoughts with Rose.

Yesterday morning, I gave Rose the package from Liza. She opened it like a rattlesnake was going to jump out and bite her. Inside was a beautiful string of carved jade beads and a delicate gold pendant I knew was Liza's favorite. An envelope addressed to Rose in Liza's sloping script followed. "Here," she handed the letter to me. "You read it, Sophie. I'm sure you're more interested in what Princess Liza has written than I."

I opened the letter and unfolded it, pausing a moment to weigh what I wanted to say. I took a deep breath and let the words fly out of my mouth. "Rose, your mother is finally reaching for you. Now, you're the one on the cold side. Does that feel good to you, to make yourself so hard?" She didn't answer. "Now, I'm going to read this letter aloud and I expect you to sit there and to listen with an open mind." Rose nodded, absently passing the jade beads from hand to hand as I read.

Dear Rose,

This letter reaches you on your way to a new life as a married lady. I hope you enjoy and wear the beads and the gold pendant. Mr. Fong from the Oriental Treasures shop says to wear them when you want good luck. The pendant is an heirloom from your grandfather's family and was given to your grandmother when she was on her deathbed. I carried it from the state of Louisiana to San Francisco when Sophie and I had to leave in a hurry.

I have never told you about my past. The story of your heritage is a long, complicated one that would take too many pages to write in the scant time remaining on this morning of your departure. I have given Sophie permission to tell the secrets buried in my past, and hers, too. I am ashamed to admit that what took place long ago shaped my actions and helped create my failure to be a loving parent. I only ask you to keep an open heart after you hear the worst in my tawdry history.

I live in hopes that someday you will understand just a little and let yourself love me like you did all through your girlhood, until I sent you to Most Holy Name. I promise I will never hurt you again, dearest daughter. I know it is hard for you to overcome my past cruelties and to forgive me. You might never come to forgiveness, but I want you to know I love you more than anyone in the world, until the end of time.

Love,

Mama

We were quiet for a moment, then Rose laughed, but there wasn't any humor in it; her laugh was brittle and sharp. "Don't you think it's a little late for Mother to pour on the love?"

"It's about time you heard some of the things that went on in your mother's life before you were born. Maybe if you heard what she went through, you'd understand why Liza is the way she is."

"I've had years of Mama acting like I was a nuisance. I tried so hard to get her to love me, and finally, I just gave up. I don't think anything you say could make me understand her better."

"Well, maybe you'll think differently when you hear the whole story." We sat in matching armchairs in the cozy stateroom, and for next few hours I told her everything, starting with Fern Dumond and her affair with Hugo Laurent. "Fern would be your grandmother if she hadn't bled to death when your mama was born. Fern named her baby girl Elizabeth before she passed out of the mortal world. My parents, Addie and Garvus, stepped in to raise the child. We called her Lizzie, and she was my best friend."

Rose listened to the story, asking an occasional question, but mainly listening. I watched the expressions on her face jump from curiosity, to anger, to disgust, as I told her the story of Liza's childhood. I told her about crazy old Miss Lucille, when she got the inkling to take Lizzie away from our family and raise her herself, and how her real father, Mr. Hugo, up and died and left Sweetbrier in the hands of his son, Bert. I shuddered when I said his name, and Rose asked why.

"Bert Laurent was a monster. He terrorized the slaves and went around raping and mistreating those of us who had the misfortune to cross his path." I didn't spare any details; I told Rose that Bert was her father as well as her uncle.

"How could Mama allow that to happen?" Rose's face was pale.

"Bert raped her, honey."

"And this foul creature was my father?"

I nodded. "And he was the father of Jules and Augie, my two missing boys. That would make them your half-brothers, Rose." I told her how Bert had raped me and later stolen my angel babies. "Bert was cruel and violent. I stood up to him to find out where my boys were, and he near beat me near to death. It's how I lost my eye."

"This story is giving me the chills!"

"It isn't over honey, and you should hear all of it. The day we left Sweetbrier, I saw him raping your mama, and I knew I had to stop him." I told her about the axe and both of us smashing Bert over the head until he was dead, and how Liza and I buried the wicked man under a pile of coal. "Liza fixed us up with a carriage and we left Sweetbrier in the middle of the night. That's when we came west."

"Did you worry that you might get caught?"

"That brings me to the rest of the story. Someone did try to catch us. Liza had to defend us to the death. It made her as hard as nails." I told her the story of Phineas Snipe and how Liza had to shoot him.

"I can't believe what I'm hearing!"

"We pushed him down a deep crack in the mountainside where his body isn't likely to be found."

"You're saying that Mama committed a second cold-blooded murder? I wish you hadn't told me! More than that, I wish she wasn't my mother!"

"Listen here, Rose. Answer this question; do you love me?"

"You know I do!"

"Well, I wouldn't be here today if your mother hadn't stopped Phineas Snipe and his plans for us. In the end, we'd have hanged by the neck and you'd have never been born. Would that have been better than your mama stopping a bad man?" I paused to let the words sink in. "Have you wondered how she burned her hands?"

Rose nodded. "You told me years ago that she'd burned them in a campfire."

"That was a lie. Truth is, in order to save us from being abused by that man, Liza picked up a red-hot pot with her bare hands. She threw the potatoes from it right into his face, and him being blinded gave her a chance to grab the pistol. It was really self-defense."

"Oh Sophie, I think I've heard enough for one day!"

I took Rose's hand. It was ice cold. "I know it's a lot for you to take in all at once. My intention was for you to understand your mama a little better. She needs you to forgive her, Rose. She knows she's done you wrong."

"What I understand above all is that Nolan must never hear a word of this. He might regret marrying into a family with such a soiled, shameful history. I couldn't bear him thinking less of me because of the despicable story I've heard today. Promise me you'll never speak of it again, Sophie."

Thus, my attempt to open Rose's heart to her mother's affections was firmly rejected. Even so, I never stopped trying to mend the hurt and pain between Liza and Rose.

Rose MacDonald

Vancouver Island

Fall 1878

I refuse to let Sophie's revelations about Mama dampen my mood. I will never speak of Mama's grimy secrets and the skeletons in our family closet; I can't risk tainting my marriage to the most perfect man in the world. It frightens me to think he might find out. I would rather die than have Nolan feel disgust for me. He must never know; it is all the more reason to distance myself from Liza Laurent and her unsavory business. I am closer and closer to blocking her from my thoughts entirely.

Sophie and I have been here less than a month, and I am in love with Vancouver Island already. No wonder Nolan is so enthusiastic when he talks of the island with its stunning landscapes and the incredible sea surrounding it. Sophie has not taken to this perfect island as readily as I have. She grumbles about the rain and claims the damp plagues her joints. Even so, she tries hard to forge a life here. She is a good sport and she makes an effort to be enthusiastic, but I can tell that it is an effort. It worries me a little.

Nolan, a skilled outdoorsman and canoeist, couldn't wait to show us the eastern seaboard between the island and the mainland. A mere week after we'd arrived, Nolan arranged a water tour. "I learned to paddle from the local tribe when I was a lad. I spent a whole summer at a Songhee camp, and at the end I was as brown as the

Indians. If you saw a crowd of us lads together, you couldn't tell I was a white boy. It was one of my finest summers, learning how to canoe and fish alongside the experts. I hope you like boating as much as I do."

"I'm sure I'll love it."

Nolan set a departure time for eight sharp. "We'll need the whole day to make the scenic tour I have in mind."

The next morning our carriage driver took us to the sandy cove near the harbor where we'd launch our canoe. A gentle mist was falling, and Sophie shivered. "Is it going to keep on misting like this all day?" she asked.

"Don't worry, it will burn off in an hour or two. I predict that the rest of the day will be warm and sunny." Sophie looked skeptical. Nolan helped Sophie and me into the boat and talked over the basics of safety. "You don't want to lunge from side to side or jump around. A canoe is actually quite stable, but it pays to move mindfully." He pushed the boat into the shallows and waded out to scramble aboard. Ka-kay-un, a member of the tribe and great friend of Nolan's, paddled at the bow, with Nolan taking the rear.

"We'll keep the eastern shore in sight this time and find a nice little island to stop for lunch," Nolan said. "I asked Ka-kay-un to bring along a couple of extra poles so you ladies can try your hand at fishing." Despite the mist glistening across the surfaces of the canoe and beading in Nolan's close-cropped beard and Ka-kay-un's thick black hair, Sophie and I stayed warm and dry under oilskin caps and outerwear.

Gliding through the gentle swells in the fresh sea air satisfied all my senses. I couldn't get enough of the invigorating fragrance of the breeze and the thrills of riding beside a whale one moment and a school of dolphins the next. Wherever the eye turned was a splendid view. I could see why Nolan liked canoeing; it suited me as well. Sophie, on the other hand, was not enthralled. The smile on her face was frozen and unnatural. "Are you feeling all right?" I asked.

"I'm just trying not to drown is all."

I squeezed her hand. "Relax, Sophie. Ka-kay-un and Nolan know what they're doing. They'd hardly take us somewhere unsafe."

"Easy for you to say," she muttered.

"Why, it's wonderful fun, Sophie! I don't understand how you could find it otherwise."

"There are two kinds of dogs, Rose. One variety likes water and swimming and the second kind is scared to death of sinking and won't go near water except to take a drink. I'm a sinker, Rose. You, on the other hand, are a swimmer."

"You told me that you and Mama went swimming when you were little girls."

"Liza did the swimming. I waded mostly. Besides, it was just a shallow pond where we dogpaddled around; this here is what I call big water, with big fish in it."

"Do you want Nolan to take us back home?"

Sophie took a deep breath and shook her head. "Don't pay any attention to me. I'm starting to enjoy it more," she said. I was unconvinced, but happy she hadn't insisted on returning to the shore. I was enchanted by the beauty around us and would have been disappointed had our trip been cut short.

The sun was overhead when Nolan suggested stopping for lunch. "My stomach is growling to be fed. Be on the lookout for any promising shorelines.

"What about the island ahead of us?" Sophie asked.

"That's D'Arcy Island, and a splendid place to stop off," said Nolan. It took several minutes for the men to maneuver the boat into a sandy cove. We unloaded the picnic and some folding stools that Nolan had stashed under the stern deck. Ka-kay-un built a fire in an old pit he found on a bluff above the beach, and Nolan pulled a grill and a tin teapot from his equipment sack. He filled the pot with water from a canteen and set the grill and pot over the flames.

We sat around the fire pit eating beef pasties, slices of cheese, butter pickles and applesauce cake while the water warmed up for a cup of tea. After lunch, Ka-kay-un led us to the ruins of an old Indian encampment on the northern side of the island. "This was place for summer camping. The salmon go up the inland strait, and this good place to catch and prepare fish. We smoke it and dry it for food in middle of winter."

"If I never eat another piece of salmon I wouldn't shed a tear. The only way I can stand the stuff is when the taste is covered up by a good sauce," Sophie muttered softly.

I laughed. "Don't let Ka-kay-un hear you say that. He'd never forgive you!"

"Rose, if you and Sophie are game to try your hand at fishing or exploring this little berg, I'll leave you here with Ka-kay-un and go sink a crab trap. I forgot on our way in, but if I set one now, we have a chance of catching a few when we head back home. We'll hopefully have crab for supper."

Nolan pushed off in the canoe, and Sophie and I followed Ka-kay-un down the beach. He carried a bucket and a shovel for the clams he hoped to find. At a sandy low beach that met the shallows he stopped. "Clam make little breathing hole. You need have good eye to find." He pointed out several possible holes and finally chose one. He dug his shovel deep underneath the hole and overturned a pair of palm-sized clams with creamy yellow shells. Soon, with our help scanning the sand for telltale breathing holes, he had filled his bucket.

An hour passed pleasantly. I continued my walk along the beach looking for interesting shells and brightly colored carnelians. Sophie found a shady spot at our picnic camp and settled down with a book she'd brought in her satchel. Ka-kay-un put a clam for each of us on the grill, and the cooked product with a sprinkle of salt on the top was a most delicious treat. When Nolan returned, Ka-kay-un handed him a plate of two of the largest clams. "Has nature ever made a more perfect food?" Nolan swallowed the tasty creature, obviously savoring it. "And on the way home, we'll check the trap I laid to see if nature left us another gift of perfect food."

We set out on our return voyage in the late afternoon, stopping along the way to pull up Nolan's crab traps. Between the two he'd set, he'd caught three large crabs and a smaller fellow that he threw back into the water. He withdrew a wooden barrel from under the port deck, put the crabs inside with a bucket of water, and fastened down the top. "We'll stop at the harbor where a fellow cleans the crab and steams it in a big pot in just a few minutes. It will save us some work when we get home."

The sky began to cloud up as we made our way towards Victoria Harbor. A sprinkle of light rain fell as we reached the shore. "Just in time," said Nolan. He and Ka-kay-un landed the canoe on the sandy spot where we'd launched. The driver was waiting with our carriage. "You and Sophie go on home. I'll get the canoe put away and the crab cleaned, and I'll follow as soon as I can." Sophie was the first to scramble aboard the coach. "I'm tired to the bone," she declared. She was quiet as a church mouse on the drive home. Sophie was a landlubber from then on; no amount of wheedling convinced her to board a canoe ever again.

To me, that first canoe adventure is a cherished memory. Late in the evening after we'd gone to bed, I told Nolan I wanted to learn how to paddle. "I think I'd be an excellent crew member."

Nolan pulled me into his arms. "We'll start your training next weekend, Rose." For the rest of the evening we tried to make a baby.

Liza Laurent
San Francisco
1878 - 1879

I am alone in the house on the hill. Though surrounded by people: my girls, Max, our clients; I have been abandoned by Sophie, my dearest friend and sister in soul, and by the daughter I've not loved and cherished as I should. It was heartless and cruel, the distaste I had for motherhood; the aversion I felt toward Rose. None of it was Rose's fault. I see that so sharply now. I've turned a mirror of inspection on myself and the war between detachment and guilt is over. Guilt has won. I'll never feel peace until Rose forgives me, and she might not.

There is more to forgive than she knows. I had carnal relations with her husband the night before he met Rose in the library. He was returning for a second helping of pleasures of the flesh. I told Nolan to wait for me in the library. It was my turn to deal the cards in our poker room; I always dealt hands when Max set up a high stakes game. I am a skilled dealer and known for being fair and straight and running a table where no one throws a bloody punch or shoots their firearm.

The game dragged on longer than usual, and when I finally opened the library door at half past midnight, Nolan was gone. I was surprised, but assumed he was tired from our exertions the night before. I'd spent much of the day napping and had fully recovered my strength by the time the poker game commenced at 8:00 p.m. Nolan, though young and strong, may not have had the benefit of a restful day. I shrugged and carried on with the now uneventful evening. I asked Max to pour me a rarely partaken nightcap, which I drank and then retired to bed where I slept soundly.

The following day, I discovered the reason for Nolan's earlier-than-expected departure when he announced his intentions toward Rose. I admit I was hurt and angry at first, but when reason prevailed I saw clearly it was a perfect solution for the problem of Rose. Though it meant the loss of Nolan, it also meant that Rose would no longer be a fly in the pudding. I gave my blessing and stepped out of the way of the rapid and steamy romance.

Rose and Nolan were perfectly suited; they were healthy and handsome and radiantly happy; together they sent off a glow. My breath caught when I looked at the two. An absence of jealous feelings over losing Nolan surprised me. In fact, I was happy for them. On the occasions when Nolan and I came face to face, we were polite and formal, like strangers, as if the times we'd lain together were erased. I was thankful for our mutual understanding; it relieved a nagging worry that Rose might find out. An unusual wave of love for my daughter overwhelmed me; for once, all I cared about was Rose.

I envied Sophie's position as her confidant, friend and stand-in mother. I vowed to do everything I could to make up for my past treatment of Rose. My efforts were fruitless: well intentioned, but too late. Rose had erected an armor of indifference that nothing could penetrate. I had to accept what I'd caused after I came to my senses and realized everything I hadn't been for Rose. In bed at night, Sister Margaret's offer to counsel my lost soul repeated through my brain until I wanted to scream from the relentless persistence of the thought.

By nature I am not superstitious, yet the night before Rose and Sophie's departure, out of a desperate hope to enlist any means to heal relations between Rose and me, I set up a little altar in my bedroom. I pulled a small table to a pool of moonlight. On top of it I arranged my farewell gift to Rose: the pendant from the Laurent family and a beautiful necklace of carved jade beads I'd purchased especially for Rose. I drew a chair to the table and placed both hands atop the jewelry. "Please let Rose's heart soften toward me each time she wears one of these necklaces." I repeated it five times, remembering the instructions for an old voodoo charm that Sophie and I learned many years before at Sweetbrier. "In matters of the heart, five is the magic number," the ancient wrinkled woman had said.

For a final touch, I lighted a two-cent bundle of sage from the curio shop run by a Mexican couple. "Sage good for clearing up any cloud over your relationship," said the shop owner's wife in her thick accent. I climbed into bed when the sage was still smoldering and fell into a shallow, troubled sleep. The next morning, the sight of the makeshift altar embarrassed me. I moved the table back to its proper place and packed the necklaces carefully into a box for Rose.

It was one of her greatest rejections, that she didn't take the box from me when I tried to hand it to her. I deserved it, but it didn't make it hurt any less.

In the weeks after Sophie and Rose left for Canada, I began to wonder about my mental state. I felt so unlike the calm, collected, successful Liza Laurent, the center of her own universe, the mistress of her own destiny. Inside my shell of a body was an ache of loss and remorse that made me weak. A feverish malaise overcame me, and I took to my bed. Ten days later, when I finally rose from my cocoon to assume my customary duties, I deduced from the usual symptoms that I was carrying my son-in-law's child, and based on simple calculations, it was near five months along.

Pure sexual passion with Nolan had upended my usual thoroughness at preventing unwanted pregnancies. I'd abandoned my guard and thrown precautions aside. Now, I paid for it with a swelling belly and agonizing guilt over the perversion of carrying Rose's half-sibling and stepchild.

I knew immediately that the baby must be sacrificed. I'd proved to be a miserable failure as a mother to Rose, and the idea of giving birth to a child spawned with Rose's own husband was unbearable. I sent for Doctor Cline who usually attended the Wayside Inn ladies when they needed his special services. "You should have paid heed sooner, Liza. You'll have to come to the surgery for this particular case, it being so advanced and all."

"When can you take care of it?" I asked.

"We need to act quickly, before the fetus grows larger."

I shuddered, but quickly recovered my resolve. "I can make arrangements whenever you are ready, Doctor."

"It will cost $115.00, Liza. Up front."

"That's a lot."

"It's gone beyond a simple procedure. And I must factor in the risk to my practice. I am breaking the law, you know. I hear some doctors are arrested and thrown in jail for doing these procedures."

I nodded. "I can pay half today and the rest when you do the operation."

"All right, I'll set up the surgery for Thursday after office hours. I must ask that you arrive at the back door, discreetly, to avoid drawing attention. Come at dusk and do your best to conceal your condition; the child you're carrying is definitely showing. A cloak might be useful, and a tighter corset could help. I have to use extra caution these days. I don't need busybodies nosing into the services I provide."

The Thursday appointment meant two dreadful days to think in morbid detail of the child I was giving a death sentence. I tossed and turned through both long nights, suffering terrifying nightmares. In one, a dog ripped a baby apart with its teeth. I woke in a cold sweat. During the daylight hours I was afflicted with a sick headache, and persistent nausea brought up the contents of my stomach. Cherie insisted that I eat and prepared my favorite clam chowder to tempt me. I took one bite and pushed the bowl away.

It was a relief when Thursday evening came. Like a person headed for the gallows, I no longer suffered the anxiety of waiting. Max helped me into the sedan, as I was not my usual sturdy self. The carriage rumbled down the streets toward the busy Mission District where Dr. Cline lived above his surgery. To avoid attracting attention by clattering up to the front of Dr. Cline's clinic, Max dropped me off at the end of the block. "I'll pick you up when the doc sends word." I walked the rest of the way, turning down an alley leading to the back entrances of the row of buildings. Dr. Cline opened the back door as soon as I knocked. "Good, Liza. You're right on time. Come in."

He led me to the clinic through a long hallway dissecting the ground floor living quarters. I stood in the chilly room while Dr. Cline lit several lanterns. "We need good light for this!" he said, heartily. I shivered. "Go ahead and remove your skirts, Liza, and put on this smock." He ushered me into a closet-sized dressing room, and I changed from my gown to the cape-like garment he'd provided. "Now, you'll need to lie on the table." I was shivering so hard that my teeth chattered. "I'll cover you with a blanket, and when you're ready, I'll start the chloroform."

I am generally in control of my emotions, but as I sat on the edge of the operating table, a sudden shower of tears flooded down my cheeks onto the surgery smock.

The doctor dabbed my tears away with a ball of cotton. "There, there, Liza." His tone was soothing. "It will be over before you know it. Drink this draught of calmative." He handed me a cup of a thick, dark substance. I gulped the bitter stuff down. "Here is a mask that I'm going to fit over your mouth and nose," he said. "Be sure to breathe deeply. You don't want to be awake while I'm poking around."

A pungent but not entirely unpleasant smell filled the mask. I felt myself drift into a land where figments of the imagination come to life. I lingered in the nether world until the chloroform took me to a state of unconsciousness necessary for the Doctor to perform his gruesome task. I have no recollections of the actual procedure. Doctor Cline said I screamed and became hysterical. "You told a person named Sophie about blood seeping from under a pile of coal. 'We've got to stop it,' you said. 'Bring a bucket and a mop!' and then you carried on about someone named Mr. Snipe and that your hands were burning up."

"Did I say anything else?" My voice was weak to my own ears.

"I couldn't make heads or tails of it. You were talking gibberish, and you were thrashing around so much I had to increase the chloroform and put restraints on your arms and legs. There was quite a bit of bleeding, Liza. You will undoubtedly feel weak. I recommend staying in bed for a few days. Don't push yourself until you're fully healed. You don't want to risk hemorrhaging."

I hadn't realized I was crying again until Dr. Cline used another wad of cotton to wipe away the tears. "You made a hard decision, Liza. I hope you don't regret it."

But I did regret it. Although the decision was made to protect the daughter I'd wronged, I was haunted by thoughts of the baby I'd killed. Now, added to my guilt and remorse about Rose was the execution of an innocent.

Sophie Washington
Vancouver Island
November 1881

Rose and Nolan are going to be parents. I am so happy for them. They are overjoyed, and I understand why. Poor Rose was half crazy from miscarrying twice since we moved here; the first one was bad enough, but the second time she lost the baby I feared for her, it sent her so far down in spirits. This pregnancy has saved her, and once again she shines with happiness, beaming her delight out to the rest of us mortals.

The way she fusses over every detail in preparing for the new baby is almost comical. I can't tease her about going overboard; she is deadly serious about doing the right thing, and she doesn't take a joke. Her latest project is the addition in the upstairs washroom of an actual porcelain baby's tub she ordered from Vancouver. Nolan picked it up at the harbor shipping office, and Rose is having a special counter built of marble just for the baby, which is an extravagance if you ask me, particularly since they don't plan on being in this house after the new house is finished. I can only shake my head over it. A nice little basin set in the kitchen sink works just fine, in my opinion. But Rose will have nothing but the best, and she reads all the books about raising an infant that she can get her hands on.

I can't help comparing Rose to Liza and marveling at the differences. From the beginning of Liza's pregnancy, she hated her condition and the coming baby. I thank God every day that she didn't succeed in getting rid of my precious Rose all those years ago. After she used the crochet hook to try to poke out the baby, I made her promise not to hurt the poor innocent unborn creature. She agreed, but her mind was set against the baby. When Rose was born, she handed her over to me, and from then on, she avoided her daughter. Rose is the reverse; she has already established herself as a doting parent. Maybe she is trying to make up for the way Liza treated her.

Liza is paying for it now. I read between the lines in the letters she sends every week or so. She sounds lost and lonely; I feel how forlorn she is. I am tempted to pay her a visit to straighten things out, but I dread the ocean travel. Plus, Rosie needs me now more than ever to help with the newest member of the MacDonald family. I will tide over with Rose and Nolan as long as I can bear living on the island.

I am not a complainer by nature, but for the life of me, I cannot get used to this infernal gray, clammy, cold climate. My bones long for the warmth of Sweetbrier, though home could be on the swampy side during the warm season. Walking around in that weather all you do is ooze little beads of sweat. Still I'd take Louisiana weather any day over weather on the island. In winter, which lasts a good six months it seems, Victoria makes San Francisco feel balmy. On the coldest days I can't get my feet warm, and my bad eye aches something fierce. My mood gets sour, and I end up dwelling on a bunch of stuff that would be better if it was forgotten. Rose, on the other hand, loves everything about life on the island.

I've done a lot of thinking since Rose and I moved here. When we left San Francisco, I thought I might never see Liza again. Now I know I couldn't bear it. She is as much my family as my own parents and brother, as my own missing sons. I have resolved that I will return to San Francisco in the future. It may be years before I go, but I will go. We have unfinished business, Liza and me. The way Liza sounds in her letters, she needs a sister.

Rose MacDonald
Vancouver Island
January 1882

I am worried about dearest Sophie. Though she doesn't complain much, I sense she isn't her usual happy self. In the months after we landed in Victoria Harbor, she didn't seem to know quite what to do with herself. I felt terribly guilty for begging her to move away from her familiar life. I was grateful when she made strides to truly embrace Victoria instead of treating it like a place she was paying an extended visit. Now that her life is more full, I hope the darkness in her heart lifts. I want more than anything for Sophie to be happy.

It was a relief when she made friends with Emma Lou Shuggs, a Negro woman who lives in a cottage near the Chinese district. Emma Lou has a husband named Otis who is gone most of the year, earning his living as a mate on ships taking the island lumber to ports down the southern coast and around the Horn to the eastern states. In the long months when he is away, Emma Lou makes a modest living sewing dresses and fancy hats for women up and down the island, and Sophie earns extra spending money by assisting her.

Though some of the women of higher society on the Island balk at the thought of Negro hands fashioning "the very same clothes that lie next to a white woman's skin," there are sufficient numbers of open-minded ladies who use her services, partly due, I am proud to say, to my efforts. I have led a quiet campaign among the women of my station. I've been quite outspoken, and because of my recruitment efforts, several ladies have become clients. A wise choice, since the clothing Emma Lou and Sophie fashion is equal to the dresses, suits, and overcoats made by the Chinese tailor and a far better quality than the handiwork of Zeta Bagatskis, the Latvian dressmaker whose store, which consists of the front room of her house, reeks of fish and cabbage, and something I can't quite identify. Perhaps it is a problem with her outhouse. Why anyone prefers Zeta's services is beyond my comprehension.

Emma Lou's cottage fitting room smells of cinnamon and cloves due to the pies and turnovers she sells to workers at the mill a mile or two down-harbor from Victoria. I hate to be disloyal to Sophie who makes a fine pie herself, but Emma Lou's crust is beyond compare; its tender flaky texture caresses the mouth when you bite into one of her apple pies or berry tarts. I've begged for the recipe, but she refuses to share it. "It's a secret I'll take to my grave, Missus MacDonald," she said, her tone grave but her eyes merry.

"Please call me Rose. Mrs. MacDonald makes it sound like I'm a hundred years old, and I'm still nineteen for six more months!" But addressing me by my first name is too familiar for Emma Lou, who has accepted the role society dictates: that a Negro should maintain a formality with white-skinned folks. No matter how I try to break through the barriers of skin color with Emma Lou, I will always be 'Missus MacDonald'.

I have commissioned from Emma Lou and Sophie a set of clothing to wear as my stomach swells with the child I am carrying. Finally, after two false starts, a child has taken hold in my womb. With luck, I'll carry this one to term. I can't help feeling apprehension after the disappointment of losing the first two, but Mrs. Beasley, the cheerful old midwife with a beaming smile and rosy cheeks, says all is as it should be. "There isn't anything to worry over, Rose. Your baby is thriving this time. Just don't fall down the stairs or get kicked in the stomach by a horse, and you'll see a fine specimen leap from your loins! I can almost swear to it, my dear, and I've delivered over twenty little ones on this Island alone. I should know by now when the unborn is thriving, and your baby shows all signs of robust growth."

It is true; the rate at which I am expanding indicates the delivery of a babe of hearty proportion. I shall have to work at restoring my girlish figure when all is said and done. Nolan treats me like I am ill and cautions me against doing too much. "I've heard of mothers-to-be staying in bed around the clock. Perhaps you should ask your midwife if it is the prudent thing to do," he said solemnly, kissing my forehead as he prepared to leave for work at the MacDonald Enterprises, a thriving shipping and logging business that he and Martin, his older brother, run. Mrs. Beasley chuckled and said I shouldn't listen to him on this issue. "Why, he would coddle you to the death if he could! The best medicine is to take a brisk walk or two every day, out in the fresh air. It will make you and your babe strong, Rose."

Every morning, after Nolan leaves for the ship works, I walk along the harbor and through town, regardless of the weather. We are nearing the end of winter, and though the clouds insist on sharing their bounteous cargo, I stay dry by carrying a sturdy umbrella and wearing a pair of new-fangled rubber galoshes Nolan brought back from his last trip to the mainland. "Mark my words, Rose, this material will soon revolutionize industry and the way we get around. Some folks are even suggesting it might be used for tires. Think of it, darling! No more carriages bouncing on wooden rims and pig iron. I foresee this new material changing the way factories work, Rose." I can't say I share Nolan's enthusiasm about the potential uses for vulcanized rubber; I can only say that the galoshes, though a bit clunky and cumbersome, do keep the feet dry. Dry feet are a good thing to have in this climate.

The climate on Vancouver Island is what Sophie complains about most. "I thought San Francisco was damp, with the fog and mist and so forth, but this weather grows mold on my insides!"

I laughed. "You grumble too much, Sophie! No amount of wet weather can grow mold on your insides, for heaven's sake!"

"Well, I can feel the chill all the way to my bones. They'll dissolve and turn to jelly if this rain doesn't stop."

There is no doubt; Sophie is homesick, and nothing I do or say takes away her melancholy. When a letter comes from Mama or one of her friends from the Free Negro Society, she can hardly wait to tear it open and pour over the contents. Mama's letters to Sophie and me arrive faithfully every few weeks, and Sophie usually gets double the pleasure, for I always hand her the unopened letters Mama addresses to me.

I don't much care what Princess Liza has to say. My mother is a fortress made of ice, after all. Sophie ignores my feelings about Mama and reads the letters aloud. I can't escape hearing the news from Wayside Inn and the latest happenings in the rapidly growing city of San Francisco, and in spite of my feelings of indifference toward Mama, I am always interested to hear of the doings at home.

Now, however, my home is in Victoria. Nolan is building a splendid and spacious new house for us. If all goes well, it will be ready for occupants before our baby's first birthday. I hoped I could deliver in the new house, but construction is slow and dependent on clear weather. The house we live in now was Nolan's parents' home, and it is perfectly adequate and quite comfortable. Our new place, however, will have all the latest advancements including an upstairs and a ground floor washroom, and most exciting of all, we'll have indoor plumbing, which only the newest homes have.

"We can afford a few luxuries, Rose," Nolan said, when I expressed concern over the expense. It seems that MacDonald Enterprises is a thriving business, and while Nolan remains modest and underplays his success, we're quite well off. The best part is that Nolan has given up skippering the ships except for an occasional trip down coast or to the mainland. He is home most of the year, as the business requires him to oversee all the various enterprises of a growing company.

Our new home in the James Bay area is a brisk walk from where we are now. I am especially excited since I helped Nolan design the interior. We'll have three stories with a cupola on the roof, accessed from Nolan's and my bedroom suite. I begged for a glass-walled solarium off the kitchen, where even the weakest sun will warm the room. In addition to the usual parlor, sitting room, kitchen and dining room, there are six bedrooms to accommodate our future family and guests, a nursery and schoolroom, a sewing room, an office, a sleeping porch overhanging the back garden, four fireplaces and a wood stove in the kitchen, a great room for parties, and a finished basement with a cold chamber for our pantry goods as well as a cozy apartment for Erma Laney, the full-time housemaid.

Nolan insisted we employ a servant to help with the day-to-day household responsibilities, though I told him Sophie and I could manage quite well on our own. "No wife of mine will slave in the laundry room or ruin her hands mopping the floors," he said, "nor should Sophie." We are building a separate cottage for Sophie, so she is truly her own person.

I can hardly wait for the house to be finished so I can start planting the garden. The island is a paradise for plants of all kinds. Gardens grow even more lushly than the gardens in San Francisco. The beauty is breathtaking. I am planning an outdoor fairyland with fishponds, topiaries, and a little bridge over the creek cutting across a corner of our acreage. I have started to collect some root-stalk and cuttings, so when the house is habitable and the grounds cleared of the construction debris, I can start immediately with the transformation into the charming fairy garden in my mind's eye. Nolan has even promised a fountain, which will be the center point of our front yard. Any guests who arrive will be mesmerized by the tranquility, I am sure.

There is only happy anticipation for me here on the island, but Sophie is not in the same frame of mind. I know my dear Sophie well; I read her like a book. She pretends everything is fine, yet just the other day I heard her crying in her room. When I asked what was wrong, she said she just felt weepy. She lies for my sake, and though she has good days, I sense she hides her general melancholy. I only wish she could enjoy life here as much as I do. Perhaps time will take away her homesickness and she will grow as fond as I am of Vancouver Island and learn to embrace Victoria as her home.

<h1 style="text-align:center">Sophie Washington</h1>

Vancouver Island

January 1885

After several delays from storms, failed deliveries, and a sometimes unreliable workforce, we are finally settled in our new homes built side by side on a spacious lot in James Bay. Our new place is up on a ridge with a view of the Sound. My cottage is tucked off to the south side of the big house. It's a wonderful, cozy little house that I'd never dreamed of living in all those years ago when I shared a one-room cabin with my family.

I am enthralled with my cottage, just as Rose is delighted with the house Nolan built for her. He outdid himself in planning the three-story mansion. The result is a true jewel in the crown, and the envy of the ladies of Victoria. Among the features are generously sized rooms painted in beautiful hues, polished wood floors and trim, and just about every modern convenience. The kitchen alone could prepare a feast for a hundred guests. Rose furnished the rooms with simple, elegant pieces, and both the house and garden are the talk of the town.

Though I loved our apartment at Wayside Inn, my new quarters beat it hands down. Nolan didn't skimp on the cottage; he planned out every detail for comfort and ease. He even had a covered walkway built from my little house to the kitchen door entrance at the big house. "I don't want wet weather stopping you from visiting Rose," he said. A picture window in the kitchen nook faces the Strait of Juan de Fuca. One of my entertainments is watching the big ships and an occasional pod of whales swimming past on their way to the icy north.

Young Robbie often joins me. He sits on my lap or in the little rocker next to mine, and we look through a pair of binoculars kindly donated by Nolan. Robbie, like his father, loves boats and everything to do with them. We watch the sea together, and Robbie's imagination works overtime wondering about what kind of ship is sailing past, and what sort of cargo it might be carrying. I have a bond with Robbie. He is a sweet child, gentle and kind.

Yet as strong as my bonds are to Rose and her family, I long for Mama and Daddy and the old home place. I wonder what happened to my parents and to my brother. Anxious question about Jules and Augie consume my thoughts, awake and asleep. Where are they? Are they in good health? Do they still finish each other's sentences? Or were they separated? It made me sick to think of Jules and Augie being ripped from the brotherhood of twins.

My sons, if they survived, are grown men now. For all I know, they are married and have children of their own. I'd make a deal with the devil to see the young men they've become. Nolan has done some inquiring among his connections in the states and has put together a list of names for me to contact in my search for the whereabouts of my family. "You'll never rest your mind until you've done everything you can to find your sons. Rose and I will help any way we can. You can count on that, Sophie." Nolan is a good man and has become a kind friend. I took the list of addresses to my cottage and wrote a dozen letters by midnight. The next day I wrote six more.

Wind whipped through the branches of the fir trees and rattled a few leaves hanging on threads from the maples lining the walkway to town. I clutched the letters under my shawl and spoke softly to them. "Please, letters, go to the right place where I can find out about Jules and Augie and my folks." My heart pounded as I handed the packet of letters to the ferryman. I didn't turn away until he carried the canvas sack of mail into the cabin of the mail boat.

I have near given up all hope, and if nothing promising comes back from these names and addresses, I will abandon my search.

Glory to every power that exists in the realms! Finally, in answer to the dozens of letters of inquiry I sent forth in a mission to find my sons, one letter of response provides a hint of encouragement. Mr. Vanderleaf, an independent detective from New Orleans, has written me with the assurance that he is a specialist in the field of finding lost and misplaced former slaves, and for a small retainer, he is prepared to begin a search for Jules and Augie immediately. He also promises to look into the whereabouts of my parents and Jerome. His letter comes with testimonials from some of the people he searched out and found. If it can be believed, the man is a genius. At last, I have a shred of hope.

He asked for a list of particulars, and I've written everything: the year the twins were born and their age now, where Sweetbrier sits, Bert Laurent's role in stealing the boys. It was a sadly short list, all considering, but I wrote down the pertinent facts I knew and sent it to Mr. Vanderleaf with a check for $70.00. Nolan insisted on paying, and I let him, though I have a decent pile of money between what I make working for Emma Lou Shuggs and what I've accumulated over the years. Happily, I have more than enough to pay Mr. Vanderleaf his final charges if he is able to uncover the whereabouts of my lost sons.

I hurry to the mail boat whenever it comes in, eagerly awaiting Mr. Vanderleaf's response. How I hope for even a trace of knowledge that the twins are alive, safe and whole! I pray they are unscarred by their rough journey. There is no word yet, but as Rose says, it is probably too soon. "It's only been two weeks since you sent it, Sophie. Give the man and the mail time to answer. It could be several months or more before you hear from this Mr. Vanderleaf." She sounded so practical, exactly like her mama.

Rose is like Liza in many ways, but when I mention any similarity, she protests. "You are deluded in imagining that I am like Princess Liza. We are as different as an apple is to a strawberry."

"Which are you, the apple or the strawberry?"

"I'll leave it for you to decide, Sophie. Now dear woman, could you help Robbie get dressed? We are going to visit his daddy at work, and I am packing a picnic lunch for us to share in Nolan's office. You're always invited, you know. Robbie will be beside himself with joy if you come with us."

"Not today, Rose. I'm helping Emma Lou. She's fitting half a dozen gowns she's making for Kathleen Campbell. They are supposed to be ready by the end of next week."

"Six gowns! That's quite an undertaking. What's the hurry?"

"Kathleen is traveling to Scotland to meet her cousins for the first time. I have an idea her folks are hoping she'll attract a husband. She certainly isn't having any luck here, poor thing."

"What a shame! She's such a nice girl. You and Emma Lou must make especially pretty gowns, Sophie." Rose pecked me on the cheek and went off to the kitchen to make sandwiches. I helped Robbie dress. Little Robbie has Rose's eyes, but the rest of him is pure Nolan down to his strong cheekbones, dimpled chin, and a wavy crop of blond hair. "Could I wear my fur hat, Sophie?" he asked, pointing to the ratty old native relic given to him by Indian Sam.

"Sure thing, honey."

I was reminded of dressing my own little boys on the morning they were ripped from my life so many years ago. A tear spilled out my good eye.

Robbie looked up at me, his face puzzled. "What are you crying about, Sophie?"

"I was thinking of the twin boys I lost a long time ago. I still miss them."

"What were the names of your boys, Sophie?"

"August and July, but everyone called them Jules and Augie."

"How'd you lose them?"

"It's a long story, Robbie. Maybe, when you're older, I'll tell you all about it." I wiped away the tear with my free hand.

Robbie nodded solemnly. "I hope you find Augie and Jules, Sophie."

"I might be lucky enough to find them someday soon. I'm waiting to hear from a man in New Orleans who's an expert at finding people who got separated from each other."

'Where's New Orleans?"

"Way on the southern side of the continent, next door to the state of Texas, about a thousand miles away, I'd guess." I handed Robbie the fur cap. "Now, get going. Your mama is waiting for you."

After he clattered down the stairs I sat on his bed, daydreaming about what I'd say when I met the twins face to face, after plenty of hugs all around. Please God, I prayed, bring my sons back to me.

Rose MacDonald

Vancouver Island

December 1888

Nolan surprised me one evening at dinner with a suggestion for an excursion he was longing to take. "It's high time for us to travel a bit. How does a second honeymoon sound to you?" It sounded wonderful to me. I had grown jealous of MacDonald Enterprises; though the company provides bounteously for our financial needs, Nolan's obligations as the head of the Victoria branch weigh on him and stretch him too thin.

"What about the business? Can you get away without things falling apart?"

"Martin will make frequent trips from the mainland to check on everything while I'm gone, which alleviates any worries about the business. What do you think, Rose?"

I was thrilled at the idea of an adventure and having Nolan more or less all to myself. "Where would we go?"

"I've been daydreaming about a wilderness trek staying as close as possible to the west side of the island and ending at the new MacDonald logging camp between Tahsish Inlet and Fair Harbor." Nolan spread the map on the table and pointed out the Inlet. "The roadways are not always reliable, and they're often nothing more than Indian trails. It might be rough going at times. I hope that doesn't scare you off."

"You should know by now that I am capable of surviving a bit of rough travel should it come along."

Nolan traced the route we'd follow. "It's by no means a straight course, which adds kilometers to the distance. We'd do it in eight or nine weeks, taking our time and making stops along the way. The Bryants and the Parks have homesteads along the route, and if it is agreeable to you, we'd visit briefly at both farms. For the rest of the journey, we'd either camp or stay in lodges when civilization provides such comforts. In all honesty, there isn't much in terms of established lodging the farther north we go. We'd set up camp the last few weeks."

"What about the return trip?" I asked.

"We'd meet a MacDonald Steamer up at the logging camp and come back on the waves, which is much faster. Of course, if these ideas don't suit you, we can plan a different trip entirely."

"Oh, Nolan, I'd go anywhere with you, and you know it. Exploring the island is something I long to do. I want to see the big trees and climb to the top of the Golden Hinde, and if there's time, I'd like to sketch totems along the way. Not every totem, of course, but some of the more outstanding examples. I think they should be recorded for posterity."

He reached across the table and took my hand in his. "You are an Amazon type, aren't you, sweetheart, ready for action! It's one of the things I love about you."

"When will we go on this adventure?"

"By late July most of the mud traps and road washouts are repaired or detours are in place. Unfortunately, it is also the start of fire season, but we can always retreat if we find ourselves faced with a wall of flame."

"I'm confident you'll steer us in the right direction, whatever the obstacles."

"As to the right direction, Ka-kay-un knows the island from top to bottom. He said he'd guide if we decide to take the trip."

"Of course we're taking the trip! There's no question!"

"I'll tell him he's hired, then. He'll be pleased."

"I suppose it is wise to have a native guide." What I didn't say was that I was hoping to have Nolan all to myself.

"It's not only wise, it's essential. Some of the country we'll pass through is rough and wild. The natives know the land instinctively. When I told him about the possibility of taking the trip, Ka-kay-un mentioned that he'd like to bring his grandson, Tal-a-quil along. He's turned eighteen, and Ka-kay-un wants to get him away from his friends at the reservation. 'They drink whiskey and do stupid things, these boys. Besides, the younger generation should see the Island before white men destroy it. No offense, Boss, but white men not good for Island,' were his exact words. It made me wince when he said it."

"How is the white man destroying the island?" I asked.

"Some old groves of giant trees are being sacrificed to clear land for farms, and there are a few greedy logging enterprises that cut down entire swaths of prime forest, leaving debris and mud slides behind. Canadian lumber is in high demand."

"Does MacDonald Enterprises do this kind of forest cutting?" I asked.

"Not on your life. I believe in thinning and replanting forests, not butchering them. That's one reason I want to visit our logging operation, to make sure the superintendent is doing his job as a steward of the forest. The day will come when loggers realize that unless they leave something behind, there won't be a second timber harvest. Cutting everything down is like shooting yourself in the foot. Eventually, law will dictate what loggers can and can't do. Meanwhile, it leaves some ugly scars in the forest."

"You'll have to point out examples on the trip."

"Speaking of the trip, if you're game we could spend a few days exploring the Clayoquot Sound by canoe. There's a hot spring in the Sound that's wonderful to soak in. The local Indians claim it cures most ills. My father took us there when I was eleven. We camped on a little island that I've always remembered. I'd love to find it again. It was one of the prettiest places I've ever seen."

"It sounds like a wonderful side trip, but wouldn't we need boats?"

"When the time is right, Ka-kay-un and Tal-a-quil will ride ahead to negotiate with the local tribe for a loan of canoes."

"Isn't that chancy? Are the Indians from the area friendly? And willing to loan their boats?"

"The coastal tribes are quite generous and welcoming, and they benefit, too; I'll pack tools to trade, like axes and knives and steel fishhooks. Tobacco is always highly prized, as are awls and needles for sewing."

"I'll bring along beads and ribbon for the women."

"You'll have the native ladies eating out of your hand, Rose. Once we get the canoes, we'll paddle in the Clayoquot area and do some island hopping. Then we'll get back on the carryall and head north with Ka-kay-un leading the way."

"The whole idea is thrilling!"

Nolan leaned in and kissed me, a kiss of passion and promise. I wished we could start our adventure the next day, but we had to wait seven long months for July to arrive.

Nolan prepared for the trip with his usual thoroughness and careful attention to detail. He collected every possible article of gear we might need. "I'm dedicated to making our accommodations along the way as comfortable as a lady deserves."

I laughed. "You needn't take special measures, Nolan. I am happy to sleep on rocks as long as you're next to me."

"Neither of us will have to sleep on rocks, I promise you, Rose.

There's a feather mattress in our gear, and pillows, too." He was quiet for a minute. "When we take the canoe to the island in the Sound, we might have to sleep on mother earth. The feather mattress is too bulky to carry on a canoe, and wet feathers are a real liability. But don't you worry, a comfortable bed can be made with what nature provides, and if we're lucky, we'll chance across an abandoned Indian lodge to shelter in."

"I am not in the least bit worried."

My excitement grew as July came closer. Nolan put me in charge of packing our clothing and gathering the kitchen staples we needed for camping out. I spent weeks locating powdered milk and dried potatoes, smoked beef and salmon, salt cod, salt pork, flour, cornmeal, dried fruit, tins of green beans and pickled beets, a case of apple sauce and another case of preserves.

"We'll pack eggs and onions and such and replenish them along the way with produce from the farms we pass. When we head farther into the northern wilderness, there aren't any more farms. We'll resort to what we bring along in cans and what we can fish or hunt along the route," Nolan said. "I promise, you won't be a slave to camp, Rose. Ka-kay-un is a fine cook, and I'm pretty handy myself." I rolled my eyes at him. Nolan was handy at many things, but I hadn't seen much of him in the kitchen. "I'm very good at chopping," he said.

"I'll remember that whenever there's an onion around."

Anticipation made me impatient; the consequence was that time passed at a snail's pace. Fortunately, our July departure date was insured by a stretch of pleasant, dry weather. The night before we left I tucked Robbie into bed. "I wish I could go with you and Dad," he said.

I hugged him. "We'll be back home before you've had a chance to miss us, Robbie. We both love you very much and will think about you every day we're gone."

"Can you and Dad collect shells for me?"

"If we find any interesting ones, we'll be sure to put them in a box for you." I kissed his forehead. "Good night, sweetheart." His sleepy eyes blinked, then he was fast asleep.

I felt a pang of guilt about Nolan and me leaving our only child behind while we traipsed off on a traveling holiday, but I knew Robbie would be well cared for by Sophie. The added treat of a two-week visit from his cousins Matthew and Morris would also help fill the void of us being gone. "Don't you worry about a thing," said Sophie. "Just concentrate on having a wonderful time. Robbie will miss you at first, but he'll survive. I promise I'll keep him entertained and happy."

Sophie's reassurance made my heart light when I climbed in bed that night. In spite of my excitement I slept soundly and woke feeling exceedingly well. Dawn was just breaking as Nolan and I climbed aboard the carryall and set out on our Island getaway.

Summer 1889

My initial worry that the Indians might intrude on Nolan's and my privacy melted away after the first day. Ka-kay-un and Tal-a-quil were discreet and respectful, as well as invaluable guides. They were essential to the passage of our carryall when it got stuck in mud or had to cross a rushing stream. The two often rode ahead to scout the trail, stopping at a spring or a spectacular meadow until the carryall rumbled up. Ka-kay-un proved to be an exceptional guide. He was a wellspring of knowledge about the areas we visited, and a wonderful storyteller. I urged him to write down the fables and legends handed down by his parents and grandparents. "Your mind is full of history, Ka-kay-un. You should preserve it for your people. Otherwise the history will die."

He shook his head. "I can write my own name, but that's about it."

"You can tell me the stories, and I will write them for you." From then on, I penned the stories he told of the island natives and their customs. By the end of the trip I'd filled a blank journal with Ka-kay-un's tales interspersed with sketches of the most notable totems and carved house fronts we came across on our route.

Ka-kay-un and Tal-a-quil forged onward to the coast while Nolan and I took a slight detour east to our friends, the Bryants. "We'll visit for two or three days and meet up with you and Tal-a-quil at the Indian village on Tofino Inlet." Nolan pointed to the place on his well-worn map.

Ka-kay-un nodded. "Can't miss rock as big as house looking like woman lying on her back. You'll find it on the north side of the road when you come across first good view of water. Village not far after you see her." We parted ways at a fork in the road that took us east and took our guides west to the ocean.

Christopher Bryant and his wife, Alice, left Victoria almost three years ago to establish a mission in the coastal foothills, where the Indians are considered especially heathen and in need of Christian conversion. When we met a handful of the natives in question, I didn't find them any more heathen than the natives who live near Victoria, or for that matter, white people. Their customs are simply different.

We stayed two days at the Bryant's. Their quarters are comfortable and clean, but because of their growing family, a little short on space. "We'll expand the cottage next spring. I designed an addition, with Alice's input, of course." Christopher draped his arm over his wife's shoulders. The couple had five children; the last two were twins delivered by Christopher himself as they'd been snowed in during her labor.

"He was a trooper," she said. "Why, he was as good as the midwife who delivered Tommie!"

Christopher laughed. "I only fainted when it came to cutting the umbilical cord."

"He's teasing, of course." Alice smiled at her husband. Their affection for each other is endearing.

Alice was obviously thrilled to have another woman for company and talked my ear off with details about life on the frontier and the harsh winter they'd gone through. "Why there's wolves and bears and who knows what else! If you're not careful, a mama bear and her cubs can empty a whole cold cellar. I know from experience. Christopher insists that I carry a little pistol when I go for a walk or gather firewood," she said. "The mountain cats tore apart a woman a couple of years ago, and everyone around this neck of the woods still talks about it." We both shuddered at the thought of the poor dismembered victim.

"Alice, next spring, you must consider a visit to Victoria. You are welcome to stay at our house as long as you'd like. There's plenty of space for company."

Alice's eyes brightened. "I'll ask Christopher. We'd love to come."

Although I enjoyed visiting the Bryants, I was glad when we said our goodbyes. I relished having Nolan all to myself. At the Bryant's place I hardly saw him except at meals; he spent both days helping Christopher build a section of fence to protect their garden from herds of elk that had no regard for rows of cabbage and potatoes. After hugs and handshakes, we climbed aboard the carryall. "Now, straight to Clayoquot we go!" Nolan's voice was enthusiastic, and I knew he was also happy to be back on the road headed for the Pacific Ocean.

At midday, Nolan pulled the carryall off the road to picnic next to a lovely sparkling creek where a beaver family ignored us and continued building a dam. Nolan carried out the feather mattress and unrolled it in a little meadow, and we made love before we ate our lunch. The traveling life is an aphrodisiac to us; along the way we take every opportunity we can to make a sister or brother for Robbie.

After lunch we made slow progress, stopping to watch the abundant wildlife: bear families ambling across the road, birds fishing in a highland lake, a vast herd of deer feeding in a meadow bordered by a band of wildflowers. The sun was edging toward the horizon when Nolan took a turn down a rutted dirt road. He stopped our buggy at a panoramic vista overlooking the coast and pointed to a rock formation that matched Ka-kay-un's description of the landmark marking the turnoff to the Indian Village.

As Nolan and I admired the shapely woman carved from stone by wind and rain, campfire smoke wafted up from the coastal plain below. We turned the rig in the direction of the sound. A ride down the hill on a thickly forested lane brought us to a large circular encampment bustling with Indians. They stopped their activities to stare at us curiously as we climbed off the carryall. Eight longhouses built of huge timbers surrounded a common area with several fire pits and benches hewn from cedar logs. The fronts of the homes faced the center yard, each of them carved with elaborate figures and creatures from Indian lore.

Ka-kay-un spotted us as soon as we rode up. He took the reins to the carryall and helped Nolan and me untether the horses and corral them with the Indian mounts. "You didn't stay long," he said.

"We got the traveling itch," said Nolan. "Besides, the Bryant's newborn twins kept up a good caterwauling until the wee hours. We needed to move on so we could get some sleep."

"I'll take you to the chief." We followed Ka-kay-un to a second village common larger than the other, also surrounded by a ring of wood lodges. It was the exact layout as the first group of lodges, but the carved fronts of the long houses were even more elaborate. In the center yard a stately man draped in a combination of animal skins, colorful cloth and woven blankets sat on a log bench. His long black hair was tied in two thick hanks and adorned with leather strips and feathers. "That is Chief Makah'aht," said Ka-kay-un. The man rose as we approached. Nolan and I bowed our heads in greeting. Ka-kay-un spoke to the chief who nodded his head gravely and spoke rapidly in his native language. "He invite you and Mrs. Rose to lodge in his house," Ka-kay-un translated.

"Tell Chief Makah'aht thanks very much, but we'll set up camp wherever he says it is convenient to do so. Tell him that we would love to share a meal with the tribe this evening. We have a barrel of smoked beef I brought for an occasion like this, and lots of ingredients to contribute to a stew pot."

Ka-kay-un spoke earnestly to the chief who nodded and grunted in response. He pointed toward a grove of cedar trees just outside of the circle of homes. "Chief says there are good flat spots for sleeping among the trees, and nice and quiet. As soon as you set up camp, he say to come for feast."

The sun sank to meet the horizon, throwing shadows across the courtyard in kaleidoscope patterns. Gradually, the people drifted into the yard to join a dozen squaws preparing food at smaller fire pits spaced in a uniform sphere around the main campfire and sitting area. Several pots of stew hung suspended over the flames of the fire pits. Women called back and forth as they stirred the iron cauldrons. Meanwhile, the elder men sat in rows on the long log benches fanning around the central campfire. A group of younger men sat cross-legged in a drumming circle, beating out a hypnotic rhythm that accompanied perfectly the mercurial, shifting rays of light.

Torches were lighted when darkness fell, and all the pots of stew and plates of salmon and venison were brought to a stout table. The chief insisted that we eat first. A round-cheeked squaw handed Nolan and me shallow bowls carved of wood and pantomimed that we should serve ourselves. I ladled a small portion of each offering onto my bowl and tasted carefully. A pretty young woman with soulful eyes presented a tightly woven platter piled high with slender, thumb-sized fish that had been threaded on sticks and roasted in the fire. "You can eat the whole fish, even the bones," she said in clear, precise English.

I didn't want to appear squeamish, so I popped one of the morsels into my mouth. It was much tastier than I'd anticipated, as were the nutritious stews seasoned with seawater and flavored with native herbs. The young woman who'd brought the platter of fish and taken us under her wing turned out to be the chief's wife. Her name was Me-kit-su'uk.

At the end of the long and leisurely dinner, the men gathered around the large campfire pit in the center of the yard. Me-kit-su'uk took my hand and led me to a separate fire ring around which the women gathered. They were singing, and the sound was haunting and soulful. I listened with fascination to their melodies, wishing there was a way to capture the magical sounds to share with Robbie and Sophie when we returned home.

Me-kit-su'uk sat by my side and softly translated the words. They were songs that told native legends, songs to ward off bad weather, songs of old battles between the ancient tribes, and a particularly lively tune was sung to honor salmon, which is such an important part of their diet. When the women grew tired of singing, the storytelling began. Me-kit-su'uk interpreted, speaking softly as the storytellers acted out their narratives. I asked Me-kit-su'uk where she'd learned to speak such clear English.

"I was taken from my parents when I was six and put in an Indian school on the mainland. That was where I learned the white man's language." A look of pain crossed her face.

I shook my head sympathetically. "I can't imagine anyone forcibly taking my son, Robbie, and putting him in an institution. What a horrible thing! It should be stopped." I took her hand in mine. "When we return home to Victoria, I will speak to the Women's Society I belong to. We need to protest such barbaric practices."

Me-kit-su'uk threw her arms around me. "The sisters of the world will be the ones to cure all the ills."

"We can only hope so."

The women broke into song once more, their clear voices ringing like bells in the otherwise quiet night air. A brilliant half-moon had risen in the eastern sky by the time the singing session ended. One by one each squaw gave me a gift. Nolan had warned me of this custom, and I'd brought a canvas sack filled with tokens to give in return for the gifts accumulating in a pile: a lovely woven basket, a carved bone awl, a shell bracelet, a lap blanket, a feather necklace, a bone whistle. As the treasures collected, I dug deeper into the sack to pull up spools of thread, packets of needles and balls of yarn for each woman.

Me-kit-su'uk was the last to give her gift. It was a fist-sized object wrapped in a supple piece of deerskin. I folded back the creamy chamois wrapping to reveal a carved figure of a woman with a swollen belly and prominent breasts. "This figure is known to help when a woman wants a baby. Keep her close to you at night, and you will find your womb full with child," she said. The other women giggled and nodded, murmuring soft words in their language. One of them patted my flat belly.

"How did you know I want another baby?"

Me-kit-su'uk shook her head and smiled. "I have good intuition."

That night, tucked comfortably into our tent, Nolan and I made love for the second time that day. Before we commenced, I perched the figure on a rock near our feather mattress, where she could enjoy our lust and where her spirit could work its magic.

Sophie Washington
Vancouver Island
Mid-September 1889

Rose and Nolan are home at last! They are the picture of health and fitness after their expedition. Rose is lovelier than ever; her skin glows and her willowy build ripples with muscles she didn't have before. Nolan looks five years younger. He has grown a mustache and a close-cut beard, which give him a dashing air. Robbie was beside himself with joy when his parents arrived on the doorstep this afternoon. Though he was the perfect little trooper these long weeks, it was time for his beloved mama and papa to come home.

Robbie doesn't know yet that there is more happy news; he will have a brother or sister by next spring. Rose took me aside and told me in a whisper that she has missed her second menstrual cycle. "It's too early to make a fuss, Sophie. You are the only one I've told. I haven't even said a word to Nolan. I don't dare to jinx the baby. If I miscarry again, his heart would be broken."

"Just get those thoughts out of your head." I laid a hand on her belly. "I have a powerful feeling that this baby is going to be just fine. But I won't tell a soul until you're ready to make the announcement, I promise." I hugged Rose, and she went off with Robbie to see the fort he and his cousins built in the enormous red cedar tree in the patch of forest that meets our yard.

As much as I adore Robbie, I am happy his parents are home. Being a round-the-clock grandparent is much more demanding than the many casual daily visits Robbie and I were accustomed to before Rose and Nolan's trip. Now, we can go back to our usual routine. I look forward to spending an hour or two with Robbie in my cottage sunroom; Robbie with his binoculars trained on a stray whale, a tuna boat, or a cormorant family diving for their dinner. And in the meantime, I will get back to work with Emma Lou Shuggs. "I need your help, Sophie! I can't keep up with the orders without you. When are your white folks coming home? There's a rumor going around about a hard winter coming, and I already have orders from seven different women for overcoats!" Emma Lou has become a good friend. It is comforting for both of us to be with someone of the same color who knows from experience the injustices Negroes face.

Of course, if Rose needs me to care for Robbie I am always willing. Robbie is like one of my own. For now, I enjoy my freedom to come and go, which means a lot to someone who was once a slave.

February 1890

My heart flutters like hummingbird wings from the news I've gotten through the mail! I have heard from Mr. Vanderleaf, the private detective I paid a retainer some three years past, for finding Jules and Augie. I'd given up on Mr. Vanderleaf long ago, but he never stopped working on the case. Imagine the thrill of hearing from him at last! I continue to read his letter over and over to let the joyous words sink in.

```
Dear Mrs. Washington,
     I apologize for the long months that
passed since you hired me to try to locate
your grown sons, July and August Washington,
twin brothers who were taken when they were
```

toddlers from the Sweetbrier Plantation in
Louisiana where your family served as slaves.
Regrettably, it takes considerable time to
sift through information found in county
records, newspapers, and so forth, but I
believe I've found your son July Washington.
I also have information pertaining to your
parents, Addie and Garvus Washington, and
your brother, Jerome.

The information is waiting for your
perusal at my offices in New Orleans. A final
remuneration of $75.00 is payable at the time
of the consultation. Because of your location
and the necessity for travel across the
continent, I have set a tentative conference
date for six weeks hence, on Tuesday, April 5
at 9:00 a.m. If this date does not suit you,
please communicate post haste in order to
change the appointment. If you can make the
date, let me know soon by post or telegraph,
and I will send directions regarding the
location of our offices.

Sincerely,

Albert R. Vanderleaf,Private Investigator

I wouldn't miss that meeting for all the gold in Cariboo or the
Mother Lode! Nolan is helping me with travel arrangements. Thank
goodness I have him handy to wade through timetables and chart out
the route by train and carriage all the way to New Orleans. "You'll
take a Ferry to Seattle, Washington, and board the train." He used
a red pencil to mark the route across country. "You'll pass through
Oregon and cut down through Idaho. The center of the western hub
is in Utah. In Salt Lake City you'll board a train that takes you across
Colorado and the corner of New Mexico into Texas. New Orleans is
a stone's throw after that."

I traced my finger down the route he'd outlined in red. "It's amazing isn't it, Sophie? Why, twenty years ago it would have taken months to cover these distances," Nolan said. "Now, the train will deliver you in ten days or fewer, depending on how many stops it makes." I shook my head in wonder and thanked him for setting up my travel itinerary.

Rose isn't as thrilled as I am. "Why, you won't be here when the baby comes! I don't know what I'll do without you," she cried when she heard the news. She is seven months along and as cranky as I've ever seen her. A minute later she apologized for being selfish. "I am used to thinking of you as mine alone. I forget about the twins. Can you forgive me, dearest Sophie?"

"Of course I forgive you, Rose. I think of you as mine, too, and I hate to miss the baby's birth, but I've been waiting half my life for this. I'm glad you understand."

After her first reaction, Rose went out of her way to help me prepare for my journey. The next day she took the carriage to Fagan's Dry Goods on Harbor Street and bought a beautiful upholstered valise. "This is for you, Sophie. So you'll look smart on the train." She kissed my cheek and left me to continue packing.

I packed the valise last. It would carry all the necessary day to night items I might need. I admired the handy arrangement of inner and outer compartments as I packed the bag with my toilet articles, jewelry, and delicate things. A smaller sack with a leather drawstring top was tucked into one of the inner pockets. It was heavy, and I suspected it was money before I opened it. The sack was filled with gold and silver coins and an envelope with my name scrawled across it in Rose's big, loopy script. I opened it. In the center of a folded sheet of paper was a neat stack of bills.

Dearest Sophie,

Please accept this from Nolan and me to help on your travels to New Orleans and to secure your return home to Victoria after however long it takes to settle your affairs and to establish contact with your living relations. I hope you find Jules and Augie and that they are robust men who have provided you with grandchildren. I only beg you not to forget me, your adopted white daughter, or Robbie, who thinks of you as a grandmother. Though we don't share the same blood, I feel that you are my closest relation.

Plenty of hugs and adoration sent your way, dearest Sophie.

Your loving Rose,
(and Robbie and Nolan, too.)

Between the coins and the paper bills, I counted $1,000.00. I'd already gone to the bank and withdrawn a travel allowance of $500.00 intended to cover the costs of transportation and to secure modest accommodations along the way. With a tidy sum of $1,500.00 I could travel first class if I wanted. The thought was tempting, but I felt a stab of guilt about taking their money. Rose and Nolan were generous, and I was amply compensated for the things I did out of love. I replaced the coins and the billfold into the leather bag and went to eat dinner with the three MacDonalds in their magnificent dining room.

"Thank you both, but I can't accept this," I said to Rose and Nolan. I placed the bag on the table and sat down.

"What is it?" asked Robbie, forever and a day a curious lad.

"It is a gift for Sophie," Rose said.

"Why don't you want it, Sophie?" Robbie asked.

"For one, it's far too much. Besides, I have my own money. I'm not a beggar, after all."

"Of course you're not a beggar, Sophie. You are a member of our clan," said Nolan. That man has a way of making you feel good with his sweet tongue.

The new cook, a French woman from Toronto, rolled in a cart laden with serving dishes and dinner plates. "Let's talk about this after supper," Rose said. We were quiet while the cook set plates piled with lamb, mashed potatoes, gravy, and a bowl of thinly sliced green beans on the table.

"Sophie, I want to show you the baby horse after dinner," Robbie said.

"I'd love to see him, honey." We chatted as we ate our meal, staying on neutral topics and carefully avoiding anything having to do with my upcoming departure. I took a last bite of the vanilla pudding cook served for desert, and before Rose or Nolan had the chance to say a word about their gift, I left with Robbie to see the foal in the barn.

"He was born in the middle of the thunderstorm last week. I named him Thor." Robbie brushed the foal gently and hugged its neck. "Good night, little Thor." He gave the colt a final pat and placed an armful of hay in the feeding bay. I drew the big latch that shut the barn door for the night, and we parted at the fork in the flagstone path leading to my cottage. "I love you, Sophie," Robbie cried as he tore down the path to the big house.

"I love you more," I called after him. I let myself into the cottage and turned up the hurricane lamp that I'd damped to low flame before I left. There on the hall table, in plain sight, was the bag of money. A folded piece of paper stuck from the neck of the bag. I unfolded it. This time the letter was penned in Nolan's hand:

Dear Sophie,

If you try to return this again you will break my dear wife's heart, and mine too. Your safe and comfortable passage to the lower states means the world to us. Your presence in our lives is immeasurable in terms of monetary worth. Perhaps you don't realize the extent of our love and esteem for you.

The money in the envelope is yours to use however you wish, and there is more whenever you need it.

Yours with love and sincerity,

Nolan

P.S.: Do not even try to return this gift! Please accept it gracefully, Sophie.

Nolan's letter brought tears to my good eye. I took the bag of cash to my bedroom and packed it into the embroidered valise. Then I took a sheet of paper and wrote a note thanking dear Rose and Nolan for the generous gift.

The ferry to the mainland was preparing for departure and the purser had blown the final boarding whistle. Rose hugged me fiercely. "Do you promise you'll come back, Sophie?"

"Of course I'm coming back. I've got to meet the new baby eventually." I kissed her cheek and didn't add that I might be just visiting the next time I came to Victoria. "You are my daughter, Rose. I share that with Liza."

"You are my mother far more than she is."

"The relationship between you and Liza is tied in a bunch of nasty old knots that I sure would like to see untied before I'm dead and gone. It's up to you now. Liza's ready to mend fences and she has been for a while. All it would take is willingness on your part."

"I'm afraid you might never witness a warm and cozy kinship between Mama and me."

"Just the same, I want you to promise me you'll do two things: First, read Liza's letters, and second, spend some time sending your own news to her. We're all getting older, and it's time to heal. Now, promise me."

"You never give up, do you Sophie?"

"Did I hear a promise?"

Rose laughed. "All right! I will write to Princess Liza, I promise. I won't respond to every darn letter she sends, but I will try to scratch out some news once a month. That's all I can manage."

"Just be sure you do it." I gave her a last hug and boarded the ferry. I waved from the top deck until Rose, Nolan and Robbie were mere specks on the blurry dock. Other travelers had stopped waving long ago and were making their way out of the chilly breeze. I followed the crowds to the inside lounge and took a seat on a bench tucked away in a corner. It was one of the few times on my journey that I didn't have to seek a seat or a room or a toilet where Negroes were allowed.

Mr. Vanderleaf is a treasure. He is helping me in every aspect of my mission, starting with lodging arrangements at this own home so I don't have to pay for a hotel while I wait for Mama and Daddy's headstone to be finished. The room he has so graciously provided has an outside entrance and a private washroom. I can come and go as I please. Since it is walking distance to town, I spend my days trying out different cafes and restaurants, and I've gone to the museums and art galleries and musical extravaganzas that make the city of New Orleans a mighty fine place. I am not sorry that I have to wait for the headstone to be finished, though I am sad about the purpose of the monument I commissioned for my folks' gravesite.

I suspected Mama and Daddy had passed by now; it's been about thirty years since I'd seen them last. On our first meeting, Mr. Vanderleaf confirmed my suspicion that they were dead. He'd found their names in the records from the colored people's Baptist church in Smithville. Mama and Daddy dragged Jerome and me to church for special services a few times a year, mainly Easter and Christmas or someone's wedding.

The record shows Daddy died first with Mama following a few months afterwards. I'm sure Mama's death was partly from a broken heart. When I was a little girl, I remember Mama telling Daddy, "I don't know what I'd ever do without you, Garvus. I hope I go before you." They were truly a pair of lovebirds. I wish I'd had that kind of love for someone in my own life, but after Mr. Bert finished with me I vowed no man would ever touch me again. Besides, with my ugly, scarred face, no man has ever really attempted anything other than polite conversation. But I refuse to give into feeling sorry about what I don't have, for now my life is richer than ever with the family members I have found.

Mr. Vanderleaf knows the whereabouts of my first-born twin! He is married and has two children, and he works as a brakeman on the Baltimore and Ohio Railroad. Though I have not yet seen July and his wife and children in person, I have written a letter and asked if he would mind a visit from his long-lost mother. His letter in response was an enthusiastic yes. As soon as Mama and Daddy's headstone is in place, I will take the train to meet my son and his family.

Unfortunately, Mr. Vanderleaf has no information about August. "Perhaps your son, July, can tell you more about what happened to him. I am sorry to say I couldn't find a single record that identified him."

"What about my brother, Jerome? Were you able to locate him?"

"I have a passenger list with Jerome Washington's name on it. It doesn't tell us much other than he went to Liberia in 1877."

"Liberia? In Africa?"

Mr. Vanderleaf nodded. "I assume your brother emigrated in the hope of escaping violence and racism. The brutality and ugliness perpetrated by the Ku Klux Klan and other groups still terrify people of color all over the South. It's a crying shame!"

"Is there any hope of finding Jerome?"

Mr. Vanderleaf sighed. "Unless one traveled to Liberia, the chances of locating him are slim, and even setting foot in that country for a direct search in no way guarantees a repatriated person can be found. Many of the emigrants didn't survive the move, being unused to tropical diseases and hostile tribes with no intention of honoring land grants to American Negroes."

A few days after our first meeting, Mr. Vanderleaf arranged transportation to Sweetbrier so that I could visit the slave cemetery on the knoll behind the Negro cabins. 'The Settlement" is what the white folks called it; I guess 'slave cabins' is too harsh for the people who owned us. Stepping out of the carriage at Sweetbrier brought back an orchestra of thoughts and feelings, and nothing was melodic about it.

On the road out of Smithfield, I walked past new farms flanking both sides of the old plantation property. A chill crept down my spine when I came to the overgrown driveway leading to the house. An image of Mr. Bert smeared with coal dust and blood wavered in my head. I took a deep breath to steady myself and started down the long driveway.

The big house evidently burned to the ground long ago. The only remains were a few mounds of rubble barely detectable from the overgrowth of weeds and honeysuckle vines. It was comforting to know that Mr. Bert, entombed under the pile of coal and the charred remains of the mansion, would never hurt another living creature. I hurried past, heading for the cabins that were home to so many of us who labored on the Laurent Plantation. I stopped in front of our old cabin; it had fallen to the ground, crumbled into a pile of rotting boards. None of the cabins stood, only mounds of debris remained, marked by an occasional stovepipe or rusted tin pot declaring that people once lived here.

I walked the familiar path leading to the slave cemetery and the fields of sugar beets and cotton that lay beyond; fields where Daddy and Jerome spent their days hoeing, planting, and harvesting crops year after year. Huge elms and a few old swamp oaks shaded the cemetery. I had no idea where Mama and Daddy were buried, but I hoped I would find them. Most of the graves were marked with wooden crosses but no names. It broke my heart to think of the living families who couldn't properly honor their dead ancestors because they couldn't find their resting place.

Thank heavens my brother Jerome had carved *Addie and Garvus Washington* into the wood cross marking their graves. I spent the afternoon weeding the plot and gathering an armful of wild lilies and Black-eyed Susan to spread on top. Then I sat down next to where they were buried, and I told them everything that had happened since Liza and I left Sweetbrier in the middle of the night those many years ago.

Liza Laurent
San Francisco
1895

After spending nearly four years with July and his family in Baltimore, and another year with Rose on Vancouver Island, Sophie is home at last. "You sure took your time coming back," I said when the shiny black and red cab delivered her to the roundabout driveway in front of Wayside Inn. "How many years has it been since you and Rose left for Victoria? Seventeen or eighteen? I'll never forget that day. It was one of my lowest points."

"Time has a way of going faster and faster, that's for sure. Even so, it doesn't seem like it's been as long as eighteen whole years!" She hugged me. "You look exactly the same, Liza!"

"Thanks, Sophie. It's sweet of you to ignore the wrinkles." I stepped back a pace and gazed at her. "Why you're the one who looks amazing." She did, too, partly because she shone with happiness.

"I got an expert Baltimore doctor who did a pretty good job on my bad eye." It had been a scarred raggedy mess, the skin around Sophie's eye, and somehow the ridges of scar tissue were reduced and the eye socket itself reconstructed to look more like her good eye.

"You were beautiful before, don't get me wrong, but you look ten years younger now!"

We hugged and kissed and carried on like long-lost sisters do while the driver unloaded her luggage. From the sheer number of bags the driver took out of the luggage hold, I felt hopeful that she was truly home for good. "I've missed you, Sophie."

"I missed you too, Liza. Now, let's get out of this fog."

"You're lucky I didn't give up on you and rent out the apartment a long time ago!"

"I wouldn't have blamed you one bit," said Sophie, "but, I'm sure glad you didn't, because I might want to stay around for a while."

"I hope you do stay, Sophie." I carried an armful of the smaller valises and totes down the back steps to the apartment entrance. "I had it aired and dusted when I got word you were on your way." Sophie opened the door and stepped in. The driver stacked her luggage in the entrance hall. I tipped him generously while Sophie disappeared on a tour of inspection. "I had new quilts made for the beds. Other than that, I haven't changed a thing. I think it's high time to overhaul some of the furniture."

"It feels real homey, Liza, like I just made tea in the kitchen yesterday!"

"I'll let you get settled in and used to the place again, and around five, if you aren't otherwise engaged, we'll have a cozy dinner at the Inn. Cherie is still cooking up a storm, and she promised to make all your old favorites. I reserved my favorite booth where we can spill the beans and tell each other everything."

"I've been waiting to sit down at the table with you for a mighty long stretch. I wouldn't miss it for the world!"

After Dr. Cline delivered the unborn child conceived with my daughter's future husband, I became more and more disenchanted with Wayside's business of the flesh. The very idea of sex aroused such feelings of revulsion that I gave up the handful of regular clients I kept company with and retired from the physical demands entirely. My feeling of distaste led me to offer Max a larger interest in the profits for managing Wayside's erotic services and other endeavors. He accepted and took over the job of scheduling liaisons, supervising the girls, and managing the kitchen and lounge staff on top of his regular duties as head bartender.

I kept the books as usual and oversaw day-to-day operations, but for the first time in my life, I found myself with time on my hands. These empty moments were torturous; I was besieged with feelings of guilt and loneliness. I threw myself into town doings to avoid constantly dwelling on my sins and shortcomings. San Francisco had become a more broadminded city. Once shunned because of my occupation, now I was treated as a person of means and invited to attend gala events, commemorative ceremonies, ship christenings, and grand openings of new stores and businesses.

As a businesswoman, I knew that I must replace the lost income from my generous clients if I wished to continue my role as a respected benefactress in the rapidly growing city. I diversified our offerings at Wayside, adding musical entertainments and more gaming in the Gentleman's Lounge, and our restaurant business expanded; we now served dinner five days a week and were open to the public as well as to our gentlemen callers. Business boomed. I sacrificed an adjoining parlor and had a wall removed to enlarge the dining area, and I commissioned the construction of booths around the periphery of the room.

The space was exotic and charming when I was finished. The polished mahogany booths were cushioned in red damask. Matching draperies curtained the sides, creating an intimacy perfect for a romantic dinner and discreet enough to conduct a private business affair. Intricately carved lattice panels divided the central area and separated the tables enough for privacy.

The former *Wayside Café* was rechristened *Mon Cherie* in honor of the amazing and resourceful cook herself. Six months later, *Mon Cherie* was one of the most popular eateries in town, and the Gentleman's Lounge hopped with activity until the wee hours. A consequence of our success was hiring several staff: two assistant cooks to help Cherie in the kitchen, a day cook to prepare breakfast and lunch for the girls and their clients and wait staff to serve customers.

Sophie and I sat in my usual booth where a plate of stuffed mushrooms and a dish of antipasto stood next to a basket of sourdough bread. "My-oh-my, this is high rolling, Liza. I'm impressed," said Sophie. "And every table is full! You must be proud!"

The mustachioed waiter with a French accent poured us each a glass of wine. "The cook recommends the Bouillabaisse tonight, and there is also a very nice leg of lamb. Everything is delicious, though. There are no wrong choices at *Mon Cherie*." We sent him off with our dinner selections, and Sophie and I settled in for a serious visit.

"I want to know about July and his family first," I said. "You were in Baltimore a long time. I wondered if you were going to stay forever."

"I thought about it, but I just hate the miserable weather; snow and ice all winter and nasty humid heat in the summer. Besides, Della and Jules needed my room for the new baby. They didn't say so, but it was obvious that the house was getting kind of crowded." Sophie took a packet of photographs from her purse and showed pictures: a two-story brick house on a street lined with identical houses; Jules and Della dressed in formal attire; portrait photographs of the children, Sassafras, Jackson, and Abraham. "The baby, little miss Emmy, wasn't born yet, so I don't have any pictures of her. Della promised to send the latest when they have their annual pictures taken."

"They are good-looking children, Sophie. It's wonderful that you found Jules and his family." I hesitated, wondering if the subject was too painful and decided to ask anyway. "Your letters never said what happened to Augie. Did you ever find out?"

Sophie shook her head. "Jules remembers that a few days after he and Augie were taken away from Sweetbrier, they were sold at a slave auction to two different owners. 'I never saw my brother again,'

Jules said. Mr. Vanderleaf speculated that Augie might have been shipped to the rum distilleries and sugar factories on the islands. 'There was a big need for laborers then, because some kind of plague had wiped out most of the work force,' he said. 'If August was one of the unlucky Negroes who got caught up by the distilleries, I wouldn't be surprised if he was dead. The rum runners had a reputation of working their slaves to death.' "

We were quiet, thinking about Augie's unknown fate. The waiter removed our plates and brought slices of pie topped with dollops of whipped cream. Sophie finally broke the silence. "Above all, I am thankful that I got to know my grandchildren." She took a second envelope from her purse and drew from it another set of photographs. "While we're on the subject, here are some pictures of Rose and Nolan and your grandchildren," she said. My hands trembled as I held the photos. I hadn't seen Rose since she left San Francisco. The first photo was a portrait of Rose seated behind an imposing desk in front of a wall lined with Indian baskets.

"She is more stunning than ever. Is that her basket collection?"

Sophie nodded. "Rose has turned into quite the crusader for the local Indian tribes around Victoria. They suffered a peck of miseries when the whites arrived on the Island, and Rose has taken it upon herself to preserve their history and way of life. She's collected all the baskets and artifacts that she can with the hope of displaying them to the public. She's working with the West Canada Society for Historic Preservation to build a natural history museum in Victoria."

"It suits Rose, that she is doing something useful and noble," I said.

"She is a busy bee, that girl. Her latest project is putting together a book of tribal legends."

"I wish I could tell her how proud I am of her."

"You can write and tell her."

"It's not the same as speaking in person." I turned over the next print, a picture of the whole family standing on the front steps of a magnificent house. Nolan, lean and tall, has one arm around Rose. Robbie, his expression serious and sweet, stands next to his father and is the spitting image of him except that he has Rose's nose. My granddaughter, Aurora, is at her mother's side and is holding her hand. Her eyes stop me in my tracks. The pupils are light and they glow eerily from the monochrome print. Her lips form a perfect rosebud and I can imagine the pale pink color of them. Ringlets of fair hair fall to her waist. I've never seen a child who resembles an angel more than Aurora, the granddaughter I long to meet.

Sophie read my mind. "You can always take a steamer up the coast and visit Rose and your grandchildren. It's high time you traveled anyway. You've stuck to this city like glue. Believe me, travel expands your horizons, and that's from someone who never expected to go farther than the slave settlement at Sweetbrier."

I shook my head ruefully. "You've forgotten one thing Sophie: Rose has never invited me to Victoria. When and if she does, I will take the first available boat."

Though I am not a true believer, I pray that someday Rose will forgive me enough to invite me to her home and into her heart.

Letter from

Rose MacDonald
to
Sophie Washington
1900

September 20, 1900

Dear Sophie,

    I apologize for not writing in a timelier fashion. I've been terribly busy with life in general, but in particular with the museum plans that we've worked so hard for. My dream is finally bearing fruit; the Canadian Historical Society and the Royal Commission on Preserving Culture and the Arts have agreed to put up the bulk of funds for construction, and the ground will be broken next summer for Victoria's own Natural History Museum! It's been hectic and challenging; there are so many details to address. Between the museum demands and family obligations, I haven't put my feet up for more than a minute at a time.

Nolan, as usual, is a wonderful support. He has an architect's eye and has given invaluable advice regarding the plans. His ideas about a restoration room and a massive basement workspace and storage were met enthusiastically by the newly established museum board. I am presently serving as chairwoman on the board, but I hope to step down from that role soon, as I am yearning for another honeymoon trip with Nolan and need more flexibility in my schedule. I have every intention of seeing the project through, and I will tide over until we find a suitable replacement. Knowing the way the Board works, it might take years.

Aurora and Robbie are thriving. Robbie is quite the grown up these days. He is through with his schooling some six months now, and he has refused my pleas to continue his education. Instead, he is joining his father and uncle as a junior partner in MacDonald Enterprises. Though I hoped he would continue to develop his fine brain (and become Prime Minister someday!) I accept his wishes. MacDonald Enterprises is a wonderful company, after all. Robbie is learning the ropes and is eager and enthusiastic about his new career. Nolan is sending him to apprentice in the shipbuilding yard at the MacDonald offices on the mainland near Vancouver. I will miss him terribly, but I wouldn't say so because I don't want to spoil his excitement. He is determined to double the production of MacDonald ships by opening a shipbuilding factory at the Victoria branch.

Aurora is a delight to everyone. She is very musical and plays both the flute and the violin with equal ease. She is good enough that she plays in the Victoria Youth Symphony, and once a year, at Christmas, she joins the full symphony for the Christmas concert held in one or other of the bigger churches in town. Besides her music, she is fascinated with canoeing and fishing and she steals away with her precious daddy whenever she gets the chance. She is a daddy's girl through and through, which I understand; I'm crazy over Nolan too!

I insist that you come for a visit soon, Sophie. You mustn't miss Aurora's entire childhood. The last time you saw her she was a four-year-old. It would be a crying shame if she forgot her Nana Sophie; I want Aurora to love and treasure you as much as I do.

Heaps and buckets of kisses and hugs sent your way, darling Sophie.

Love,

Rose

P.S.: Victoria is enchanting at Christmas time these days. The whole town is decorated with cedar swags tied up in giant red and gold bows and hung from every lamppost, hitching post and street sign.

The shop owners light their storefronts with candles and lanterns that twinkle onto the streets and throw patterns across revelers who pass. Hot cider and candy apples are aplenty, as is a cup of grog and plates of clams if that's your preference.

Please come for Christmas, Sophie. You can attend Aurora's Christmas concert, and Robbie is dying for a game of checkers with his Sophie. Emma Lou Shuggs asks, "When is Sophie coming back?" every time we cross paths. She wants to introduce her new fiancé I don't doubt! So, do come! Please, please, please! The best present of all would be your arrival.

Liza Laurent

San Francisco

December 1900

Sophie was invited to spend the holidays with Rose on the island. Once again, I am left to my own devices at the loneliest time of the year. Though I loved holidays as a child, I now find them to be grim times that I suffer through. I dwell on memories of the past, and melancholy weighs anchor when I face the season with no family of my own to share the celebration.

My first adoptive parents, Addie and Garvus, were especially merry during the holidays. Papa Hugo gave all the fieldworkers a week-long break from working in the fields, and Addie brought home gifts of fabric, honey, dried fruit, slabs of beef and bags of brown rice and flour bestowed on her by Mama Lou and Papa Hugo. She'd cook up a storm, joining the rest of the settlement women in a race to turn out the best pie or fruitcake.

On Christmas day we gathered together at the Negro church just outside Smithville. A proper and solemn service was followed by skits and musical offerings performed on a makeshift stage in the meeting hall to a cheering, laughing crowd. After the boisterous entertainment, the women piled the table with side dishes while the men finished roasting baby pigs threaded on a long spit and suspended over wood coals in the fire pit. The sliced meat was the most delicious food I'd ever tasted.

I was almost six when I went to live with Mama Lou and Papa Hugo at the big house. To my new white guardians, Christmas was a way to win my heart by spoiling me. My first Christmas spent at the big house was a fairy tale come true. Mama Lou decorated the place with hundreds of hanging crystals and we spent hours stringing long popcorn and cranberry garlands to drape around the fir tree Papa chopped down and set up in the ballroom. You needed a ladder to reach the upper third, and I begged for the job of decorating that part of the tree. Papa Hugo steadied the ladder while I tied red satin bows on the highest branches and placed a golden angel on top. "She's almost as pretty as you are, Liz," said Papa Hugo. He was always my champion, and I miss him to this day.

Though I'd already started down the gilded path of the white race, my first Christmas with the Laurents solidified my conversion from a white Negro to a full-fledged, privileged member of the paler tribe. I was spoiled, indeed. Mama Lou wrapped big boxes of ruffled gowns and dollhouses in festive green paper and striped ribbons. Papa Hugo gave parcels of books and drawing pencils and practical things: a dainty saddle for Nance; a new pianoforte for Mama Lou, umbrellas and mud boots for the rainy season. I was the ruling princess of Sweetbrier until Papa Hugo died and Mama Lou crumbled like a dry cracker.

At dinner, Sophie announced her plan to spend Christmas with Rose and family in Victoria. We were sitting at the table finishing our Cherries Jubilee. "I've decided to accept Rose's invitation for a holiday visit. I'm dying to see her and the children. Aurora is ten now. Can you imagine! The last time I visited she was only five, but my-oh-my, could she talk up a storm! That child is the apple of everyone's eye. And of course, Robbie and I are old pals. Nolan, too." Sophie took a bite of the dessert. My silence must have given away my state of inner turmoil. "You should pack a trunk and join me," she said. "It would do you good to get away from the Inn for a pace."

"I wasn't invited, Sophie. In spite of my longing to see Rose and my grandchildren, I refuse to go where I am not wanted."

Sophie shook her head and sighed. "It's a crying shame that she still carries such a grudge! Maybe our Rose will come to her senses some day and give you a chance. I've been working on her, but she's stubborn, just like you. Like mother, like daughter!"

"It isn't Rose's fault. I'd carry a grudge, too, if I was her."

"Oh, now, Liza, don't be so hard on yourself."

"Sophie, there are good reasons for Rose to hate me! I look back and see myself clearly, and the reflection isn't flattering. If only I knew how to make up for my treatment of Rose. I ignored my own daughter when she needed me, and there is no bloody excuse for it. Thank God you were there for her." We were quiet while the waiter poured two snifters of cognac. "I am resigned to being shunned by Rose, yet I will never give up in the effort to make amends."

"Someday, Liza, she'll forgive you. I know she will."

Meanwhile, I shall spend Christmas at the Inn surrounded by my employees and profoundly alone.

Letters from

Sophie Washington
and *Rose MacDonald*

1903-1905

April 16, 1903

Dear Rose,

I hope this letter finds you and the whole family in good health. All is well here, and especially so: July is bringing the family to San Francisco for a visit. He is taking a month off work, (can you believe he has worked at the Baltimore and Ohio R.R. for twenty six years now!) and he and Della and the children are riding the train across the country, stopping briefly in Mississippi to see Della's sister. After that, they follow a straight route to

San Francisco. Shamus picks them up from the station exactly three days and sixteen hours from now! Can you tell that I am counting the minutes?

Your mother, bless her heart, has offered to put them up at the Inn. She was quite insistent; "The apartment is fine for two or three people, but a family of six needs room to spread out. There are three rooms upstairs that are perfect: a nice big room for Jules and Della and two rooms across the hall for the children." Liza had the housekeeper clean the rooms from top to bottom, and she spent a small fortune at Marino's Dry Goods Emporium buying toys and games to entertain the young folks.

You might be wondering why three rooms are available at the Inn instead of being occupied by the usual tenants. I think you'll be pleased to hear that your mother is out of that line of business. Max bought a rooming house a few blocks away and established a separate enterprise with the girls and their clients. It was with Liza's blessing, of course. Though it was hard for her to even partially lose Max, they will always be good friends. Why, Max has been with the Inn since Liza started the business!

Max still runs the Gentleman's Lounge two days a week, and the old partners help each other out; Liza refers the gentlemen who make inquiries about pleasures of the night to Max, and Max sends his wealthier clients to play cards at the Wayside Inn gaming room. Liza hired a new manager to take over the jobs Max had to give up. She grumbles about the fellow although he seems pleasant and capable to me, but what do I know? Fortunately, the changes didn't affect Cherie; she is still the head cook. We can only hope she never retires. Your mother will be in a world of panic trying to find a replacement for Cherie.

Between the restaurant, the Gaming Room and the gentleman's lounge, Liza is making a small fortune: more than enough to make up for the loss of her original line of business. I help Liza with special events, and I still bake once a week. For this, I am paid amply; in fact, I am overpaid, but that's your mother in a nutshell. She's always been generous to me.

You may wonder where all this talk of Liza is leading. Rose, it would mean the world to her if you visited San Francisco. And, no matter what feelings you have about your mother, Aurora and Robbie should get to know their grandmother. She is a different person than the one who raised you. People can change, Rosie, and she has. Liza and I were on shaky ground when you were growing up, and now she is back to being my sister in everything but blood. My heart tells me she'll never be fully happy until you let her into your life.

Think about it, dear Rose. The children would benefit from seeing the sights in California and connecting with their grandmother. She is a woman of means and could help them in the future.

I will say no more. I hope you don't think I am an interfering old nanny.

All my love to you, Nolan, Robbie, and Aurora,

Sophie

P. S. Liza and I are planning an excursion into the foothills. I have heard such stories about the beauty of Yosemite that I want July, Della, and the children to see it. Liza will also take the trek. She hired an expert guide at the advice of an old acquaintance and is paying for the whole trip. I argued about that, but she won't take no for an answer. We'll cross the bay to the northern end and take a ferry up the Sacramento River Delta to the town of Stockton. The guide is meeting us at the Port of Stockton with horses and a wagon. And off we go to Yosemite! Liza arranged for the head guide and his men to set up camp and do the cooking and cleanup. Hallelujah! I intend to put my feet up and enjoy myself! I will report the details in my next letter.

June 10, 1903

Dearest Sophie,

Your newsy letter was high entertainment. Reading it made me miss you terribly. I need to see you more often! Your last visit was two years ago. Hard to believe, isn't it?

You certainly packed in a lot of activities while Jules and family were visiting. I found myself wishing I'd been with you all. Your description of the trip to Yosemite was thrilling. I could smell the sweet fragrance of the forests and see the plunging waterfalls. The bear family fishing in the pond must have been a sight, and one the children will always remember! Poor bears have a job of it, catching fish in their paws. It must be tedious at times.

When you wrote about the boys wading into the river a little too far and suddenly losing their footing. I felt as if I was actually there, watching helplessly as the current swept the boys downstream. My heart was racing! I hope Jackson and his brother are recovered from the icy river water. Thank God the guides saved them! They could have been smashed to death against the rocks. I've always heard that Yosemite is a dangerous place, but the beauty makes the difficulties one must overcome worthwhile.

I am facing my own difficulties with the administrative workings of the Victoria Natural History Museum. Now that we are in the twentieth century we must make every effort to preserve what has come before these modern times. The board members, all well intentioned, are in perpetual disagreement over what to display, how to display it, which bricklayer to use, whether there should be a fee schedule, how to raise funds for the future advancement of the museum, etc.

My original reason for suggesting the museum was to preserve the cultural heritage of the first people to inhabit the island. The trip Nolan and I took, with Ka-kay-un and Tal-a-quil as our guides, inspired a deep admiration for the island tribes and their way of life. Now, I have to fight the mastodon and taxidermy interests for space. Don't get me wrong; there is no doubt that natural science is a crucial element in a museum. Unfortunately, a few members of the Board are inclined to dismiss the native people's archeology as less consequential than other disciplines.

One particularly stubborn fellow wants to take up half the building displaying relics from Hudson's Bay Company! He believes the most important thing to preserve is white man's arrival on the island! I've told him we have limited exhibit space and may have to take turns for public displays. I'm sure some of the board members find me annoying, as I continue to fight for the preservation and exhibition of the natives' rich culture, lifestyle and art, in direct opposition to what others feel are priorities.

Family life soothes me after the demands

of the museum; Nolan is wonderful as always, and Robbie and Aurora are happy and healthy. I may suffer from motherly prejudice, but I can't help the admiration I feel for the children. They excel in their abilities and talents as well as the human kindness and sensitivity with which they conduct their lives.

We see Robbie on holidays mostly as he is finishing an apprenticeship with his Uncle Martin at the MacDonald Ship Works. The factory is in the heart of the port district, and Robbie is learning from the best craftsmen in the field. "By next year we'll have our first Victoria-built MacDonald schooner," he announced the last time he was home. I wish he wrote more often, but I know he is busy at the ship works, and I hear he is courting a young lady he met at a cotillion. I have to wrestle information out of him, and most of the personal news comes from his aunt and cousins.

At thirteen, Aurora astonishes me. I don't tell her so because I don't want her to get a swelled head. She is a beautiful young woman, but she ignores her own good looks; a quality that people find delightful. There is nothing flaunting about her behavior; she is comfortable to be around and has many friends. A few months ago, she decided to switch her main instrument from the violin to piano. She asked her father if he could find a suitable piano that she could buy with her savings. (Aurora earns an allowance every month, and you and Mama have also contributed to her bankroll. I hope she always thanks you for the money you send her.) Nolan told her he'd look into it, and not a word more was said until a baby grand arrived from the mainland last week.

A crowd of twenty workers carried it off the ferry to a flatbed trailer pulled by a team of six horses. The piano proceeded with much fanfare through town and then out to the house. Luckily it wasn't raining! "Why I'll never be able to afford it!" cried Aurora when she saw the beautiful instrument.

"This is a gift from me to the MacDonald household," Nolan said. "You'll not pay a penny, Rori."

Aurora didn't waste time; she is already practicing up a storm. I must admit that I am impressed with her progress! She is so musical; Nolan and I are urging her to keep the violin and play both instruments. Besides music, I am delighted by Aurora's signs of interest in the doings around the museum. She helped set up an exhibit of Women's Artifacts: baskets, clothing, feather and bead adornments, shell jewelry, carved bone and tusk tools and a variety of ceremonial objects. She has a good eye for creating pleasing and attractive visual arrangements, and her neat lettering in ink names many of the objects and identifies their use. We had a jolly time setting up the displays, and Aurora said she wants to help with the next exhibit when we change in the spring.

I must broach a subject that is difficult and potentially hurtful, Sophie. I hope you understand my position. You have tried now for years to convince me to forgive Princess Liza for her lack of affection when I was growing up. My request to you is to please stop trying. I have wounds inflicted by Mama that are not healed and perhaps never will be. It is for me to decide, dear Sophie. I know you and Mama grew up like sisters, and you love her. I don't, plain and simple. She extinguished my love for her long ago.

Perhaps my feelings will soften in time. Until then, I am staying where Mama can't hurt me, and nothing you say will move me an inch.

I hope you don't take this the wrong way. I still love you as much as I always have and always will; I just wish you'd stop nagging me about Mama. When and if I change my mind, I shall do it on my own. By the way, I have encouraged Aurora, and Robbie when he was a youngster, to communicate with their grandmother, so they do know her through letters. Aurora is especially curious about Wayside Inn and her grandmother and begs to visit San Francisco. Perhaps someday I will send her on her own! Even better is the possibility of you accompanying her when you return to San Francisco after a visit to the MacDonald residence on Vancouver Island. (Hint, hint!)

I am sorry that I didn't meet July and his family. Maybe the future will throw us into each other's path, and I will meet my half-brother. Sophie, it pains me to say this; no one must ever know that July and I are related. There is absolutely no rhyme nor reason for Nolan, Robbie, and Aurora to learn about the distasteful and unsavory matters tainting the Laurent side of the family. Again, I hope this doesn't hurt your feelings, Sophie. I am thrilled that July is my half-brother, and my need to keep our blood relationship a secret has nothing to do with the color of his skin.

The hour is late, and I will climb into bed soon. With all my heart I ask for your understanding and forgiveness for my shortcomings.

Love,
Rose

March 17, 1904

Dear Rose,

I am sorry to report that I must postpone my visit to Victoria. I am disappointed that I won't see you as soon as I'd hoped. I always look forward to visiting the MacDonald clan. I hope you aren't too upset by the news. I will miss you terribly, and at the same time, the event responsible for the postponement is cause for celebration: July, Della and the children are moving to Oakland, right across the bay from San Francisco, an easy ferry ride from here! Why, it's just a stone's throw away!

I'm so excited that I could bust open like the jack-in-the-box that scared the dickens out of you when you were a toddler! You can imagine how thrilled I am. July was missing for so many years, and I longed for him and his brother every day of my life. I'm resigned to missing August for eternity, but at least I will have July and my grandchildren close by in my old age.

Your mama is delighted. She developed a bond with all four children, but she gets on particularly well with Emmy, the youngest. Though Emmy is obviously a Negro, she has lighter skin and wavy hair like a white girl. She reminds me a lot of you when you were a little girl, in both looks and her spunky attitude. I think the resemblance is what captivated Liza in the first place, (but I know you don't want to hear about your mama still longing to make amends for the way she was when you were growing up. Sorry, Rosie.)

You might be wondering how it came to pass that July and family are moving to Oakland. When they were here last year, July took the ferry over to Oakland to tour the Southern Pacific Railroad lines and a new-fangled electric train that runs around the town. He didn't tell a soul that, besides sightseeing, he applied for a job. Well just six weeks ago, the Southern Pacific Company sent him a letter offering a job out of Oakland. He'll be a brakeman, same as his job on the Baltimore and Ohio Railroad, but he'll be paid twice as much! Apparently, the Southern Pacific is in need of trained brakemen. The newspapers have stories every week about the expansion of trains all across the Bay Area and into San Jose and the San Joaquin Valley. Business is booming, and thank heavens for it!

Your mama and I have taken the ferry to Oakland several times since July sent the telegraph with his good news. We found a nice house split into two apartments and put a deposit on one for the family to rent until July and Della find a house to buy. It is an unfurnished flat, and we spent a few days ferrying over to hunt down furnishings and basic equipment for the family. July and Della are selling most of their belongings in Baltimore to avoid the troubles involved with long-distance shipping. We are purchasing beds and a dinner table and so forth. Your mother fights over paying the bills!

She got meaner than a polecat when I insisted on paying the deposit for the apartment. She finally gave in, but she races to pay for the every-day necessities we are gathering.

The family arrives five days from now. I am spending at least a week in the flat to help Della organize her household and get accustomed to the area. July starts work at Southern Pacific the day after the train delivers the family to the station, so he won't be around during the day to help with the children. His one day off is Sunday, so Della is sure to have her hands full to overflowing. I will do whatever it takes to help them settle into their new neighborhood.

I meant to write to Aurora but have been so busy that I haven't done it yet. Please tell her that I am sorry to miss her performance with the Victoria Symphony. I know it's the first time she'll play piano in the orchestra, rather than her usual violin. Wish her luck from me for a wonderful performance.

I will write a note to her soon and send along a letter from Sassafras, who desperately wants to be pen pals with her.

Give my congratulations to Robbie for finishing his apprenticeship as a shipbuilder. I'm proud of him and know that he will build the best ships on the west coast. On the nosy side, is there any progress toward a marriage proposal from him to the girl he's been courting? Your description of Kate makes her sound charming and like she'd be a perfect addition to the family. Hopefully, Robbie and Kate will announce their engagement soon and end our nervous wait!

Dearest Rose, I must sign off. Liza needs help with a special dinner she's hosting at the restaurant. The Chamber of Commerce is renting Mon Cherie's for a meeting followed by a seven-course meal. Liza says the shopkeepers and businessmen are intent on coming up with plans to deal with the terrible crime that rules the streets.

Love to all the MacDonalds, and especially to you, Rose.

Sophie

P. S.: I hope your invitation for July's family to visit Victoria still stands. I'd love to show them around the island! I assure you that any potentially embarrassing secrets are held in strictest confidence. July knows I was nanny to you, and that is all. Liza will uphold the story, which means there are no worries about discovery regarding any deeper ties. Burn this after you read it!

December 1, 1905

Dear Sophie,

We are coming to San Francisco for a visit! If all goes according to plan, the MacDonald family will arrive in town on the ninth of January to deliver the fruits of Robbie's hard labor. After months of grueling work, Robbie and his crew of twenty have finished construction on 'Island Queen', the first boat turned out by our own Victoria Ship Works branch of MacDonald Enterprises. The Dollar Steamship Company from San Francisco bought the boat to add to its fleet. Have you heard of it? Their ships go all the way to China, and other far-flung destinations, loaded with northwest lumber and various commodities.

Robbie invited us to join him on the maiden voyage of 'Island Queen' to the new owner in San Francisco. The boat is a compact iron-hulled steamer built primarily to transport cargo, but it also accommodates a modest number of passengers. There are cabins enough for twenty bodies give or take a few. You will see how beautiful it is when we dock. Robbie had it painted white with the tricolor Royal Union Flag emblazoned on the steam stack and on both sides of the bow and stern. It immediately catches the eye. Judging from the bidding competition when Robbie put 'Island Queen' on auction, he is going to be a very successful young man. Nolan and I are terribly proud of him! He is twenty-five years old and already running a boat works!

Robbie announced the other day that the sale of 'Island Queen' provided him with sufficient funds to take care of a wife and family, and to that aim he finally proposed marriage to Kate Turnbell, the young woman he's been courting since he started his internship on the mainland. Kate accepted, and the marriage will commence on May 25th at her family's home in Vancouver. You are invited to the wedding. Invitations will be sent out in March.

We are thrilled that Kate is joining us on the trip. She is a wonderful young woman and quite the role model for Aurora, who is under her spell. Rori copies the way Kate wears her hair, her gestures, her style of dressing, and she's taken on Kate's pet sayings. Everything is "the cat's meow," or "let's skedaddle," or "horse feathers and applesauce." The two have hit it off like long-lost sisters. Indeed, Kate is darling, and such a perfect match for Robbie. Their devotion reminds me of Nolan's and my courtship. I hope that's a sign they'll be deliriously happy.

Nolan and I have such fun keeping up with the young folks and watching them develop into adulthood. If the heavens took me tomorrow, I would enter the gates full of thanks for the gift of my children. They give me reason and purpose. They fulfill me, and Nolan is the crowning glory. What a lucky woman I am!

Sophie, would you please ask my mother if there is room at the Inn for us to tide over until January 20th, when we board the SS City of Puebla, a steamer headed for home. If there isn't room at the Inn, perhaps you could look into lodging for the five of us. I know you would gladly offer to share the apartment, but I fear the numbers would make for a crowded space. You can reassure Mama that we will fend for ourselves and mostly stay out of her hair.

I realize that January is not the choicest time to visit San Francisco, but we will make the best of it. I hear there are new museums and art galleries throughout the city, and I am longing to ride the cable cars. If there are any decent titles playing at the opera hall, I would love to attend an opera! Do you remember when you and I went to the opera some thirty years ago, Sophie? I was home from school, and you had tickets to see *La Traviata*. It is a memory I cherish. Aurora will be mesmerized by an opera experience, I know!

I'm looking forward to seeing the dear old City of San Francisco before it gets so built up that I don't recognize it. Maybe it already has. It will be fun to visit some of my old haunts. And you finally get your wish about Princess Liza meeting her grandson and granddaughter. I hope she can rise to the occasion.

Please let me know about lodging as soon as possible, dearest Sophie. I look forward to seeing you.

Love,
Rose

Aurora MacDonald

Victoria

January 2, 1906

The worst luck has fallen like a black shadow across our happy plans! I have the measles and must stay in quarantine for the next three weeks until Doctor Peters says I am completely well. It means that I have to miss the voyage to take Robbie's boat to San Francisco. I was so excited about going! We haven't had a family vacation since we took an excursion to Lake Louise three years ago. Imprinted forever in my mind's eye are images of the thrilling scenery along the way. I fully intend to return in the future, when I have a sweetheart. Lake Louise drips with romance, and Mom and Dad cooed and cuddled like turtledoves. Robbie and I took lots of walks in order to let them carry on.

But back to the present: I am particularly disappointed because Kate, my future sister-in-law, is going on Robbie's boat, too. She will be part of the family soon, and I already love her to pieces. She is so much fun! I am a bridesmaid for the wedding in May, and Kate was going to help me find the perfect dress! I could cry because of this bad luck! Blast and damn, stupid measles!

The other thing that miffs me is that I've waited my whole life to meet Liza Laurent, my mysterious grandmother who I know only from her letters, and to see Wayside Inn for myself. Mom and Sophie have told me stories about the Inn, where Mom grew up in a big house on top of a hill. She talks fondly about the tree fort the gardener built in a giant oak, and the separate apartment she and Sophie shared, and she talks about Most Holy Name School and her favorite teacher, Sister Margaret, yet I never can coax Mom into talking about Gran. She shuts the conversation off immediately.

Once, I overheard Mom telling Dad that her mother was so cold she could freeze bricks. Sophie was visiting at the time, and I asked her what Mom meant. "Well, your grandmother had some rough years when she wasn't at her best. Liza is much better these days. Now, the tables have turned; Rose is stuck back in the past, and she won't let go of being mad at her mother. Please don't repeat any of this. Rose gets all hopped up like a boiling teapot when you bring up Liza."

Despite Mom's feelings, I'd like to have a real-life grandparent around once in a while. Dad's parents died before I was born, so Gran is my only living relative besides Uncle Martin and Aunt Claire and three cousins who are all ten or twenty years older than I. And, dear Sophie, of course. Gran and I have written letters faithfully, but it isn't the same as meeting her in person.

There was a big fuss over whether Mom would go on the trip to San Francisco or stay with me. Dad and Mom were talking in the doorway of my bedroom where I lay in bed with my runny, itchy eyes tightly shut.

"I hate to miss the adventure, but I'd never forgive myself if anything happened to Rori," Mom said. "I'll have to forego the trip."

"I'll stay home with you," said Dad.

"You certainly will not! At least one of Robbie's parents should go! It means so much to him! I can manage Rori's measles on my own, Nolan. You must not miss the milestone in our son's life. He would be greatly disappointed."

Dad put his arm around Mom's shoulders. "Rose, if you are certain you don't need me here, I'll go ahead with the original plan and crew for Robbie on *Island Queen*."

"I think it's an excellent decision, Nolan." Mom gave Dad a little kiss on the cheek. "What about Kate?" she asked suddenly. "She may have to cancel her plans. Gossip's tongues love to wag about a young woman traveling alone with two men."

"What if Kate asks her Aunt Harriet? She loves to travel, and she's just a hop, skip and a jump away. I bet if Kate wired her, she'd take the ferry over to join us."

"That's a perfect solution!" Mom cried.

I sat up in bed and squinted at Mom and Dad through puffy eyes. "The whole trip is ruined because of me!" I burst into tears.

Mom rushed over to try to sooth me. "You are not at fault in this matter, Rori. You didn't ask for a case of the measles. Now, don't get overly excited."

"You and Kate mustn't change your plans. I don't feel sick enough to die. You don't have to stay and babysit me! I mean it!"

"Let's hear what Doctor Peters says this afternoon. If he thinks you're in the slightest danger, I'm not going anywhere."

Doctor Peters took my temperature, listened to my lungs and peered into my mouth. "Say 'ahhh,' Aurora." He poked the back of my throat with a long swab. "When you're recovered, we should remove those nasty tonsils."

Mom nodded. "We'll cross that hurdle when we come to it." Dad explained to the doctor about Robbie's boat delivery, and the intended family outing that was now uncertain.

"I won't even think of leaving Aurora if there is any chance that her health is in jeopardy," Mom said. "What are your thoughts, Doctor Peters?"

"Aurora has a strong constitution, which would indicate a quick recovery, but honestly there is no way of predicting the length or severity of measles. I don't mean to frighten you, Rose, but the fact is that measles can lead to more serious conditions. The worst cases can cause swelling of the brain and occasionally death. Whether that will happen in Aurora's case is doubtful, but I can't guarantee it."

Doctor Peters put two fingers on my wrist and used his stopwatch to time my pulse. "Excellent. Steady and strong." He patted my shoulder. "You'll feel better in a few days, Aurora." Doctor Peters packed his stethoscope into the black leather valise he carried. "It's up to you, Rose, to decide whether or not to go. I'd hate to lead you to the wrong decision." The Doctor handed Mom a slender bottle. "If her throat hurts and she starts to cough, give her a tablespoon of this horehound syrup. It will also help her sleep."

"Thank you, Doctor Peters."

"If you decide to take the trip and are concerned about leaving Aurora alone with the housekeeper, you can always hire a nurse. I recommend Ada Perry. She is capable and steadfast. You couldn't have a better person look after her."

"Thanks, Doctor Peters, but I am inclined to stay here with Aurora. The only thing that would make me change my mind is if she makes a recovery overnight."

Mom and Dad walked the doctor downstairs to the front door. I fell asleep to the sound of their muffled conversation and drifted into troubled dreams of dragons shooting flames at my eyes. In the morning I woke with a high temperature and a dreadful earache that made me cry from the pain of it. My poor eyes were swelled to slits, and I was covered with a nasty rash. Mom brushed her cool hand across my forehead. "I'm not letting you out of my sight until you're better. Nolan, you must tell Kate to wire Aunt Harriet to take my place."

Two days later, Dad, Robbie, Kate and her Aunt Harriet said their goodbyes and set course for San Francisco. Their departure was a melancholy moment for me. I had so looked forward to the trip. My only consolation is that Kate promised to look for a pretty dress for the wedding. "I shall try to find something in cornflower blue or a soft violet. Both colors would complement your eyes and complexion, Rori."

Mom did her best to console me. "We'll plan another trip to San Francisco, I promise. And as soon as you feel better, we can play cards and dominoes and backgammon and drink hot chocolate. We'll make a lark of it, Rori. After all, it's not the end of the world."

I am resigned to missing the fun and making the best of my quarantine. I will read the stack of novels sent by the town librarian, who knows my taste in books, and Dad gave me a thousand-piece puzzle to work on while I'm confined to the sickroom. I am grateful to have Mom keeping me company through what is turning out to be a nasty case of measles. I'm glad she stayed. I have her all to myself for a change.

When Robbie, Dad, and Kate come home, I count on hearing every detail of the trip from Kate. I hope she brings me an especially pretty gown for the wedding!

Sophie Washington
San Francisco
January 10, 1906

Liza and I, bundled in our winter coats and mufflers, waited on the pier as Robbie and his crew maneuvered *Island Queen* into the slip. We'd brought two folding stools with canvas seats and a canteen of hot tea, knowing that landing a boat can involve waiting. We watched a dozen dockworkers secure the beautiful craft and attach a boarding ramp. I could feel Liza's excitement; though she stood an arm's distance away, she pulsed with anticipation. It took several minutes before a group of sailors carrying luggage ambled down the steep ramp. They stacked the bags on the wooden pier and continued walking toward the wharf. We waited for the MacDonalds to appear.

"Where are they?" Liza's voice was impatient.

"It won't be long now, I'm sure," I said. "Take a few deep breaths and relax, honey. You're as wound up as a clock spring!"

"I most certainly am not!" she said, but she took a bunch of deep breaths and calmed down.

Finally, two women I didn't recognize made their way down the ramp followed by Robbie and Nolan. "Sophie!" cried Robbie. He ran to where we stood waiting and threw his arms around me.

"Why, you've grown taller than your Daddy!" I said, hugging him back.

He held me at arm's length. "Gosh, it's good to see you!"

"The feeling is mutual!" I planted a kiss on his cheek.

"What do you think of *Island Queen*? Isn't she a beauty?"

"She is stunning, Robbie. I am so proud of you!"

Robbie turned to Liza and took her hand. "You must be Gran," he said.

Liza's eyes got moist as she hugged her grandson. "I've waited a long time to meet you, Robbie." She dabbed her eyes with a handkerchief extracted from her bosom. "I hope you understand that my tears are from happiness."

The young woman standing next to Robbie tugged his arm and whispered something. "Kate has just reminded me of my manners. I'd like everyone to meet Kate Turnbell, my fiancée, and her Aunt Harriet, who came to the rescue and joined us at the last minute. And of course, you both already know Dad."

Nolan bobbed a little bow and reached out a hand to Liza. "Why, you look the same as you did when Rose and I got married," he said.

She gave his hand a quick, formal shake as if he were a complete stranger. Nolan didn't seem bothered or offended by the lukewarm greeting. He smiled sweetly. "It's good to see you again, Liza." There was a rush of everyone talking all at once, and there were hugs and handshakes flying back and forth. After everyone was properly introduced, Nolan took charge. "I'll round up a porter with a cart for the luggage."

Liza turned her gaze on the boarding ramp. "Shall we wait until Rose and Aurora come down?" she asked.

Nolan looked questioningly at Robbie, who gave a little gasp. "Oh gosh, I could kick myself. I told Dad I'd stop in the telegraph office in Victoria and send a telegram about Mom and Rori, but I was so preoccupied with putting finishing touches on *Island Queen* that I completely forgot. It's all my fault, Gran."

"What were you going to tell us in the telegram?" Liza asked.

"Aurora came down with a bad case of measles a couple of days before we were scheduled to leave Victoria. Doctor Peters put her under strict quarantine. Rose stayed behind to nurse her," said Nolan.

Liza turned pale and began to sway. I was afraid she was going to faint, so I put a steadying arm around her waist, and Kate rushed over to take her elbow. "I'm fine. Just a little dizzy," said Liza.

I unfolded the campstool and made her sit. "Rest here until you feel less lightheaded," I said.

"I apologize for springing the bad news, Liza. It must come as a terrible letdown," said Nolan.

Liza's mouth twisted into a weak smile. "Why, there's nothing to apologize for! I hope I don't seem ungracious. The news about Aurora's measles is disappointing, of course; I was looking forward to seeing her and Rose. At the same time, I am overjoyed to finally meet Robbie, and I'm delighted to meet Kate and her Aunt Harriet."

"There's a porter." Nolan waved his arms at the man pulling an empty cart. He wasn't looking our way, and Nolan set off in a sprint to catch up with him.

"I have rooms at the Inn for Kate and her aunt," Liza said. "Sophie insists that Robbie and Nolan stay in the apartment with her. I suggest a sightseeing tour of the waterfront area and winding our way to the Inn through downtown with a side trip to Chinatown. Does that suit everyone?"

"It sounds perfect, Gran," said Robbie.

"I'd love to see all of the city!" said Kate.

"Let's start with a short excursion today, and every day we can explore a new area. If we're all in agreement, I thought we'd end up at Wayside midafternoon, so everyone can settle in the rooms. Afterwards, if you are inclined, we'd meet at *Mon Cherie* for an early dinner."

Aunt Harriet nodded enthusiastically. "I hoped we'd have the chance to eat at your restaurant, Mrs. Laurent. It is famous as far away as Seattle!"

"Please call me Liza."

"All right, Liza. And please call me Harriet as well."

Liza nodded. "After supper, if you're not too tired, I have tickets to the theater for a vaudeville show. If the reviews can be trusted, it is a delightful performance. A generous friend offered us box seats."

"I wouldn't miss it if I was dead tired, which I'm not," said Robbie.

"Me either," said Kate.

Nolan returned with the porter, and he and Robbie helped load his cart with luggage. The carriage was waiting where we'd left it when we'd arrived at the pier to greet the family. Liza and I followed Kate and Harriet into the sedan. Nolan climbed up to sit next to the driver, and Robbie sat in the rumble seat. It was a stunning winter day in San Francisco. The bay sparkled, and the crisp air smelled of evergreen trees and the sea breeze. Liza and I pointed out the sights to Kate and Aunt Harriet on the ride to the Inn. The ladies craned their necks to see out the windows on opposite sides of the carriage. We stopped at points of interest along the way, showing the visitors all the new buildings shooting up around the city. Liza insisted on taking our guests for a snack at Yee Lin's Dim Sum. We made our way home, and by mid-afternoon the cab driver delivered us to Wayside Inn.

I was proud of Liza. Though it was obvious that her heart was breaking over Rose and Aurora staying behind in Victoria, she made a heroic effort to be the perfect hostess. She showed our visitors the best San Francisco had to offer and used some of her highfaluting connections to make special arrangements. "Tomorrow morning, Mr. Sutro is closing the doors to the public, and he's giving us a personal tour of the baths and Sutro Gardens," she announced the next morning. "I thought we'd take the tour and then have lunch at Cliff House. It has such a marvelous view, and though the food isn't as good as *Mon Cherie*, it is tasty enough."

Robbie and Nolan had business to conduct in San Francisco, which meant they were sometimes unavailable to join us in the pursuit of fun. When their obligations drew them to the dockyard or warehouse, Liza organized shopping trips and luncheons to please the ladies. Aunt Harriet had the time of her life browsing in all manner of fascinating shops, and after discovering a thriving church bingo circuit, she branched off to try her luck. Our group expanded on the weekend; July, Della and the children took the ferry over to join us for a sailing tour of the bay and a thrilling performance of one of Mr. Mozart's symphonies.

"Aurora and Rose would have loved the concert tonight," Nolan said. "Rori is particularly fascinated in all things musical. I wish they were here."

"You and I aren't the only ones missing them." I pointed my chin toward Liza.

He nodded. "It's a great disappointment for everyone, including the two left behind in Victoria." Nolan is such an understanding and kind soul and the perfect mate for our Rosie.

On the eve of their departure, Liza ordered a grand feast at *Mon Cherie*. Our table was lively with conversation during all six courses of the most delicious food you could imagine. When the waiter brought glasses of port for dessert, Robbie proposed a toast. "Here's to Gran and Sophie for making this a bang-up trip." We clinked glasses.

"And here's to the next visit with the whole family," said Liza. "I hope I don't have to wait so many years this time!"

"Why, it won't be long at all if you and Sophie come to Vancouver for the wedding," said Robbie. "It's only four months away now."

"And look at the engagement ring Nolan found! Isn't it beautiful!" Kate held out her hand, and we all admired the ring sparkling with sapphires surrounding a single diamond.

The next morning was filled with the usual hustle of travelers preparing for departure. A quick breakfast followed last minute packing. Soon it was time to meet the cab. We waited in the misty fog for the men to stow a considerably larger amount of luggage than when they'd arrived into the hold of the carriage. Kate and Aunt Harriet had taken full advantage of San Francisco's wonderful shops and had packed their purchases into additional wooden crates. Liza had also packed a trunk for Rose and Aurora with gifts and souvenirs from the various attractions we visited.

Our goodbyes were muffled in the swirling fog. Robbie wrapped me in a tight hug. "You and Gran take good care of each other," said Robbie. "I love you, Sophie."

"I love you too. I only wish you were closer so you could visit more often."

Liza kissed her grandson and Kate and gave Aunt Harriet a hug. "Now remember, Harriet, you have a standing invitation to come back for a visit. You are always welcome to stay at the Inn," she said. Nolan extended his hand, and Liza shook it. "When you get home, please give my love to Rose and Aurora and tell them how much we missed them."

"I'll do it first thing," said Nolan.

"Have a safe trip home," I called as the cab pulled away from the Inn and disappeared in the thick fog. A chill swept down my spine. I shivered and pulled my cloak tighter across my chest. "It's cold. Let's go inside and have some tea."

It was like old times; we sat in the back apartment at the scarred-up kitchen table, and I poured cups of hot tea for the two of us. The rays of cold morning light fell across the table. I looked at my dear friend's face and was taken aback by the deep sadness I saw in her eyes. I reached over and patted the back of her hand. "That was a real nice vacation you put together, Liza, in spite of being disappointed about Rose and Aurora."

In an unusual display of emotion, she burst into sobs. "Though it is my most earnest hope, I am afraid I shall never make amends to Rose!" She left the table and rushed through the connecting door to the Inn. For the rest of the day she stayed locked up in her bedroom. I knocked on the door a couple of times, but she called out that she had a sick headache and to leave her be.

I felt sorry for Liza. I'd hoped a family visit would heal the torn relationship between Liza and Rose. It was a pity all the way around that poor Aurora had caught the measles.

Aurora MacDonald

Victoria

February 7, 1906

Coming down with the measles was the beginning of my life falling apart. The happy world I knew a few short weeks ago is destroyed forever. I have only one parent now; Dad, Robbie, Kate and her Aunt Harriet drowned at sea aboard the steamship *Valencia*. It wrecked on the 22nd of January, a day I wish I could wipe out of history as if it never happened. Mom and I would have died too if it hadn't been for the measles. The sad truth is that Mom wishes she'd gone down with the ship, so she wouldn't have to live life without Dad.

I imagine myself drowning with Dad and Robbie and Kate every time I think about the shipwreck; first the bitter cold of the icy sea closing over me, the stone weight of wet skirts and winter boots dragging me to the bottom, my mouth and nose flooding with salty brine until I become one with it; until I become food for the sharks and sea worms, perhaps the same creatures that chewed away pieces of Dad and Robbie, or Kate and her Aunt Harriet. It makes me shudder to think of beautiful Kate and my wonderful father and brother dissolving into the ocean until only their bones rest on the seafloor. I feel guilty to be alive.

I am tormented by sleeplessness; for hours I toss and turn and relive the night we learned of the shipwreck. It is indelibly etched in my brain. Over and over the events replay: there was a sharp knock on the front door at eight. Mom and I were in the library, playing games on a table pulled close to the fireplace; it had rained in sheets for days, and the wind howled and pelted our house with furious wet gusts. It was a chilling wind that turned the rain to sleet, and I remember hoping it would snow. I'd been confined inside since my sickness, and I had cabin fever. "If it snows tonight I want to build a snowman tomorrow."

"We'll check your temperature in the morning. I wouldn't want you to have a relapse," Mom said.

"I'll bundle up really well, and if I feel fatigued, I'll come in immediately," I assured her. Loud knocking on the front door interrupted us. The knocking was sharp, insistent and startling. Eight was late for a social call on a winter evening. Erma thumped down the hall toward the door. "I'm coming, I'm coming!" she muttered. "Lord 'a mercy, have some patience."

We heard the muted sound of a man's deep voice, and then Erma rushed down the hall to the library where Mom was beating me in a game of Chess. Mr. Palmer, who ran Victoria Telephone and Telegraph, and Officer Collins, the new deputy from the Mounted Police, followed her. Their expressions, grim and pale, yanked Mom to her feet. "What's happened?" Her voice squeaked like a broken step. I crossed to her side and took her hand.

"You might want to send the young lady out with Miss Laney." Mr. Palmer spoke softly, looking away as if he was afraid to meet Mom's eyes.

"I'll stay right here," I said flatly. "I'm not a child. I'm almost sixteen."

Mr. Palmer and Deputy Collins looked at each other, shrugged, and turned their pitying eyes back to my mother and me. The deputy took off his wet hat and handed it to Erma, who held the dripping thing through the terrible news. "It pains me to say that Mr. Palmer here received a telegraph with some bad tidings."

Mr. Palmer cleared his throat nervously. "It's come across the wire from Cape Beale Light Station. Apparently, the steamer *Valencia* ran aground on a reef some 48 hours ago. Your husband and son are believed to have been on board."

Mom looked relieved. "For a moment you had me scared to death. Nolan booked a return trip from San Francisco on the steamship *City of Puebla,* not the *Valencia.*"

Mr. Palmer shook his head sadly. "Apparently *The Puebla* was pulled from service to undergo repairs, and *Valencia* was substituting on the San Francisco to Vancouver Route." My mother made a sound like a wrung-neck chicken and turned the color of a freshly bleached sheet. Mr. Palmer put a supporting arm around her to keep her from falling. "The authorities believe that Nolan and Robbie are among the victims who perished in the maelstrom. I'm sorry to bring you this dreadful news, Mrs. MacDonald."

"It can't be true," wailed my mother.

"I'm afraid it is, Mrs. MacDonald."

"How?" The question trembled on Mom's lips.

"The same God-awful series of storms causing mischief up and down the island caught the SS *Valencia.* The ship landed on a reef, and for hours it was battered against rocks by huge waves. The boats that tried to come to *Valencia's* rescue didn't have much of a chance in this weather." He took off his glasses and dried the lenses before he spoke. "So far there are only twenty-eight passengers and crew accounted for. Over a hundred are missing. Nolan and Robbie are among them."

"What about Kate?" I managed to squeak.

"Who?" asked Mr. Palmer.

"Kate Turnbell, my brother's fiancée."

Both men gazed at the floor. "Her kin will be informed whether or not she survived," said the deputy. "You can make inquiries to them. We can't give out that information."

Mr. Palmer's tone was grim. "In light of the circumstances, I wouldn't get your hopes up. I don't remember that name being on the list of survivors."

"Oh my God!" Mom clutched her throat and sat with a thud in the chair she'd occupied in the carefree moments earlier in the evening. She looked like a sculpture of herself done of white marble.

"There must be some mistake," I said. "Dad and Robbie know the sea like the back of their hands!"

"I'm afraid that no human is a match when the conditions in the Strait are so treacherous. It wasn't many years back when my brother Michael died a few miles from where *Valencia* went down. During a heavy storm, that stretch is a veritable death trap." Mr. Palmer passed a gnarled hand across his eyes.

It was quiet for a minute or two. Finally, the deputy spoke. "The ships that went to the rescue couldn't do anything in such rough conditions. One sailor, who by the grace of God made it to shore, said it was the worst storm he'd weathered. 'The sea wanted human flesh,' he said."

I waited for Mom to insist that Dad and Robbie were undoubtedly alive and well and would be found somewhere on the shore, but she just made little panting moans. I wasn't ready to accept the news. "What about lifeboats? Is it possible that not everyone who survived has been found?"

Mr. Palmer shook his head sadly. "The outlook isn't hopeful. In the first hours of the wreck several lifeboats set out, but the wind and heavy swells sank them or crushed them to splinters on the rocks. One of the survivors saw Nolan and Robbie board a lifeboat that was swallowed by a huge wave just minutes after it launched." His voice lowered to a hoarse whisper. "No one could survive for long in the cold water." Mom let out a strangled wail.

Deputy Collins bowed his head respectfully toward my shivering mother. "A search party has gone out overland, Mrs. MacDonald. If there are any survivors, they'll find them in the next day or so. Unfortunately, there will probably be more remains washed ashore than living passengers." Mom wailed again, and I felt like I was going to be sick to my stomach. "If anything comes to light, you'll be the first to know, ma'am."

In the days after the shipwreck I prayed that Dad, Robbie, Kate and her Aunt Harriet had somehow survived, but good news failed to come. Searchers found a few bodies, but the corpses were ravaged by sharks and in most cases unidentifiable. As the number of days mounted, my hopes sank. Now, I've come to accept the dire truth; my dearest father and brother and Kate, the sister I longed for, are truly lost at sea, and my mother is lost on earth. Part of her died along with Dad and Robbie. She reminds me of something hollow and lifeless: an empty box or a broken eggshell.

It doesn't help that every inch of the house brings memories: Dad's favorite chair and ottoman, Robbie's intricate model sailboats constructed of exotic wood, Dad's overcoat and fedora in the closet, Robbie's telescope set up in the second-floor window alcove. The house is full to the rafters with Dad and Robbie, yet the real men are gone forever to a watery grave. Three days from now we are leaving Victoria to flee from their ghosts.

I will turn sixteen in May, but I feel ancient. The carefree young girl has disappeared in a fog of death and sorrow. I want my mother to be her old self: dependable, happy and loving. She was powerful and strong; now she is weak and weepy like a newborn, and I can't rely on her for anything. I've done my best to bring Mom out of her grief, but it is impossible. She stays in her bedroom with the door shut, and she refuses all visitors. She hasn't even glanced at the sympathy cards pouring in, and she's eaten barely enough to keep a bird alive.

I lost my father and brother just as much as my mother lost her husband and son, but I must hide my despair. Only my pillow knows the true measure of my sorrow. Sometimes it grows so damp from tears, I have to turn it over for a dry spot. I keep my suffering to myself, as I suspect a mere inkling of it could add to the burden of Mom's grief.

Thankfully, Sophie is here. Mr. Palmer sent a telegram to Gran and Sophie with the news of the wreck, and Sophie sent a one-line reply. "Will arrive in Victoria per travel arrangements." Dear old Sophie! Though she hates traveling by sea, it was the fastest way to get here on such short notice. Her arrival in Victoria was a huge relief. After one look at Mom, she sent Erma to fetch Dr. Peters. "I'm going to prop some pillows behind your back so that you can sit up," she said.

"I can't," Mom wailed. "I'm too dizzy."

"Nonsense, Rose. You're dizzy because you've been lying here crying your eyes out. Now, sit up, honey. It'll make you feel better, trust me. I'm going to comb your hair and give you a little sponge bath while we're waiting for the doctor."

The doctor listened to Mom's chest with his stethoscope and took her pulse. "Your heart is racing too fast, Rose. You must eat properly, you're losing far too much weight," he said. "Are you having trouble sleeping?" Mom nodded and began to weep. "Rest is the great healer, Rose. Here is a tonic to help you relax." He turned to Sophie. "Is there any chicken soup in the house?"

"No, but I'll be happy to make a pot," she said. "Aurora can help."

"Make sure Rose eats a decent portion of soup and follow it with an ounce of the calmative in a cup of hot water. She needs to eat regularly and get plenty of rest. In a few days, she should improve. The state of overwhelming sorrow will lessen with time." But Doctor Peters was wrong; Mom's will to live in the real world had died. By the time we arrived in San Francisco she'd erected a shell and retreated into it like a sea snail.

Liza Laurent
Wayside Inn, San Francisco
March 1906

I've waited in hope for twenty long years for Rose to come home to the Inn, and now that it has finally happened, she is no longer the Rose of old. Aurora put it into words perfectly. "Mom's mind is with Dad and Robbie at the bottom of the ocean. She can't find her way back to life in a world without them."

Rose has withdrawn from everyone including poor Aurora. She doesn't respond to Sophie, either. My chance to make amends for being a lousy mother is once again thwarted; Rose looks at the three of us with blank eyes as she sits with her arms wrapped tight across her chest. She murmurs words of love to the ghost of Nolan, and every so often she rocks from side to side and lets out a deep gasping sigh. I wonder if she has a damaged brain from her broken heart.

I sent for Doctor Walheimer, a specialist in evaluating mental problems, to make a house call. He examined Rose, testing her reflexes and measuring her vital signs. Finally, he lifted her eyelids and shined a light on her pupils. When he was done with his examination, he patted Rose on the shoulder and gestured for Sophie and me to follow him into the hall. He closed the door gently.

"She's not blind, and she hasn't gone deaf," he said. "I believe that Rose has entered a state of catatonia."

"I'm not sure what that means," I said.

"Catatonia describes a condition where the patient becomes unresponsive to everything and everybody outside themselves. They are frozen in some kind of mind limbo that renders them incapable of relating normally."

"But Rose was never like this!" cried Sophie. "She's smart and strong and kind. The Rose I know can handle any obstacle that comes her way, just like you, Liza. What on earth happened?"

"The pain of her grief is so intense that her mind has shut down. I've come across it several times before."

"What are her chances of snapping out of this?" asked Sophie.

"The severity of episodes varies from person to person, but generally, if the patient has the proper support through a mental specialist, the chances of recovery are improved. I'll give you some names of mental therapists, if you're interested."

"Of course, I'm interested in doing everything possible for Rose!"

He handed me a card with the names he'd written. "You'll need to exercise patience and to shield her as much as possible from any more shocks," he said as he took his leave. He paused at the open door. "In the long term, if Mrs. MacDonald doesn't respond to outpatient treatment, there are institutions for the mentally ill."

"Never," I said. "Rose will recuperate right here at the Inn. Having family surround her is far more healing than a mental ward. Thank you for the names, Doctor Walheimer." I closed the door gently and turned to Sophie. "We will bring Rose back to the living if it's the last thing I do."

Until she is restored, I will devote my undivided attention to the daughter I mistreated and have come to love so deeply. I will do it for Rose and myself and for Aurora, as she is the one who suffers the most. I won't stand by and see my granddaughter damaged like I damaged Rose.

Aurora MacDonald
San Francisco
May 1906

My dull and dreary spirits matched the winter weather when Mom, Sophie and I arrived at Wayside Inn. Gran understood my despair. She took me in her arms as soon as I stepped from the cab we'd hailed at the wharf. Though it was the first time we'd met in person, love streamed through her eyes and her tender embrace. I felt a bond, like I'd known her forever and could tell her my deepest secrets. I buried my face in the soft fabric of her dress and wept. Gran hugged me tight. "There, there, child. You're safe now. Everything will be all right. I know you've been through hell." Her words soothed me, and for the first time I felt there might be some hope for the future in spite of the loss of my entire family: Robbie and Dad by drowning in the ocean and Mom by drowning in sorrow.

Gran and Sophie took charge of Mom, which helped relieve the growing burden of worry I'd carried since SS *Valencia* wrecked. From the moment we'd heard the horrible news, Mom was like a sick baby bird that needed to be kept warm and fed or she'd leave this mortal world. Unfortunately, she didn't cooperate in trying to get better. I did everything I could to reach her, to bring her back to her old self, but she shut me out along with everyone else. Although I understood Mom's pain, her abandonment was a wound I bore silently. Worry and hurt stalked my waking hours, but Gran gave me hope. "Rose will heal, we just need to exercise patience."

The earthquake brought Mom to her senses. The angry gods intervened in her deep and afflicting sorrow by shaking the earth so hard that she finally woke up and found herself back in the real world. It shook us all to the very foundations of our souls and defined our path as survivors. The monstrous shaking took place a few minutes past five on the eighteenth of April. The grandfather clock in the hallway alcove announced the hour, and I'd pressed the pillow over my head to muffle the sound.

I went back to sleep and fell immediately into a terrifying nightmare; I was aboard SS *Valencia* as it wrecked. The boat shuddered and twisted as it was battered against the rocks by huge waves and hurricane gusts. Dad and Robbie stood next to me, and Kate had her elbow crooked in mine, but the force of the crash parted us, throwing the three of them to the opposite side of the cabin. Sounds of wood splintering and glass shattering joined into a noisy, roaring crescendo as a wall of water burst into the ship and swept my father, brother, Kate and her aunt into the sea.

I woke, screaming frantically as my bed rose and fell like a bucking bronc at the rodeo. "Help!" I screamed. The room rippled as if monster waves were under the floorboards, and the pretty knickknacks on the dresser and side tables danced and jiggled like they were possessed by demons. I managed to get out of bed and was thrown to the floor. I dragged myself up by holding on to the side of the bed, and, stumbling like a drunk, I made it to the door, steadying myself along the way by clinging to bedposts and chairs for support.

The shaking kept on and on, and with it an infernal moaning roar. I was certain it was going to kill us all; I wondered if I'd join Dad, Robbie and Kate in the afterlife. At last, a final shudder rattled the house, and suddenly there was blessed stillness. I stepped cautiously into the hallway. The paintings and fancy mirrors had been shaken off the walls, and broken glass glittered across the dark floor. I risked a dash back into my room for slippers and a robe and returned to the hall.

"Rori! Rori!" shrieked my mother running down the hall in the dim light. "You're alive! Thank God!" she cried when she reached my side. "I couldn't bear it if I'd lost you, too!" We clung to each other and she showered kisses across my face. In spite of the circumstances, it felt wonderful to have her arms around me. It was the only real attention Mom had paid me since Dad and Robbie died, and it marked a turning point.

Gran joined us in the hall. She threw her arms around both of us. "Thank heavens," she said over and over as we hugged.

"Oh, Mama!" Mom collapsed into Gran's arms, and they held onto each other like there was no tomorrow.

"Oh, Rose!" Gran kept making little cooing noises, and they both forgot about me standing next to them in the hallway. "We should see if Sophie is all right," I said at last.

There was no electricity, so Gran found an unbroken lantern and lighted it. Shards of glass and fragments of China vases crunched underfoot as we followed Gran downstairs to the apartment. Sophie stood in the doorway connecting the Inn and the apartment. "Can someone tell me what in hell just happened?"

"I believe we had an earthquake, and a sizable one," said Gran.

"Well, I don't know about you all, but I'm afraid this house is going to come down on my noggin if Mother Earth starts another free-for-all. I think we should hightail it to the street or someplace place clear of falling objects."

Outside, we met a steady stream of people, many of them still in their nightclothes, carrying overflowing baskets and luggage and pushing wheelbarrows or carts filled with haphazard piles of belongings. "Everyone's heading for higher ground. The quake was bad enough, and now the fires are chasing us out," said a surprisingly cheerful young woman. "The rescue workers told us to get out and hurry up about it. The smoke is so bad in some places that folks are practically choking to death!" She carried a baby in a sling on her back and led a toddler with her free hand. "My husband stayed behind to help fight the fires. We're walking to the Presidio to set up camp and wait for him."

By midmorning, the clear sky disappeared in the gloom of over-hanging smoke and falling ash. The sun shone a bloody red through the layer of black smoke, casting an eerie light on the ruins of San Francisco. We learned of new developments from the refugees. "All the water mains busted from the shaking, so they're trying to stop the fires with dynamite. They blow up a whole city block to try to halt the fire in its tracks," said a man pushing a big two-wheeled cart filled with bread and salami and other items he was able to gather from his delicatessen. "I lost my store and my house, but at least I'm alive. Would you be interested in buying a salami?"

Gran bought five salamis, a couple of loaves of bread, and a large round of yellow cheese. Sophie sliced up oranges and apples she fetched from the cold cellar, and Mom and I sliced the salami and cheese. We set the eatables on card tables. Soon the front yard collected a crowd of hungry people. Many of the earthquake victims escaped their homes before they'd eaten breakfast. Mom and Gran and I risked another trip inside to raid the kitchen at *Mon Cherie*. "We can't feed the whole world," said Gran, "but we'll be as generous as we can while our supplies last." Some of our more fortunate neighbors, whose homes were still standing and sound enough to enter, brought offerings from their pantries, and the hungry people kept on coming.

Except for one of its three chimneys, Wayside Inn was left in relatively sound shape; however, we were wary of going indoors, fear-ing that another shock might bring the walls and ceilings upon us. While Mom and Gran served the hungry folks, Sophie and I took another quick trip inside to gather blankets and wooden cots. When the food tables out front were empty, the four of us set up camp in the backyard. Gran and Sophie strung some old canvas awnings together to form a three-sided makeshift tent, and we dragged out a set of small armchairs to sit on.

Our view from the hilltop showed plumes of black smoke rising across the city. "I used to hate walking up, up, up, sweating and panting to get home," said Sophie, "but everyone who lives down below us is trying to get to higher ground! I'll never complain again, if we live through this mess. Now I appreciate the elevation, to say the least!"

"And I appreciate Stuart McCurdle, who built the Inn so sturdy and sound that it stayed in one piece. Verna was sure right about him being a fine carpenter," said Gran. I asked who Stuart and Verna were, and Gran told the story of how the Inn became hers.

I had a curious feeling during that whole unreal day, a feeling of happiness brought on by the togetherness I felt with Mom, Gran, and Sophie; happiness at joining forces and becoming one in purpose. For once I did not picture in my mind's eye the faces of Dad, Robbie and Kate. The earthquake brought out the best in all of us, and it shocked Mom out of her round-the-clock grief. It is undoubtedly wicked to be thankful to a terrible earthquake, but I am forever grateful to it for the return of my Mother.

All afternoon and evening weary folks fleeing the ruined, burning city walked past the Inn. The fires continued to rage, and the sound of dynamite blasts became more frequent and more frantic. Max and Cherie joined our group. Their home, in a district close to downtown, lost both the front and back walls "You can see through it," said Max, shaking his head. "I told the girls to find a safe place. There's no way we can conduct business as usual. Everyone is on his or her own in pandemonium like this."

"You must stay here," said Gran. "There's plenty of room, and a whole closet full of blankets and extra pillows." Max and Cherie camped out with us that night and the next.

On the third day we decided the earth had calmed enough to move back inside. Gran gave Max and Cherie the big bedroom nearest to the kitchen. "It will do my back good to sleep on a real bed again!" said Max. "Thanks for letting us stay, Liza. I know it's an imposition."

"Bite your tongue, Max! Such talk!" cried Gran.

Though there was no electricity or running water and no cooking allowed indoors, it was good to be surrounded by four walls. The aftershocks finally stopped enough to trust that the walls wouldn't shudder and shake and crumble into heaps. Max examined the Inn for damage. "The side porch buckled and needs new boards, and the chimney needs rebuilding. There are a few cracks in the plaster. Other than that, I don't see much wrong." It was happy news for Gran. Poor Max didn't have such good fortune; the remains of his and Cherie's home and most of their possessions were completely destroyed by the raging fires.

We all pitched in to clean up broken glass, shattered china and plaster dust and put away the many household items that were scattered across the floors. I volunteered to reshelf all the books in the library, and Mom joined me. We worked quietly, sorting through the titles to group them by subject matter. "This is where I met your dad," she said softly. I held my breath, expecting her to break into sobs, but she didn't. Her voice was calm, and I found it comforting. "I broke your Gran's rules and sneaked over to find a book one evening."

"What were Gran's rules?"

"The library was off limits unless I asked permission, and only during the morning hours. There would have been hell to pay if she'd discovered me. Your grandmother was stern when I was growing up. She's developed a softer side over the years."

"Why was she so strict?"

"That's a story for another day. I promise I'll tell you, but for now, I'm thinking of some lovely memories of your dad." I listened as Mom told about meeting Dad and falling in love with him. "He was the most handsome man I'd ever laid eyes on and so smart and understanding! The next day he showed up at the apartment with an armful of roses, and he sweet-talked Sophie into inviting him for supper. Nolan had a way of wrapping the ladies around his finger."

"I miss him so much," I said.

Mom put her arms around me, and all the tears I'd kept to myself for fear of adding to her misery came streaming out. Mom held me and stroked my hair. "Go ahead and cry, Rori. I know how much you miss him, and Robbie and Kate as well. Just let it out." I sobbed and sobbed until the tears finally slowed. Mom passed me her handkerchief. "I've been a bad mother, and I apologize for it."

I shook my head. "You've never been a bad mother," I managed to squeak.

"I was, and I hope you can forgive me. In my wretched state after the ship went down, I left you to fend for yourself. I didn't provide any comfort to relieve your suffering. I didn't pay attention to the fact that you'd lost your father and brother just as I'd lost my husband and son." She was quiet for a moment. "I'm not proud of this, but until the earth shook some sense into me, I wished I'd gone down with the Valencia. I couldn't see life without your dad by my side." She wiped away a tear and took a deep breath to collect herself. "When the earthquake struck, all I could think of was you; hoping you were safe and unharmed. You are my main reason for living, Rori! And though I loved your Dad and Robbie, I am glad that I wasn't on board the ship; I wouldn't have the pleasure and honor of your company. I am sorry it took so long, but I am back as the mother who loves you more than anyone else in the world."

We clung to each other, rocking gently from side to side. Peace swept over me, and a burden of worry I'd carried since the wreck lifted. Mom would face the future without her husband and son, and she would survive.

Liza Laurent
San Francisco
Late summer 1906

A few weeks after the quake, Sister Margaret Kirkpatrick from Rose's old school paid Wayside Inn a visit about an urgent need for lodging children orphaned in the catastrophe. "I'll be frank, Mrs. Laurent; I am here to beg your assistance. We are overflowing at Most Holy Name. A shipment of cots and blankets arrived last week, and every bed is occupied, every pillow allocated. If they're small enough, we have them sleeping two to a bed."

"Why, the poor children! As if losing parents and home wasn't enough, they have to sleep like sardines in a tin! I'd like to contribute to your efforts, Sister Margaret. May I write a check for any particular amount?"

Sister Margaret smiled. "Actually, my intention is not to gather charity funds. Our coffers are happily overflowing with donations from the dioceses across America. People have been wondrously generous. Our problem is lack of space. There are hundreds of orphans and newly widowed women with children who are homeless. Those who haven't found shelter in a church or community center are still camping in the parks and empty lots. I thought of Wayside Inn, Mrs. Laurent. It is so spacious, and I knew, due to the nature of your former enterprise, that there might be several empty rooms."

I was taken by surprise and momentarily speechless. "Why don't you come in for a cup of tea," I finally managed. "Rose will be delighted to see you."

"Rose is visiting? I'd love to see her, of course!"

"I believe she's in the kitchen helping Sophie make soup." Sister Margaret followed me down the hall.

Rose's eyes grew wide when she saw her favorite teacher. "Sister Margaret!" she cried and ran to embrace her. "Why, this is a treasure and a surprise! You must have read my mind because I've been thinking about you and wondering how the school held up in the earthquake."

"There was damage to the gymnasium and the chapel and a few broken windows. Other than that, Most Holy Name made it through the shaking in one piece."

"Wonderful!" cried Rose. "What good fortune! I'd hate it if the dear old school had crumbled."

"I didn't know you were in San Francisco, Rose, or I'd have visited sooner."

"You must forgive me, Sister Margaret," said Rose. "My mood was too dark to speak to any living soul."

"I forgive you, of course." The nun looked at her questioningly. "I hope your dark mood has lifted, Rose."

"It has taken a turn for the better, thankfully. This is my daughter, Aurora," Rose said. "I'm terribly proud of her. She is everything a mother could ask for!"

Aurora shook Sister Margaret's hand. "Mom's talked about you for years," she said. "Pleased to meet you."

In conversation over tea, Rose told Sister Margaret about the death of Nolan, Robbie, and Kate. "What horribly sad circumstances! I had no idea," said Sister Margaret. "No wonder you didn't contact anyone. Such deep suffering, and then to find yourself in the middle of a natural disaster! It's a wonder you and Aurora are still standing!"

Sophie passed around a plate of shortbread cookies, and we finished our tea quietly. I broke the silence. "Sister Margaret has asked if we could take in some children who were orphaned by the quake. Since we are all in this together, I thought we should discuss it."

Rose lifted her chin. "I don't think we need to discuss it, Mama. Of course we'll help the children." Sophie and Aurora both nodded.

"It's decided then. We'll get the extra rooms aired out and the bedding freshened. When will the children come, Sister Margaret?"

"As we speak, there's a family of four children camping at Golden Gate Park. The eldest child, Caleb Wilson, is nine, and the youngest, Lilly, is only four. Caleb is doing his best to be a father to the other three, but he's just a boy himself. They need a warm house and steady meals. Little Lilly is skin and bones." Sister Margaret paused. ""I should add that there is relief money available to cover the costs of food and lodging until the children are placed in permanent homes. There's some paperwork involved, but once it's in place there would be a monthly remuneration for each orphan."

"I'll volunteer for paperwork! I'm an expert at it. I had lots of experience from serving on the board for the Museum," said Rose.

"You're good at everything you do, Rose," I said.

"Thank you, Mama."

"I should have said it years ago, Rose. I need to make up for it if you'll let me."

Rose nodded. I slipped an arm around her, and she leaned against me. My heart raced with happiness.

"The agency could bring the Wilson children as early as tomorrow," said Sister Margaret.

"What agency?" I asked.

"The Catholic Humane Resettlement Society has formed to place the orphans in permanent homes within the outlying communities. Is tomorrow too soon?"

"Tomorrow is just fine," said Sophie. "We'll have the rooms spic and span in no time."

"I'll help," said Aurora.

"Very well, I'll have someone from the Society deliver the children in the afternoon."

"We'll plan for it," I said.

Sister Margaret pulled a timepiece from her bodice. "I'd better go. I'll have just enough time to stop by the Society headquarters on my way to the ferry."

The Wilson orphans arrived at Wayside Inn at five the next day, marking the start of the Inn's new mission. By the end of the summer, our numbers soared to two dozen. Sister Margaret sent Sister Bernice, a young nun, to help oversee our flock, and Sophie, Rose, Aurora and I were busy around the clock caring for the homeless children.

In September, Sister Margaret suggested that Aurora attend Most Holy Name School, which had resumed classes for the first time after the earthquake. Rose lost all the color in her face. "I don't know if I could bear being apart from Rori! She's all I have left."

Sister Margaret nodded sympathetically but kept on with her recommendation. "She must have some relief from the hard work at the Inn. She needs to be a carefree young girl again. Both you and Aurora are still in mourning from the loss of your loved ones. It's hard enough for an adult, but we must not forget that Aurora is only sixteen, and she's away from her home and school and friends. The poor child needs to feel normal again and to be with girls her own age."

Sophie nodded. "I agree with Sister Margaret. I've been thinking the very same thing."

Rose turned to me. "What do you think, Mama?"

"I think you should ask Rori what she'd like to do."

Over supper, Rose told Aurora about Sister Margaret's suggestion that she board at Most Holy Name for the fall term. "I couldn't leave you, Mom," cried Aurora.

"Though I would miss you terribly, Rori, I assure you, I'll be fine. If you're thinking you have to take care of me or I'll fall apart again, you must not feel that way. I promise I won't. I'd hate to have you hold up your life because of me. Sister Margaret says the music program has a top-notch new teacher. You don't want to get rusty on your instruments."

"But I'm needed here," said Aurora.

"You're a wonderful help, Rori, but it's time for you to branch out. I think you should try Most Holy Name for the fall term. If you don't like it you can always come home," said Rose.

"Why not think about it overnight and make a decision after a good sleep?" I suggested.

On the following Monday, Aurora boarded the ferry to Benicia. Sophie, Rose and I waved until the ferry was nothing more than a distant speck on the bay. I clasped Rose's hand in mine. "I can't help remembering when I sent you away to Most Holy Name so many years ago. It was unfair and cruel. I will never forgive myself for it, Rose. I hope that I can make up for my past actions. My whole purpose in life is to gain your trust and to earn your love."

Rose linked elbows with Sophie and me as we stood on the dock, the last spectators gazing after the long-gone ferry. "I count myself lucky to have two mothers." She smiled and kissed us both. "Shall we walk home instead of getting a cab? It's such a lovely day."

Wayside Inn gleamed invitingly in the rosy light when we climbed the last steep hill to our neighborhood. "Who's ready for a piece of apple pie? Cherie baked five of them this morning," said Sophie.

"You two go ahead," I said. "I'm going to sit on the porch for a minute and put my feet up." The view from the back porch overlooks the city and the bay beyond. I gazed across the panorama, musing about the Inn. From boarding house, to brothel, to restaurant and lounge, to its current function as a refuge for orphans, it had transformed in response to prevailing circumstances.

Like the Wayside Inn, my life has been subject to the whims and vagaries of circumstance. I forgive myself for what I couldn't control; I did the best I could with the hand I was dealt. I am no longer the cold madam of the early days at Wayside. I am no longer the secretly tortured, guilty person who loathes herself. Rose's forgiveness releases me. I feel blessed, and as if possessed, my spirits lift and merge with the flock of gulls flying toward the sea. I have longed for this moment. It does not disappoint me.

Acknowledgments

Thanks to everyone who cheered me on and read through the various drafts of Sisters of the Soul. Cindy Roberts, dear friend and mentor, has faithfully read Sisters of the Soul from original inception to final manuscript—if a manuscript can ever be really final.

I thank Shirley Nelson for her thoughtful suggestions and reflections and for urging me on with this endeavor.

Also thanks to Susan Thoms. Without her encouragement I might have given up as soon as the going got rough.

Thanks to Ann Wallace, Hope Slifert, Beverly Ginn, Beverly Britts, and Beverly Hayes for all their help and insight.

Thanks also to the ladies in the WOW writing group and the Inklings writing group for their perusal and insightful response to selections from Sisters of the Soul.

The Tuolumne County Library staff was invaluable in the process of locating and procuring research materials needed for historical accuracy.

Finally, a special thanks to Melody Young of Word Project Press for her fine work designing and laying out the book.

Thanks to all for supporting the process and providing the wisdom needed to complete Sisters of the Soul.

Dear Reader,

I hope you enjoyed Sisters of the Soul. If you have a moment to give some feedback, please leave a rating–and if time permits–a review! Or just send me an email. Reader reviews count a lot and are much appreciated!

Email: kf@KristinFulton.com
Amazon: https://www.amazon.com/dp/B0CC3TNRKH#c\customerReviews
GoodReads: https://www.goodreads.com/book/show/44564084-sisters-of-the-soul#CommunityReviews

ABOUT THE AUTHOR

Kristin A. Fulton is the author of middle grade novels **Snake Food** and **The Haunting**; a fable for all ages, **Henry Bingle's Transformation**; a picture book, **Is THAT a Hat?**; a two act play, **Christmas in July**, and the novel **Sisters of the Soul**. **A Dangerously Close Encounter**, the second book in the **Hazelsmith Family Adventure series**, will soon join Broadway Pacific's list of published titles. When she isn't writing, the author strums with a garage band, paints watercolor landscapes, and goes on hikes. She is currently working on a novel that takes place during the California Gold Rush.